CAIN'S COVEN

God bless you,
Kristin King
2012

Cain's Coven

Begotten Bloods One

This is a work of fiction. All of the characters, organizations, and events portrayed in this novel are either the products of the author's imagination or are used fictitiously.

Three Kings Publishing
115 Canterbury Court
Princeton, Kentucky 42445

For information contact: threekingspublishing@gmail.com

To my family and those like it, bound by love more than blood, and especially you, Ryan. This is all your fault.

Prologue

On the outskirts of Tulsa under cover of darkness, Jeff Adams pumped another shell into the chamber of his shotgun as he approached the figure writhing in pain on the hard packed dirt that served as the parking lot of the Copperhead Bar. The bitter taste in his mouth was from disbelief that the scrawny punk on the ground with the big belt-buckled Wranglers had been chosen for immortality when Adams had not.

Checking for stragglers and satisfied they were alone, Adams turned back and blasted another round of his homemade mercury filled shot into the creature's chest. He smiled at the pain he inflicted enjoying the wheezing, gasping and scratching as it tried to claw away its own skin to release the liquid metal burning through the flesh in dozens of places.

"I'm not what you think," the creature choked out, "I'm not a killer."

"Unfortunately for you," Adams spat, "I am."

He kicked at its head. "What have you got that I don't?"

No response.

Certain the vampire was beyond fighting back, Adams dragged it over to his old blue Ford F-150 truck. He hoisted his prize over the tailgate before tearing up the dust of the old highway. Adams intended to drain as many syringes of blood from the creature as possible before leaving the thing to burn in the coming dawn.

By then Adams would be back on the computer playing the game that started all this madness, the web hosted ultra-game Mission 2B Immortal. He would read and reread all the postings linked to a fellow subscriber named live4ever. The persona claimed that the ultimate payout to those who triumphed over every level of the game, as Adams had, was recruitment for an immortal life. Most players considered the posts a marketing ploy, but there were true believers, like Jeff Adams who diligently worked two long years to win and then be denied his rightfully earned place.

1

"Someone mistook me for a fool, and they will pay dearly," he thought. On the warpath now, Adam's new mission possessed him even more than the game. A sneer settled across his face as he gripped the steering wheel. It wasn't immortality he had coming to him, he knew better than that. But it was the closest thing this side of the ever after and "Daggone, I earned it."

If injecting all the creature's blood into his own system didn't work, Adams already had his own web-based recruitment to form a team of vampire killers. His ulterior motive was still to find a way to join them, but his fellow slayers needn't know they might end up as his first meal.

Chapter 1

On the hunt for an altogether different sort of female, Justice Cain caught his brother looking longingly after a trio of co-eds decked out for a night on the town. The reflection of the lights from the downtown bars and restaurants on Albuquerque's rain-wet street mirrored each other in the hazy way Chess's eyes reflected how hard it was to be on the wagon even after two years. Chess with his dark Italian ancestry still dressed for the scene in black jeans, a trendy button up shirt, and a fitted black leather sport coat while Justice's cargo pants, Henley, and worn rain gear plainly expressed his lack of interest in the surroundings. Justice was strictly business as he stalked the streets for the third night running.

A recent series of disappearances and deaths had Chess canceling a trip north to investigate with his younger brother. The most recent report said the victim, Dale Mitchell, age 28 of Los Cruces, New Mexico, was last seen coming out of Club Durango in the company of two young women. Copies of other less public reports obtained by their northern neighbor noted the victim's unaccountable pre-mortem blood loss. There were also inconsistent accounts of a bouncer, who said the victim was clearly intoxicated, and the bartender, who swore he had served the man nothing stronger than soda.

"There she is," Justice nodded toward a couple coming out of the Cadillac Lounge further down on the left. There was a tall man with the well-dressed look of a business traveler. His companion, with her sweeping brunette curls, form fitting dress and stilettos, resembled a music video dancer.

The brothers tailed the couple up the wide brick sidewalk past mimosa tree planters. They weaved in and out of occasional pedestrians intent on their own nightly activities. Their quarry led them to the upscale Regency Hotel where they entered the thickly carpeted brass gilded lobby almost on their heels.

Too close, Justice realized belatedly. The female turned her head as if catching the pleasant whiff of a nearby bakery. She honed in on Chess and Justice.

Her twinkling eyes raked over them, and then she smiled flirtatiously whispering into her companion's ear and knowing the two brothers could hear her from across a crowded room if they chose. "My sister and I like to share everything. The more the merrier we always say."

She threw Chess and Justice a wink, then arm in arm she led her doomed companion into the hotel bar. Just across the threshold, Chess stopped short and placed a restraining hand on his brother's arm.

"What?" Justice's irritation flared.

"I can't do this."

Justice stared at his brother in disbelief. He stepped aside with his brother and pointedly crossed his arms, waiting for an explanation. None was forth coming, only Chess's pained and slightly embarrassed face. Justice turned and saw the couple at the bar meeting with another woman whose face was blocked from view by a mirrored column. The mirror cast Justice's own hard reflection back at him. He turned from it quickly.

What had he expected? His brother had never been a hunter, never hunted wild vampires to survive. A lover not a fighter, Justice thought, and not even that. Chess engendered love, made a marvelous game of it. That game usually concluded not long after he got a hold of what he needed to carry him through till his next diversion. Chess never violated the letter of coven laws, he was far too smart for that, but he certainly broke the spirit of them. After his last relationship ended so badly, Chess finally acquiesced to his brother's appeals to live a more honest life, one that might even be a benefit.

Finally giving in to Justice, Chess made repeated trips north to learn to hunt from their elder, Arvon. Chess's unique abilities lie in tracking rather than taking down the young out-of-control vampires. Called the wild ones, they often drank so much blood that handling them was like containing a cocained bear. Their elder was the best, though, and Chess was presumably adjusting well to his new lifestyle.

A hunt like the one tonight should be easy for someone trained by Arvon, Justice thought. Maybe hunting with me is throwing him off.

Shoving his short bangs off his forehead, Justice struggled to suppress his frustration. "Chess. The wild ones gorge themselves while out on frequent deadly sprees. Never make nor take. Remember? These kill with no care and reproduce without caution. It's intolerable, and they are beyond reform.

"This," Justice pointed toward the bar, "this is what we do. It's how you live now, and it is in fact better even if it's more difficult." Justice caught himself and attempted an appeal instead of a lecture, saying with control, "And tonight, with the two of them, so recently fed, we're safer together."

Chess shook his head vehemently and turned away from Justice. Justice swore and leaned over far enough to view the man, rhapsodic, taking the room key from the black haired beauty. Chess wanted to have his brother's back, he very much wanted to.

"I should have told you last night when we picked up their scent. I suspected then who it was. There was just too much death taint to be sure. Did you see the sister?"

"No." Justice stole a look around the mirrors and saw her at the same time Chess spoke her name.

"It's Jenny."

Justice jerked his head back out of sight, his shock clear. Jenny had been Chess's latest and greatest failed attempt to make them more of a family. For Chess, it might not have been true love, but it was truly something. Now Justice saw the irony of the sister's words to her victim. Jenny did like to share; she liked to share everything with anybody who took her fancy.

The trio at the bar slid off their stools walking toward the bank of elevators, the man trailing the beautiful women who walked with their arms around each other's waists. The sister whispered in Jenny's ear as they approached the entrance. Jenny shook her head then warily watched Chess and Justice from across the room, one uncertain and conflicted, the other focused and defiant. She pulled the man up to her side between them like a shield as she headed to the elevator.

In the foyer, the brothers stared as the elevator doors closed, and Justice watched to see where it would stop. Jenny obviously gorged so often and so deeply that the death taint inherent in even the healthiest human's blood now flowed behind her like a contrail of disease. Unfortunately the time it would take for the death taint to kill Chess's ex-wife was too long to wait. Four or five decades of mayhem and chaos were beyond the bounds.

Justice, finally understanding, rested a hand on his anguished brother's shoulder.

"I can handle this. You go north. Arvon is expecting you."

Justice took the stairs to the eighth floor and found the fourth door on the right standing open a few inches. Justice cautiously peered inside and saw the woman Jenny had left with. Obviously a newer wild one, she crouched over her now unconscious victim. The beautiful brunette gazed up at him curiously, but without fear or comprehension.

Justice looked around, where was Jenny? Behind the wild one, sheer curtains billowed in the breeze from the room's balcony. Could she have left that way? Alert, Justice inspected the possible hiding places for Jenny even though his nose told him she was no longer nearby.

Confident there wasn't a man alive or undead who could resist her charms, the brunette began flirting with him.

"Jenny said you weren't the type to share, but then I have so much more to share than she does."

She pushed her dress off one shoulder and flipped her hair out to the other side revealing more of her smooth skin. "Do you like what you see?" She ran the side of one hand down her bare throat across her chest and between her breasts before letting it drop beside her in a gesture of open invitation.

Justice stood firm though his mind wandered to another young woman with a smooth throat, smaller more subtle curves, and the French countryside of his past where she had stirred up an undeniable attraction in him so many life times ago. Thirst wasn't the only drive he always kept in strict control. Challenges one conquered, he told himself. Sometimes, though, it felt like pure deprivation.

The female perceived indecision and appreciation. She sashayed over to him, laid her hands flat on his chest and leaned close, her ruby lipstick the color of the blood that freshly scented her mouth.

"I'm Candy. What's your name?"

"You've broken the laws, Candy." The urge to ball his hand up in her hair and have at more than her throat tried to rise and was immediately punched down. He focused on the scent of tainted blood and death, wondering how many humans she killed to smell this way and why a vampire did not pass the taint on to others of their kind. At least one drive would be satiated tonight.

He shook his head at her. "I've come to bring you to justice."

She scowled as she shoved him away violently and made for the balcony only to find him blocking it. Her eyes went wild with rage, and for scant seconds she hissed and tore uselessly at his face as his jaw clamped over her jugular. Under his bite, her struggles soon lost their intensity and slowed to weak sleepy-like movements, but Justice only stopped drawing out her lifeblood till it ran so sparingly her larger blood vessels collapsed under his force. Efficiently done Justice dropped the lifeless and surprisingly light husk of a body to the floor beside her unconscious victim who now had more blood left in him than she did.

On the sidewalk in front of the hotel, Chess wanted to get out of sight. He needed to get away from this scene, out of the city, away from it all. But then he saw Jenny dart out of the alley. Spotting him, she stood riveted for a moment before turning to flee back into the alley's comforting darkness. He did not give chase; he merely watched her disappear into the darkness and out of their lives again. Part of him yearned to go after her. Instead he hailed a taxi to the airport, reassured that his brother was no longer outnumbered.

JT is always fine on his own, Chess told himself. JT didn't need anyone, least of all Chess.

Chapter 2

Glancing in the rearview mirror of the packed minivan, Claryn Anderson smiled as her best friend busily re-teased already huge blond hair and readjusted the bachelorette tiara and white flowing train which weren't holding up too well on a night barely begun. Pulling into the Burger Shack's almost empty parking lot Claryn nodded at the maid of honor who was riding shotgun with the plan of attack for their evening of frivolity. The warm-up party and prep had included a makeover for Claryn whose straight mouse brown hair and pale face was almost unrecognizable but for the delicate high cheekbones and light gray eyes. She thought that was probably for the best, since at nineteen, Claryn was nervous about using someone else's ID at the bar which was only one town further down I-40 toward Flagstaff.

"Thanks for the food stop, Chelsea." Claryn hoped it would stave off any accidents while she was driving someone else's car but was disheartened by the booming reply.

"The Shack's chili-cheese-fries are an absolute must!" Chelsea boomed to their companions. "The best tried and true hangover prevention in Hallston, Arizona-guaranteed."

Jay's last night behind the fast-food counter was passing uneventfully when he heard the raucous group of girls in the parking lot. Seven of them stepped, slid, and stumbled out of an 2002 green GMC Safari minivan. The ones wearing bright green, purple and hot pink bridesmaid dresses with great balloon sleeves drew his attention first. Their hair competed with their sleeves for height and width.

Some aspects of an era, he thought, were best forgotten.

They traipsed through the glass doors, a regular entourage for the bride-to-be. The three closest to her, talking the loudest as they tripped over nothing, were in obvious need of something other than libations. Still, Jay grinned at the 80's night bachelorette party. Those not in dresses were decked out from their heels and leggings, past lace gloves, beaded necklaces, and straight up to big hair tied at all sorts of interesting gravity-defying angles.

These gals could have walked off the set of a Cyndi Lauper video and were certainly doing their best to party like rock stars. All but one of them, he noticed. Keys in hand, she held the door, put the bride's tiara back on when it fell off, was soft spoken and evidently the designated driver.

"At least they have one," he said under his breath to no one in particular.

"I've got it, no, go on. Have a seat," she said stopping to help a friend before stepping up to place their order while half the ladies scooted tables together and the other half headed to the restroom. Thankfully, none of them looked sick…yet. Turning his attention back to the slight figure at the counter, he was arrested by her air of innocence so like his younger sister's, by the selfless care she demonstrated like his sweet French mother, and most of all by the haunted look in her eyes that reminded him of how his fiancé appeared when he returned from war. In a moment long shelved feelings for the only women he had ever loved as a human surfaced, and all he could think was I need to know this young woman.

The only register open this late had the new girl, Rae, who seemed to need a lot more assistance than most. The designated driver's first special order had Rae searching him out for help, and he dutifully stepped up, but not too close.

Several times in her first nights Rae leaned, bumped or fell into her tall, blonde trainer with his serious and, she thought, seriously good looking face. It was all unwanted attention as far as he was concerned. He and his brother referred to girls like Rae as "barely legal" though they used the phrase to reference physiological maturity rather than the urban law.

Claryn noticed the little dance of space going on between the girl and the guy behind the counter. He stood with an almost constant ten inches of distance between them even though the girl was quite pretty and markedly interested in him. His rugged handsomeness seemed more appropriate for the Eddie Bauer catalog rather than the Burger Shack's clown suit. Impossibly, he made the gauche colors and jaunty paper hat look almost chic. He probably made everything he wore look good where Claryn saw herself as awkward in anything other than jeans and t-shirts. However, what she liked was the way he was maintaining the space between himself and his coworker. Claryn could appreciate a guy who gave her the personal area she needed. His name-tag read "Jay."

Their names are Jay and Rae? Seriously? Claryn almost laughed but noticed that she had the oh-so-attractive young man's full attention. With a concentrated effort she managed to keep her view elsewhere.

Jay thanked her for her patience as Rae went about filling the order, found no fries were up and proceeded to drop some into the fryer.

"Looks like your party started early this evening," he remarked. Jay was used to getting overly favorable responses to most any conversation starter he dropped, but the slim brunette seemed distracted.

"Yeah," she turned her head to see her companions excitedly waving her over.

"I can bring your order out," he offered.

"Oh, great...thanks," she said without a backward glance.

He watched her go, a perfect girl-next-door with that elusive je ne sais quoi, or I-don't-know-what as his French mother used to say. His eyes followed her unflinchingly as she joined the others. She might not have noticed him, but her friends obviously had. Their eyes darted to him as they animatedly gestured toward something the bachelorette was holding and they talked behind their hands.

The girlfriends' conversation turned to Hollywood hotties as Claryn slid in next to her best friend and bride-to-be, Kelley, who was still observing the fast food worker. Claryn followed her friend's gaze, and

11

they both watched him assist an elderly couple in the door. The wife steered her husband's wheelchair toward a handicap table, where Jay moved a seat to make room for him, held the old woman's chair for her, and took their order waiting on them as if the Burger Shack were a fine restaurant. His "yes, ma'am" and "yes, sir" carried to his audience of two. Kelley peeked over at Claryn whose unusual interest held while the young man entered the order and went to the back line before reappearing to wipe all the salt from the fry area for the next batch, apparently a low sodium special order.

Jay barely relieved Rae of the party goers order in time to deliver it. As he passed the elderly couple holding hands, he could not help but wonder how long they had been together. He had lived longer than their combined years, yet they shared something he had never had.

The babbling 80's rockers were ready for him, all bright attentiveness except for the one whose notice he desired. On impulse Jay bent lower than necessary next to the designated driver to set down the two trays.

The bride-to-be raised a speculative eyebrow while paying close attention to her space conscious friend. Pleased, and with a look of determination, she launched into a little speech, "Hi, I'm wondering if you could do me a huge gi-normous favor? Jay, is it? I'm Kelley, and this is Natalie, Shelly, Jill, Mary, Chelsea, and Claryn."

With an impressive attention to detail, he greeted them each by name resting a bit longer on Claryn's name, just as Kelley had done. Then he offered Kelley his congratulations.

"Why thank you, thank you very much." Kelley smiled.

As Claryn's only long time pal, Kelley felt a certain responsibility for marrying and moving away from her unsettled friend. Struck by her own imminent marital bliss, Kelley was determined to find a love interest for her friend. But Claryn didn't make it easy. She refused to be set up, and rarely accepted subsequent dates after the first, for reasons not entirely unknown to Kelley.

Reflecting on Claryn's odd issues with personal space and the guys who entered hers, Kelley was fast losing hope. Her friend did little to present her best, wore little makeup, and generally dressed as if already wearing her boyfriend's shirts and jeans. But that was not the worst of it, in Kelley's opinion. Few guys approached someone who displayed such complete disinterest. The only upside Kelley saw was that Claryn, with her sleek shiny hair, wide-open features, and trim figure, was cute in whatever she wore.

Tonight was a little different as the pre-party prep required everyone to indulge the bride. Kelley took advantage of her status to the fullest extent and was pleased with the way she'd highlighted Claryn's fine features.

Cupid himself seemed to be indulging her as well, guiding them here after only one bar hop, and then striking this Armani in polyester with an arrow for her own dear Claryn. Why else would he deliver the food when his coworker took the order? Kelley the matchmaker spied the way he delivered the tray and watched with bright hope as Claryn allowed the bubble around her to be violated. As far as Kelley was concerned Fate had spoken, and now she must as well.

"So, Jay, are you familiar with the ritual of the bachelorette party?"

"Somewhat."

With a flourish Kelley said, "I have in my possession a to-do list the completion of which my happily ever after could very well depend." Drama queen personified now, Kelley's more jovial cohorts jumped on board with all manner of supporting actress's lines on their vividly colored lips.

"I must dance with each and every type of partner on this list between the hours of midnight and 4am or face the doom of my dancing shoes by matrimonialization.

"Would you? Could you join us at the O-Zone to sign the fast-food-worker line on my dance card?" Kelley folded her hands together and batted her eyelashes, slid the briefest of glances toward Claryn and back saying, "Please tell me you are able, willing and available?"

Although Claryn did not look at him as he knelt beside her accepting Kelley's invitation with chivalric aplomb, she wasn't surprised he accepted. The other partiers were so bright with admiration and encouragement.

It wasn't till much later that Claryn realized the direction of his interest.

Chapter 3

The O-Zone was fairly busy for a Wednesday night and people cheered the bachelorette gang, shouted congratulations over the music and joined in the girls' heightened revelry. Claryn bought a round when it was her turn even though she wouldn't partake, but she also got a cup of ice water for Kelley.

The press of a crowd could sometimes make Claryn dizzy, but whenever the throng threatened the bachelorette partiers too much a couple of the gals would cut off the encroachers from their dance circle. Even so, the closeness of the gyrating bodies became too much for her personal space issues, and Claryn spent a good deal of time guarding their tall drink table and suppressing the fear and panic the mass caused her. From Claryn's perch on a bar stool she saw him enter the mob, the people parted in front of him unconsciously as if their instincts knew what their brains did not. Still wearing his wide striped red and white work shirt and dark slacks, his square shoulders and lean figure turned the ridiculous outfit into a trendy fashion statement.

A look of pleasure lightened his features when he saw her and nodded acknowledgement. It took Claryn several moments to realize that seeing her had elicited his response. But just as the pit of her stomach threatened to react to his interest, he turned toward the troop with the veiled Kelley in its midst. Even on the dance floor the waves parted, so he made his way easily to the center. "Poetry in motion" came to Claryn's mind quickly followed by a vision of a shark swimming into a large school of fish.

One song later Kelley was arm-in-arm with her dance card companion and headed to the table with her faithful followers in tow. Jay offered to buy the next round then walked purposefully to the large kidney shaped bar in the back center of the room.

"Promise me something," Kelley was waving her other friends out onto the dance floor as she raised her voice over the din.

15

Claryn frowned, "What?"

"No, Claryn, promise first," Kelley was sounding a bit like Elmer Fudd at this point, so Claryn doubted she would remember the promise regardless.

"Okay."

"Okay, what?"

"Okay, I promise."

"Good." Jay was headed back, stepping through blue lights carrying six mixed drinks with the assistance of a waitress. "Promise if he asks and is a gentleman around you, that you'll go out with him at least three times."

"Kelley, I . . . "

"No, you promised."

"He's not even interested in me."

"An Honest Abe promise."

First dates were okay, usually. Second dates without a kiss goodnight, highly questionable, but a third? Just the thought of it made Claryn's heart beat heavy. She concentrated on her breathing for a moment. Kelley was demanding her full attention.

"You promised already. So just say it."

Almost forehead-to-forehead Claryn grumbled, "I promise," as drinks were set on the table.

Jay's notice was all for Claryn who pointedly ignored him even when he placed a glass in front of her saying, "This one is yours." The other girls saw Jay return with the drinks and surrounded the table.

Kelley smiled broadly, certain her only obstacle at this point was to keep Natalie from throwing herself on the poor chap. She determined to keep herself between them.

When Jill wanted to buy them the same drink for the next round, Jay declared his drink a secret concoction, which only he could procure. Deftly pointing out a young man with an interesting haircut he mentioned the next dance card entry, "Someone my parents would not approve of."

Kelley seized the opportunity to lead Natalie and the others onto the dance floor leaving Jay with Claryn.

Claryn alternated between clenching fists and tensely splayed fingers under the table as she gave herself a little self-talk. It didn't matter what she promised. There was no way someone like him would ask out someone like her. Why had she let Kelley dress her up so much tonight? Apprehension squeezed her chest.

Jay pretended not to notice her tension. He was actually visually monitoring her pulse rate under the skin of her pretty neck and was concerned by how much it had slowed since her friends left the table. Oddly her heart rate was going down as her tension increased.

"I feel like some fresh air, how about you?" he commented.

"Air?" Air. Air sounded really good actually, the music and crowd seemed to press down on her.

"There's a patio out the other side past the bar."

The place was so full she couldn't see what he was referencing but she felt almost desperate for open space. Nodding she tried to start that direction but was blocked by a wall of humanity.

Jay eased around her without touching her, "It's faster this way."

Following him Claryn felt she was floating in a peaceful wake between waves of people. By the time she stepped through the door he held open she was more relaxed. Most of the tables were open as she hesitated.

"Over there we'll be upwind from the smokers," he pointed.

She chose the chair furthest from the other seats as he sat down their drinks.

The silence was companionable for a few minutes as they took in the view into the club windows on one side and the dimly lit park on the other. Looking at nothing in particular, he listened to her heartbeat slowly return to normal.

He's not going to ask me out. Why, he's hardly noticed me at all. Kelley has it all wrong. He's probably waiting for Natalie or Jill to join us. Likely thinks I can help set him up with one of them.

Thus assured, Claryn was first to speak. "This is really good. What is it?"

"Secret recipe."

"You know I'm the designated driver, right?"

"I got that." His half smile was reassuring, friendly but not overly.

He shifted toward her with a conspiratorial look but saw her discomfort and relaxed back saying quickly, "My secret concoction doesn't contain alcohol."

She stared, smiled and started laughing, little bursts that got louder and freer after a moment. It sparkled in the night air. She raised her glass in a toast, "Here's to Jay's Secret Concoction!"

Her drink half gone, a waitress came by to get them refills. Jay ordered water with a lime and paused as she ordered a Sprite.

"You're drinking water?" She assumed his clear beverage was a gin and tonic or such. She almost asked if he was in AA, but he looked too young and the question was intrusive.

"I am. Are you always the designated driver?"

"I, uh. . . I actually don't get out to parties or the scene much."

"Too many people."

The comment was off handed but very insightful. She wasn't sure if he meant too many for him or her.

"It's much better out here. Thanks for suggesting it."

"My pleasure."

After their new drinks arrived they sat quietly for a bit, she gazing into the park at the shifting light patterns under the non-native deciduous trees.

Claryn found she wanted to talk, to find out more about him especially if he wanted to go out with one of Kelley's friends. "You don't

18

look much like someone who'd be working fast-food, if you don't mind me saying."

"I don't mind. I like to hear the truth." They both turned as the cover band played the first few bars of "YMCA" eliciting whoops and shouts from the dancers. "So what do I look like I should be doing?"

It was on the tip of her tongue to say modeling but she couldn't bring herself to offer a compliment that might intimate any special notice on her part.

With practiced distraction, she changed directions. "You also don't look like a Jay."

This sincerely amused him. "Then I shall confess . . . I am not."

"Not what? A fast food worker or a Jay?"

"As of--" he glanced at his watch, "—midnight, neither. It was my last night at the Burger Shack and the Jay on my name tag was supposed to be my initial. It's not my name."

Rather than ask the more obvious question Claryn inquired, "Why were you working at the Burger Shack in the first place?"

"It was on my bucket list of jobs."

"Really?"

"Truly."

"That's weird. I've never heard of a job bucket list, and I'm not sure I'd put that on mine if I had one."

"Different positions in society lend themselves to various insights about people and places."

"Are you a grad student?" she asked.

"No."

"Then what are you?" Claryn was sorry she asked as his face fell flat.

He looked at the table. "You mean what do I do? What is my vocation?"

"What do you usually do?"

Claryn glanced over through the large plate glass windows beside the dance floor. Kelley and crew had found them and were variously waving or dancing at them. Then headed toward the rear of the bar for the double glass doors of the patio area.

"These days I rebuild old cars, usually." His light air returned. "You don't seem very interested in knowing my name. Vocation first, huh?"

Embarrassed, Claryn waved Kelley and her friends over with relief. She couldn't say why she hadn't asked and contemplating it made her nervous again. Grateful for the diversion when Kelley asked how things were going, Claryn told her "J" was just his initial.

"How does not even being on a first name basis rate for how things are going?" Claryn said.

But Kelley seized the moment to introduce a new drinking game whereby each person got to guess Jay's name and drink for incorrect answers. All the other girls starting throwing out J names like they were on a rapid fire game show. John, Joe, Jim, James, Josh, Jacob, Joseph. Claryn enjoyed watching them from the sideline as Jay turned his focus away from her.

Chelsea said, "He wouldn't have us guess if it was something that common."

Mary wanted a rule clarification, "Does it count as the right answer if your name is Jonathan but you go by Jon?"

"I would count that, but it's irrelevant."

"Names without nick names," Kelley said.

"Or he just doesn't go by one," Mary responded.

The names got more creative after that: Jackson, Josiah, Jace, Jarrod, Jeremiah. The game went longer than expected. Natalie declared the guys at the next table over "hot" and enlisted their help to no avail.

Finally Kelley demanded to know the correct answer announcing her privilege as the bride and her constitution as Kelley unable to endure the game's extension.

"And what do I get if I give you the answer?" Jay asked.

She stood and threw her hand out toward Claryn as if she were a prize, "What do you get? Why a date with none other than the lovely Claryn Anderson!"

His grin was only surpassed by Kelley's beaming when he stood and shook her hand saying, "Justice, Justice Cain. Pleased to meet you."

"Ugh, we never would have guessed that!" Natalie said.

"Speak for yourself," said Jill. "I was getting closer."

With the now game over the others gals were engaged in flirting with the guys at the next table as Claryn angrily pulled Kelley back into her seat. "I only promised to go if he asked me!" Kelley was triumphant and continued smirking.

A little too close right at her elbow, Justice asked, "Claryn, would you go out with me tomorrow night?"

It was a mistake. Claryn's heart rate plummeted, and she rocked dizzily in her seat going pale.

"Oh great," said Mary, "the designated driver is passing out."

Justice reacted immediately to steady her, as did Kelley, but Claryn's flayed hands pushed him away weakly as she fell against her friend, eyelids fluttering and breathing shallow.

Kelley pushed him away more forcefully, "Just back away for a minute. I've never seen her this bad."

Justice reluctantly moved away. Concerned, Jill was asking if there was anything she could do and Chelsea wanted to know if Claryn was all right.

"She's not drunk, she doesn't drink. It's sort of an allergic reaction," Kelley said, "but she'll be right as rain with some air and space. Why don't you all go dance? Seriously, she'll be fine."

Claryn did look a little better already. She was sitting back up blinking at the faces around her.

Justice leaned back in his seat as the others set off for the restroom. Seeing Claryn dizzy seemed to make Natalie realize how she felt. She was looking a little green around the gills.

"I'm so sorry," Justice said. "I didn't think to ask about allergies before I got drinks."

Kelley shook her head, "It's not that kind of allergy. I just said that because it's the easiest explanation."

"Kelley?" Claryn's voice was weak.

"Yeah, honey, I'm right here."

"I'm sorry, Kelley."

"Oh, girl-friend, this is not your fault."

"I think I need to go home, but I don't think I can drive for a while. I'm sorry."

"That's all right. That's why God made cabs, you know?"

Justice was genuinely bewildered by what had happened to Claryn and wanted to assist. "I could take you, I mean, I could take you all wherever you need to go."

"That's kind, but probably not a good idea," Kelley was quick to answer.

But Claryn cut in, "No, that's a good idea. Just give me a few minutes.

Claryn put a hand on Kelley's arm. "If he takes me, you all can stay, and I won't have ruined the night."

"Silly Claryn, you aren't ruining the night. Natalie is two sheets to the wind and has already been sick once. It's past time for the after party to begin."

Chelsea was behind the glass again now holding her hand up like a beverage to ask if she should get another round. Kelly exaggeratedly pointed at her watch and toward the door, then turned back to Claryn.

"And I know I was pushing this thing, but I'm not going to put you in a car in this shape at this hour with someone we just met."

Her look at Justice was apologetic, "But I will accept a ride…or rather a driver unless you also brought a minivan tonight?"

Justice shook his head.

"Okay, if you help gather the troops," she passed him a set of keys. "We'll meet you at the car."

"You sure?" He thought she might need assistance getting Claryn to the vehicle.

"I've got this willow wisp."

Ten minutes later the van was packed and Justice was chauffeuring seven young women through three drive-thrus and back into a Hallston suburb. Claryn's house was the locale for the after party as her stepmother was out of town again.

She sat in the second row seat mostly recovered and wondering how to explain. At her place everyone else piled into the house as Kelley, Claryn and Justice paused on a brick-paved patio out front.

Justice had been nothing but a gentleman even in the midst of the club scene and Kelley, though she felt bad, had made up her mind.

"Justice," she said, "Claryn can't go out with you this week because she'll be getting ready for my rehearsal dinner, the rehearsal, and the wedding."

"Oh."

"But if it's okay with you, Claryn, I'd like to invite Justice to the wedding. Is that okay?"

"It's your wedding, Kelley."

"Yes, but this isn't about me. Well, okay, it actually is about me. By Sunday I'll be flying off into the sunset with the man of my dreams. The movers have already taken our things to Dallas and who knows when I'll see you again? I just want to know that you're, well, if not with someone, at least trying to get out there. Here's a guy that likes you and wants to go out with you, right Justice?"

"True."

Claryn started breathing more heavily and sat down on the metal garden chair.

"I'm not saying he's Mister Right, but I think he's awfully nice and would follow any kind of ground rules you wanted to set for going out a couple times. Right, Justice?"

Still baffled and with growing curiosity, he nodded.

"So, Claryn, how about you bring a date to my wedding. Make my special day all the more so, and after that I'll be out of your hair. How's that sound?"

"Miserable?" Claryn teased her friend and tried to avoid eye contact with Justice.

"I'll start things off for you then, now that we're all agreed."

Kelley dug into her purse and produced a wedding invitation for Justice.

"The only ground rule is that you can't get within eighteen inches of Claryn, not your foot, not your hand, nothing. That's her move. And any explanation is also her prerogative. No questions. Are you okay with that?"

"Yeah, I'm okay." He turned to Claryn, "Are you okay?"

She nodded her head and groaned. "Yeah, sure."

"Okay, then. I'm going inside. You two should sit here and chitchat a bit. Try to pretend like this evening ended less awkwardly. See you Saturday, Justice."

"See you Saturday, Kelley."

The screen door slammed shut behind Kelley. Justice stood quietly listening to the music and laughter coming from inside. He could smell the rose bushes next door as well as mesquite wood and the trimmed lawns. The neat drives hemmed by narrow sidewalks with evenly spaced mailboxes appealed to him even though he'd never spent much time in neighborhoods.

Finally, Claryn spoke, "I'm so sorry about all that, about what happened at the club, driving us home, having your weekend commandeered. Kelley is just used to getting what Kelley wants."

So am I, Justice thought.

"She's a good friend," he mentally measured the distance to the next porch chair before crossing over to sit down.

"They'll be lots of fun folks at the wedding and reception. All the girls from tonight will be there. You don't have to hang out with me."

He turned his body to face her squarely across the small outdoor table between them.

"Claryn?" He waited for her to look at him and held her gaze captive when she did.

"I haven't been out with anyone in a very long time. But I knew before you finished placing your order at the counter tonight that I wanted to ask you out. I just didn't think I should." He looked down for a moment before continuing. "But the night took on a life of its own and now, here we are."

He shook his head and smiled, "My brother is going to laugh at me. He's kind of my Kelley, always pushing, saying I should get out more." The invitation was in his hands. "I've never even been to a wedding, but I'm really looking forward to going to my first one with you."

He studied her face for a moment before he stood up to go. "I hope you'll be looking forward to it as well."

Claryn rose unsteadily. "You noticed me at the counter?"

He smiled a bit. "No, I noticed you at the door. It wasn't till the counter that I knew I wanted to go out with you."

She smiled tentatively. "Should we meet here or at the church?"

He looked at the time of the ceremony embossed on the creamy card in his hand. "The church would be best. I think. You've got girl duties to do before that anyway, don't you?"

"Yeah. Getting Kelley ready is a pretty big job."

"I'm glad you're feeling better, and you all are in for the night now, right?"

In for the night sounded like a phrase Claryn's father would have used. "Yeah, in for the night."

"Are your folks around?"

"No," she looked at the house she'd grown up in thinking how glad she was it was empty this weekend. It gave her a little more time to think about how she was going to explain that she'd dropped out of school. "My step-mother is traveling with her new boyfriend."

Justice and his brother had lived with a sort of stepmother of their own until her suicide. It was odd to think he might have even more in common with Claryn, odd and disconcerting.

Claryn waited for the obvious questions about her parents but they weren't forthcoming. The heavy pinch pleat curtains on the large picture window beside them swayed as someone tried to figure out where the opening was. Giving up on that, heads began popping up from underneath. Girls waved, smiled and kissed the windows.

"I'll see you Saturday?" Claryn turned her back and took a few steps toward the driveway. Her voice still sounded uncertain.

"Definitely. And Claryn?"

"Yeah?"

"You go on in and lock up, okay?"

"Okay. Goodnight."

He waved a hand back over his shoulder as he headed down the drive. Claryn hadn't thought of how he would get home and had no idea how far it was. Even walking down the driveway, Justice had, true to his word, carefully maintained the gap between them. She couldn't have known how practiced he was at keeping his distance.

Claryn turned back to the window seeing on all the faces except Kelley's the disappointment and the mimes of "what, no kiss?" On the top step Claryn paused with the screen door in her hand and looked off in the distance at the young man standing under the street lamp on the corner. He waved one last time, waiting for her to go inside. As she pulled the door closed and turned the lock, her own disappointed look would have startled Claryn.

The Darkman stood in the shadows watching the house. It was a thrill to walk through the floor plan in his mind, rehearsing his every movement. Right now the house was brightly lit and crowded with guests. But soon, one night this very week, the lone female occupant would check all the doors, leave the TV on for company, and turn off lights as she headed to bed. But she wouldn't need the TV for company that night. No, he would come to her and she'd never have to spend another night alone.

Chapter 4

Kelley cheerfully declared the rehearsal a disaster, which meant the wedding itself would go off without a hitch. By noon Saturday the patchwork hail on the green grass of the church lawn was melting under a light drizzle. In the church parlor where the girls were dressing Kelley reminded everyone that rain on your wedding day promised a happy marriage. She was indomitable. Everything around her added to her glow, and Claryn was her pet project, just the distraction she said she needed to "avoid nervousness."

Claryn had tried to pass her bridesmaid duty on to someone else, anyone else. As fate would have it, the groom had no sisters or close friends or even distant cousins he wanted to stand up with his bride. He did, however, have a number of good buddies who populated the slots for six groomsmen and three ushers. Surely, Claryn hoped, no one really paid that much attention to the sixth bridesmaid no matter how she looked in her pink dress.

Not much of a girlie-girl, Claryn thought she would look like a stick wrapped in bubble gum. Kelley had chosen well, though. The pale pink set off every skin tone perfectly, and each girl wore a different cut dress suited just for her. By the time the cosmetician finished her hair and makeup, Claryn was uncomfortably "stunning" according to Kelley.

In spite of the way she looked, Claryn calmed herself, instinctively knowing that if a gal smiled little and made minimal eye contact, guys took the hint. Kelley had long maintained Claryn's need for therapy, so much so that developing a heart condition was actually a relief because it sidetracked Kelley's dogged attention to her friend's "man-allergy".

As much as Claryn loved Kelley she had to admit she was looking forward to being alone and mostly on her own. Her stepmother, "Sissy," had tried to be more of a pal over the years and was, unfortunately, neither the picture of responsibility nor the sharpest tack in the box. Her one saving grace was that she had made Claryn's dad very happy. Their small ceremony before the Justice of the Peace was Claryn's idea of wedding bliss.

Waiting her turn to walk the aisle Claryn's remembered how close she and Sissy had been after his death. They had really been there for each other, but it just hadn't lasted. When Sissy started dating again things went from bad to worse, so Claryn sought refuge in solitude or with Kelley's dysfunctional family.

Mom gone when Claryn was six, Dad at eleven, Claryn never expected life to be safe. But always before there had been one person she could count on and who really counted on her just as much. Putting on a happy face, Claryn hugged Kelley and stepped down the aisle.

Who are these people? Claryn didn't see a single face she recognized till the front rows where Kelley had contrived a family arrangement to keep her divorced parents apart. Standing in front of the church Claryn frowned at the large floral arrangements placed so the dueling parents didn't even have to see each other.

How would my parents have ended up? Claryn did not often dwell on what if. You play the hand you're dealt, her father often said; Kelley sure had.

Traditional wedding roles were mostly cast aside; Kelley was escorting herself down the aisle and her aunt whom she'd lived with down the street from Claryn since ninth grade had the place of honor. As the bridesmaids and groomsmen waited for the bride's entrance, Claryn thought rather ruefully that it wasn't a very good first wedding for Justice.

She had been rather successful at putting thoughts of him aside. When she'd put on her dress she tried to wonder what her father would have thought of it rather than what her date might think. When her hair and make-up were finished she focused on wondering if she looked like her mother. Even standing in front of the altar she tried to pay attention to the seating at the front rather than who might be entering from the rear.

Finally she couldn't help herself. She scanned the rows of people looking for that one too-fine face, the remembrance of which made her stomach flutter. He wasn't there. She breathed, well, that's for the best. Studying her bouquet for a moment, a strange mix of emotions whipped her insides.

Then the music changed. The sun was back out as if on cue to correspond with Kelley's exact choreography. As everyone took notice of the familiar music the evening rays shone through the stained glass bathing the entire room in liquid gold as a radiant Kelley took her first steps down the aisle. The effect was stunning. All heads turned to follow the bride as she neared the front of the assembly. But a more spectacular sight greeted Claryn.

Justice slipped in the back and stood like a golden vision admiring not the bride but the sixth and last bridesmaid. Unconsciously Claryn beamed an uncharacteristic but dazzling smile before turning her face resolutely toward the bride for the rest of the service.

Rick Court sat on the cot in his prison cell flipping through the Hallston Weekly thinking about his return home. The middle school girls' soccer team lined up across the sports section; he turned the page quickly. Oh how I've missed the girls. No misstep now, though. He'd been on his best behavior for over a year. It saddened him to think how much older his favorite girl was now.

He turned to the classifieds and as if his thoughts conjured it up by magic, there was a photo of his favorite girl petting a mutt from the shelter. Rick was mesmerized by her slight frame and the child-like smile she gave the animal. She had to be close to nineteen but she sure didn't look it. Not too old for a reunion after all, he thought. Rick folded the newspaper on his chest and began dreaming of holding her again. The first of many only a few weeks away.

At the reception, Claryn found Justice easily whenever she glanced up from her bridal party duties. As she went from the buffet line, to the head table, to the cake cutting there he was. Standing across the room, leaning against this wall then that, a relaxed figure taking no interest in the people, food or small talk swirling around him. Natalie was the only party go-er Claryn saw try to engage him in conversation and, finding no encouragement, wandered off disappointed.

At last Claryn found her excuse. She gathered her courage to walk two small plates of cake across the room. Seeing his intense gaze and lopsided grin, she didn't even make it halfway. Her pulse slowed and weakness swept over her. In slow motion she saw one of the plates begin to slip from her hand. Miraculously someone took it and she sat not in the expected empty space between tables but in a white folding chair.

She concentrated on breathing evenly as she hoped against hope that she hadn't drawn too much attention to herself. The closest table was just being repopulated with guests carrying cake plates. No one asked after her or noticed her at all, except for the very concerned young man looking intently at her . . . neck?

"It's not polite to stare," she said to hide her confusion and embarrassment.

"Is that one of the ground rules?"

"Most definitely."

"And I'm not supposed to ask about what just happened."

"No," the harsh note in the word made her wince.

"Anything I can do?"

"No, except, maybe…" He looked anxious to assist. "Try the cake. I helped pick it out and. . .it's the best."

Justice looked at the cake as if contemplating eating mud. He plucked the silver fork from the plate and picked at the wedding cake. A crystallized pansy capped the confection.

"Small talk, you know, that would help."

31

"Oh, I probably forgot to mention that I'm not very good at small talk." He gestured around the room. "Been carefully avoiding it all evening."

Claryn couldn't blame him as she looked over the room full of strangers. "What did you think of the wedding?"

"It was beautiful," he said.

A shaky bite of cake tasted different under scrutiny. She spoke with her mouth half full. "Too much staring."

"Right." They sat quietly taking in the scene around them till Kelley's aunt came over. She gushed just a bit about the ceremony, the turn out, the meal. Claryn then introduced Justice who was all "yes, ma'am" "I agree" and any other two word responses that would suffice.

Tiring of carrying the conversation, the aunt let an awkward pause lengthen before saying with a slight frown, "Well, I'll report back to Kelley that you two are getting along fine, then. See you later. A pleasure to meet you."

"Sent to check up on us," said Claryn. "Well, Kelley is nothing if not relentless. And you really are bad at small talk."

Claryn cleaned the last bite of cake off her fork. She was fine now. It was fun to think he might be less comfortable than he looked. It set her more at ease.

She stared at the cake he barely touched. "Can I have your pansy?"

"Sure. It's all yours." He tried not to notice how close she leaned, how near her hand was to his. As a diversion, he looked off at the bride who made a visit to two tables before being called to the dance floor. Most of the guests had cameras and half the people rushed over each other like paparazzi trying to get the best shots.

Claryn laughed at a memory of her friend's planning and proceeded to tell Justice how Kelley chose the songs, the fun they had at the bakers, how her aunt had talked her into having flowers when Kelley wanted to forego them entirely. The constant distractions served well, and the comfortable silences reminded Claryn of people watching with her dad.

32

Justice was careful with his sidelong glances, trying to measure how much staring was too much according to the pulse rate at her throat. The music was too loud to rely on his hearing.

Claryn stole glances at his hands, his profile, even his shoes. He was still and comforting in the midst of the hustle and bustle.

A little boy came by with one of the disposable cameras from the tabletops in his hand and one in each pocket. He had obviously decided how best to spend his time and Claryn could only imagine what was on those cameras.

"Can I take your picture, please?" he said standing close.

"Sure, how's this?" said Claryn.

Not thinking he might need to back away he told them, "Ya'll aren't sitting close enough." He directed them to move and Claryn obediently scooted her chair to sit almost right in front of Justice. He sat very still admiring Claryn's pile of loose curls as the photo was snapped. Then, as she turned her chair back around, loose strands wisped across his face.

The moment she sat, he stood.

"Excuse me, please," he mumbled as he walked away.

Claryn wondered what she did wrong. She nibbled a couple more bites of his cake before Jill and Mary accosted her and proceeded to drag her out on the open dance floor. Claryn was the queen of line dancing and had promised to teach them a new one.

Justice took a stroll around the parking lot for fresh air before manning a post near the entrance adjacent to a lit fichus tree. Kelley finished her table rounds and made her way over.

"Felicitations," he said.

"That's one I haven't heard tonight," she said. "Thank you." She spotted Claryn on the dance floor.

"I'm surprised to see her enjoying dancing so much," he said.

"Ah, well. Her Dad taught us both when we hardly reached his waist."

"There is more space out there too," he murmured. "Can't say it's my preferred dancing style, though."

He didn't seem too pleased.

Undaunted, Kelley smiled, "Aunt Mel said your first date was going pretty well. Was she wrong?"

He exhaled. "I honestly find that very difficult to gauge."

"How many . . . incidents?" she asked as they both watched Claryn shimmy.

"Just one, I think."

"Oh my, well you're doing very well then." She gave him an encouraging pat on the arm. "We might just try to keep you around."

He glanced at his shoes for a moment, thinking before returning his gaze to the dance floor.

"She has no idea how beautiful she is, does she?"

"My Claryn?" Kelley sipped champagne. "Clueless. I probably couldn't stand her otherwise." She said thoughtfully, "I hate to leave her but maybe she was telling the truth. Maybe she really is doing better." Kelley looked at him pointedly, "She just needs time."

"I've got plenty of that," said Justice.

Kelley smiled at Justice's comment and then smacked the side of her head. "Ah, I've got an idea!" She bummed a cell phone off the next person who walked by and sent a text from it, before handing it back.

"Come on then," she grabbed his hand, leading him on the dance floor. The next three songs in a row were line dances, all noticeably new to Justice.

Kelley tried to teach him the first one, but as Claryn pointed out over the din, "He can't see your feet for the skirt!"

So Claryn took charge and Kelley moved off with her beau throwing Justice a wink. It was great while it lasted, but the DJ called for the money dance after that.

Justice got Claryn some water and they stood side by side as she absently inclined her words to his ear to explain the dance to him.

34

"How much do people pay?" he asked.

"Just whatever they want, I guess. I usually do a five or ten dollar bill but I'm not even carrying a purse tonight."

"I've got a twenty."

They waited in line, and when Justice put the twenty in Kelley's white satin purse she declared it too much for one person, grabbed Claryn's hand and had the three of them dancing in a circle holding hands.

Justice felt rather than saw the moment Claryn's pulse slackened; he cut out early leaving the two friends to finish the song.

When Claryn stepped off the dance floor he suggested some fresh air.

Cutting her eyes at him, Claryn thought, it's not possible he sensed I was losing it, right? What she said was, "That's your standard line, isn't it?"

"I don't have a standard line."

"Except for me, apparently."

"Well, if it works, you know. . ."

"I don't know, Kelley and George will sneak off soon . . ."

"But you know she'd be delighted to think we sneaked off together first. Maybe we should cut out all together."

Claryn couldn't help but laugh. Taking in the people, the loud music, her own catchy breath she said, "You know what, that actually sounds really good. Meet me at the door."

She cut in to a slow dance with the bride and groom, swayed with them a couple bars and then gave her friend a goodbye hug. Usually she felt more relief when leaving a crowd behind. Heading out with her date robbed the fresh air of its oxygen.

Jeff Adams turned the rifle over in his hands appreciatively. It was certainly a step up from his own sawed off shotgun. The smooth polished stock reflected the care its owner gave it. Adams nodded his head at the self-proclaimed marksman as he returned the firearm.

"I've never been much good at distances, but it sure would come in handy." Adams admitted. "Have you ever killed a man?"

"You do what needs doing in the service," the man known as Fleets responded. "But this isn't about men."

Fleets had seen something or lost someone and didn't much care to talk about it. A very useful combination of skill, commitment and discretion, Adams thought, as long as he remembers who gives the orders now.

Adams left his new team member with the task of modifying ammunition and told him he would call as soon as he had solid targets. Fleets nodded, pleased with his new mission.

Chapter 5

Claryn braced herself for being alone with Justice who was all caution and care as he opened the reception hall and car doors for her. He followed the ground rules so well. Too well. Why should that bother me? Good grief, she thought, the money dance coming to mind. We held hands before I even realized it.

She reflected as she watched him driving on automatic back into town. As if on cue he had left the dance floor the moment her heart flagged, but he couldn't know that. Could he? She decided the rules only went one way and proceeded to stare at him while he drove. It was hard to get a handle on all her mixed-up feelings. Attraction and fear came out on top, so she turned to distraction.

"You drive awfully fast."

"Is keeping the speed limit one of the ground rules?"

No such thing as too fast. Sometimes she imagined taking off so fast her problems would be left in a plume of dust.

"Not one of mine," she said.

"Noted," he smiled over at her.

"But keeping your eyes on the road is." She wasn't concerned about traffic safety. Oddly enough, she felt safe with him. All the more frustrating because it meant her issues were there regardless. She pushed the thought aside.

"You didn't eat one bite of that wedding cake."

Justice changed direction. "Where are we headed?"

"The church, if that's okay. I need to grab a couple things there."

He turned on High Street to go that direction.

"You are also very aware of personal space," Claryn said.

"What do you mean?"

"I watched the little dance you did with that Rae the other night at Burger Shack."

He liked the way she said 'that Rae' but said nothing.

"I've never seen someone as conscious of it as I am."

"You," he said, "are very observant."

His tone was off. Was he irritated or complimenting her?

"Not really," she cocked her head. "What happened when that boy took our picture?"

Justice stopped by a curb and pocketed his keys. Then he faced her squarely and reached over to unbuckle her seatbelt. The reaction hit immediately. Couldn't be helped. She felt trapped and suddenly weak. He turned away giving her room to breathe before he opened her door. Claryn blinked. They were already at the church.

The side door lock was stubborn. Claryn jiggled the key this way and that before Justice offered to try. He put his ear close like he was cracking a safe, wiggled the key, and they both heard the satisfying thunk of the bolt.

In the dim security lighting he followed her studying her silouette and thinking about her reactions. She turned left to the parlor door, but he was drawn by the red glow of the exit sign shining on the sanctuary door.

Claryn turned her questioning eyes on him.

"Do you need any help in there?" he asked.

"No."

"Then I'll just wait in here."

She nodded.

He sounds sad.

Collecting the little items left here and there in the parlor, she tried to figure out how to salvage the rest of the evening. She'd just seen her best friend happily married and was on the best date of her life.

She, Claryn Anderson, was hoping for a second date. Amazing. And Justice? He seemed to sense when to back off. Thoughtful, concerned, and, on both a positive and negative note, he was very attractive. She'd just never met anyone like him. But now a pall hung over the end of the evening.

How do I fix this?

She took her bag to the side door, left it and entered the sanctuary. It was already tidy and ready for the next day's service. The light scent of the Murphy's oil soap used on the pews permeated the dimness. It smelled clean like a fresh start. The way a church ought to smell, she thought.

Her eyes took a couple moments to adjust to the pale moonlight filtering through a veil of stained glass. Justice sat a few rows back, his head bent over his knees as if in prayer. She closed the space between them, slid down the pew behind him and sat in the dark. No words came to her, so she just sat. It was a good place to simply "be" she thought. In the quiet she closed her eyes, knowing he was an arm's length away though the hum of the electricity was the only sound her ears detected.

After a while he spoke. He was still facing forward, half talking to her, half talking to himself.

"Why are you so afraid of me? I mean--" His muttering sounded like, "Lord knows you probably should be but no one's that observant." He sat back seemingly talking to the altar…reasoning with it.

He exhaled and hesitated before resolutely going forward. "I thought it was a man thing, you know. I'm pretty observant myself and there were a couple times at the bar when I thought . . . but then no, cause Kelley's George is fine."

Justice stretched his arms out down both sides of the pew speaking to the vaulted ceiling. "George you can embrace and dance around with, but me? No . . . it's . . . you don't have to talk about it, I've heard of it before I've just never met anyone that has it."

"Has what?"

"That inverse fight-or-flight reaction." He pulled his arms back in close and hunched over like a boxer bracing for a side blow. "You're afraid, mostly of me, but instead of getting an adrenaline boost with a racing heart, your energy drains and your pulse drops like you just lost a liter of blood, maybe more. I get that. The whole vasovagal thing. It's wild to see, but I get it.

"And I get not wanting to talk about something in your life. I've got stuff like that. I guess everyone does. I hadn't thought much about it before. But why just me? Everybody else is fine."

He appeared to be turning it over in his mind, and Claryn felt badly about not helping with an answer.

Her voice was so small. "Not everybody."

They sat in silence together, a silence that wasn't so much companionable as heavy. She guessed from the set of his shoulders against the back of the pew that his hands were folded in his lap. His head tilted down again and he seemed to be barely breathing.

In the dark of the church, sitting behind him this way, she wanted to talk. She wanted to confess. But even contemplating how to start made the weakness slip over her. Breaths came short and shallow; her heart grew sluggish.

"Stop. Please stop." He pressed his hands into his face. "I don't have to know anything. You don't have to tell me."

How do you tell someone things you can't bear to think about? Things you only half remember. She'd never really told anyone. Even with Kelley it had been more of a "me too" thing.

"I'm sorry," he said. "I wasn't supposed to ask. I'm sorry." He shook his head. "I should take you home."

Neither of them moved, though.

Claryn wrestled with herself. She leaned forward, immediate weakness. But she waited it out till her breathing was almost back to normal.

Then quickly, before she could change her mind, she ran a hand through the back of his hair. Her arm got so heavy she could hardly move it. It dropped back to her lap.

She was so close behind him that every short breath she took felt like she was breathing him in and out. A scent so soft and appealing that a vision of making daisy chains as a child popped into her head followed by something more elusive and incredibly tantalizing. At first it made things

40

worse, but after what seemed an eternity she felt herself relax ever so slightly. It was enough. It gave her hope.

"I'm sorry too," she whispered.

If she had sat back at that point Justice would have accepted the dismissal. But she stayed where she was.

He knew he had an unfair advantage. Yet, there she was so close he could feel her breath on the back of his neck.

Nothing ventured, nothing gained.

"Would you consider going out with me again anyway?"

She smiled in the dark; he could hear it when she answered.

"Yes."

So he smiled too.

Chapter 6

Justice drove home more slowly than usual, unsure of how to approach his brother. Chess was due back from his hunting trip north. Justice had spent a great deal of time over the years trying to convince his older brother that the way their stepmother, Sephauna, had trained them to survive was not only dishonest but wrong. Seducing humans when they should be protecting them just wasn't right.

Chess was big on talk and Justice didn't know what he wanted to say or not say. Honestly, he didn't know what he was doing with Claryn, but at this moment he felt like hypocrite. "You don't have it out with temptation," he'd said, "because she'll have the first and the last bite." Chess was coming round to Justice's way of thinking. He made regular hunting trips now and dated less. It helped matters that the human population was increasingly contaminated.

Justice backed his black 1969 Plymouth GTX into bay three of their auto shop. He hadn't expected Claryn to comment on his car. He figured it wasn't the kind of thing to impress her and that wasn't the reason he drove it. He enjoyed the power of the motor and the idea that he'd brought it back to life.

Chess was waiting with his feet propped up on an oversized toolbox they used for a coffee table. A new blu-ray movie still in the plastic lay there as Chess worked over a game console trying not to break it in frustration. Justice liked to mess with his brother about how mashing the buttons harder was the key to winning any game.

The brothers had worked on vehicles together since one of them first crank started a Model T, though it was a greater passion for Justice than Chess who became enamored with the silver screen and then the digital age. For Justice, driving one of the cars he worked on was an extension of the pleasure on a job well done. Chess drove his muscle car more as a reflection of the image he had of his own personality and for the artistry of the model.

Chess grinned to see Justice out of the frump he'd been wearing for work. "There he is and no longer in your bling from the Shack. Is that a new suit?"

Justice picked imaginary lint off his suit as he contemplated an excuse for going outside and using another entrance. Nothing came to mind as the other entrance was emergency access.

One thing the brothers Cain had were noses like top line bloodhounds. Sephauna had recognized their talents before she brought the humans into her coven and thereafter taught them how to use their heightened senses.

Diagnostically there were very few predilections for disease that a DNA test would find better than a Cain inspection. Sure, a few items required a tasting, but that wasn't their business. The human body's capacity to function and repair while absorbing abuse across every operating system continued to amaze Justice.

In today's day and age, excess was the abuse of choice, at least where they lived. Justice thought about Kelley's bridal party. Mary indulged her sweet tooth and consumed too many trans fats. No surprise to anyone that Natalie partied too hard and too often, forcing her liver to process a lot of alcohol, but most of them would be shocked to learn she was experimenting with a pharmaceutical chest of drugs as well. Kelley ate a balanced diet, which unfortunately included a high mix of certain pesticides, food colorings, and additives typical of the "healthy" American diet. Her Aunt Mel was a borderline diabetic. Chelsea was struggling with bulimia. And then there was Claryn. She and Chelsea got the most exercise in the group and had the highest metabolic rates not just of food but also of everyday "poisons." The things Justice and Chess could tell after one evening in a crowded bar were mind-boggling.

Justice assumed for the longest time that their abilities were common, but their elder, Arvon, assured him they were not. Chess was especially gifted. In one evening at a place like the O-Zone, he could tell with an 80 percent accuracy rate which people would tolerate vampire venom and benefit from its healing effects. He had confirmed this through experimentation sometime ago, and now knew these people made up only half the general population as compared with two-thirds just a couple hundred years in the past. Venom deaths were on the rise, though untraceable, and the numbers of those who could successfully be changed diminished over time.

Chess once asked their oldest acquaintance if there might have been a time when their presence was primarily a benefit to mankind. Chess theorized that the original relationship was actually a natural symbiosis beneficial to all.

The elder, Arvon, had laughed derisively. Would it sooth his conscience as he seduced his victims to dream of a time when all was right with the world? What difference could it possibly make to fantasize of a time when humanity might have been purer and their own longevity thus incalculable? Follow the rules, Arvon said. Neither make nor take. Live long and prosper. If you by your "gifts" occasionally make one miserable life a little better for a fleeting moment in time, think on that. Arvon ended the conversation saying the general direction of the spiral is down and it is widening into chaos.

Chess thought he caught Arvon on a particularly bad day, maybe a bad decade. He never revisited the conversation.

Despite what Justice knew about Claryn, Chess would have known so much more in the short span of an introduction. Justice knew she tended to drink water or tea with a slice of lemon, she had a great metabolism, moderated her intake of and exposure to just about everything. She was either prone to wellness or averse to medication. Chess would know which it was. And the things Chess was gifted at discerning, and would consider the most vital to know, Justice told himself didn't matter.

It's not that kind of relationship, not going to be.

Justice walked over to their "customer waiting area" which served as their living room and was open to the auto bays. They did most of their business online these days and through a reseller, so no one actually ever sat in the waiting area except for them or the occasional free lance elder.

A black leather sectional faced an entertainment center built entirely of engine parts. The thing weighed a ton but Justice had patented several versions of the design and sold the things to specialty shops for an incredibly exorbitant amount.

Edging around the far side of the couch Justice saw that Chess was once again playing the online "Mission 2B Immortal" game that Arvon had turned them on to.

"Damn," Chess threw his remote console which skittered down the couch. "I'll never become immortal at this rate." Chess had yet to make it past level three.

He looked up at his brother, "Which bucket list job requires a suit?"

"I went to a wedding."

"Seriously!?" Chess sat up quickly. "You should have told me. I totally would have come back into town a day early for that."

Chess got up to turn off the red button on the power strip with his bare toe. For someone who probably had stacks of gold stock piled somewhere, Chess was a little obsessive about saving electricity. Doing our part for the environment, he said.

He started toward his brother. "So are you adding wedding planner to the list?"

Chess stopped dead in his tracks, turning his head first one direction and then the other. He walked over and sniffed around his brother's head. Justice turned and shoved his face away.

"Holy. . . ." Chess hopped over the couch to sit closer to his brother.

"I don't know whether to be pleased or upset. I finally decide to start living clean and you go and fall off a hundred year old wagon. Wassup, dog?" Chess's fascination with the culture of whatever age he lived in tended to extend to every facet including popular vernacular.

45

Justice had worried over nothing. Chess was Chess. He took life as it came, made few judgments, and was a great friend. The other possible reactions he had envisioned were Justice projecting.

"I had a date."

Chess nodded encouragingly but Justice decided to inspect his fingernails.

"So how'd it go?"

"Mixed bag. Good mostly, I think."

Chess feigned nonchalance but his mind was racing with questions he knew better than to ask.

"You got a second date lined up?"

"I do." Part of Justice wanted to ask for advice. Chess had more experience with girls than, well, than anybody. But he also had an agenda with them.

"You still headed north this week?" Chess's eyebrows were half up his forehead as he asked.

Justice had forgotten his scheduled visit, but the question was a little loaded per the eyebrows. He ignored it.

"Okay." Chess thought this was what people meant by pulling teeth. Justice wasn't volunteering anything. "What's she like then?"

Chess looked past his brother to the car. The easiest thing to do would be to sniff around the vehicle and track this chick down, answer a lot of questions. But Justice Cain had gone on a date, against his better judgment and without any input from his personal peanut gallery. And he was going again. This girl might mean something or have the possibility. Chess wasn't about to jeopardize that.

Justice didn't want to analyze and describe Claryn, so he tried a different tact. "She has an inverse fight-flight reaction."

"Really?" Chess contemplated that a moment. "Wow, how did you find that out?"

"She's afraid of me."

46

"Wait. She's afraid of you, but she went out with you? She didn't--see something, did she?"

"Nope. She says it's not just me, but that's all I've seen."

Chess was grinning so broadly now that it annoyed Justice.

"What!"

"You really know how to pick 'em." He rested his weight on the back of the couch. "So what triggers the reaction?"

"Oh, you know. Look at her too long, stand too close, touch her arm."

"Ha!" Chess simply had to laugh. There was nothing else for it. "And the hair thing?"

"She did that from behind. Nearly made her pass out."

Chess sank back down into the black leather. This news meant most of his questions could wait. The relationship, whatever form it ended up taking or where it may or may not go, was on the slow track . . . the incredibly slow track.

"That's . . ."

"Yeah."

The atmosphere in the room was subdued. Chess was amused but his good buddy, JT, obviously was not. Keep it simple, he told himself.

"What's her name?"

"Claryn."

"Claryn," he rolled it over. "That's a nice name. Does she have a last name to go with it?"

"Not that I'm telling you."

In other words, stay away.

"Oooo, protective, territorial, I see how it is," he said, scrutinizing his brother. "I'm intrigued already. So when am I going to meet this Claryn?"

In his mind Justice thought, never, and was surprised by how possessive he felt.

"Let's see if I even make it to a third date."

"Yeah, cause we both know you ain't makin' it to first base!" Chess gave Justice a friendly punch in the arm as he got up.

"You living in that suit now or what?" He was talking to himself now as he went. "How was your week, Chess?" At the bottom of the stair he answered. "Fine, real fine. Thanks for asking."

Chapter 7

Candace Fortner was the fifth missing person reported in the Oklahoma City paper in less than two months. Adams picked up the story from an internet news service that mostly dealt with outlandish tales of the strange and unusual. In their pages every death, missing person, corrupt politician, or underhanded business operation were connected.

His hacker was hired rather than part of the team but found the Quest Institute connections to the Mission 2B Immortal game fairly easily. Unable to get what he wanted from the institute, he had tried to kidnap suspected members. It was difficult because they were so insular, tended to travel in pairs, and were so strong. It was also rife with danger.

So he hung out at some likely bars and continued recruiting his own lackeys before kicking his plans into high gear. He called himself The Slayer and was intent on at least becoming that. If he couldn't join them, he'd see them pay.

With input from the game he tested for suspected weaknesses and discovered a natural weapon. From there it was a simple matter to pick off some low members of the institute. He knew Tulsa was too hot after their third slaying, so he began looking for other big game to take down.

When the third missing person in Albuquerque turned up bloodless with his throat cut, Adams sent a man down to see if their quarry was afoot there. Additional information supported this theory. Adams was more confident than ever in his own investigative prowess. Hadn't he found the Quest Institute on his own? He was certain he'd turned up another target.

Fake credentials on hand, Adams offered his investigative services to Candace's family and eventually got a lucky tip; she was spotted in the company of another woman headed southwest along a trail of scattered missing person reports. He did not inform the family, rather he advised them that their daughter was, as the police had said, either dead or did not want to be found. He solemnly collected his fees from the family and then, with photos of her still in hand, Adams began his pursuit.

He caught up with her on the streets of Albuquerque and used his own surveillance photos of both women to ask around and find their lair. His accomplices needed more proof of what the women were and delay ensued. Then abruptly Candace disappeared from their radar, but her companion fled the city, not realizing she'd picked up a tail.

Chapter 8

Claryn was happy to be back at work even at six a.m. on a Monday morning. Mrs. Smithson, the shelter owner and manager, had jumped at the chance to have her on full time and said she would look into benefits for her as soon as possible.

She let half the dogs out the east door into a high fenced play area and talked to the others while she cleaned out kennels. Felix, love struck lab mix pup that he was, opted not to play but to tag around at her heals. She waggled his ears up and down in opposite directions as she asked him, "How am I going to tell Sissy I'm college a drop out? Huh?"

Felix blinked his doe eyes at her slowly, completely contented with this smidgen of direct attention.

"Lucky for us, we've got another two weeks to ponder that thought." She returned to her mopping.

She held the mop for a moment like Carol Burnett's stage prop and loudly asked the other wall of full kennels if they would like to hear about her latest love interest. Several of the dogs whined and whimpered, which she interpreted as universal assent. By mid-afternoon the dogs knew more about her thoughts and feelings on Justice than Kelley would probably ever find out. And that was day one.

Chess watched Justice pace back and forth across their living room with much less patience by Wednesday night.

"Just call her already."

"What if she's having second thoughts? If I call I'll just give her an opportunity to cancel."

"Fine. Good thing we don't have carpet." Chess was also frustrated with this stupid online game. He'd promised to tell Arvon about his progress, but at this point it was simply too embarrassing. Dead again on level three, he set the console down carefully on the tool chest. He'd broken two others this week and was down to his last one.

"I've got an idea. Let's go check in on her."

Justice stopped pacing and glared at Chess, "What?"

"And by let's, I mean you. You go check on her."

Justice considered. "She's not expecting me. I'd probably give her a heart attack. Besides, it's what, two o'clock in the morning?"

"It's perfect! You've got to do this at least once. You sneak over, check out her room--"

Flaring nostrils accompanied the glare this time.

"I mean, of course, you see if she's okay, sleeping good and all that."

Justice's eyes went back and forth as if he was reading his own thoughts at arm's length like air writing from a sparkler.

"I should check on her. Her step mom's out of town and she's all alone in that big house."

"Yes! Exactly." Chess was so pleased he was getting JT out of the way. Now he could really concentrate on this ridiculous game.

"Yeah, I should have done this earlier." He headed to the door but stopped mid-stride.

"You don't think it's sort of...an invasion of privacy, do you?"

"Absolutely not. She's just sleeping, and you're making sure she's safe. That's what's important."

By the time Justice reached Claryn's house, Chess had already died twice on level two and broken the last console.

The night caressed the Darkman's face like a lover as he walked through the backyard to his access point. He slipped between sage bushes breaking off a piece of the aromatic plant to inhale more of its sweet fragrance. At the door he dropped the sprig, stepping on it as he went to work using his locksmith skills. Had to be one of the most useful classes I ever took, he thought. He worked the tumblers with the rake until all three fell into place and felt the satisfying release of the lock as the tension bar turned the lock in his hand. With a last glance around in the darkness he disappeared into the interior of the house.

He had taken his time choosing this first home. In this one he had to be exceedingly careful. Leave no trace the Nat,ional Park Service said. No trace for those who came after; in this case, the police, the worried friend, a family member, and, eventually, the crime lab. Here he took extra care because he might not be done with his vacation playtime even after the investigation got hot.

The Darkman sometimes thought if he could only explain his need, how desperate he was for this two months out of his year when he could play to his heart's content, they might understand. Dull, dreary, lack-luster living, if you could call it that, filled his existence the other ten months of the year. The only thing keeping him going was the plan. Choosing the town, finding a playhouse to rent, watching the real estate ads for the area. This particular home had a virtual online tour. How helpful was that.

The layout of the home was so clear in his mind, he didn't need a light at all. Still, the television sent pulses of eerie illumination across his path as a nighttime chase scene roared across the screen. The squeal of tires covered any light squeaks the floor made as he crossed the living room to the hallway.

Her bedroom door stood slightly ajar, inviting another to the inner sanctum. He lightly pressed the door with one finger careful for any noise the hinges might make, but the door was obligingly silent. He opened it wide for that first view of his new doll laying so still in her perfect display. He could have stood admiring her for hours, but now was the time for collection.

He positioned himself over her, carefully pulling the chloroform-soaked washcloth from a zip lock bag. With an intense rush of excitement, he firmly pressed the washcloth over her mouth and nose. Her eyes fluttered open making him angry. Dolls don't open their eyes when lying down. It was wrong. Her weakly flailing arms dropped to her side once more resting as they should be, posable.

He so wanted to touch her, to position her and play. But, no. That has to wait. He slipped his gloved hands under her, slid her over his shoulder and stood. Her weight was light as he walked down the stairs to the garage collecting her keys from the dish in the hall along the way.

Too excited to move slowly, he bumped her head against the doorframe leading to the garage with a dull meaty thump. It left the smallest scrape of blood from her temple on the wood. Safely stowed in her own trunk, the Darkman opened and closed the garage with the remote hanging from her sun visor. His doll rested unaware of their voyage to another house with a similar garage, a playhouse of nightmares.

When the phone rang, Claryn popped up completely disoriented. The clock said 3:00 am. She tried to ignore the ringing but the phone screamed at her like a banshee. She rolled over with a groan and picked it up.

"Hello?"

"Hello! Miss me yet?" Kelley's exuberant voice. "George had some sneaky romantic plans to finalize so I thought I'd call and see how you're doing, and what plans you've got for the weekend. Stuff like that."

"Kelley, it's the middle of the night."

"No, I knew you were getting up early for your job and timed it just so we'd have a good talk time before you go into work."

"From 3:00 to 5:00?" Claryn yawned. "Seems like a long time for George's secret mission."

"Heavens to Betsy! It's 3 am there?! I'm so sorry, sweetie. I'm surprised you answered the phone. But since you're awake now, tell me everything."

Claryn sighed. She couldn't imagine calling anyone from her honeymoon.

"I should be asking if everything's okay with you. You're calling from Spain during your honeymoon at nine o'clock in the morning?"

"George has funny ideas about romance."

"Like?"

"Well, yesterday he surprised me with a snorkeling trip and the day before that it was a hot air balloon ride."

"But you're afraid of water and heights. Didn't that come up when you were dating?"

"Yes, but it's like he's on some personal mission now to help me overcome my fears – all in one week."

Claryn thought of her set up with Justice. "That's ironic."

"What?"

"Nothing. That's lunacy."

"I know! Isn't it? So I'm a little nervous about today's plans. Oh, I think I hear George. So you'll call me Sunday afternoon with all the news, right?"

"I didn't say we were going out again."

"You promised!"

"Maybe he didn't ask."

"Now *that* is lunacy. I've never seen a guy so smitten. Oh, gotta go. Love you!"

Smitten. Now Claryn really wanted to hear how Kelley made that assessment. Claryn had spent much of the wedding trying not to notice how much he was looking at her. She rolled over and pulled the covers over her head. I should at least try to get a little more sleep. Once awake she was usually awake for the day.

Justice rolled in with a look of thunder on his face. He walked part way over, stopped to face the wall, and gave the cinder blocks a couple good punches that left dents.

Better the wall than me, Chess thought.

"What happened?"

"She has nightmares. Horrible, gut wrenching nightmares." He turned to hit the wall again but leaned his head into it instead. His arms dangled uselessly at his side.

"There's nothing I can do. Somebody hurt her bad, and she's reliving it in her dreams, and there's not one thing I can do about it."

55

Chess was thinking two things. First, this girl came with a lot of baggage. Second, JT was way too serious after a single date.

The only thing he said was, "I'm glad we don't dream."

"Yeah, me too."

"Maybe it was one bad night, comes and goes."

"Maybe, but I'm going to find out. And if I ever find the creep that did this to her, he's a dead man."

Chess held his fist out, a gesture of solidarity.

"Justice," he said, not meaning his brother's name.

"Justice," was the fist-to-fist reply. JT headed for the stairs but Chess stopped him.

"Arvon called with some interesting news."

"Can it wait? I'm going to bed."

"Yeah. It'll wait."

Chapter 9

When Claryn heard a car roll into the driveway Thursday around 6 p.m. she thought she'd gotten her date night wrong. A quick peek through the drapes showed Sissy, sans the boyfriend, dragging luggage out of her Kia Sport. Claryn unlocked the door and went to help.

"Claryn! I didn't expect you here till tomorrow night after school. Is today Friday? Is everything all right?"

"It's Thursday, and everything's fine with me. What about you? You weren't due back till next week, right?"

"You're such a smart girl. Here," she handed her a small duffel. "I'm so glad you're here. I've got news!" She sang the word "news," so it was apparently good news from Sissy's perspective.

After dropping two pieces of luggage, several small totes and a small trash bag in the middle of the living room floor, Sissy turned on one heel.

"I can't wait another minute." She thrust her hand out toward Claryn. "Brad and I got married!"

Claryn's mouth dropped. The proffered hand had a flat corral ring on the left finger, the kind of cheap trinket you buy at the beach one week and break slapping your hand down on the table at home the next.

"Of course, we'll pick out a real ring later, money being so tight and all right now. But, yeah! Say something!"

"Congratulations?"

"I knew you'd be happy for us. I told him not to worry about it." She put her arm through Claryn's, directing them toward their old hide-a-bed couch for a chat. They sat on the burgundy faux suede slipcover they'd chosen to hide the psychedelic green upholstery.

"But of course he'd think of you. He's such a thoughtful man. Isn't he?" Sissy gushed.

Claryn had to agree. After an incredible string of the scummiest boyfriends imaginable, Sissy had found a thoughtful, indisputably nice guy.

"He reminds me of your dad. Is it okay to say that? I just mean he's a keeper, you know?"

Claryn nodded. Sissy really needed to hold onto a good man, because she attracted so many rotten ones. Impulsively, Claryn gave her a big hug, and Sissy started crying. That made Claryn cry and soon they were a blubbering mess.

"I just love you. You are the best sort of daughter-friend person I could ever have. So I knew you'd be okay with this and with my other decision."

Claryn nodded, not trusting her voice.

"I've decided to sell the house."

"The house?"

"Yes! It's too big for just the two of us, and you're off at school most the time. And soon you'll be making your own life. I'm hardly ever going to be here now. The realtor said--"

"The realtor?" Claryn was looking around only half listening to Sissy. Of course Sissy could sell the house, Daddy had left it to her. For a moment Claryn could hear her father reading to her before bed in this spot. In the kitchen they'd cooked Saturday morning waffles together. How could someone without these memories do anything more than occupy the space? It was the only home she remembered.

"It's ours outright," Sissy said, "so we could split the money. Just think, you could have your own townhouse or condo. How grown up would that be? I hope it's not too fast, but the listing comes out in tomorrow's paper and the realtor will be here first thing in the morning for a walk-through. That's why I came home early."

The house was too big for Claryn alone. This was a good decision, really. Sissy had made a good decision, and if she had consulted Claryn? Well, it wouldn't have gone over very well. Looking around the room, out the patio doors, down the hall, Claryn knew it was a good decision. She just kept saying it over and over to herself.

"Good decision," slipped softly from between her lips.

"Oh, Claryn! I'm so glad you think so. I was so worried."

Sissy was all hugs and more tears, not noticing how limp Claryn was in her arms.

Out past the ghost town of Los Cerrillo, New Mexico, Jenny checked the roads and dirt tracks leading to the homestead for any recent disturbance. Other than the regular access of the side road for turquoise mining, the rest of the property lay abandoned like numerous other holdings in central New Mexico.

In the late 1800's the area had been bustling with settlers and miners who dug out the gold, silver, lead, zinc and turquoise from beneath the hard packed earth. Untapped uranium deposits waited in the hills now, where mostly hobbyist mining operations poked around for the silver and turquoise.

Not far from Santa Fe, the old Cayne homestead was off the beaten path where tourists now trekked from one historical town to the next along the Turquoise Trail National Scenic Byway. Los Cerrillo had some residents, but they were there to cater to the tourists dutifully delivered by the scenic byway. Raised outside of Santa Fe, Jenny had always wondered what it would have been like in the mid 1880's at the height of the boom.

This was the one place the brothers would not think to look for her. It felt welcoming, as if she was coming home, but she knew her thirst would drive her back into the clubs or a nearby city soon. For now she would rest.

Jenny spent more time in repose these days rather than less. Chess had said she would need less down time as she grew older. Of course, he had assumed she would follow his ridiculous rules. Neither make nor take, he said like he was quoting a nursery rhyme. But the taken blood didn't weaken her. Indeed, she was stronger than ever. So what if I need a little extra rest, she thought. Jenny Cayne lay down for the day wishing her long life extended back in time instead of forward.

Adams saw there was no way to access the rural property without tipping his hand to the female vamp. So he had decided to wait southwest on the edges of Albuquerque while the team watched the roads north and south.

When their pigeon finally did fly the coup past him in the south, he sent his men after her while he searched the old house and outbuildings. Considering the old world paintings, the diverse library in several languages, and the lack of kitchen equipment so different from the female's other lair, he figured this place had once been home to an older coven.

Adams spent the next two days going over every small item looking for leads like he was panning for gold. Disappointed but not disheartened, he latched on to the idea that the property itself was the end of the rainbow where others of the coven would eventually turn up. Since he hoped to catch them unaware, Adams covered his search of the place by hosting a keg party for some local youths.

Chapter 10

When Friday evening finally rolled around, Justice found himself ready a full hour early, pacing back and forth in his room as he practiced various conversation starters.

Chess stepped into JT's bedroom doorway, enjoying his brother's unease. JT, who was so sure in every other area of life, was venturing out into the minefields of dating. All the while Chess, the voice of experience, found his advice unsought.

"Big night, huh? What have you got planned?"

"Dinner and a movie?" he hated that it came out as a question.

Chess's face said it all as his head shook emphatically back and forth.

"Bad move, bro. Yowser!"

"I thought a movie was pretty standard, even for you," JT held up a couple ties against his shirt rethinking his choices. Chess began giving dating pointers as he walked over throwing both ties back in the locker that served as the closet and untucking JT's shirt.

"Yeah, for me. It's fine. But for you? What does a movie say? I want to get close to you in the dark, drop an arm around you, get a little squeeze, maybe even make a move. With this chick?"

JT cringed as he imagined sitting in the dark and hearing her suffer with anxiety throughout an entire movie.

"Okay. Fine. I get it."

"And dinner? Really? When was the last time you tried to eat something, anything, or pretended not to eat with any success? Especially with someone scrutinizing your every move."

Claryn noticed one piece of uneaten cake, so a whole plate of food would be as inconspicuous as fireworks.

JT's face was pure resentment, which thoroughly amused Chess.

"What would you suggest?"

"Bowling. There's activity, good views," he was making hour glass shape with his hands. "Food with an opportunity for disposal while she's faced away. And let's face it, you've already been to a wedding together. You need a little light fun."

It was ideal. Chess knew it and was already smug even though there was no way JT would admit how perfect his brother's plan. JT grabbed his keys off a shelf in the locker.

"Later."

"And don't be early!" the final advice trailed him up the stairs.

Sissy looked out the bay window and spotted the black muscle car parked across the street with someone sitting in it. Not again. Sissy had a boyfriend once who sent someone to check up on her every time he was out of town on the weekend, but she didn't think Brad would do that sort of thing. She edged over to the window figuring it was too light outside for him to see in.

"I tried to wait." Justice knew he'd been spotted twice now by what had to be Claryn's stepmother. He didn't want to appear altogether creepy. When he'd turned down their street and parked, Justice knew he'd spent at least five minutes staring at the shiny new For Sale sign in the front yard. There was no indication that Claryn was home, but her room was on the back of the house. He slid out of the car without bothering to lock it and strolled across the street.

Sissy backed away from the window and called out, "Claryn? Are you expecting someone?"

Her head popped out of her bedroom door.

"He's here already?" she sounded a bit frantic.

Sissy was greatly relieved and suddenly excited. Claryn has a date. Then she checked her enthusiasm. Claryn has a date with a very good-looking boy in a hot car. She went into Claryn's now open door.

"What time is he supposed to be here?"

"Uh, six?" She had been so focused on putting on her make-up the same way the woman at the wedding did that she hadn't paid much attention to the time or her hair. Now it was a quarter till and she felt she

62

was wearing a mop on her head. Her reflection in the vanity mirror did nothing to reassure her.

"What am I going to do?"

"Well, he's unconscionably early." Sissy cocked her head sideways for a moment to study Claryn's unruly tresses. They both jumped when the doorbell rang.

"You blow dry, upside down, while I meet and greet. Then I'll come back and do a quick French braid."

Claryn's concerned eyebrows went up.

"Too school girl? Okay. How 'bout a French twist?"

"How about something not French."

Sissy slapped her hands together. "Ooh, I know just what to do."

She and her wide smile skipped off to answer the door.

Justice wondered if he should ring the bell again but footsteps were coming down the upstairs hall. The house was split-level with an entrance in the middle. Downstairs was a two-car garage, half bath, den and utility room. Upstairs left was the living room, dining and kitchen. The three bedrooms and other two bathrooms were along a hall on the upstairs right. But, of course, he wasn't supposed to know all that, after all he'd only seen it all in the middle of the night.

"Hello. I'm Sissy," she said as she invited him in with one hand. "And you are...?"

"Justice, but most my friends call me JT."

"Justice. Gee it sounds so Old West."

Older than that, he thought. He took a polite look around and followed her up the stairs.

"Would you like some--" she realized she had no idea what was in the fridge, "--water or juice?"

"No, thank you."

They both looked around awkwardly for a moment listening to the dryer down the hall.

"Actually, water sounds good."

63

"Yes! Just a minute. Have a seat."

Justice sat but popped back up when she reentered with a glass. She handed him the glass and waved him to sit again. The blow dryer was still going, so Sissy sat down in the rocking chair that creaked with her movement as Justice sat back down on the couch.

"That's an awfully nice ride you've got out there. Is it yours?"

"Yes. Ma'am. My brother and I actually rebuild old cars."

"Really," Sissy couldn't help batting her eyelashes, "I'd think there'd be pretty good money in that."

"Can be," the dryer stopped, so Sissy was already turning away as he said, "but it takes a lot of time to do the job well."

"Uh-huh? I'll be right back."

She patted him on the knee as she stood.

"Don't you go anywhere."

Justice sipped his water and flinched when the residual tastes from the water treatment plant gave his tongue a taste lashing. Sissy went down the hall to the second door on the left.

It had been a long time since he had water that wasn't purified with a reverse osmosis machine. He was pretty sure he could taste every chemical the local water treatment plant used, and none of them were to his liking. The spider plant sitting on the end table was the immediate beneficiary. The empty glass abandoned nearby. Justice listened to the voices carrying down the hall.

"You may not date much but you sure know how to pick 'em. Oh my—like Thor and the Mayhem Man rolled into one. Just gorgeous, and have you seen his car?"

"Uh, yeah. It's kinda old."

"It's not old! It's a classic. You should definitely say something nice about it."

There was silence for a few minutes.

"There. I think that will do it."

"Thank you. You should have your own shop or something, Sissy. You're really good with hair."

"Yeah, but you've got to go to school, get a license and all that. It takes a lot of money just to get started. But maybe when the house sells, I could do it. In the off-season, maybe. Oh, Claryn, that would be so great!"

"Wouldn't it?" Claryn tried to sound encouraging but she had been trying to ignore the fact that the house was for sale. When she went to check the mail at the curb this morning, she gave the for sale sign as wide a berth as she had the pretend alligators and sea monsters when scrambling up her maple tree fortress in younger days.

Justice stood as the ladies came down the hall. Sissy did a little "ta-da" and stepped aside to present Claryn who blushed instantly.

Sissy didn't seem to notice.   "So where are you two headed?"

Claryn's uncertainty caused stepmom to do a double take.

"The bowling alley," Justice answered and then said to Claryn, "if that's okay?"

After a pause she said, "I haven't been there since I was a kid."

It was difficult for Justice to tell the direction of Claryn's nostalgia, and he started to ask when Sissy cut in.

"What fun!" She was ushering them toward the door. "The perfect place for a first date, JT."

Justice and Claryn exchanged hesitant looks but Sissy already had them out the door and was waving goodbye. She couldn't wait to call Brad and tell him about Claryn's big date. She wished she knew more about cars or had asked because Brad would be as interested in that as anything else.

"Have fun!"

Claryn waved back only to see Sissy pointing and pantomiming, "The car, say something about the car," and then without a beat smiling and waving the moment Justice glanced back.

65

Claryn grasped for something to say as Justice opened the door for her. It's black. It's shiny. It smells like a shoe store? She smiled nervously and slid in across the horizontal stitching of the leather bench seat.

When he reached to turn the ignition she finally blurted, "Your car has such nice wide seats."

Justice swallowed a laugh, "It does, doesn't it."

The engine roared to life and they headed across to the older part of town where the lanes were. My side of town, Justice thought of it.

"Sorry about that whole 'first date' thing." Claryn hoped she hadn't hurt his feelings.

"Sissy didn't know I was coming." His voice was pleasant.

"No, and she's been so busy with this whole realtor thing," Claryn couldn't keep the distress out of her voice.

Justice felt a little distressed himself.

"Where are you moving to?"

"Here. Somewhere close I guess. She came home early and just kind of sprung it on me. It's a good decision." The line she kept saying was as flat as the first time she'd said it.

"Could take a long time for the place to sell," he offered.

"Really?" her voice was hopeful.

"Oh yeah. The housing market is terrible right now. Every sector of real estate. Nothing's moving."

Claryn brightened considerably and started noticing other houses that looked like they'd been on the market for a long time. Even the usually depressing empty storefronts downtown made her more chipper.

Passing an old rundown historical home she couldn't resist saying, "That place has been for sale a really long time."

"Over two years," his comment was rewarded with such a big smile he added, "maybe three."

Arvon's call, although disturbing, relieved Chess on multiple levels. Jenny was dead. Neither he nor JT had had a hand in it, and the sweeping consequences his mistake had thrust upon the world were at an end. Most surprising, he owed his release to a bona fide vampire slayer.

Course, now the trick was to insure he and JT didn't become the slayer's next targets. Chess was pretty sure Jenny hadn't visited their homestead in years, but her body was found closer to it than one would expect. Close as well to her birthplace in Santa Fe.

There was no reason to suspect the slayer knew about their rural property south of town. Arvon was sending him on this roadtrip to take care of the remains, but Chess thought he would swing by the homeplace if possible. He texted JT to tell him he had wrecker detail, their code for body retrieval duty, and not to expect him home till well after dawn. Chess lit out through the night in one of their restored cars on a back road shortcut to the highway leaving clouds of dust in his wake.

Chapter 11

The bowling alley, already half full, was much smaller than Claryn remembered. Her dad had brought her here fairly often after her mom died and then later with Sissy. She hadn't deliberately avoided the place, but after he was gone there didn't seem a reason to go.

They got their shoes and went to search for appropriate balls. Justice found one almost immediately and began setting up the computer scoring system, looking only moderately challenged. When Claryn passed by their lane to look through the other racks, she stopped to inspect the scoring program.

"Wow. That's high speed. The last time I was here this was a tall wooden desk with paper and little pencils."

The good old days, Justice thought. When there wasn't a computer keeping track of the ball speeds on every lane.

She went on searching for a good ball. Her long fingers forced her to settle for a ball that felt too heavy but had a nice fit for her grip. It was previously owned, as indicated by the worn Betty Boop cartoon etched into the dull black surface.

"Clairyn" was first on the screen followed by "JT."

"It's just C-L-A-R-Y-N." She sat in a bright red space chair that matched his in front of the console. The chair beside him was yellow and corresponded to the other two seats facing her on the opposite lane.

"Kelley's wedding program had it wrong then," he was backtracking and correcting the input.

"The programs were done by her cousin. Kind of a last minute thing. Kelley wanted to skip them, but someone in the family put up a fuss."

After explaining she teased, "Aren't you the observant one, JT?"

"Don't you know it, Betty," he nodded at the cartoon on her loaner ball, "and I've got my eye on you, young lady." He instantly regretted it as she bit her lip and looked decidedly uncomfortable.

Searching for a way to recover he saw that several people had pizza sitting on the tables behind their lanes. Food wasn't allowed in the bowling area past that point.

"How about some food?"

"Okay," she answered relieved at the diversion.

Standing in line at the counter, Justice positioned himself slightly behind Claryn and tried not to grimace at the odors coming from the kitchen. The alley was definitely a step down from the Burger Shack and needed to replace their fryer oil in the worst way.

"It's a junk food wonderland, isn't it?" Claryn said examining the menu.

"We could probably have Chinese food delivered."

She shot him a strange look and stepped up to place her order.

"Chicken tenders and French fries." She couldn't get completely away from the French thing this evening.

Justice was pulling out his wallet but spotted her frown.

"Aren't you eating?" Claryn inquired.

"Yes, of course. I'm eating." He looked over the menu, "I'm . . .eating. . . pizza?"

"Messy fingers. You won't drop the ball will you?"

He was rethinking what most people were eating and considering the fact that pizza would be hard to throw away bit by bit.

"Uh, make that two chicken tenders and fries, please."

Claryn grabbed a bottle of malt vinegar from the condiment table, a huge stack of paper napkins, and plastic knives and forks. They set the food where they could stand to eat it at the back of the lane where the rows of balls ran along the wall below the eating booths. Justice spotted a large trash can on the corner beyond their table.

Claryn shook a large bottle of dark liquid up and down till her fries were drenched and swimming in vinegar. Then she stabbed a fat one with her plastic fork and put the whole thing in her mouth at once. It was too hot, so she puffed a bit before offering him the bottle.

Justice tried not to stare. The vinegar smell was an improvement, but now he figured it was the only thing people could smell for at least three lanes in either direction.

"Maybe just a spot." He shook the bottle once over his fries and saw a lady two booths down lock in on the smell she'd been trying to identify as she crinkled her nose at him having caught the offender.

"I'll just put this away. Ladies, first," he indicated the lane.

Claryn was a fairly bad bowler. She knew how to approach the lane, swing the ball, and follow through, but she did it differently every time and was all over the place. One time she'd swing wide with no curve, the next her ball curved straight into the gutter.

Twice she dropped the ball on her backswing and blushed right through to the roots of her hair. He could have caught it for her but decided against such a display.

Justice, on the other hand, walked to the end of the lane, had no form whatsoever, barely swung the ball, and had a hard time missing. But Claryn was just as pleased with his accomplishments as any of her own, and they exchanged high fives whenever one of them got a spare or a strike. Every high five felt electric to Justice, but Claryn seemed not to notice as they walked closely past each other taking their turns. He observed that Claryn's inverse adrenaline reaction seemed to only occur when she was conscious and focused on the fact someone was close to her. Now she was distracted by the game and seemed completely at ease.

Meanwhile at the table opposite the trashcan, a little boy with big sad eyes looked positively mournful each time he caught Justice tossing fries or chicken tenders in the trash. At the end of the first game, Claryn took a restroom break, giving Justice the opportunity to dump the rest of his plate. He wished he could have slipped them to the kid somehow, but from the looks of him the child did not often miss his junk food quota.

When Claryn threw her fourth gutter ball of the evening, Justice quipped about having the bumpers put up on their lane. She, however, pounced on the idea.

70

"Do you think they'd let us?"

"It's our lane. I don't see why not."

Their last game was played off the inflatable bumpers. Claryn declared a new rule saying every ball thrown had to hit the bumpers once in order for the score to count. It certainly made getting a strike or spare much more challenging. She was delighted with their almost tie game.

"It's not really fair," he said, "you've had a lot more practice aiming for the gutter."

All in all it was a great first date and neither of them wanted it to end. Thinking of ending what was really their second date was enough to give Claryn heart palpitations, so while she changed her shoes she racked her brain for something else to do. Thinking along the same lines Justice asked her if she had a curfew.

"Not since I went to college. Actually I never had a curfew, per se. More of an understanding I would check in until I was about sixteen and Sissy retired from parenting."

"I could give you a historical tour of town, it's very exciting stuff."

She placed her shoes on the counter and made a face.

"That's just weird. Who knows the history of Hallston?"

She was thinking he was a bit of an odd duck anyway, or more of a rare bird. She'd never seen somebody so quick to open doors, and occasionally he used some word or phrase that she might have heard in an old movie or from Kelley's grandma. Maybe.

Walking out the glass door he held for her, Claryn said, "I've got a better idea. Why don't you show me where you live?"

Justice thought this all manner of bad in the idea department. If she thinks a historical cruise through town is weird, wait till she gets a load of home sweet home. The only up side was that Chess, according to the text he'd sent, planned to be out till after dawn. It was a good opportunity in that respect.

Climbing into the car Justice kind of wanted to discourage her. People had a tendency to drop by places of business unannounced, which

71

is why theirs was the only automotive shop set up like a mail order supply company with a post office box listed as the address.

He placed his arm on the back of the bench seat and gave her his best southern drawl, "That seems a might bit forward for such a pretty young miss."

Someone needed to give him a swift kick. She didn't even look at him, just splayed her fingers out on her jeans in a gesture he now recognized from her nightmares.

"I'm sorry, Claryn. I tend to think I'm much funnier than I am."

He got going and basically started driving zigzags through the downtown blocks till she spoke. Frequently he did better with her by keeping his mouth shut. When she said something it sounded very much like "all's forgiven" to him since she made a little joke.

"I've lived here since I was three. I don't think you can get me lost. Or have you forgotten where you live?"

"All right," he took a sharp turn. "One weird bachelor pad coming your way."

Claryn recognized the road they were on as one headed nowhere. Eventually it led to an even less consequential town best described as a wide place in the road, but since all the highways linked up on the other side of town, it was a pretty deserted area.

The only reason she'd driven this road at all was because out near the county line a couple roads branched off it. You could drive into town from a completely different direction from the way you drove out. It was a common route for teenagers who, having just received their licenses, roamed the longest route possible while remaining in the boundaries of the county.

So Claryn recognized the old auto repair shop with its four bays. She didn't recall the sign on two poles outside that said "Chess & JT's" at the top and "Automotive" at the bottom. There was a drawing of bishop and rook chess pieces, both black, tilted away from each other in the middle.

The building was completely dark as Justice stopped the car in front of one of the bays.

"This is where you live?"

"It is. Would you like to go inside?"

She reached for the door handle but he revved the engine and deftly took a garage door opener out of the glove box in front of her.

The last bay on the left slid open, lights flooded the shop, and she got her first view of the shop laid out to her right as he pulled in.

An old car was perched up in the air beside her on hydraulic lifts. The bay beyond that had various engine and body parts spread around the floor. The distance beyond the bays to the back was large enough for several other automotive projects and work areas. She felt a faint pang thinking how her father would love this place.

"Watch your step." Justice pointed out the areas of the floor painted yellow for caution and car parts or machinery that stuck out into the walking areas. Claryn wandered under the old car on the lift getting what was for her a very strange perspective of a vehicle.

"What's wrong with it?"

"Nothing. She's almost done." He put a hand up on her chassis as if giving her a friendly pat. "We're waiting for a muffler and she'll be ready to roll."

Claryn admired the skill it must take to work on all those parts of which she was seeing only the underside.

"You enjoy your work."

"I do."

"So why the bucket list of other jobs?" she asked.

"Even something you enjoy can get monotonous if you're always alone. My brother, Chess, doesn't do much of the auto work anymore."

She nodded as if this made sense perfect sense and wandered further back where she saw that the section of the shop that jutted out from the back had another much taller side entrance.

73

"Previous owner worked on mobile homes back there. That's why there's such a nice large space and the extra entrance."

Meandering over to the living area, Claryn stopped here and there to look at some part or tool. A half wall faced the bays separating them from the living area, and on the bay side the wall was lined with red tool chests on wheels. An HD flat screen television of enormous proportions backed up to the far wall on the other side. Justice followed her at some distance wondering what she was thinking when she spoke aloud.

"Oversize sectional sofa, boxes for coffee and end tables, incredibly overpriced entertainment center with . . ." she paused to count, "no less than three game systems, a satellite receiver, blue ray and a laptop? This isn't weird. It is a carbon copy of every bachelor pad I ever went to at college, minus a high end system or two."

Justice brows furrowed as he speculated how many bachelor pads she might have seen.

"Where do you cook?" she asked looking around.

He pointed toward the break room where one sink, an old coffee machine, and a couple hot plates sat next to a large unidentifiable kitchen appliance. The walls contained neon signs of various auto parts and tool companies. Car manuals and diagrams were spread across the kitchen table. It was all surprisingly clean. The whole thing made her feel more relaxed somehow. The space suited him and she could see him there. Justice rebuilt cars. He was a mechanic and lived in his shop. It made sense. She liked it.

Continuing to wander she poked her head into an oblong office with a desk and a futon. A coed toilet lay beyond the last door off the customer service area.

"Okay, this is a little weird."

Justice tensed.

"Your restroom is entirely too clean for a bachelor pad."

She turned in a circle.

74

"Where do you shower? There's two of you right? Where do you sleep?"

"That's actually the coolest thing about this place and the reason we bought it." He pointed back to the first bay where steps went down the concrete pit looking like any other quick lube place.

"There are old bunkers built under this place."

She headed toward the stairs and he stepped into her path.

"For the purposes of tonight's tour the additional living quarters are strictly off limits."

"But I paid good money for this tour," he raised one eyebrow at her, "or would have. At least a quarter." He wouldn't budge so she went to sink down into the over stuffed sofa.

"Fine. Then I at least get to see what you've been playing."

It was bizarre to see her sitting there looking so comfortable and a little too appealing.

"Would you like some water?" He bee-lined for the break room not waiting for her to answer and needing a distraction. He turned off the excess lights as he went.

"Sounds good."

He listened to her picking things up and putting them down again.

"Good grief. I've never seen so many remote controls."

"That's mostly Chess's area. He's a TV addict, game-aholic, and general couch potato," he said from the other room.

She managed to get the TV and the laptop turned on so the last death screen from Mission 2B Immortal lit up the almost life size screen. Claryn laughed out loud causing Justice's brisk return with her water.

"Oh, thanks. This is the last thing your brother was playing?"

"Yes. What's so funny?"

"Wow, this water is really good. Have you played this game?"

"No. Games aren't my thing."

"Oh, me neither, but Natalie was all into this for awhile. At school she hosted a girls' weekend all around this game and had a party that

75

Saturday night to meet your vampire lover. I know you're thinking how ridiculous all the vampire fever is--"

"Not exactly."

"--but Natalie was so into it. She was pretty annoyed that I had the high score that weekend."

Justice choked on his water. "You had the high score on Mission 2B Immortal?"

"Yep. If your brother comes home anytime soon, I could help him out."

"Sure. He'll be back bright and early tomorrow morning."

Claryn's ring tone sounded out. Justice recognized it as Danzig's "Mother" and she held up the picture of Sissy.

"Hello?"

Justice practiced looking like he couldn't hear both sides of the conversation.

"Yes. It's going good. No, we left there a while ago. I don't think I'll be able to lift my arm tomorrow."

Claryn got up and walked over to the window peeking out through the blinds. "Now? I'm just checking out his bachelor pad."

Listening, she shook her head, "Nothing inappropriate. No, he's not like that. He opens doors and kisses ladies' hands, I imagine."

She glanced over her shoulder before turning away and huddling over the phone.

"I'm not talking about this right now. Gotta go. Nope, no idea when I'll be home but certainly by dawn. Bye."

She turned back around abruptly.

"That wasn't embarrassing at all. I don't think she's checked up on me since middle school." I never gave her any reason I guess.

"You could give me the fast track on the game so I can beat my brother. It would really aggravate the heck out of him."

She came back to her corner on the couch and looked around.

"I think all your game consoles are broken. They're easier to play than the laptop mouse pad and keys." She looked around and threw up her hands.

"Doesn't matter, I can tell you. The key to this game is patience, and a lot of it. Also, you can move forward pretty quickly and get to level two or three, but you'll die there without fail if you didn't do enough on level one. So you've got to move sideways, check out everything on each level, collect as many skills and resources as you can before entering the next level. Essentially, you have to figure out how they want you to play and do it their way, not yours."

"How far did you get?"

"I don't remember exactly," she scrunched up her face thinking back. "I guess most sites collect some personal information, link to your social network. But at some point this one asked for medical history type info that I thought 'do I really want that out there on the web?'"

"Are you on Facebook?"

"Not anymore." She started wringing her hands. "I had some stalker kind of issues with that. You can set all the security levels you want, 'Just Friends', but if someone is determined enough they'll get in."

Claryn's breathing went shallow again. A quiet settled over them and the winds kicked up around the stone building producing a distant sounding howl. Justice turned his head away toward the front windows as if his attention was elsewhere, listening to the night rather than focusing on her issues.

"Do you have anything else to drink?" Claryn asked nervously.

"What would you like?"

"Oh, I don't know. Maybe a beer?"

"Not a one."

"Okay, I take it back. This is definitely the weirdest bachelor pad e-ver."

Justice could see she wanted something to take the edge off her nerves and was racking his brain as he took a mental tour of the storage area below them.

"I might be able to scrounge up a bottle of wine."

"That'd be great."

"Why don't you see if there's any music on that thing you'd like to listen to?"

"Okay."

Justice jogged off to the bunker and started ransacking the storage room. There has to be something down here, he thought. Not finding anything, he relocked the door and fingered his keys while thinking.

Making a decision, he unlocked Chess's room and slid a wooden crate of wine bottles out from under the bed. His eyes ran over the dates on the bottles, they all looked old and likely rare. He pushed that flat back and pulled out another examining it more quickly. That one! He double-checked with the contents of the first crate to make sure he was actually holding a duplicate bottle. Course that might just mean he'll be twice as angry with me, he thought. Oh well.

Back upstairs he walked past the couch holding the bottle up.

"Found one. Can't vouch for the contents other than to say it's red."

Claryn had picked a Gypsy Kings CD and turned off the lights, but the music was low. The colorful circles from the media player threw patterns of light all over the large front windows and from there to the walls and high ceiling of the room. The entire arrangement was hypnotic and soothing.

Justice carried two highball glasses identical to the water glasses he used earlier from the break room. He would now have to wash glasses in order to serve another beverage, but since there were no other beverages, all was well. He gave her one and took the water glasses back to refill them as well, leaving the bottle on the machinist chest.

He chose to sit further away this time hoping the increased physical space would help. He sipped his wine and watched the light patterns while

78

surreptitiously observing her do the same. When the song ended he closed his eyes to concentrate on her slower than normal but steady pulse.

She changed the song, tossed back the rest of her wine and joined him in the middle of the couch holding out her glass out for a refill Reclined on the couch with his head leaned back he decided to openly watch her. She didn't seem to mind so much now. He didn't inspire her fear. Having watched her sleep, he knew it wasn't personal.

"You seem really patient, when you're not driving." With her glance his lips barely curled up at the edges. He forced his gaze to the ceiling.

"My dad was good at waiting, and I think it killed him. Not literally but he was slow to go to the doctor, didn't push for more information. By the time they knew what was what, the cancer had…well, it was too late." She folded her legs up under her hip and faced him straight on, but he didn't move except to sip his wine.

He closed his eyes to speak. "I'm sorry."

"Sissy didn't take it too well. She was a basket case for over a year. Then one day it was like," Claryn snapped her fingers loudly, "she was back on the market. Her dates would have made a great reality show. Awful, just awful."

She paused for a couple drinks and changed the music again.

"Did I tell you she got married? Yeah, she's married her boyfriend, Brad, and I am so happy for her, 'cause he's a nice guy. Sweet, sincere, completely into her. Treats me like . . . a nice kid."

Hands shaking, Claryn put her wine glass down now and pulled her legs up in front of her to hug them.

"He's a good guy. She needs that." Claryn swallowed. "She had this one on again off again boyfriend that totally took advantage of her."

She began rocking, and it was all Justice could do to sit still and listen. He smelled the salt of her tears but otherwise wouldn't have known she was crying.

Claryn rested her head on her knees because it felt too heavy to hold up. When she spoke again it was just a whisper.

"He thought we were a package deal." Claryn choked out. "And he wasn't the only one, but he was . . . the worst. He came to my room at night."

Justice was the one sitting with clenched fists now, eyes tightly shut. After a while, the quiet music began clearing out the thick atmosphere of the room.

"Sissy can't know. She can never know."

After a couple minutes, her pulse started to recover. "Kelley knows, at least partly. I think I blocked out a lot. Don't remember some things.

"So now I have these personal space issues, but it's really just with people, guys, who are interested, you know, or worse, guys that I, uh, that I could really like. How lame is that?"

She was obviously waiting for his response, but he was seeing red, literally. He kept his eyes shut knowing if he opened them they would glow unnaturally with reflected light.

Several moments later, he laid his hand out palm up between them. Claryn looked at it for minute, so still just lying there, open. But hands could close like a vise. She rocked again trying to alleviate her nausea. Men's hands were strong, stronger than they looked.

Hot tears spilled over again. "I can't. I just can't."

Justice abruptly went to the break room. He stood with his palms pressed onto the counter-top watching the reflection of his eyes glowing white back at him in the stainless surface of the cabinet door. He thought about Claryn bowling and line dancing, about the way the sun caught her hair in the church. The glow faded back like a panther disappearing into the underbrush.

He returned with a cool damp dishcloth for her. It was the only thing he could offer that wouldn't make things worse. The only way he knew to reach out to her.

In the recesses of time he remembered a woman wiping away his own tears with such a cloth. He didn't know who she was or why he'd been crying, but he remembered the cool soft material on his face and the clean damp smell of the water. The years were too many to count, but the emotion returned fresh and tugged at his heart with Claryn's pain.

She accepted the cloth, grateful for the gesture as she wiped her face clean.

Claryn took a deep breath and stood to pick her way to the restroom. The shapes of the man and woman so close beside each other on the door, yet not touching, mocked her.

When she came back there was soft instrumental music playing, it sounded like Vivaldi's 'Four Seasons'. She took the pillow from the end of the sofa and lay down with her head just on the corner seat.

When she closed her eyes, Justice did the same and completed the "L" their bodies made. He heard her relax to the gentle melodic strains, but found he could not.

"Does that guy still live around here?" He tried to keep his voice soft and even, but it came out hard and flat. Hers sounded sleepy.

"No. He went to the state pen about five years ago. Go figure."
A few minutes later her even breathing assured him she was asleep. He carefully propped the laptop on his lap. Someone from around here was convicted and sent to the state penitentiary about five years ago. It wasn't much to go on, but Justice intended to discover the identity of this walking dead man.

Chapter 12

After midnight Claryn's phone lit up just before ringing so Justice plucked it up and answered ahead of the noise that could disturb Claryn.

"Hello?"

"Oh…is this JT?"

"Yes, ma'am."

"I didn't expect you to answer. That's a good thing, though, right?"

Justice had no idea what was good about his answering.

"Well, I was just wondering when Claryn might be home. I know she said dawn but I'm sure that was just a joke. She wouldn't want to leave me here all by myself." Then, as if realizing the irony of what she said, she added, "I'm not used to being on my own, you know."

"Of course not. Should I wake her?"

"Wake her?"

"Yes ma'am. We were listening to music and Claryn fell asleep on the couch. Should I wake her?"

Sissy paused, "How's she sleeping?"

"Pretty soundly right now."

"Hm…and what are you doing?"

"Surfing the internet."

"OK, well… no, I guess not. Claryn doesn't think I know, but sometimes she has nightmares, so if she's sleeping peaceful like we'll just let her be."

"Nightmares? That doesn't sound good."

"Poor thing. I think it's about her father dying. Seems to me they started about that time and have just never really gone away."

"If she has one, should I wake her?"

"Oh no. She can wake up really disoriented and a strange face might scare her. Not that your face is strange."

"Would you like me to call you when we head back to your house?"

"Oh, well, that's very thoughtful, but . . . no. I think I'm going on to bed now. I just wanted to make sure everything was okay."

Justice remembered what Claryn said about Sissy not checking up on her since middle school.

"Is everything okay at your place?"

"It's fine." She said it like she was reassuring herself. "I just saw some crime drama and it got under my skin. Stupid television."

"There is one sure fire way to make your house less of a target for criminals."

"What's that?"

"Lights. Turn on all your outdoor lights, front and back porch, driveway, and leave on a hall light or two. Lights and a dog, but you can't run out and borrow one of those in the middle of the night."

She laughed, "Unless you're Claryn, of course."

He chuckled softly in response with no clue as to what was funny.

He said, "Anyway, it'll be nice for the house to be lit up for Claryn when she gets home even though I'll be sure to see her in."

"I'll bet you will," she yawned. "Such a peach. Okay I'm turning on some lights and going to bed. Goodnight, JT."

"Goodnight, Mrs. . . . "

"Just call me Sissy," she insisted. "Don't make me feel old."

"Goodnight, Sissy."

"Night-night."

Times they are a changing, Justice thought. Holding hands was once scandalous, but now you could pretty much stay out all night as long as your folks could check up on you by cell phone. He briefly wondered if cell phones promoted lying. Back in the day a lady Claryn's age, which he made a note to pinpoint, would soon be considered an old maid. Insanity.

Claryn whimpered in her sleep and Justice reached over to stroke her hair. Earlier rage had made his eyes glow, but now something else caused it. I've got to go north soon, he thought. Claryn quieted after a minute, so he returned to his internet search.

The Darkman sat in his car watching the newly listed home with interest. The woman inside was sitting in the dark talking on the phone with the TV on, but turned down low. He would have to set up an appointment with the realtor, but this looked like a very good prospect. He had two others he wanted to check in on tonight. He was already out on the main road when the outdoor lights flipped on.

The wind died down in the early morning hours and the changing sound caused Claryn to wake up enough to realize she wasn't at home. She sat up, opened and closed her eyes a few times to clear them, and looked around the garage. A strange blanket slipped down her shoulder gathering in her lap.

Justice was playing opossum further down the couch.

She grasped for her cell phone, nearly turning over the bottle of wine sitting on the tool box. Justice stirred but didn't open his eyes. Checking the time on the phone she saw it was nearly four o'clock in the morning. She couldn't believe Sissy had taken her seriously about coming home at dawn. Even Sissy wasn't that laid back.

Checking the call log produced some beeping, which she muted quickly. She saw that she had indeed missed a call from Sissy shortly after midnight that had lasted less than fifteen minutes. Shivering in the cool garage, she glanced over at Justice, suspicious now.

"Are you asleep?"

He smiled. "No. Are you?"

She hit him with a pillow. "I've got to go."

"Bathroom's over there," he said rolling away.

She hit him with the pillow again.

"Home. I've got to go home."

He sat up and tried to look innocent. "But Sissy said it was okay. I just talked with her a couple hours ago."

"I see that," Claryn held the phone up.

84

"So we're good," he yawned and tried to roll back over only to take another hit in the head with the pillow.

"We're not good. Sissy doesn't know that Claryn has to be at work in less than two hours."

"Work?"

"Work. Some peoples' jobs aren't sitting in their living rooms." She gestured around the shop as if he completed his work while sitting on the couch. He stretched and got up figuring the night was officially over.

"Where do you work?"

"Smithson's No-Kill Shelter."

"Ah."

"What does that 'ah' mean?"

"Sissy said you could get a dog in the middle of the night if you wanted one." He flipped on a couple lights.

"What on earth did you two talk about?"

"Not much." He was picking up the glasses to take back to the break room when another thought struck him.

"Are you going to go back to bed when you get to your house?"

"Let's clarify. I haven't been to bed at your house, okay?"

"Oh yeah. No problem. If you want to keep this on the down low, I'm cool with that," he winked expansively.

"Never mind. No, I am not going to sleep any more tonight. I usually can't. Once I've woken up, I'm up."

"So if I took you to breakfast would that be our third/second date or the latter part of our second/first date?"

She stood thinking about that for a moment.

"You're a morning person, aren't you?" She was very accusatory.

"Depends on how you define 'morning'."

She started picking her way across the garage to his car.

"Well, if you want a third/second date or a third/third date with this chica you better start driving."

"Yes, ma'am."

85

He was in the driver's seat fast enough to cause momentary confusion.

"So can I tell my friends I'm dating a chica?" She just glared at him.

"One that has that glower thing down really well?"

"Drive."

"Does this mean no breakfast, yes breakfast?"

"I don't do food in the morning."

"Me either!"

He bordered on gleeful, so Claryn growled at him.

"If I can't understand exactly what you mean by that I'll have to make up my own loose interpretation, so you said something like 'grrr-call me this week,' right?"

Claryn couldn't help the tiny grin spreading across her face or help feeling he understood her better than anyone else had in a long, long time.

"Just drive," she said, unable to hide her pleasure.

When Chess came roaring into the side door of the shop, Justice was downing glasses of water and working across level one of Mission 2B Immortal on the laptop. It made Chess suspicious as he walked over and tossed a couple new consoles on the couch.

"How was your date?"

Justice didn't look up from the game, "Fabulous. Girl of my dreams."

In Chess's book, such straightforward answers from Justice were dubious at best. He tasted the air.

"You didn't eat her, did you?"

Justice turned off the game and looked daggers at Chess for a moment before settling on misdirection.

"How was your night?"

Chess didn't particularly want to talk about retrieving and disposing of his ex's corpse. He was haunted by the good memories of when they met, their wedding, the happy days before she went blood wild. The past paled in importance compared with news of Justice's date.

Chess had long given up on JT growing their family and Chess's own botched attempts did not bode well for him making it happen. After they'd lost their mother figure, Chess always felt a certain emptiness that needed filling. No amount of dating put a drop in the bucket. Now there was new hope that JT would do better, and Chess wanted to hear more.

"Fabulous. Body recovered. Definitely a vampire hunter on the loose. Can we get back to your date?"

"They're not hunters, they're slayers."

Topic avoidance. Much less worrisome coming from Justice.

"So the slayee was a wild one, right?"

"Yeah, but it's problematic."

"Problematic? Hold that thought." JT came back with two glasses of water and didn't offer one to Chess.

"How many of those you had this morning?"

"A lot."

"Well, that explains . . . something."

"I'm going to head north this evening. Are you going to tell me about the problems or shall I wait and ask Arvon?" JT asked yawning.

"What the heck! Did you just yawn?"

JT put on his thoughtful face and looked around for another culprit.

"Me? I don't yawn."

"You are seriously lit. You better stop laying that stuff back." Chess took the glass of water from JT's hand.

"You are delusional."

A whiff of his brother's breath was telling.

"You've been drinking more than water, my friend."

With that, JT knew the game was up and Chess was down the stairs in two heartbeats. But he'd delayed just long enough. When Chess burst through his bunker door, JT was already out cold.

"Bugger." Chess had some time to sniff around before he too was out for the count, and he proceeded to do just that.

Chapter 13

Home in Dallas, Kelley called Claryn at work Sunday afternoon with loads to share about her honeymoon. Claryn felt like she said T.M.I. so often that Kelley mistook it to mean Tell Me Info instead of Too Much Information. At some point the newlywed ran out of steam and asked a question totally from left field.

"Do you know Carolyn Johnson?"

"Was she at the wedding?"

"No, goof ball. But she's gone missing. I did tell you that we're subscribing to the local paper, right? I just thought it would help me keep in touch, but honestly I don't know most of the people in the news and Hallston is not even that big a town."

"You're not going to ask me about my date, are you?"

"Oh, I thought if you wanted to talk about it you would."

Claryn was much better at the waiting game than Kelley. She petted Felix's furry head for a bit and then asked.

"Is Carolyn Johnson the Carolyn that works at the supermarket deli?"

Kelley exploded on the other end.

"What! You want to talk about some deli lady instead of your date. I'm hurt. I'm injured. Only gone a week and I'm not even your best friend anymore." Melodrama. Claryn hoped George liked it, because Kelley was an expert.

"It's true," Claryn projected boredom, "you've been replaced."

Kelley inhaled quickly, "I've been replaced."

She sounded happier than she ought to be.

"Have I been replaced by a guy? A tall handsome guy named Justice who sometimes goes by Jay?" Kelley broke down in giggles, completely high on life, or maybe left over champagne from the wedding. It was hard to tell which.

"No. A short hairy male named Felix."

"That won't work. I'm probably the only person in your life besides Mrs. Smithson who knows who Felix is. And I know I can't compete with him."

Kelley rattled what Claryn assumed was the local newspaper she'd been reading and was now wrestling.

"These things are impossible to get back straight. Okay, back to reality here. Your date obviously went well or you wouldn't be cracking jokes so freely. So give it up, what'd you do?

"Bowling."

"Bowling? I wouldn't have taken Justice for a bowling kind of guy."

"Me either. But he's very good."

"Very, very good?"

This was greeted by silence. Claryn didn't do innuendo. Although she could easily picture Kelley's eyebrows jumping up and down on her forehead Groucho Marx style. It made her miss her friend.

"We should do video chat," Claryn said.

"Uh, nice segue there, mi amigo. Could we go back to the date talk?"

"We could go back to the honeymoon talk."

"I don't think there's anything left to tell."

Claryn shook her head, not surprised in the least.

"Jay. Justice. Let's talk about tall, hot, and so into Claryn."

"Sissy likes him too."

"Sissy likes everybody."

"And Sissy got married last week."

"What? No way! That's...wait. Stop. You are just trying to distract me from date talk. So real quick, did Sissy really get married?"

"She did."

"Wow. Why didn't they put that in the paper?"

Claryn wondered how long it would take Kelley to discover a listing for the house in the paper and decided not to mention it. "The paper doesn't have any of the good stuff in it," said Claryn.

"Yeah, I'm liking the direction of this. Keep talking."

"Like how a girl might go bowling with a very nice guy,"

"And…?"

"And have a wonderful time,"

"And…?"

"And go back to his place for the night."

Kelley was seriously ticked, the silence at the other end of the phone stretched out. Claryn didn't think she had ever left her friend speechless and took a moment's pleasure in the feat.

"Now you're just messing with me and it is wrong. So wrong," said Kelley.

Claryn held up her hand as if swearing in court. "Honest Abe."

"Not funny!"

"Well if you're not going to believe me, why should I tell you anything?" Claryn's false indignation was clear, but now Kelley wasn't so sure.

"Honest Abe?"

"Honest Abe. I fell asleep on his couch listening to music and didn't get home till after four this morning."

"When you say it like that, it doesn't sound quite as exciting. Did you hold hands?"

"Do high fives at the lanes count?"

"In your world, yes. It's a split second hand connection, but I would have to say, yes. Did you have any allergic reactions?"

"Not at the alley and really only a little one at his place." Claryn enjoyed surprising Kelley. "By the way, dude sleeps in a bunker."

"Get out! You slept in a bunker?"

"No. I slept upstairs on the couch in the automotive shop."

"You are totally messing with me again, aren't you? Daggone it! Cell phones are useless. I can't tell if you're messing with me or not on the phone. What's that video chat thing you were talking about? Let's do that. Later, after George sets it up for me.

90

"I can't believe I just said that. I'm going to be one of those totally dependent helpless wives we would have made fun of last semester. I am not helpless," she declared. "Can I just say that it's really, really nice to have someone else watching out for me and taking care of me? Quick! Duck! I think the feminist snipers are perched on a building across from mine."

Claryn thought about her first, and last, year of college and the slant a lot of the classes seem to take. Then she saw a silhouette standing under a street light waiting to see if she locked the door, a guy catching a phone call so she could sleep, a young gentleman seeing her to the door and teasing about kissing her hand goodnight some other time when it wasn't already morning.

Claryn said, "But you'll find ways to watch out for him too."

"You bet I will." Innuendo.

"That's not what I meant."

"What? What? What's not what you meant?"

"I've gotta go take doggies for walks now."

"Wait! You've hardly told me anything about your date."

"We're going out again soon."

"Soon? What's soon? How will I know when to call?"

"I don't know. He said he had to go north for some fluids. Car thing, I guess."

"Ooo, maybe it's code for something."

"I very much doubt that. Mucho doubto."

"Ah," Kelley laid one hand over her heart. "Happy girlfriend breaks out pretend Spanish."

"Do I do that?"

"Oh yeah. You do."

"I am a goofball."

"I know. And I love you for it. Smoochies to all the puppies for me!"

"Ciao."

"Chow, chow."

Chapter 14

"Found it, sir." The information analyst working for Arvon handed him a print out from the slayer's defunct webpage. The elder had disposed of the wild one's body subsequent to examining it after Francesco, or Chess, as he liked to be called these days, stole the dead female from the morgue. It made things both simpler and more complicated that Francesco knew her.

They'd easily found the furnished apartment she'd rented before the police got there, but the slayer had already been there and found a reason to head south according to the homeless man who lived in a box next to the building. How far south and how exact the slayer's information was anybody's guess. Chess went directly home to advise Justice and arrange a visit to check to their old homestead.

With the Mission 2B Immortal game getting so many hits a day, this was bound to happen. Arvon had thought that far ahead, but the creator of the game had not. Eventually there would be players who believed, informed themselves, won the game, and were rejected by the cohort behind it.

Arvon knew a scorned wanna-be was a dangerous human being. Especially since the game inadvertently hinted at weaknesses such as the pandemic and fatal allergy to quicksilver. To keep the game interesting it naturally included half a dozen real or imagined ways to kill the so-called immortal. Cannibalization, Arvon's personal favorite, was one of the few options left out of the game.

Now Arvon was holding a lead on the scorned man, at least a lead to his past. And knowledge of the past is, as the old saying goes, requisite for predicting the future. At the moment Arvon couldn't remember the origin of that particular old saying, so he attributed it to himself, making it ancient indeed.

Chapter 15

Sissy was a veritable tongue wagging about the house. From the list of home improvements the realtor recommended to commandeer the best price to the incredibly long conversation Sissy remembered having with Justice, she simply gushed. All was bright, good fortune, think happy thoughts in Sissy's merry little world. Even Claryn's news about quitting school was simply a new opportunity.

"You have such a good head on your shoulders, like your father. You'll do well with whatever you set your mind to do," Sissy said.

Sissy's only worry concerned the caring real-estate professionals. She had it in her head that since it was a buyer's market, all the realtors were secretly working for the buyers rather than the sellers. So her strategy at this point was to ask the highest possible price the realtor thought the house might get after renovation but to do so without actually making any of the recommended improvements. To Sissy, this made perfect sense, and Claryn was more than happy to play along.

"Justice seems, well, great," Sissy was saying. "It worries me." Her every silver lining has its cloud attitude slipping back into her day.

"Worries you?"

"Well, yeah. What do you do at your age if you find a keeper?" She was peering squinty-eyed and pursed lips at Claryn as if this facial contortion helped her think about the problem.

"Can you keep him? That doesn't seem right. And is a keeper always a keeper? What if he changes? Or you change? Oh, but how great would it be to keep someone at your age and avoid all the heartbreak between nineteen and thirty…" Sissy trailed off trying to remember how old she'd decided to be. "Oh, I'm married. Who cares? Thirty-seven. No. Thirty-eight? No. All the heartbreak between nineteen and thirty-six."

Finally, Claryn was able to extricate herself from Sissy by claiming a phone appointment with her traveling "boyfriend." Sissy was very sympathetic to the traveling boyfriend phenomena and the needs thereof.

In fact, she had traveling spouse needs to be addressed herself. So as Claryn dialed Justice, Sissy rang Brad.

If resting first had few fringe benefits, waking up last had fewer still. Chess had not exacted his revenge for his brother's thievery in Justice's room, but Justice decided to check out the other areas of the bunker before heading upstairs.

One of the downsides of sleeping the sleep of the dead in a bunker in the middle of nowhere was poor cell phone reception. So the Cain brothers had a landline running underground. Never mind that no ringing on any decibel could wake them when they rested or that the only person in possession of the number was Arvon. So mobile phones were conveniently left charging upstairs, and Chess found the fact that he got to check the messages first quite fitting.

This afternoon, though, he actually intercepted his brother's first phone call from Claryn. Having done a good bit of sleuthing while Justice slept, Chess was much more knowledgeable of the previous evening's activities. He caught Claryn's call in the midst of the first ring, very much as Justice had caught Sissy's.

"Hello?"

"Hi. Justice?"

"JT is not available at the moment, but you have the fortunate opportunity of speaking with his elder brother. Would this be the remarkable, but not much remarked upon Claryn?"

Claryn thought Chess's clipped speech and over enunciated words sounded very Matrix-villainesque.

"Yeah. I guess that's me."

"I've been very concerned about you today. How are you feeling?"

"I'm fine." Claryn smiled and waved at Sissy who was walking by her room on the phone. Then she slipped off the bed to gently close her bedroom door.

"Is there some reason I might not be fine?"

"I don't know. My brother was not very forthcoming about your, how shall we say, interactions last night. So all I know is that you bowled, came back here, drank an exorbitantly expensive bottle of wine from my private collection," cried over something, he added to himself, "and left before you and I could be introduced."

"Oh, and I came home to find Justice fairly intoxicated and playing a video game he could have cared less about yesterday. It's just exceedingly strange and quite frankly intriguing. Would you consider meeting me for coffee about this same time tomorrow evening?"

"I'm a very poor bowler and Justice was not intoxicated when he drove me home this morning."

Chess sat silently waiting for more. The silence dragged out, making him chuckling.

"That's it?" he finally asked.

"Pretty much."

"Wow. You two really are peas in a pod." Chess's voice relaxed.

"Is Justice really unavailable?"

"You don't think he'd just stand by and let me talk to his girl, do ya? Yes, he is actually resting."

"Oh." Claryn was turning over the "his girl" reference wondering how Chess reached that conclusion if Justice hadn't said much about their evening.

"Did you at least enjoy the wine?"

"Not really."

"Ach," his brogue took over, "could you not at least tell me a wee white lie, lass?"

"No, but I will say I am extremely grateful for its availability. Thank you so much. And your accents are really good. I like the highlander one best so far. Does that help?"

"Actually it does." Chess liked few things better than compliments about his person.

"And just for curiosity's sake who had the last glass?" he asked.

95

"Last glass? I don't know. I had two, maybe three servings. I didn't think Justice finished one, but you said he was intoxicated when you got home? That doesn't make any sense, maybe he finished off the bottle when he got home? But I thought things went well."

"Oh they did, right up to the moment he poured the rest of a $13,000 bottle of wine down the drain to hide his villainy, of course."

"What?!" Her voice went up at least an octave.

"Wine under the proverbial bridge now, isn't it," he soothed since she was more upset than impressed.

"'Fabulous,' Justice told me. 'Girl of my dreams.' That's a direct quote."

"Are you messing with me?" Completely distracted from the wine, Claryn suddenly had a newfound sympathy for Kelley's phone woes, except she didn't know Chess well enough to gauge what he was saying even if he was standing right in front of her.

Justice came up the stairs in time to hear Chess saying, "I will not mess around with you!" then to JT as he passed him the phone, "Can you believe that? Women! They just can't get enough of me."

"Claryn?"

"Justice!"

"Claryn, you sound happy to talk with me. Of course, who wouldn't after conversing with a Neanderthal for the last ten minutes."

"He wasn't that bad. But he did say that wine cost $13,000. Is that possible?"

"You can't believe anything he says. Incorrigible liar."

"So I'm not the girl of your dreams?"

Chess had on a rakish grin. Justice wished there was somewhere he could go to have a private conversation. But anywhere around here with cell reception was also a place where Chess could hear every word of both ends of the conversation.

"Did he say I said that?"

"He also said you were inebriated at the time – no, intoxicated."

Chess was writing a note, "I Love her!" and another, "Wanna share?"

"You can forget that!"

"What?"

"Not you. Sorry."

"I take it he's standing right there?"

"Yes, he is."

"I betchya a cookie if we stop talking about him he'll wander away. It's worth a try."

"All right. So what were you saying?"

"Girl of your dreams?"

"Let me say that spending time with you is fabulous and--"

"Fabulous?" same word Chess used, Claryn thought.

"Yes, and I look forward to doing it again soon."

"What is soon exactly?"

"I don't think I'll make it back into town before Friday night, maybe Saturday."

"Oh. Okay."

Disappointment.

"But I could stop by for awhile tonight on my way out of town."

Claryn hadn't asked about his travels and, knowing how fast he drove, wasn't sure she wanted to know how far he was going.

"It would probably be safer to leave sooner as opposed to later," she reasoned.

"Yeah, but I would like to see you."

"Just a quick visit?"

"Quick visit. I'll be there within the hour."

"I'll be home from work."

"See you then."

"See you."

Chess reached over to hang up the phone.

"On to matters of almost equal importance, Mr. I'll-be-there-within-the-hour. I am willing to forget about the wine, if you promise not to say I told you so. Deal?"

This was getting off too easy, but Justice readily complied.

"The wild one Arvon and I liberated from the morgue was shot up with quicksilver, looked like homemade buckshot that burned most of her skin off." Chess shivered. "Upside is we didn't have to kill her." Chess looked uncharacteristically apologetic.

"And the downside would be?"

The next thing Chess said came out too fast for the human ear. "It was Jenny and she might have had something laying around her place that ties her to us, to me, to us."

"Jenny. Your ex-wife, Jenny. Your black-haired, Spanish-Native ancestry, wild one recently escaped justice, Jenny?"

"That's the one." He nodded and watched JT carefully for combustibility.

"So look. I know you've got this budding romance happening. But I really need you to focus, get juiced up and back down here ASAP."

"I brought Claryn here."

"I figured that out."

"I brought her here, and now you're telling me we might have a maniacal killer headed our way."

"Not maniacal. Killing vampires is just good thinking when you think they're all out to, you know…" he made fang motions with his fingers in the air, "eat you."

"Not funny."

"But hey! Claryn's not a vampire, so . . ."

"So what? So bullets will only what? Kill her faster?" Justice's eyes were turning white.

"That's debatable when they explode with quicksilver," Chess said. "I'm sorry, JT. I really am. I was in love."

98

"You're in love every decade or two. And I don't know if you noticed or not, but it's not working out very well for anybody."

Justice knew he was being harsh. Although none of Chess's ex's were still around, Jenny was the only one who went wild.

"I'm sorry," Justice apologized. "You couldn't have known."

"No. You're right. I should have been more careful. The other thread of good news in all this is it's most likely the homestead that the slayer will be headed for if he's got a lead pointing anywhere in our direction."

"The homestead. That's right. Jenny's connection to us will lead there, not here. Anything else?"

"No. Arvon said he'd probably have more information by the time you got to him and he's gotten all wiggy about electronic communication. So that's a no go."

Chapter 16

Claryn rushed home from the shelter as if hounds were on her heels, and she registered none of the town or other houses till she was pulling into the driveway of her own place wondering how she'd gotten there.

Her watch told her Justice would be stopping by in about fifteen minutes. Claryn depressed the garage door opener only to see Sissy's car still ensconced there. If Sissy is here, she thought, I might have time to wash the dog smell off before Justice gets here. She was up the front stoop in two giant steps.

"Sissy?" She called up and down the stairs. Claryn dropped her keys in a depression on the antique hall tree Sissy and her dad had picked up at some flea market shortly after they were married. There was no answer, which probably meant Sissy was out power walking the neighborhood in either a lime-green or neon-yellow tracksuit.

"I've got to bathe," Claryn told her reflection as it made a distasteful face at her.

On her last dog walk of the day she had tethered a rather excitable, oversized lab mix to a large sight-hound of questionable breeding. The two personalities struck her as destined to be great friends, and, as it turned out, great partners in crime. A jackrabbit crossed their path not twenty feet away and both dogs tensed and took off with such force that Claryn was dragged along for some distance over rocky ground and morass, the origin of which she didn't want to contemplate too closely.

She couldn't let go for fear she would never see them again, or worse she'd spend the next hour looking for them and miss seeing Justice. In her hurry she hadn't cleaned up her right forearm, smeared as it was with a mixture of dirt and blood. She hopped in the shower in high-speed wash mode, slowing down only for the tender injured area.

Powering down the sidewalk, Sissy walked around the corner swinging her three-pound weights as Justice drove by in his muscle car with the window rolled down. He gave her a wave and accelerated alarmingly down the block into their drive. She watched him spring from his car to Claryn's, look in all the windows and rush to the front door in such a manner that Sissy actually sprinted the last thirty feet to her own home.

"What's the matter? What's happened?" She couldn't get the key out of the zippered pocket of her wristband fast enough.

"I think Claryn's hurt," he said even as he registered the shower water turning off and realized he was probably over-reacting.

"Hurt what? Hurt how?" Sissy pushed through the door, calling for Claryn.

"Claryn!"

Justice pointed out the water stopping, so Sissy darted up the four stairs and down the hallway as he paced the living room.

Claryn jerked her towel up as Sissy burst into the bathroom.

"Claryn! Are you all right? You had us worried."

"What? Us who?"

"Justice and me. He thought you were hurt. Oh my goodness, what have you done to your arm?"

Claryn peeked her towel wrapped head out of the bathroom far enough to see Justice down the hall, smile, and pop it back in again. Having left her terry bathrobe hanging on the back of her bedroom door, she pushed Sissy out in front of her as she slipped around the corner wearing another towel.

"Nothing. I'm fine. Could you just go talk to him for a minute?"

"Well, I'm not dressed either." Closing her drapes, Claryn let both her towels drop to make a point as she started dressing. For once, Sissy caught it.

"But...better than you are. Okay. Hope you didn't use all the hot water," Sissy said as she pulled the door shut and went back to a still concerned Justice.

"She's fine. Scraped up her arm from here to there, goodness knows how. I've been out power walking myself." She headed into the kitchen, gesturing for Justice to follow as she kept talking.

"Power walking burns more calories, helps you sleep better, boosts your immune system, and is much lower impact than all that running Brad does. I just know his bones aren't going to thank him for that when we're older. Water? Cola? Tea?"

"Nothing, thank you."

"So, JT, what do you do?"

A soft exclamation of pain from down the hall caused Justice to lose all focus on what Sissy was saying.

"What do you do?"

"Excuse me?"

"For exercise! Don't tell me you don't work out, 'cause I can tell."

Justice took a moment to think about his activities, hunting wild ones, working on the cars and decided what it boiled down to.

"Jogging, lifting . . . even fighting now and then."

"Fighting! Oh no, you have too nice a face to chance. Mark that one off your list. Sissy says 'no.'"

"No to what?" Claryn entered from the hall with her towel dried hair still dripping on her shoulders. One yellow sleeve of her baseball shirt was pushed up to her bicep to keep it from rubbing her forearm.

Even as he spoke with concern, Justice backed away from her halfway into the dining room behind him. "Sissy, what have you got to put on that?" he asked with a note of panic in his voice.

Sissy inspected the size of the wounds, shaking her head back and forth as she held Claryn's arm up, but Claryn was trying to figure out what she'd done wrong to make Justice back away from her. It was such an odd turn of affairs. *If I hadn't showered, this would make sense.*

Sissy went to collect her first aid kit as Claryn took a few more steps toward Justice. He retreated into the living room, contemplating items on the walls as if he hadn't been seated in the same room waiting for her last Friday night.

The personal space bubble seemed to have grown from a couple feet to well over a couple yards.

"What's wrong?" She asked.

Justice shook his head thinking how badly he needed to get north as he lied "Nothing. Really, I…"

Claryn was both uncertain and determined to close the distance between them. She smiled tentatively and, without thought, reached her injured arm out a short distance as she approached him.

Justice looked at her bloody arm and fairly tripped backwards as he descended to the front door, facing her but still keeping his distance. The light reflected off his eyes strangely.

"I just have to get on the road more quickly than I thought, that's all. I'm glad you're okay." He kept talking and backing away, right out the door into the yard where he skimmed past the for sale sign.

"You should take good care of that, keep it from getting infected. I'll call you in a couple days. Okay?"

Claryn felt let down but tried to keep it out of her voice. "Kay" she said as she stepped into the doorway holding the screen door half open.

Justice stopped at the sidewalk taking in her expression and breathing the fresh air.

"I'm sorry, Claryn. I'm really sorry."

She didn't like the ring of his apology or the sag of his shoulders, especially since she didn't know what exactly he was so sorry for. Brow knit as he backed out of the driveway, he gave what looked to Claryn like a perfunctory wave before speeding out of the neighborhood.

"You're dripping on the linoleum, Claryn. Let's do this on the porch. Is Justice gone already?"

"Yep. Had to get on the road."

"Well." Sitting on the stoop, Sissy began dabbing something gooey that stung on Claryn's arm. "It is better to drive before it gets too late.

103

That's why I'm getting a fresh start tomorrow morning. Very responsible young man there."

Sissy continued talking about her drive back to Phoenix as Claryn's glazed eyes turned unseeing toward the north.

Chapter 17

Arvon was not surprised to see Justice through a security monitor arriving in the first few minutes of the new day that Monday morning. What did surprise him was which monitor. Monitor Six, Tower Gate. Patient, methodical, principled Justice stood, glowing eyes focused on the door rather than the camera, outside the Tower Gate waiting for access to the wild ones imprisoned there.

"Behavior out of character does raise eyebrows, my young friend," Arvon intently spoke to the screen even though he had not activated the com link. Erratic behavior seemed to be spreading amongst his most reliable allies recently.

Even so, Arvon's deliberation ended with a positive verdict. He punched in the access code prompts specific to Justice, who was assigned them although he had never used them, and observed Justice's manner as he answered promptly with his code. Nothing bespoke a change in demeanor other than location. Arvon, with his hands steepled and fingers lightly touching the tips of their mates, rested back as far as his desk chair allowed.

Claryn tried to refrain from randomly checking her cell for missed calls. He will call. He said he would. He does what he says. Thinking over his stop by the house she had finally concluded that whatever she had done she could undo. They simply needed to talk.

She was practicing several ways to broach the topic as she walked Aggie, a female Doberman Pit-Bull mix, on her favorite evening route out past a rock cropping to view the sunset. Her cell phone ring startled them both as 'UNKNOWN' came up on the screen.

"Hello?"

"Hey."

It was him. Claryn breathed a sigh of relief. Aggie wasn't the type to take off or wander, so she let the dog off the leash and sat on the large stone catching the last of the day's rays.

"Hey, you."

"What are you doing?"

"Admiring the sunset."

"Tell me about it."

"Don't you have one there?"

"I do. But I like the sound of your voice. Besides I'm pretty sure your view is substantially different from mine."

"Why? What's yours got that mine hasn't?"

"Uh-uh. You first."

"Okay. Well, there's this ravine leading off from where I'm sitting so the shadows are dark and growing there already giving this contrast to the last golden rays on the flats. And the sky is just huge with orange and pink and lavender. There's a whole layer though that is getting darker blue, do you think that has to do with a layer of the atmosphere?"

"Probably. Why ask why?"

Claryn had heard that phrase before, she couldn't quite remember where though.

She went on, "And my sunset has something yours probably doesn't."

"Oh, what is that?"

"A very regal large dog off in the near distance watching it with the same regard."

"Yeah. I definitely don't have one of those."

"What have you got?"

"A mountain."

"Ooooo."

"True. I think my sky has more pinks and purples around the mountain as the sun drops down. My favorite moment is when the sun has first disappeared and the mix of blues and purples are still holding their color before night rise. I never take the sunset for granted anymore."

Night rise. Claryn didn't think she'd heard that phrase before. The night fell, right on top of the sun. That made sense. Night rise conjured up very different pictures of the coming darkness. She saw it happening though, the dark shadow from the ravine reaching out to encompass more of the land, rising from the depths of the earth. An image of the bunker under the automotive shop came to mind unbidden.

"About the other evening when I rushed out so awkwardly."

He was bringing it up out of the blue. None of her practice talks began that way. She cut him off as she and Aggie headed back along the trail to the shelter.

"I understand. You needed to get on the road."

"I didn't need to rush off quite so fast, though. I thought maybe I had hurt your feelings. I did say I would stop by."

"I wasn't hurt really, more disappointed? I wanted to talk, you know?"

"Yeah." He really wanted to ask her if she realized she'd offered him her hand. Ask if she might have taken his in return. It was a moot point now. Honesty was the best policy, he thought. Every time he was honest with her, though, there seemed a built in misdirection to it. This was no exception.

"I have these blood issues, see and . . ."

This had never occurred to her. She slapped her head like the lady in the old V-8 commercials. It made perfect sense!

"Oh! Have you ever passed out?" she asked.

"No. It's not like that exactly."

"I'm sorry, I didn't even think. Oh, and Sissy said I was still bleeding! I'm so sorry."

It struck him exceedingly wrong that she was apologizing for the effect her blood had on him. He had been both shocked and appalled. His

107

impulses so mixed up and strong. It really had taken every ounce of his self-control not to lose his game face completely.

"No. You have nothing to apologize for. I should have told you before."

"On one of our countless dates?" she was teasing him now, feeling better about life in general as she locked up the kennels for the night and climbed into her Accord.

"I see what you mean. How many dates do we actually get to count? I'm so confused. Does non-breakfasting breakfast time count?"

"Definitely not."

"Then I think we have a situation on our hands."

"What sort of situation is that?"

"One where I need to take you out as soon and as often as possible."

"I'm not the one off gallivanting around the countryside."

"True. You are the one driving while on your cell phone without a hands free device," he answered.

"How do you know I don't have a hands free?"

"The sound of your voice would have changed. I notice these things."

"Observant."

"Very." She thought about asking where he'd seen the blood that alarmed him, the blood he told Sissy about when he had first arrived at the house. She hadn't been able to find any on the car or sidewalk leading into the house. Consideration overcame curiosity.

"What are you having for supper?"

The question threw him. It was probably the kind of thing for which Chess had half a dozen ready replies. Justice blanked.

"Hello?" Claryn held her phone up to see if she still had a connection.

"Hey," he responded quietly.

"Hey, you."

"I'm experiencing déjà vu. What do you think that means?" A different question was a good diversionary tactic. He heard her stomach growl.

She said, "It might mean the conversation has come full circle and should be ending soon?"

"Don't believe that for a second." He was quick to respond. "Unless you need to go? Maybe get something to eat?"

"No." Her stomach growled again, as if betraying her, but she knew he couldn't hear that over the cell. But he does have an uncanny knack for picking up on my . . . moods? No. Vibes. Kelley would say she was giving off vibrations, which she usually did in such a way as to send guys packing.

"I was thinking of driving through somewhere."

"Really?"

"Why so surprised?"

"I was under the impression you didn't do much fast food."

"You say it like it's doing drugs."

"That's not what I meant, exactly."

"Who said something? Kelley or Sissy. You never did really say what you and Sissy talked about the other night."

"We didn't talk that long." Justice saw how handy it was to leave his talk with Sissy a mystery.

"I've got it right here in my call log. I know exactly how long you talked."

"Is she home this week?"

"You're trying to change the subject. I'm on to you. And no, she's not home this week."

"I wish you weren't going home to an empty house."

Claryn glowed every time he expressed minor concern for her. She neared a couple fast food places and switched gears.

"What would you order from the Burger Shack?" she asked.

This he could answer with complete truthfulness.

109

"Ugh. Water."

Claryn laughed out loud and drove through at Taco-Mex instead. She refused to eat where he could listen while he declined getting off the phone till she had eaten and was safe at home. He did tell her numerous stories about some of the more humorous jobs on his previous bucket lists. She muted her end to eat and later to brush her teeth to get ready for bed.

The quiet house and the familiar movement of the air slowly moving to the rhythm of her ceiling fan were as cozy to her as the old blanket pulled up to her chin. She felt safer having the place to herself than when her erratic step-mother was home.

To Justice's keen ears the silence was an ominous reminder of what can happen to a young woman on her own. He remembered returning not from a trip but from war only to find his parents dead and his fiancé alone in the provincial house which had afforded her little protection when roving bands of deserters came through. Talking to Claryn brought back so many human memories, and closing his eyes, he began reminiscing to her about his family and his loss.

Great silent tears coursed the short journey to the pillow, some pooling beside Claryn's nose before slipping over to join others on their short trek. She never knew anyone else her age that had lost both their parents. Instinctively she knew this was not something he talked about with just anyone, and the connection she felt to him as they shared open heartedly with one another was like none she had ever known before. The hours went by like minutes till she was curled up in bed practically falling asleep on the phone.

"Goodnight, Claryn," he said finally.

"No. I'm not tired." She yawned out the last words then laughed at herself.

"No. Not at all, but everyone needs their rest."

"My beauty rest. Is that what I need?"

"I don't think you've left any room for improvement in that area."

"Cheese-y," she said, knowing he didn't say it that way. He sounded sincere. She was the one who didn't take compliments well.

"You are beautiful."

"Going to sleep now."

"And a very cute sleepy-head."

"Aim to please." She yawned again unable now to open her heavy lids.

"Goodnight, Claryn."

"Night-night."

Chess was slack jawed and a tad jealous when Justice told him he and Arvon were headed east to hunt together on Thursday night. Arvon hunted alone, always, at least for as long as Chess had known him. Chess's hunt training took place around the Tower Gate area.

"I think we're going after a gang of wild ones, if you can believe that. One released by the Mission 2B's coven."

"I still think he could handle them alone. This is probably more about evaluating you."

"Thanks. That's what I needed to hear, bro."

"Better you than me."

"Speaking of which, Arvon wants me to take the first turn making our presence felt in the homestead territory."

"I'm not without skills, you know."

"Yeah, but the slayer isn't a female, so . . ."

"Hardy-har-har. Well, since I'm going to have some time on my hands maybe I should meet this girlfriend of yours. She's got you so chipper you've turned into a regular comedian."

Justice didn't find any humor in Chess's remark and answered it with stony silence. Truth was Justice was half afraid whatever had drawn Claryn to him might operate on a higher level for Chess and thus lure her away. The thought that she might be able to hold Chess's hand or rest in his arms more easily than Justice's ripped at the edges of his reason.

"I'm pulling your leg, bro," said Chess.

"I know. Look, I'll introduce you when I'm ready."

"Noted. I would say be careful out there, but you're hunting with you-know-who, so I'm hoping you come back with an out of this world tale."

Sephauna had told them several fantastic stories about Arvon. The least absurd of which included an evil twin brother set on taking over the world by wanton reproduction of wild ones.

"I'm shooting for making it home tomorrow night. Hopefully I'll learn a thing or two about efficiency."

"You make the prospect sound fairly dull. No longer jealous at all, thanks."

"My pleasure."

"Leave the lights on for you tomorrow then?"

"Sure."

Justice hung up the phone and hoped it all went so well. He had an odd feeling of foreboding about this mission. Pushing these thoughts aside he went in to prepare for the hunt.

Chapter 18

Thursday, Claryn optimistically tried switching from counting the days till Justice's return to hours, even though he had only said he would try to make it home by Friday night. Counting hours only made time go by excruciatingly slower.

When she had walked the last dog at work, scrubbed the last kennel, and given every animal a bath, all before closing on Thursday, she decided it was time to call him back. As the phone rang, she sat behind the counter on a bar stool in the front room. Felix comfortably lounged at her feet, and as the phone rang she doodled her initials and Justice's on the desk calendar in front of her like she'd watched love-struck adolescents do in junior high.

It occurred to her that Mrs. Smithson might ask about her doodling and for once she smiled. It would be nice to tell someone else about Justice. Maybe it would help her put into words what she was feeling.

Getting no answer on his cell, Claryn hopped off the stool to see if there was anything else she could do before taking off for the evening. She was sure she could find something. Dogs were needy.

The Darkman opened the refrigerator as he lifted, pushed and curled his doll into the opening made after he had removed the shelves and drawers. He felt bad for his doll, who could not be played with as much now. Hopefully she would view their new addition as a welcome friend rather than a competitor for his attentions.

His shoes were heavy on the old wooden floorboards as he crossed to the kitchen table where a real estate magazine lay open next to his well-marked town map. Four neighborhoods were circled in blue, and one of them had a large "X" through it. Best not to trod the same ground twice. A missing person was still a missing person in a town this size. Tonight he would check listings in the other neighborhoods, or rechecking in several cases.

Tomorrow he would make appointments with the realtor to visit twice the number of homes as needed. He liked the realtor a lot, had actually checked out her house last week. The layout and garage were completely unsuitable for his needs. Needs. Life would be so much easier if more people understood his basic needs.

Arvon was pleased with his young friend. Hunting with Justice took him back to an age when Florence and Rome had been his stomping ground with another young, equally driven, friend. A friend who would barely speak to him these days even though the worst aspect of his betrayal remained Arvon's secret.

Arvon knew he was not the best at maintaining connections. Perhaps a favor here and there was in order, kindnesses that might be remembered when Arvon called for Justice's skills in the future. Because call he would. He already had someone doing a small research favor on something Justice said was "personal."

"You have what, an hour?" Arvon asked.

"If that," Justice replied.

"If you'd like to wake up a little closer to home, I could arrange it."

Justice displayed openly pleased speculation. He supposed Arvon could afford to be magnanimous. Still, he wasn't about to look a gift horse in the mouth.

"Not too close."

"Would Amarillo do?"

"Certainly. Flag would be better."

"Ah, yes. Trying to drive off into the sunset is not your easiest option."

Justice considered Arvon's choice of words, weighing the likelihood that the elder hunter knew about Claryn and contemplating what difference it made. None, he decided.

"Flag it is then."

Claryn checked the caller ID on her cell and sighed as she answered Kelley's call. Felix laid his head against her leg, looking up at her with sympathetic brown eyes.

"Hey, Kelley."

"Hey, hey, hey! What's the news? I'm hitting the books again and could use a diversion of epic proportions."

"Nothing new happening here."

"What! I thought you could at least give me a heads up on your big weekend plans."

"I don't know what my plans are yet."

"Speaking of plans, why did I find out your house is for sale from the newspaper?!"

"I didn't really want to talk about it and figured you'd see it there and know better than to ask."

"Ah, right. Clever friend that I am. So about your plans for the weekend, you do have some. Please tell me you have some?"

"I am expecting a phone call any minute."

"Yeah! Oh! I'm sorry. Getting off right now. But you'll call me Sunday with an update?"

"If I don't call you I'm sure you'll call me."

"Yes! You know me too well. Okay, more later then. Love ya."

"You, too. Bye."

Irrepressible, that was Kelley. She was putting the phone back in her purse when it vibrated and rang in her hand.

"Hello?"

Sissy's enthused voice rang in her ears.

"Claryn! Guess what, we have got not one, not two, but three! Count 'em, three appointments to show the house next week. What's your work schedule?"

Claryn inwardly shrank. "Still on early mornings to early afternoon week days. When are the appointments?"

"Hum. Two are lunchtime, one afternoon. Do you think I should come in for them?"

"I don't know. Do you trust the realtor?"

"Okay. You're right. I'll come in. Do you have any plans this weekend?"

"I'm working on that as we speak."

"Oh. Is someone there with you?"

"That's not what I meant. I was expecting a phone call."

"Ah, well, don't go out with anyone tonight who is calling this late in the game. That is definitely against the rules. You might plan a trip to see Kelley. Show him your life is not about waiting for him."

"Right. It's about waiting for realtor appointments."

Gleeful Sissy, "No more waiting for those! Yippee! I'll catch you later or see you Sunday evening, maybe Monday. Okay?"

"Kay."

"Bye."

This time, when the phone rang, Claryn's answer verged on peeved.

"Hello?"

"You all right?"

"It's you," she said much more amiably.

"It's me."

"I'm glad. Where are you?"

"On my way to see you, I hope."

"I'm on strict orders not to see you till tomorrow at the earliest. It's against the rules."

"Whose orders? What rules?" Justice was indignant.

"Sissy thinks it's important for you to know that my life is not about sitting around waiting for you to call or waiting to make plans."

"If I tell you I know your life isn't about waiting around for me does that mean I can see you tonight?"

"Let me ask Felix."

"What? Who's Felix?"

116

He heard her asking someone but was certain he heard no one answer.

"Felix thinks that will work."

"Is Felix an imaginary friend, 'cause I didn't hear him answer."

Piqued she replied, "He is not imaginary." She petted Felix waggling his ears from side to side making his collar jingle. "Why use words when body language will suffice?"

Justice was relieved by the metallic noise he recognized from previous calls with her at work.

"Should I be jealous of Felix?"

"Definitely. We talk about everything, he's always hanging around at work, and he sits right against me."

Funny how relief can turn to jealousy so quickly, Justice thought.

"Hello? You still there?" Claryn thought she'd lost him again.

"You should go ahead and eat without me. Can I come by your place around eight?"

"Or I could meet you out at the shop?" she offered hopefully.

"No." His response was too quick and emphatic. It made Claryn second guess how things had gone that night. She got quiet.

"I'm sorry," she said.

"What? You don't have anything to be sorry about, Claryn. Look, Chess is home, anxious to meet you in fact. And I don't feel like sharing."

Claryn smiled broadly. "Oh. Well, since you put it that way..."

"Eight-ish? Earlier if I can?"

"Earlier if you can. I better finish up work."

"See you soon."

"See you."

Claryn's buoyant steps perked Felix up till he realized he was going back in his kennel. Even there he beat the floor with his wagging tail to show he shared Claryn's happiness.

"And you know what, Felix? I still don't know what my plans are. I know who they're with though and that's all I need. Hold down the fort. Okay, buddy?"

Felix paced out a tight circle twice and lay down as Claryn locked up the shelter for the night.

"Hello?" Chess answered the shop phone expecting Justice.

"Call for Mr. J. Cain," said a very official sounding female.

"You've got Mr. C. Cain. Can I help you?"

"Are you responsible to take a message for Mr. J. Cain?"

Chess paused to reflect that others might disagree.

"I am."

"Please inform him that the person of interest appears to be a Richard Court, previously of Hallston, Arizona. Mr. Court has a parole hearing scheduled for the 22nd of this month at the Arizona Penitentiary and Camp in Tucson, Arizona."

"Richard Court, possible parole on 22nd, Tucson. Got it. Who should I say called?"

"Thank you, Mr. Cain. Goodbye."

"Goodbye," he said to the already dead air on the line.

He regarded the handheld crossly. Sure doesn't take long to lose your touch with the ladies, does it?

Chess wrote a note for JT rather than calling him. Whatever it was about could wait. Court, whoever he was, wasn't going anywhere soon. Chess decided to surprise JT by actually doing some work on the engine sitting in bay two rather than return to the Friday Fright Night movie lineup. He felt like he'd seen Night of the Living Dead, The Bat, and The Fog enough times for this decade.

Chapter 19

Claryn practically bounced out the front door when Justice pulled into her driveway at a quarter till eight. As he came around from the far side the urge to hug him caused her to almost skid to a halt. He stopped several feet from her smiling broadly in the way that dazzled her so that she noticed little else. She let herself be drawn as close as she dared and then found she felt too shy to speak. It was so different to talk on the phone with only his soothing honey toned voice as a reminder of how faultless he was.

Justice wanted to tell her how great she looked, how much he missed her, but he was certain it would make her uncomfortable. Irish eyes a smiling ran through his mind. He fell back on their phone greeting.

"Hey."

"Hey, you."

"How's your arm?"

"Almost as good as new." She held up the scab-streaked appendage for inspection.

"Lovely liar."

She turned toward the yard, gesturing at the for sale sign.

"Three appointments coming to see the house next week."

"I wouldn't be too worried. Some people make a hobby of house shopping instead of trolling the mall."

He knew just what to say to make her feel better.

"What's the plan, date-man?"

It was Justice's turn for discomfort.

"I didn't make one other than getting over here as soon as I could."

"That's okay. I'm not a big planner myself."

A gentle breeze picked up tendrils of Claryn's hair and carried the scent of her shampoo to him. He thought that with some assistance he could stand there half the night breathing her scent off the light breeze. It was his inspiration.

"Would you be up for a walk?"

"Sure. Let me grab a jacket." She turned to unlock the front door.

"Here. Take mine." He held out toward her his dark brown military-cut jacket with the short collar. She put in one arm and then the other knowing he was inches away behind her. With a light touch he drew her hair out of the jacket as it rested on her shoulders. Her heart barely slowed.

Without looking back, she led the way across the yard and down the street. He fell in step beside her, taking the position nearest the road along the sidewalk as they shared a companionable silence. A couple neighbors greeted her by name, one jogging and one walking a schnauzer on the opposite sidewalk. Justice motioned for them to cross the road when a dog walker with four dogs approached. On the other side he again changed position to walk the roadside of the sidewalk even though it left him upwind.

"My dad used to do that."

"Do what?"

"Walk on the outside. I asked him about it once and he told me it was what a gentleman should do, place himself between a lady and the danger or unpleasant things. Is that why you do it? Are you a gentleman?"

"I would like to be one for you."

"You're kind of old fashioned. Has anyone ever told you that before?"

"Yes."

Justice kept expecting Claryn to ask where he picked up his old ways. But Claryn, who sometimes found it painful to talk about her own parents, veered away from those topics as a habit. She discovered she could tell Justice about most anything though, he was easy to talk to.

At the park, she meandered between the monkey bars and the merry-go-round to sit on a swing.

"Would you like a push?"

"Sure."

"My dad used to do that too. I don't think I've been to this park since he got sick. It looks kind of spooky at night." But I feel safe with you, she wanted to say and found she couldn't.

"A couple of the lights are broken out," he said. "Probably kids throwing rocks."

With more height, her hair and scent began sweeping back across him with every push. They lapsed into silence for only a few moments before he noticed her breathing change.

"I feel dizzy," she said weakly.

He caught her on the back swing and brought her to a stop before reluctantly moving away to sit on the swing beside her.

"Is it me?"

She shook her head. "No. It's strange. I used to swing for hours but now I think it messes up my equilibrium. It's definitely the swinging."

A dog found something to bark at, setting off a relay of barking across the neighborhood. The joggers and walkers had gone in for the evening leaving the sidewalks deserted and the young couple alone in the park.

Justice registered a decidedly unpleasant odor coming from the dark side of the park as Claryn shivered again. Death was in the air.

He stood, turning his head off to the left in the breeze as he offered her his hand. "Let's get you home."

He seemed distant all of a sudden, and Claryn looked at his hand for several beats and found she could place her hand in his just long enough to pull herself to her feet. Her heart rate dropped suddenly as they both registered the feel of their hands holding each other for the first time.

Claryn quickly slipped her hand out of his and into the jacket pocket, waiting for the weakness to pass. Justice found it increasingly difficult to step away when all he wanted was to hold her close. The fowl odor stalking them didn't help matters.

They didn't speak all the way back to Claryn's house. Justice scanned the darkness on every side as they walked. Claryn felt his tenseness and

121

increased her pace to match his own which swiftly returned them to the stoop. The foul odor well behind them, Justice relaxed as he held the screen door for her, although he continued peering out through the darkness.

"You want to come in for a while?" Claryn hated the idea that their evening might be over so soon and figured there was no way he would get the wrong idea.

"Yeah. We should have left some lights on in your house." He stepped in, looked down the stairs before proceeding up to walk the circle through the kitchen and dining room back into the living room.

"Is something the matter?" Claryn turned the dead bolt before joining him.

"No. I tend to be a bit paranoid. Nothing for you to worry about."

"George says paranoia is just good thinking when everyone's out to get you."

"My brother and George would get along famously," he said pulling the drapes closed and sitting down on the couch.

Claryn almost asked about Justice's brother but decided not to. Instead she turned on a floor lamp next to the wicker rocking chair Sissy bought a few years back to replace the recliner Claryn's Dad used to have in front of the bay window. The wicker chair was nice enough, but to Claryn it was still her dad's spot no matter what piece of furniture you was in it.

She sighed unconsciously as she turned off the overhead lights and joined Justice on the couch where she took a large decorator pillow and held it on her crossed legs between them. She found she could sit closer to him with this barrier of fluff than she could without it.

Justice put one arm on the back of the couch and rested his head on that hand as he examined her face, hair, neck, and finally her eyes. She was sitting as close as she ever had, at least while conscious, and she was bearing up under the scrutiny well.

122

Claryn studied his boots, his dark wash jeans, his hand on his knee, slowly working her way up to his face, which always looked astonishingly pleased to see her. Justice seemed satisfied simply sitting and gazing at her, and although she was doing better with it, she began to feel the need for conversation.

"How was your trip?"

"Uneventful. Your week?"

"Slow." She picked at the fringe on the large pillow as she barely whispered, "I felt like you were too far away."

"I was," he frowned and joined her in regarding the fringe, "and unfortunately I have to go out of town next week as well."

"Why? You just got home."

"Chess and I have some property over near Santa Fe, and a friend of ours said someone may have been messing about the place. I have to go check it out. Been needing to look things over as it is."

"Couldn't Chess go?"

"We actually have to spend some time down there, so we're trading out weeks. I'll go this week and he'll probably go the next. The good news is I will definitely be back in town in time for a real date. Where would you like to go?"

"You're not leaving tomorrow are you?"

"No, no. I'll head out Sunday night."

"I don't have to work tomorrow. We could spend the whole day together."

This produced a far away sadness Claryn hadn't seen before, something akin to regret.

"I wish I could. I won't be able to get out till early evening." He switched gears on her changing the subject. "Are you ever afraid being here alone at night?"

"Well I haven't been before, but I probably will be after tonight. Thanks."

"Give me your phone."

"What?"

"Give me your cell phone." She handed it over as he began inputting numbers. "You have my cell already, the second number I'm putting in is the shop, and the third is Chess, 'The Number of Last Resort,' I'll entitle it."

He held the phone out towards her, emphasizing his words with it.

"I want you to promise me if anything scares you, day or night, that you'll call every one of the numbers till someone answers."

"I'd feel silly. What if I just had a bad dream? Have you looked at this place? This is the 'least likely to rob' house on the block."

"Bad dream, call me. Intruder, call 9-1-1 and then call me, then the shop, then Chess."

She reached for the phone but he held it away, waiting for her consent.

"And don't wait for your heart to stop. You're usually not scared because you've got good instincts. If you get so much as a queasy feeling in the pit of your stomach, promise you'll call those numbers?"

"You're as bad as Kelley. I promise. Next week you won't have to worry though, because Sissy is coming home on Sunday night to monitor the realtor situation."

"It won't stop me from worrying, but I am glad she'll be here."

He held the phone out to her holding it longer than necessary as her grasp brought her hand in contact with his.

"Enough of that," she said. "Do you have any TV shows you usually watch on Friday nights? Oops, I don't think I'm supposed to let on how often I'm home on Friday nights. Probably breaking one of the rules."

"I don't watch much TV. Besides, Friday nights I usually work on cars."

"On Friday? Then you're missing out. All kinds of old movies come on this time Friday nights."

She flipped through the channels till she found The Ghost and Mrs. Muir on the old classic movie station then she tossed the remote down

124

and turned to lay down on the pillow and keep the bubble of cushion between them.

She knew he was watching her as much as the movie and once when she glanced over, his instantly averted eyes looked like they were glowing with the reflected light from the screen.

She was half afraid he would touch her and half longing for him to do so. I am so messed up, she thought. After that she kept her focus on the screen till she fell asleep. In the morning she awoke under a blanket, feeling more rested than she had in a long time. A note from Justice on his seat said, "See you tonight at seven for a nice meal out. JT"

Chapter 20

Justice spent the rest of his morning reviewing online information about Richard S. Court, a low life if there ever was one. It was hard to imagine Sissy ever dating the man. Like other scumbags he had a knack for finding people who were at low points in their lives and taking advantage of them. The elderly woman with a son his age who had gone missing in action, the widow and her teenage daughter still grieving, and the teenage runaway found unconscious in a ditch with enough evidence to put the ogre away.

His was not one of those stories where people are shocked to discover the evil lurking in the form of a mild mannered neighbor. Every reporter easily located source after unnamed source with descriptions of his destructive and abusive character. Of interest, there were two vengeful accounts; the man was not above holding a grudge and Justice got the feeling the unnamed sources still feared Court.

The only real surprise was the photo attached to one article; "Rick" Court was startlingly good looking. Justice studied the strong lines of the man's face and wondered how six years behind bars had altered it. Maybe he had them at "Hello."

"Well, I for one am glad he's finally taking you out for a nice meal. We were beginning to worry that for all his other great characteristics Jay was on the cheap side of dating," said Kelley knowingly.

Claryn had caught Kelley and George going hiking for the day. Kelley might do a good bit of complaining about all their activities, thought Claryn, but she thrives on it. I'd definitely trade dinner for hiking. Claryn felt a twinge of envy for their whole day out together.

"Do you think I'm trying to go too fast?"

"Too fast! Let's face it, you're about as slow as they come. Hold on." Kelley covered the mouthpiece to listen to George put in his two cents.

"Ah, George wants to know if you tried to have the 'defining our relationship' talk. He thinks it might be too early for that."

"The what talk?"

"Oh you know. The one where you force him to put a label on what you're doing besides dating. Are you exclusive? Are you boyfriend and girlfriend? That kind of thing."

"Gosh, do we have to label it? I think a girlfriend ought to at least be able to hold her man's hand and kiss him goodnight. I'd be labeled what, the worst girlfriend ever?"

"You're doing wonderful! You've already slept together what, twice? That makes up for a lot."

"We have not slept together. Does George know that?"

Kelley put on her mysterious spooky voice, "George knows all, sees all. What?" She was listening to George again.

"You haven't asked him where he sees the relationship going, right? I think George's first thoughts of matrimony came on the heels of me asking him that one. . . . He denies it, of course."

Claryn tended to think on today, letting tomorrow's troubles care for themselves. When her father was his sickest, she caught him humming an old tune his mother sang to him, "One Day at a Time." Claryn didn't know the words, though she took the refrain to heart. It was sometimes the only thing that kept her going when things got their roughest.

"Tomorrow is not promised, so why dwell there?" she quoted a favorite saying to which Kelley had a ready response.

"But you still set your alarm clock every night. Look, we've turned onto the park road. I don't think relationship advice was why you called."

No, indeed. Claryn had been through her closet twice and Sissy's once looking for something to wear to her nice dinner. She'd discovered her own clothes were on the drab side and Sissy's on the risqué.

Finally she gave up and took a shower, thereby procrastinating the wardrobe decision. Her hair came out wild as a bramble patch and for the first time since Sissy had gone on the road with Brad Claryn wished her stepmother home a day early. Calling Kelley was an act of desperation.

"Clothes and hair emergency on a titanic scale."

"Clothes first. Choose something fitted, but comfortable, skirt above the knee, top with spaghetti straps. Oh! Do you still have the dress I loaned you for the rehearsal dinner?"

"No. I put it in one of your bags of wedding gifts."

"Darn. That would have been perfect. In lieu of that, you've got what? Seven hours? Go shopping. And then stop by the salon. When was the last time you got your hair cut?"

"I like my hair long. It's easier to pull back each day."

"I'm not saying get it all hacked off. Ask for some shape and have them show you how to fix it yourself. Okay? And if it was me, I'd get a manicure. You've got those thick perfect French manicure looking nails anyway. Half the fun is the treatment and relaxation though. Oh no, skip that and have your make-up done! Oh, I wish I was there too. You're going to have such a great day!"

Contemplating the mall at all, much less going by herself, was not Claryn's idea of a great day. She heard George comment in the background and Kelley revised her last statement.

"And I'm going to have a different kind of great day right here! Gotta go now. Call me tomorrow. Bye."

"Bye."

Claryn tried to opt out of the forty minute drive to the nearest big mall by going to the Dress Warehouse located in a strip of shops next to the All-Mart. Flipping through dresses unsuccessfully, she saw a stunning girl come out of the dressing room in the perfect dress. She did a turn and her smooth, shiny auburn hair flowed flawlessly around her neck looking for like something out of a shampoo or hair color commercial.

Claryn found herself jealous of the slender but full figured nymph, who asking the attendant how the dress looked as she smoothed the skirt over her hips and received the appropriate and abundant praise. The dress was everything Kelley said Claryn needed but after seeing it on the other girl, Claryn didn't think she wanted to wear it anyway.

As she slid behind the wheel of her car feeling sorry for herself, for the long drive ahead, for shopping alone, for everything, Claryn guiltily watched the beauty exit the dress shop, bag in one hand and long white cane in the other. The young woman tapped her way along the sidewalk to the All-Mart. Her father's words ran through her mind, "Always think on and be thankful for what you have, Claryn, rather than focusing on what you have not."

Chess amused himself by making ridiculous food handling suggestions and seeing how gullible JT was. It was fun to be the expert in an area where JT sought advice. JT had lived with Chess's mischief for so many years, he honestly thought himself now immune to its irritating force.

This was a new area and Chess was like a dog with a bone he refused to let go of. At the end of his rope and on his very last nerve, JT not only got quiet but took off his jacket and folded it over the arm of the couch as he prepared to face off against his brother. Chess saw the jokes had outlived their ability to entertain even him. Their sparing always resulted in something getting broken. Chess mentally calculated the cost, his eyes settling on his giant HDTV flatscreen lovingly. It wasn't worth it, he quickly decided. He threw up his hands in surrender still keeping the couch between him and his brother.

"Fine! Fine! I give. I give up."

"Sit."

Chess complied and began speaking in his best professor voice, "In theory you have a digestive system, it doesn't really work anymore though, so basically anything you eat is going to make you feel a light urge to hurl. The incomplete truth works to your advantage; tell your date you are on a restrictive diet extending to content and amount at one sitting. Half the

129

time girls are too and don't want to talk about it much, so you're in the clear.

"After that, your primary strategy is creative food disposal while pretending to eat. Go to one of the restaurants with patio dining so you give your bits of bread to the birds, have the waiter put half your meal in a to-go container as each course is served, push your food around on your plate trying to spread it out so it looks like you ate more. It requires a lot of vigilance to make your food disappear while she's looking down at hers.

"And I was serious about the pocket baggie. Sometimes you will get caught and have to chew up something, so as you order keep in mind items that you can fake chew and discard with your next napkin use. In an emergency you may even have to swallow, if so chew that sucker up for all it's worth 'cause your teeth are about the only part of your digestive system still working for you. As long as you're really into them, or appear that way, some dates won't care that you're not eating much."

"Claryn will care. She noticed when I only picked at the wedding cake."

"Then you've got your work cut out for you. You may have to claim slight indigestion, chalk it up to your condition and order bubbly water. You could also talk a lot, and I do mean a lot, but sometimes that backfires in terms of date quality. So...impressed, right? Am I the man or what?"

"I'm thinking 'or what.'"

"I resemble that," he said instead of resent.

Chess opted not to inform JT that Maestro's was the type of restaurant where the chef might come out to appease you with extras if your plates went back to the kitchen with too much food on them. Let him figure that one out on his own, he thought.

"What's with the Court fella?" Chess had scowled over the browser history as much as JT, only with less intensity.

"It's probable he'll return to the area if he gets paroled."

130

"The reports didn't say he went down for murder. I suspect he'll make parole. Has he actually killed anyone?"

"If he's the one I'm looking for," JT swung around with a flat stare causing Chess to cringe, "nothing else matters."

"You might want to think some happy thoughts, and erase that look from your face or you won't have a date. Nobody'd get in a car with that mug."

From Justice's "Wow" when he saw her to the moment he pulled back into her driveway it was the most perfect evening Claryn could imagine. The restaurant was elegantly lit so even the air around them seemed to dance with radiance. They talked, laughed, shared stories, so enthralled with each other they barely touched their food.

Over Justice's shoulder Claryn saw a concerned chef coming toward their table, but when she acted as if nothing else in the world existed other than the man telling her a story and making her smile, the chef had the good sense to retreat.

Riding home, she knew more than anything how she wanted the evening to end and the thought of it sent waves of dizzying fear over her. One kiss! I can do it, I can do it, she said it like the mantra of the Little Engine That Could, while her body patently disagreed, saying "You cannot."

Lightheaded she leaned back against the headrest feeling so woozy she could not even lift her arms. I must look a sight. In her driveway she felt rather than saw Justice turn in the seat beside her, tense with concern.

She spoke slowly, her eyes closed, her breath heavy. "I want to kiss you goodnight. I just can't." She breathed. "Will you kiss me anyway?"

Under his breath he sighed, "Ah, mon cherie" and then less softly, "I don't want to make you pass out, and you will. You're almost there now."

Hot salty tears broke over, spilling down her cheeks to her jaw line and cresting before running rivulets that petered out to dryness on her

131

neck. She dropped her shaky hand beside her on the cream leather of the seat.

Justice slid his own hand towards her in slow motion, listening to her pulse, her breathing, watchful of further reaction. Light as a feather he laid only the tips of his fingers across the tops of her own. They sat that way, neither speaking, for a long time. He studied their hands as he listened to her cry and silently wished for the first time in over two hundred years that he could cry too.

"I would fix this for you if I could," his voice all tenderness.

"I know you would." She raked in a ragged breath and a fresh barrage of tears rolled as she turned her head on the rest to look over at him.

"I'm sorry." Her voice was high almost squeaky.

"No, Claryn. No. You don't have to be sorry. Patience, time, this can be overcome. I truly believe that."

Her eyes said she was desperate to believe it too. How could anyone be that patient? I wouldn't be, she secretly thought, but oh how she hoped he was. She watched him rest his head back, pensive.

"I'm the one who should be sorry. There are things about me, things you should know and I'm too scared to even think about telling you."

Claryn didn't believe him. He's trying to make me feel better, she thought. They sat like that till her head cleared, her eyes dried, and she was able to turn her hand over on his to cover his fingers.

"See," he said, "improving already."

They smiled.

The Darkman was intrigued. There were too many eyes out and about on the weekend, so he was very careful when he chose the driveway of the deserted house in which he now sat in his car. He watched the young couple across the street through his rearview window.

They sat in the hotrod car an inordinate amount of time for a couple not at least necking. Sometimes they appeared to not even talk. When the young man walked his date to the door, they didn't hold hands or kiss, though their lingering gazes gave all the indications of a budding romance.

He glowered at the young man's car as it drove away, the coward. Then he turned sympathetic eyes back to the young woman who watched the muscle car drive away with obvious disappointment. This I can fix, the Darkman said to the mirror. You deserve better, my love. My dolls get all the kisses they could ever want, so you, my dear, will not be disappointed with me.

He smiled at the for sale sign in her yard, recollecting which day his appointment was. She was quite young. Age before beauty, he remarked deciding to save her for last, save her for the road. Driving to Doll Two's house, he hummed and sang like Old Blue Eyes, "Make it one for my baby, And one more for the road."

Chapter 21

Sissy called Claryn at work Sunday as she carried her one bag into the house and noted its dismal state.

"Claryn, could you not have at least vacuumed yesterday? Oh, well. Never fear, Sissy is here! When will you be home?"

"I don't think Mrs. Smithson was able to get many of the dogs out yesterday so I thought I'd stay later and try to do what I can for them. Maybe seven thirty?"

"All right then. I'll probably have everything ready before that. How does your room look?"

Claryn inwardly cringed, "Uh, not the best. I'll beat it into shape as soon as I get home. Okay?"

"I could work on it for you."

Claryn thought of the new dress on the floor amongst other things and did her best to discourage Sissy.

"No, please. It's my mess and I'll get it all straightened out." Inspiration struck, "Besides I'm going to go through some things to get rid of them," which was the absolute truth as she decided after looking at and vetoing every item in her closet as un-date worthy, "so it's easier if I only have to sort it out once."

"Good for you! I should do that in my room as well."

Confident Sissy would be busy all evening, Claryn returned to the poor keyed up creatures at the shelter.

"Justice! What a pleasant surprise. You know Claryn is working late today so she's not here yet," said Sissy.

"Yes, ma'am. I was hoping to speak with you before she gets home."

Sissy acted as if he'd given her a compliment of the highest order as she invited him in off the stoop.

"Me? Well, then, do come in. Can I get you something to drink? You're twenty-one aren't you? Or twenty-two?"

"Yes, ma'am."

She went through to the kitchen where she poured him a glass of wine from a half empty bottle.

"I see you've been getting ready for this week's appointments. It looks nice."

"Why thank you. I'm sure it's a vast improvement over the last time you were here. Oh, but I just realized I don't even know when that was."

Sissy batted her eyes at him but Justice wasn't about to reveal anything to her since he didn't know how far into Claryn's confidence their relationship extended. He accepted his wine glass and deflected.

"Does the name Richard Court mean anything to you? I think he used to live around here."

Sissy's face and entire body sagged as she sat heavily on the other end of the couch.

"Where did you hear that name?"

"Maybe I read it in the paper or something."

"Shhi . ." she covered her mouth with both hands before finishing the word but he didn't have to guess what she was saying. She jumped off the couch like it scorched her and started pacing, dialing a number in her quick list.

"They are supposed to call me if that bastard gets even a whiff of a chance at parole." She walked into the next room for a quick conversation and came back fuming.

"You were right! I can't believe it. He's up for parole in less than two weeks. Can you believe that? I can't believe the arresting officer didn't call me or something. Said he was waiting to hear. Forgot is more like it. Claryn doesn't know this, but I testified against him at his trial. Kind of a character witness for bad character."

"I hear he's the type to carry a grudge. But you'll be back on the road with Brad by the time his parole hearing rolls around, won't you?"

"I will." This thought obviously relieved her.

Justice glanced around the room. "You don't think he'd come around here, do you?"

She blinked a couple times.

"Come here? No, I mean he's got no reason to come here."

"But Claryn might be here if he did."

"Claryn? Well, she might be around if she hasn't found a new place yet, I was going to tell her to start apartment hunting this week. She'll be better off in her own place instead of rattling around in this big old house and that way the house will always be ready for appointments. But Rick would never think of Claryn.

"Oh! Unless . . . are you thinking he might mistake her for me? I'd never forgive myself if something happened to Claryn because of me, Justice. I mean, I've made some bad decisions but that man represents the absolute worst – worst three years of my life."

Three years. Three years. Justice covered his eyes with one hand to hide the sudden color change and thought he would completely lose it at any moment. His voice was tight and his eyes shut. He sank into the couch to try and relax.

"But they're going to call you if he makes parole, right?"

"Hell, yes, they're going to call me. I gave them a thing or two to think about. If he sets foot outside that prison, I'm going to know about it." She was pacing again not paying him much mind. "They've got some automated system now, but give 'em your cell phone number and it will spit you out a text message. Ain't that something."

Sissy's accent had slipped back to one from her past, probably to a time when she felt stronger Justice knew.

"Can you give them more than one number?"

"No. Just the one. I'm pretty sure. You thinking Claryn ought to know? I think it would just scare her."

"No. Absolutely not. I was thinking if he got out, I could keep an eye on her; make sure she's safe. Even if she's kicked me to the curb by then, I could still check on her."

Sissy knelt in front of him, brushing his hair back with her fingers.

"Aren't you the dearest thing," she was too close to him and when she sighed she started blinking funny. He looks fuzzy. She shook her head and stepped back thinking, I've got to get new contacts.

"You know, there was a time not so long ago, mind you, when I thought Claryn'd been put off men all together after watching everything I went through." Sissy's smile was a little wobbly, "But she had the best Daddy ever. So I shoulda knowd better."

"You'll call?"

"You bet I will. Gimme your phone and I'll put your number in on speed dial." She stepped toward him and back again. "Better yet, you put 'em in yourself. That way I won't get any of the numbers mixed up."

Sissy had her own stories to tell about Rick Court and some of her other past mistakes before she rebounded to happier times. About meeting Brad, their online dating as he traveled, and how the distance made hearts grow fonder. Justice's mind could not be budged from thoughts of Court.

A horrified Claryn came home to a tipsy Sissy and a weakly smiling Justice who she immediately rescued by telling her stepmom, "We'll be in my room listening to music while I clean."

"Oh--well, okay. Toodles," Sissy waved at Justice's retreating figure and then put her finger beside her nose to indicate they should both remember to keep their secret. Claryn frowned as she caught the motion and closed the door behind them.

"Heavens! What was that all about? How long have you been here?"

"Over an hour, I'd say, but it felt longer somehow."

"Oh! You're a saint!" Claryn flopped back full length on the twin bed she'd bought for herself between her freshman and sophomore year of high school, but then she popped back up.

"Hey. You knew I wasn't off work till after six and you got here before that? What's that about?"

137

He put his finger to the side of his nose as Sissy had done, indicating the two of them had their own conspiracy.

Claryn regarded him skeptically for a beat and then said, "I take it back. You're not a saint. You're cruisin' for a bruisin', just asking for whatever you get."

She shoved some clothes off the bed to make a spot for him and indicated the clock radio as she began picking up, sorting, and cleaning.

"Find some music?"

Justice saw no pattern to her work so quickly gave up the idea of helping. He lay back with one elbow supporting his upper body as he dialed through the stations stopping on every one that came in regardless of category so he could watch her facial expressions as she evaluated his supposed selection. She threw him a baleful look for heavy metal but sang along with anything upbeat.

Sissy couldn't resist poking her head in after a while ostensibly to see how things were coming along. Claryn had a nice row of brown paper bags to take to the Salvation Army on her way to work the next day. She was mostly down to finding a place for the small odds-n-ends that accumulated and multiplied unaided on her bureau and vanity top.

Sissy spotted two men's flannel shirts hanging among the sparse shirts and slacks populating the large wooden rod in Claryn's closet. Justice had wondered about them enough to wander over and flip through ten or more hangers nonchalantly trying to determine whose they were. The scent was faded after six years, and muddled with some salty tears, but it was definitely that of a blood relative, obviously her father.

"Oh, Claryn. I didn't know you still had these."

Sissy went to them, took one in both hands and held the fabric over her face inhaling deeply. "Nothing left is there? See, this is what Justice and I were talking about."

Claryn stood frozen to a spot on the floor by the vanity stool, feeling an irrational sense of possession about the shirts. She warily waited for what Sissy and Justice had been talking about that related to her dead father's shirts.

"It's time to move on, make a fresh start for yourself. Stop moping around in this old house."

Sissy sat down on the bed near Justice who looked out from under arched brows at her. His expression broadcast clear uncertainty about where she was headed.

"We thought you might start looking for a new place of your own this week. Justice could help you."

Unmistakably Sissy had not run this idea by Justice or she would be aware that he was going out of town this week. In Claryn's mind, he was thus innocent of all wrong doing.

"Wouldn't it be nice to start new before the house sells, sort the things you really want to take with you from those you don't?"

Sissy carried one of the shirts over to her and placed it in her hands.

"Just think about it, okay? That's all I'm asking."

"Sure."

Sissy gave her a hug, and nodded as she left the room closing the door softly behind her.

"For the record, that was not my idea," Justice spoke up.

"Obviously."

Claryn gave a weak laugh and patted the wrinkles out of her father's shirt before carefully hanging it back in the closet. She placed her hands behind it sinking her face into it and inhaled deeply. She registered memories of his pipe smoke, his aftershave, and possibly even her mom's perfume. These were favorite smells, but not the only ones. She was sometimes surprised by new smells, which brought a previously forgotten memory crashing down on her with such force it could make her cry. Something of his is there, or maybe I'm imagining it.

"Your dad's?" said Justice.

"Yeah. He had a lot of shirts like this. Said they were all the rage at one time. Can you picture that?"

139

Justice remembered it distinctly and smiled without speaking.

"You took me to the bowling alley and the park swings like he did." She sunk onto the vanity stool. "By Saturday I was half braced for a nice meal at the steakhouse we used to go to."

"I can't tell if you want to go there or want to avoid it."

She grinned. "Both. Kelley says that it's our prerogative as women to be complicated and unpleasable in at least a couple areas."

"If not more," he agreed.

"Maybe when you get back we could go to the cemetery?"

"If you like."

"I know he's not there but I like to talk to him there sometimes, the way he used to talk to Mom. As silly as this sounds, I'd like to introduce you."

"I'd like that too."

"You're too easy to please," she was doubtful.

"Someone has to be."

She growled and chucked a random object off the vanity at his head which he plucked easily from the air and placed in his pocket.

"Thanks. Nothing like a souvenir to take with me this week. Speaking of which, I have good news and bad news. What do you want to hear first?"

"The bad news."

"I won't be able to talk to you on the phone at all this week."

"Yuck. The good news?"

"The good news is I'll definitely be home by Friday evening."

"Yeah!"

"And I do have a favor to ask but I'm not sure how to go about it."

"Ask and ye shall receive."

"I'll take that as a commitment."

"Uh-oh."

"It's not that bad. I don't think you should rush out to start apartment hunting . . ."

140

"Agreed."

" . . . but I would like you to stay somewhere else the twenty-second through the twenty-fourth without asking me why."

"What for?"

"That's the same as asking why and you've already agreed not to. Maybe you could go visit Kelley?"

"I have to work those days. Oh, but that works out perfectly though because two of those nights Mrs. Smithson has already asked me to stay over because she's going out of town."

"Perfect."

"You're really not going to tell me why?"

"Maybe after. So what about Friday, shall we make plans?"

"No, we shall not." She'd taken to making fun of what she called his odd phrase-ology. "Let's just go with the flow and see what happens. No pressure. No plans. We can hang out."

He raised a hand for a high five that she slapped hard enough to sting her own hand and wince shaking off the pain. I'll have to watch out for that, Justice thought, not knowing how much would change in the next week.

Chapter 22

The Darkman's first doll could only come out to play for short periods of time now. He didn't want to play with her too much because he loved the short time when he had two dolls, his own special sort of threesome. Now, however, was his Acquiring Phase.

His own excitement was hard to contain, mixed as it was with the sense of danger that came with making a new find. He closed his eyes breathing deeply as he leaned against the front of his doll box. If all went according to plan, he would have two dolls to play with by mid-week.

Kelley wasn't too perturbed with being put off till Monday, especially since the report was so good. Claryn was obviously lonesome without her man, and they got to talk longer with George out at work.

"What do you think Sissy and Justice talked about for an hour?" Kelley asked. "That's kind of scary."

"I don't know. Knowing Sissy she talked non-stop and carried both sides of a conversation revolving around selling the house and planning my new life. Poor Justice."

"Poor Justice. But like you said, he got there early all by his lonesome. Hopefully he's learned his lesson and will stop showing up earlier than expected. Can't believe he did that for your formal evening out. Unforgivable."

In this Kelley and Claryn disagreed though pointing out such would only hurt Kelley's feelings. In fact Claryn could not disagree more. He was anxious to see her. The clock didn't keep him away. Maybe it was kind of their thing? Yeah.

"I'm thinking turn about's fair play and I'll show up at the shop early on Friday."

"Not sure that's a good idea."

"Why not?"

"I don't know. Say, you haven't met his brother yet, have you?"

"Have not."

"Will he be around Friday? It might be fun to talk with him for awhile before Justice even gets home like he did with Sissy."

"Won't do. His brother isn't due home till later."

"Oh well. It was a thought. What's the brother's name again?"

"Chess."

"Is that short for Chester?"

"No, let me think . . . I know this."

Kelley was about to give up and move on to something else.

"Fran-ces-co!" Claryn burst out in a moment of inspiration.

"Ha!" Kelley broke out laughing.

"It's not that funny a name."

"No, ho-ho-ho, it's how you said it. Ridic-cu-lo-so!" Kelley imitated. "Like a spell straight out of Harry Potter."

"Fran-ces-co!"

"Fran-ces-co!"

"If it's a spell, what do you think it does?" Kelley asked.

"It definitely gives me the giggles," Claryn said.

"And makes me hungry. I want a Frisco burger now. Do you remember all that talk about the freshman fifteen? No one tells you, but there's a new wife weight gain as well. Beware!"

Kelley had fought the freshman fifteen with a passion and succeeded where most of her friends had not, as evidenced by the bridesmaids' fittings. To Kelley's chagrin, Claryn had one of those enviable metabolisms that processed anything you threw at it. She still had the same petite figure from their sophomore year of high school.

Their conversation rambled on through three more dog walks before Kelley announced she was running late for a class. That was Kelley for you.

The short man with the wide spectacles was interested mostly in security at first. He went to all the exits of the house and inspected them first before asking any questions. This gave Sissy and the realtor a chance to exchange looks. Sissy whispered, "Is this normal?" The realtor responded, "Not really."

In Claryn's room he pawed through the clothes to ascertain the size of the closet space, and the realtor saw him smelling them as he did it.

"So you're not in residence?" the short man asked Sissy.

"No. I got married recently."

"But it's not sitting empty? Empty houses deteriorate so rapidly."

His comment made Sissy rethink the encouragement she'd given Claryn to find a new place.

"No, it's not. My stepdaughter lives here right now."

The realtor cleared her throat to interrupt and directed his attention to the larger master bedroom with attached bath. In that room he couldn't be bothered to even open the closet.

His examination of the house seemed so inconsistent to the realtor. Some rooms he paced off, the dining room, living room and hall, others he hardly stepped into, such as the two smaller bedrooms on the front side of the house. He didn't test the water pressure which was usually on everyone's to-do list, but he did open and close the automatic garage door several times, once with the wall button and twice with the available remote control. He was even perturbed by the fact that the other remote was unavailable since it was in Sissy's stepdaughter's car.

Sissy too felt odd about the visit. She found the whole process much less exciting than she'd hoped and more painstaking. Her presence did not seem to be a selling point as far as she could tell, and the strange man poking about the place left her mildly disturbed.

The realtor was better at fielding off the wall questions, so Sissy changed her assessment of the woman and decided to leave the rest of the appointments in her capable hands. As she packed to rejoin Brad the next day, she made a mental note to schedule future appointments when Claryn was also out of the house.

If Claryn thought last week was slow, this week simply refused to progress at all. She eventually called the shop hoping to hear Justice on the voice mail recording and heard a canned electronic voice instead.

The only break in a week of fastidious housekeeping and overzealous doggie care was the lone woman who came in wanting to adopt a dog. One of her neighbors had gone missing and the scared lady was highly motivated to take a fearsome dog home that day.

Claryn explained that the adoptions took a couple days under normal circumstances. She was always wary of people who had limited dog experience, had no great love of the animals, and who wanted one fast. The woman was diligent, though, spending a couple hours interacting with various groups of dogs before narrowing her choice down to two.

She spent one-on-one time with each of them and by lunch was plainly taken with a shepherd-lab mix, who responded to her with the tentative admiration and affection typical of those breeds after experiencing abandonment.

Trusting her own judgment as much as the rules, Claryn started the paperwork and added to it a form for temporary custody. The woman and her new companion went home together without delay. By Friday their new relationship was solidified and Claryn experienced once again the greatest pleasure of her job derived not only from saving an animal from euthanization, but also adding a new member to a now happier home.

As she closed up the shelter later than intended Friday evening and went home to get ready for her no-plan plans, she found herself humming along with the radio and checking the clock. Soon Justice would be home for an entire week, and she was going to talk to him every single day for as long as he could stand. Being apart had done one good thing. Without a doubt, she now knew she was head over heels for Justice Cain.

Chapter 23

Justice skidded through the gravel in front of the shop stopping with his right rear tire on the concrete entrance ramp. The pain was almost unbearable now as each pellet burned like its own incandescent flare under his skin.

It was reminiscent of the uncomfortable tingling from a limb gone to sleep, but each tingle was more molten stabbings running across the left side of his chest, around his side and into his back. He knew his flesh was burning away and trying to recover moment by moment.

He would not have been able to drive much further. He didn't have much time.

His left arm didn't seem to function properly, so he awkwardly shoved his body against the car door and half stumbled to the customer door of the shop.

Fumbling the keys with one hand, his body convulsed in reaction to the toxic metal within and caused him to drop the keys. He bent over painfully to retrieve his keys from a crevice between the concrete walkway and the foundation of the building. Justice considered just breaking the glass out, but his better judgment was still weighing in.

The slayer had carried a shotgun of modified shells, and he had not been the only one. On your average cattle range a shotgun might be loaded with rock salt to discourage coyotes, stray dogs, or rowdy teenagers. Instead, these shotgun pellets had burst on impact injecting quick silver into what felt like a million holes in his screaming skin. Justice was sure he could actually smell his flesh burning inside.

Vampire skin being what it is, it had healed over the mercury in seconds before his body had time to expel the poison. The vampire blood was rushing to the mercury to try to fight the invader much like white blood cells in humans, but that ancient compound didn't stand a chance.

First things first. Start with just opening the damn door. The formidable task of getting the quicksilver out of every fiery pit before his body used up its liquid reserves was too far in the future to consider.

Opening the door was taking all the concentration he had, so he didn't pay attention to the car in the distance.

Didn't matter. He was confident he'd lost his pursuers before cutting across country on dirt tracks that weren't on any maps or GPS. It helped that he could race through the desert without the need of headlights.

The door burst open, rattling the customer bell Chess had hung mostly as a joke. It seemed to set off a ringing in Justice's ears that got deeper and louder till it sounded more like a jet engine landing on his brain. Got to think, he told himself, or you're dead.

The silver plated blade he needed was supposed to be in the top drawer. He pawed through three drawers before spotting the long knife. He'd worry about why things weren't in their proper place if he survived the next hour.

He stumbled across the room and braced himself against the table. Justice gripped the knife with his right hand forcefully enough to bend the handle and let himself collapse onto the nearby sofa.

Tearing off his shirt to expose the wounds, he didn't even notice the new one he made with the blade. No more pain could register, it was already too much.

The convulsions came and went as he excised the bulging mercury. The liquid silver was actually burning away the flesh under his skin even as his body worked to restore it. For now his body was holding its own. It just wasn't able to generate the force necessary to break through his Kevlar like skin from the inside.

A wooden splinter would spit back out as fast as it went in. And the silver coated blade cut through his hide like it would into butter.

Shaking hands botched jagged cuts as he perforated the bulging skin. The mercury oozed out and burned a trail down the top of his skin before it balled into the deeper seams of the leather upholstery.

147

The trick was to get all the quick silver out of his body before his physical reserves got too low. If that happened, he'd be pockmarked with growing craters that would burn him alive from the inside out.

Every wave of pain threw his mind into darkness. A vision flashed behind his eyes of Chess returning too late and finding Justice's body as ravaged as Jenny's.

Life is in the blood, do not drink of it said the Torah, but death was also in the blood. Humans carried it around in various degrees, some more than others.

A vampire who took what was not given freely produced an exponential death taint from every source in the human's body. No one knew why.

Hence the rules that Sephauna taught them. The rules for life, at least for a long life.

Take only what is given.

Chemically it made no sense that the blood given carried inconsequential traces of the death taint except what manifested presently. Yet taken blood carried the death taint of diseases the person wouldn't develop for another thirty years.

Given blood was lifeblood. On- going abuses or illnesses that added to the death taint were somehow negated by the nature of the act of giving. It was ironically miraculous.

In theory, any death taint was bad, thus the honing of their keen sense of smell and an on-going concern about the corruption of the human populace.

Justice made progress where Jenny only suffered. Most of what he could easily reach was cut out.

Now if he could only get the rest with enough blood in his system to wait for Chess. He suspected he was beyond that point already. Rest seemed like a wonderful idea. Go into an oblivion of pain beyond reason. Let death finally bring him justice.

The idea of giving up the fight, any fight, grated. It went against his character. And what would he be to Claryn but another resounding death toll? Justice twisted and stretched till he could drag the blade in a sweeping arc on his back. Two more fireballs erupted from his body.

Claryn thought she had the hibbie jibbies. She didn't actually see the man standing in the thicket between the neighbors' properties, nevertheless gooseflesh broke out on her arms and her heart rate slowed as she climbed from her car to check her mailbox, one of fifteen grouped together like outdoor post office boxes on the street.

She had promised Justice she would call if anything at all didn't feel right, or looked wrong, or affected her. Following through on a promise is a good thing, she told herself.

No answer on Justice's phone. She slammed the car door and pulled down the block to her driveway.

Hang up and try the shop. Still no answer. She reached up to push the button for the garage door opener at the same moment the moon went behind a cloud. The button failed to work.

The street was too dark and too empty. Dogs barked warning tones. One of the brothers would be back later tonight. Claryn put her Honda in gear deciding to go to the shop and wait.

The Darkman watched the young woman sit in the car on the phone after pulling up. He could be patient, didn't want to scare the little doll before she had a chance to know him better. A hint of anger and frustration bubbled through him as he watched her toss the phone down and look around suspiciously. She couldn't possibly suspect anything, but there she was driving away. He growled angrily. Patience, patience. The Darkman jogged down the sidewalk to her mailbox. He rested his hand where she'd placed hers hoping to feel a hint of her body's warmth on smooth metal surface.

There was nothing.

Rather than disappointment he felt only a heightened sense of anticipation. Tonight he would jog and return to his rental unit hot. Too hot to be missing this bit of warmth.

On the contrary, the cool bodies of his other dolls would be a balm. Unfortunately one of them would have to go soon. But he could wait a few nights to replace her, maybe more if he was waiting for the right doll.

The sight of Justice's car angled awkwardly in front of the shop did not alarm Claryn. Her heart soared. I must have just missed him.

The car door hanging open gave her pause. Her feet slowed with apprehension. Opening the front door she'd never used, the customer bell welcomed brightly.

She felt for the light switch, and fluorescent bulbs flickered at the same time she heard a moan across the room. Two steps in, Claryn spotted Justice's form on the floor in front of the sofa.

Another three steps and she froze, realizing the moan was actually his rasping, weak voice telling her to go away. Misery soaked words degenerated till "go away" was only "ho ay."

In his effort to reach his wounds, Justice had rolled off the couch and onto the knife blade. This time he felt the excruciating pain and noted how slow it was to heal.

Not good.

Claryn's arrival?

Even worse.

His thirst was so great she resembled a walking popsicle to his parched burning throat. If the popsicle passed out next to him, he knew what the beast would eventually do.

Concern overcame confusion and Claryn rushed to his side. "What happened? I've got to get you to the hospital!"

She tugged ineffectually on him with soft juicy hands that found their way to the cell phone in her pocket.

"Noooo!"

150

He roared against his instincts as he half lunged toward her and smashed the cell phone with the hand that began to reach for her arm.

Mercifully he was slowed by the poison and she drew back to the wall in bewilderment.

He couldn't hear if her pulse weakened or not with those jet engines thundering through his skull, which was probably a blessing in disguise. As it was he could barely tear his eyes away from her pulsing carotid artery.

Focus. Focus. Focus.

The quick silver must come out.

He rolled his back to her and contorted enough to release one more pellet of pain.

Claryn couldn't quite fathom what she was seeing.

Justice looked so strange. His eyes were almost white and reflected the lights in the way animals' eyes did.

What appeared to be small rocks were embedded in his skin which he sliced at ruthlessly. But when these pebbles hit the air they melted into sizzling tiny mirrors burning their way across his skin like eggs down the side of the skillet.

An odd calm settled over Claryn.

It doesn't have to make sense. Justice needs me. Needs my help. She edged back over behind him, seeing what was needed as if from a distant trance.

Justice was flaying desperately trying to reach further across his back when he realized how close she was.

At that moment he was glad his left arm hung useless instead of clotheslining her like it wanted to. Her hands cupped his right hand from behind and took the knife.

"I can do this. Let me do this, Justice."

He barely had the presence of mind to tuck his face as far into his right arm as he could and bite his own flesh.

151

The shiny sharp blade required a surprising amount of force to cut through and release the . . . Claryn's mind refused to give her the right word till the third flattened ball made its hissing way down to the floor to join its brothers . . .mercury.

She recognized it not so much by color but because of the peculiar way the liquid moved. She let her thoughts veer to fifth grade when she thought she could take care of herself and had been shaking down a thermometer in the hall bathroom when she accidentally thwacked it against the porcelain sink. The glass tube shattered and poured its contents on the two-inch squares that made up the tiled floor.

The mercury droplets rolled into the lines of grouting, each drop a little different from the others. She couldn't resist poking them around with her fingers where they left no trace.

They moved like flattened water balloons and joined together to make larger and larger ones. Later when a science teacher told her class about mercury poison and warned against ever touching the fluid, she'd wanted to say, "But it is so fun to play with."

It wasn't fun now to watch it burn down Justice's back.

It didn't make sense; the mercury felt decidedly cold. The way it dribbled out of the incisions she made didn't make sense either.

My poor Justice, she thought, all those cuts.

But there weren't many cuts. She paused, blade poised. The cuts he had made were gone and hers were something out of a band aid commercial where time lapsed photography showed in seconds the healing that normally took a week. In moments there was only a faint scar and soon after, even that was gone.

Impossible.

She lost count of how many cuts she made.

Justice didn't move or speak as the last one came out. The jets were leaving and Claryn's heart pounded in their stead.

"Go away." He said it with his face still pressed into his arm.

"I think they're all out. Justice?"

152

He was silent for what seemed a long time. This was a comfort to Claryn, their silences being what they were. There was no way she was leaving him like this.

At last he thought he could turn over and keep his eyes shut long enough to ask her to leave.

Unforeseen he rolled over into the quick silver on the concrete floor. With the unexpected burn he sat up suddenly on his elbows, glaring and cursing the foul metal.

Claryn was quite near.

Her concerned face maybe half an arm's length from his rather altered countenance.

Her worried expression remained unchanged, even as her gaze traveled his face from one iris to the other and back again before resting on his elongated canines.

In his current state Justice was afraid to move a muscle, terrified that if he did he would hurt her without volition, taking what he so desperately needed. He stopped breathing and waited for her inverted fight-flight reaction.

She blinked several times and leaned to see his side.

Claryn noticed for the first time how pale and smooth his skin was. She had never seen so much of it. His bare chest brought to mind posters she'd seen of Michael Angelo's David. He was a statue.

Without thinking she reached out to touch his hand more fully than she had before, but it didn't move.

She studied his face again, moving closer almost as if she intended to kiss him.

Grave alarm instantly etched his features. She was reaching up with both hands to the sides of his face when Chess exploded through the front door.

Claryn heard the statue that was Justice roar incredibly loud at the newcomer, "Get her out of here!"

She was swept up off the floor and out the door to the side of her car before she knew what was happening.

Chess leaned in close to her face, eying her. "Claryn, I know we haven't had the pleasure. I'm JT's brother." His voice was low and urgent, "Claryn, are you okay to drive home? JT needs me right now."

Her voice was small and so far away. "Justice was hurt bad. The mercury burned him."

"Yes. I should go help him. Do you think you can drive home okay?"

"He looks so . . . strange."

Chess took her by the arms and the physical contact she hadn't registered coming out the door now made her snap out of her daze and pull away.

"I'll be fine." She touched Chess's forearm tentatively. "Maybe I can help?"

Chess had taken in the whole scene in an instant.

He'd smelled the quick silver burning his brother's arms even as he rested them in it right where he'd rolled over, afraid to move.

Claryn had seen what she wasn't meant to see and probably hadn't fully processed. All the same she stood offering her help, her complete desire focused on getting Justice whatever it was he needed.

"Aren't you a jewel? But no, you need to go home now. He'll feel better once he knows you're safe at home. Text when you get there, okay? I'll take care of my brother."

She responded with quick nods, and he turned away after a reassuring smile, heading inside.

"It'll all be better tomorrow," he said over his shoulder. "Goodnight, Claryn."

He closed the door, turned the deadbolt and ran a hand over the blinds to smooth them shut.

Claryn went to her car and started the engine glancing at the big shop windows. Then she slipped back out of the car and up to the place where two pair of blinds met. She could see a sliver of the room through them.

Justice was still sitting on the floor with a few inches between him and the mercury. Chess sat behind him with his left hand propped on one knee and his other arm around Justice's neck.

It almost looked like he was holding his brother in a headlock except that Justice's face was turned down with his open mouth was on Chess's arm.

Chess's placid face looked toward her with glowing white eyes.

Claryn jerked her head back from the window, got in the car and drove home in a daze.

Absently, she ran a stop sign by the rental property at the corner of 10th and Market where the Darkman was spooning the lifeless corpse of Julia Anthony. Inside his double garage, he'd just finished regretfully slipping the over-ripe body of Carolyn Johnson into the trunk of her own car for later disposal.

Kelley knew she was starting to sound huffy, but she was worried and did not like being put off. This was the third voice mail she'd left Claryn today.

"Final warning, my friend. If you don't call me back in the next hour I'm going to call Sissy and send out the hounds." Her voice was very heavy and authoritative.

Then more naturally, "Seriously, don't leave me hanging like this or I might just call the cops. I was going to tell you later, but Timothy Anthony called me yesterday wondering if I'd heard from his sister. And now today, I see in the paper she's listed as a missing person. That's two women this month. Oh, Claryn. Please call me. I should call the police, but--" Kelley continued talking till the voice mailbox cut her off.

Chapter 24

Chess still kept in touch with two of his area good time girls of which JT heartily disapproved. Yes, they gave him anything he wanted, but they didn't know what they were giving. As far as JT was concerned it was immoral.

That weekend, though, it helped save his life.

Chess's blood barely gave Justice the strength to stand, much less walk down to his room. Chess carried him, left for several hours, and returned to replenish his brother's system once more. A process that took repeating before JT rested the next day, Chess did what was necessary and wasn't about to apologize for it.

By Sunday evening, JT had regained his physical strength.

Emotionally and mentally he might as well have still been filled with burning holes.

No matter how Chess talked to him, reasoned, tried to tell him how Claryn had offered to help even after everything she'd seen, JT was having none of it.

"It's over."

Claryn, who could almost pass out at the thought of holding his hand, had handled Friday night like a rock star. Even then, knowing he owed her his life, JT had almost eaten her alive. He couldn't bear it. He couldn't stand to be around himself now. She deserved better.

When JT announced he was going west for an interminable amount of time, Chess practically helped him pack. Watching his brother agonize, berate himself, throw things around the garage, and generally fall apart was excruciating and finally intolerable. JT tried to give Chess his cell phone saying he would call with another number down the road, but the thought of the upcoming parole hearing and changed his mind. He told Chess he needn't bother calling because he did not intend to answer anyone.

"If she calls, tell her I said I'm sorry. If she's scared . . ." his eyes searched the ground for an answer but he ended saying, "take care of her for me."

"I never thought I'd live to see the day you ran away from anything. It's an act of cowardice, brother. Mark my words, this is the biggest mistake of your life."

Chess wasn't able to get a rise out of his brother. He felt powerless as he watched JT trying to drive away from his irrational shame and heartache.

Between her sophomore and junior year of high school, Claryn had spent six days a week working at Smithson's Dog Shelter. Mrs. Smithson was a widow in her mid-sixties who had decided to sow some belated wild oats. Claryn got a lot of extra hours that summer whenever Mrs. Smithson ran off to Vegas a few days every week. It was Mrs. Smithson who offered for Claryn to stay at the kennel anytime she needed. There was a fold-out cot in the storage closet.

At that time, Sissy dated what proved to be another loser of great proportions, so Claryn jumped at the offer to be away from the house as much as possible. She never unfolded the cot, though, except to remove the small mattress from it. She took a sleeping bag and bedded down in the common area outside the dog's kennels, letting her favorites out to cuddle around the pallet.

It became her little refuge her last two years of high school even when she had to cut her hours back to only a couple days a week. Mrs. Smithson called her the dog whisperer and then felt ripped off when they stole her idea and used it for a TV show.

Now it was the real-estate agent Claryn was trying to avoid. She was sitting on her pallet with all the dogs except one out for the evening. Helene was the only irritable old biddy in the bunch that could not get along with the others. The rest socialized swimmingly. Felix rested his head on Claryn's knee listening sympathetically as she talked.

157

"It's Kelley again, not Justice. I wish she'd quit calling already." Twice yesterday she'd called Claryn without leaving messages. Then three times today.

"I can't call her back till I have something to say." She looked guiltily at Felix. "Okay, we both know that's not true since she'll probably talk enough for both of us. But she's not the person I want to talk to right now. I don't know what to say."

She knew what she had seen, the teeth, the healing skin, Justice biting down on his brother's arm, their hypnotic eyes. She also knew there was no way she could tell Kelley or anyone else for that matter. Who would believe her boyfriend was a...she couldn't wrap her mind around the word and so distracted herself with the other. Boyfriend? Yes. Nothing she knew of Justice shook her desire or her basic belief that he was a good person.

The phone rang again and Felix's ear popped up with excitement as if he were expecting a call. This time Sissy's photo was the one on screen. She couldn't put Sissy off like she did Kelley.

"Hello?"

"Claryn! There you are. Darlin' you've had us all worried."

A vague hope loomed, "Us?"

"Yes, Kelley told George about you not answering and how worried she was and he said she should talk to me and maybe call the police if you didn't answer. Then I got here this morning and Mr. Fowler said you didn't come home last night."

"I just talked to Kelley a few days ago."

"She was half hoping you'd run off with JT, but I told her you definitely did not."

"How do you know that's not where I am?"

"JT's brother Chester came by this morning to tell me JT was out of town for a couple days but I was to call him if I needed anything."

"Chess, not Chester. And what would you need?"

"Oh, well, you know, manly help getting the house ready to sell."

Claryn figured if Sissy was home unexpectedly it had something to do with fixing up the house for a prospective buyer.

"I thought your fella was mighty handsome, but oh my, this Chester is something else all together. Where did you find these boys?"

"Under a rock." It slipped out and Claryn thought of the bunker and laughed at her own little joke.

"Un-huh. Well could you scoot out from under your rock and come help me work on the house? I've got a big list to get done before I get back on the road tonight."

One of the dogs whined like he knew she was leaving them.

"Sure, I'll be there in twenty."

"Oh thank you. You're the best."

"Bye."

"And call Kelley!"

Claryn took her time putting away her bed and letting the dogs out one more time. But she did not call her friend.

Sissy's to-do list was much longer than her time allotted. Claryn wanted to revolt, not because she minded the work, being busy ought to help, she told herself, but because the house would really look significantly better if they got the entrance and living room repainted.

Chess rolled up about thirty minutes later and Sissy stopped painting just to watch him walk from the car to the door.

But she let Claryn answer it. "Hi. How are you?"

"I'm good. How are you?" he put a little emphasis on the "you" bending his head down and cocking it sideways. She knew he was watching her for some sort of reaction now that she'd had a few days to think things through.

Sissy couldn't stand it and came over to talk by the banister.

"What brings you back by here? That's twice in one day, you know?"

"I came back to help paint. You said you might need some muscle." Then more to Claryn "and I do like being the muscle around two lovely ladies."

Sissy tittered and almost spilled a roller pan off a nearby ladder.

"How's Justice?" Claryn asked.

"Almost as good as new."

"Did JT get hurt?" asked Sissy with genuine concern.

Chess came in and walked over to the supplies, picking up some paint and a brush.

"Oh, you know these young folks. . ." Chess answered with a reassuring smile ". . .injured one minute and out climbing trees again the next."

Justice had said his brother was quite the player, but to see him in action was another thing altogether. Sissy was excessively pleased that he lumped the two of them together as opposed to that younger crowd of Claryn and his brother.

Good grief, Claryn thought, if he keeps this up, Sissy will come down off that ladder and slit a vein for him. The random thought stopped Claryn in her tracks, trying to ascertain how she felt about that. The term "player" took on a whole other aspect now.

This set the ball rolling in her mind to all sorts of questions she should probably ask but was determined not to. She was staring at him with a spaced out but thoughtful expression. Chess was slowly stirring the paint in his can while watching her wheels turning. He brought the small can over to her.

"Why don't you use this one? It's easier to walk around with as you're doing the edging."

"Sure." He's testing me, she thought, to see if I'm scared.

Claryn's phone rang and that reminded Sissy, "Did you call Kelley back?"

"No." She intentionally walked so closely past him to answer her phone she almost brushed his arm. "It's Kelley."

160

"Hello?"

"Thank God! Girl-friend, do not do that to me again. You have got to answer your phone at least once a day. You had me worried sick. Did you get my messages?"

"No, assuming by 'get' you mean did I hear them."

"Okay, well, George is almost home so I can't talk too long." Kelley used her megaphone voice, which wasn't all that loud, but the way Chess glanced over, Claryn knew suddenly that he could hear the whole conversation. "Listen to your mes-sag-es! Now, what up with you and Justice?"

"We're, uh, getting to know each other a little better."

"That sounds mundane. Listen, don't find out too much, okay? Makes it too easy to find excuses to run away."

Chess cough-chuckled; he could definitely hear the conversation.

"Is he over there right now? I thought I heard someone talking to Sissy."

"No, that's his brother, Chess."

"You finally met Chess! If he's anything like Justice you better not let Chelsea find out, she'll be all over him faster than a . . . I used to know some clever pithy saying that fit perfectly right there, but it escapes me now. Any who – oh, there's George! Love you!"

"Love you too."

Sissy was saying something about Claryn's hairy best friend. "Yeah, Kelley used to be her best friend but she's been replaced by Felix now, hasn't she, Claryn? You tell him everything in spite of his creepy night eyes and big teeth."

"I'm listening to my messages now."

"Claryn's other best friend is a dog, I take it?" asked Chess.

"Oh sure, she says he's just a dog, but I'm pretty sure he's actually a werewolf." Sissy bared her teeth and chomped them together audibly causing Chess to fall out laughing.

Claryn couldn't hear the first two messages but the last one from Kelley shocked her. Chess sobered up quickly as he heard it too.

"Who's Carolyn Johnson?" he asked Sissy.

"Have you not heard about that?"

"I've been in and out of town a lot recently."

"She worked over at the All-Mart Bakery and went missing over a week ago. I don't know when exactly, but it gets much worse."

Claryn and Chess were both waiting and listening.

"Around lunch time yesterday they found her dead in her house."

"Why didn't they look there in the first place?" Claryn asked.

"Oh, they did, they did. But she and her car were gone for more than a week. Then both turned up today."

Sissy came down off her ladder as if someone might be listening in on their conversation.

"And I hear tell she's been dead since near the beginning of the week if not longer. So, it's no wonder Kelley wigged out when Timmy Tony called asking if Kelley had seen her friend, and then with you not answering your phone since who knows when. . . ."

Claryn felt bad for not calling Kelley back earlier.

"You shouldn't let your friends worry. That reminds me, I promised Brad I'd be on the road before eight. Would you two mind finishing up? Oh--and since you're here, Chester, there are some door handles that need replacing on all the hall doors and kitchen cabinets. The realtor said that's the kind of shine gets noticed. The hardware is on the dining room table."

"No problem."

"Sissy, this is a big paint job. And it's going to take two coats," said Claryn.

"I know, but it's going to look so nice. It's not too much for tonight, is it Chester?"

"No. It is definitely not." Claryn threw him a baleful look, but Chess was clearly not threatened by her.

162

"I'll see you next Tuesday, Claryn. Bye, Chester."

"Bye, Sissy."

They worked quietly for a while before Claryn spoke up. Being alone in the room with him made her filter through her thoughts again. Justice had mentioned Chess going north. Then last time Justice came home from his trip north, he was different, more relaxed around her. Now she had a sneaking suspicion why.

After sustaining injuries over half his torso, he refused to move and basically had Chess throw her out. And of course she'd seen them, saw how both of them had looked.

"So Justice went north?"

"He is out of town, Claryn." This was sincere Chess.

"I know I should wait and ask him about things. That's the right thing to do."

Chess cleared his throat and got really focused on painting.

"I am going to have the chance to talk to him?" He didn't respond. "Chess?"

"I don't know." He turned from his work. "Honestly, I do not know. He has unique perspectives sometimes."

"I could call him."

"Wouldn't make any difference right now. His cell phone is laying on the counter in the break room." Chess thought a little white lie was better than telling her Justice wouldn't answer her calls.

Claryn's heart skipped a beat; it slowed as her breathing turned shallow.

"Wow! That is something else." Chess was fascinated for a couple beats before he realized he was being a lunk.

"I'm sorry. What is it? What happened?" Chess asked concerned.

"What if he needs help? Or get hurts again? How will. . . How will...." Claryn sat down unable to hold her own weight.

Chess came over and squatted down near her.

"We were looking for one guy, and the dude showed up with three. That won't happen again, nor will they get the drop on JT more than once. I guarantee it. Besides right now, he's gone elsewhere to rest and recover, not into danger."

Chess watched her like she was a bird of paradise dancing in the Amazon. Hearing her pulse rate and respiration, seeing the slight pallor of her skin, her unsteadiness, it was all so fascinating. He squatted down again resting his elbows on his knees with his hands folded together looking for all the world like a college basketball coach on the sidelines.

"Just so I have this straight, you're okay with spending half the night alone in this house with a vampire, but you're so worried about my bro JT that you're about to pass out? Wow."

She was distracted now. He'd said it out loud like it was nothing. Mentioning your darkest secret in such a casual manner. What did it do to that secret? I'm a victim of sexual assault, she thought. You're a vampire. A regular conversational context with irregular content; maybe it took some of the stigma away.

"Sissy knows you're here. And I guess I've spent several evenings alone with a . . . vampire recently. I just didn't know it."

"Yeah. You're not really supposed to know. So, now I'll probably have to kill you."

Chess narrowed his eyes and pursed his lips waiting for her response. He was thinking of the elder coven called the Consortia. Secrecy was a given rule, but he and JT had never had dealings with them.

Arvon was their only Elder, the one Sephauna gave them, the only one they'd ever needed. He said the Consortia worked to protect human lives from rogue vampires. As long as the Cain brothers were careful, in other words followed most of the rules and exercised self-control, the Consortia left them alone.

Claryn was thinking Chess was easier to read in person than he had been on the phone.

"Who says?" She was feeling better each moment.

"The great coven of elders on high, of course."

"Well, all right then." She stood back up looking around the room. "Do we finish the room first so there's a silver lining for Sissy, or just cut to the chase so I don't have to smell these paint fumes anymore?"

"That's not the proper response to my threat."

"My responses seldom are proper. What's it supposed to be?"

"You are supposed to plead for your life by telling me your deep hidden desire to join our ranks, and then you throw yourself in my arms."

He noted her modest Mona-Lisa smile. "That will never happen," she said.

"Which part?" he asked.

Her phone rang, saving her from answering his question at least. While opening the phone she watched him close the drapes that Sissy had inexplicably left up during the paint job.

"Hello?"

"Claryn?" asked a highly agitated voice.

Chess was moving around in the room, painting the edging with a speed and precision that made her feel like she was stuck in slow motion.

"Yes."

"Hey. It's me, Tim, Timmy Tony."

"Yeah, Tim. Kelley told me you were looking for Julia. Have you gotten a hold of her yet?"

"No. I was actually hoping maybe you'd seen her around town or heard something. I don't know what to do. I should really get back to school but how's that going to go when all I can think about is my missing sister? Especially since they found Mrs. Johnson. You know?"

"Oh, Tim. There's no reason to think there's any connection from that woman to your sister." Claryn was trying to be reassuring. Tim was beyond consoling.

"Oh yes there is. Mrs. Johnson lived by herself over in Hopi Hills. And Julia lives by herself just a couple neighborhoods over. They're both working service jobs. And Julia is making some big changes in her life, just like Mrs. Johnson was doing."

"Sounds like you knew Mrs. Johnson pretty well, Tim. I'm so sorry."

"Not that well. I mean, thanks, but I did some work for her at her house. She was really nice and not bad looking and always understanding about my work schedule and stuff. She was only about six years older than Julia is."

Chess finished the edging with Claryn's wide eyes on his back. Then he came to the middle of the largest wall and wrote something in the middle of it in paint. 'What major changes?' appeared in cream against the faint green background.

"Tim? What sort of major changes is Julia making?"

"She's going to night school now, and she broke up with that Gerald Hayes. He never gave her the keys back to her place and I told her to replace the locks, but that costs money. School costs, gas going up. I don't know. I told her I'd come home and change the locks for her. That's why I was headed to town, really. We were supposed to go to the hardware store together as soon as I hit town Thursday night, but she wasn't there. Her car was gone, just like Mrs. Johnson. The police won't listen to me. They seem more interested in the fact that I've been working for Mrs. Johnson."

Claryn couldn't imagine the police suspecting Tim Anthony of anything. He was one of those quiet, keep your head down folks, the kind who never hurt a fly.

Chess painted words again. 'Be back soon.' He gave a wave and was out the door before she waved back.

Hopi Hills was not that far away and it wasn't hard to find the home with the crime scene tape. Chess never fancied himself a do-gooder who might take this new life and make a difference in the lives of others. Truth be known, he'd been mostly self-serving in both his lives.

166

Then Sephauna brought Justice into their world. Even his name placed a burden on Chess' thought processes. JT wasn't on a mission or anything, but he attracted certain types of people, often broken people, like Sephauna herself, who saw something in him that soothed or encouraged.

JT had a peaceful strength about him even at the age of seventeen. Sephauna watched him longingly. It took a lot to ruffle JT's feathers. A threat to those he cared about did it, though, and brought resolve.

Sephauna finally brought him into her "family" at twenty-two. His visage was always older, his movements deliberate as well. In the five years they'd observed him, he'd lost those he cared about most one by one.

JT believed in retribution and vengeance, finding both on more than one occasion. He fought for what he believed in. And Chess often thought JT was probably the only vampire in existence who had killed more people as a human than he had in the time since then.

Maybe some of JT's attitude was rubbing off on Chess. Chess was more motivated by reason than passion in spite of the cavalier facade he wore. Often times his reasoning wasn't very sound, but his instincts saved him. Did he sympathize with Tim? Or see a kindred soul trying to reason with what was purely instinct?

Either way, he checked out both Carolyn Johnson's and Julia Anthony's places not liking the result. The intruder was fastidious, to be sure, but not enough so. The women both left their residences in their own vehicles. Whether they had been the ones behind the wheel backing them out of their garages was uncertain; however, they did leave alive and one of them was injured.

The intruder went with them, though, and in the case of Mrs. Johnson brought her back home, dead in her own trunk. Here was an ill neither of the Cain brothers would tolerate on their turf. Chess couldn't track the fiend, much to his consternation. Maybe the paint fumes got in the way. He'd probably have to wait for another woman to go missing to get a bead on the culprit.

The Darkman made no rounds the night and subsequent evening after a body was found. People would be on edge. Everyone would be on guard patrolling their little area of the world. In two days, ninety-nine percent of them would be back to their old habits. A few evenings at home suited him fine. He had his new doll for amusement, and she was holding up rather well.

Chapter 25

Claryn's house stood silent. Light raps on the door produced no answer. Chess made his way around the house to look for another entrance. This also doubled as the home security inspection Chess wanted to do regardless. It was the sliding glass door he breached with a little jimmy to its ineffectual lock. It was the elderly retired infantryman whose chain linked yard backed up to Claryn's that saw him do it.

Inside, Chess found Claryn's succinct note painted on the wall. Nap. A quick peek confirmed. Chess took up the painting with alacrity until a disturbance on the front lawn interrupted his considerable progress.

Out the window he saw a patrol car was parked behind Claryn's car and a policeman was disarming a feisty old man who'd evidently been carrying a shotgun through Claryn's front yard.

Seeing the drapes part the old man cried, "There he is! He's the one you're after! I'm telling you, I live here! I called this in you morons!"

The officer walked the old gentleman to Claryn's door. Chess opened it before the doorbell rang.

"Hello."

The officer started talking but was eyeing the plastic laid out on the entryway floor at the same time.

"We received a call reporting a prowler at this address. Is everything okay?"

"Yes. Everything is fine. Just doing some renovation work."

The old man was having a fit. "He doesn't live here. I do. Ask anybody."

"Are you acquainted with Mr. R. J. Fowler?"

"I am not, but he's correct. I don't live here. I'm helping a friend."

"She's here alone a lot. I bet you he's got her tied up somewhere right now." The old man was straining against the policeman as if he just wanted an opportunity to go after Chess.

169

The officer frowned and asked permission to enter the house. Chess wasn't much on having people in his place, much less inviting them into someone else's. He declined to permit entry. The officer was unsure what to do next. Mr. Fowler wasn't. He launched himself against the doorbell and started hollering for Claryn.

"Make a noise, honey," Mr. Fowler cried. "We'll hear you!"

Chess highly doubted that anyone but himself would hear thunder over all Mr. Fowler's racket.

Roused by the bell, Claryn made her way down the hall blinking at the scene. Chess backed out of the doorway to make room for her as she stumbled down the stairs.

"Mr. Fowler? What's going on here?"

Claryn vouched for Chess and for Mr. Fowler telling the policeman where her life-long neighbor lived. Chess returned to painting after Claryn invited everyone in. He gave the authorities as little face time as possible while still participating as needed. Mr. Fowler eyed him suspiciously.

Claryn was more concerned by the cuffs on Mr. Fowler than anything else. He had been detained while walking between homes carrying a weapon.

"I'm the one that called you. I told you that. I wasn't about to wait to see how long it took for you to arrive. Claryn, why was this so-called friend of yours sneaking in the back patio door?" Then more to the officer, "I saw him breaking in, I tell you! He still might be your man. Wasn't the Johnson woman getting renovations too?"

"I didn't want to wake Claryn, sir."

"So you break in to paint?"

Claryn took over talking about how tired she'd been and gone to nap without considering how her friend would get back in.

"This is all a misunderstanding." Claryn pleaded. "Can you please let Mr. Fowler go, Officer?"

"Officer Jones, ma'am."

"Officer Jones, please. Mr. R. J. Fowler is a decorated war veteran. He has lived in the house behind ours since before I went to kindergarten."

Chess could see Claryn was going to have her way. Young Officer Jones had that wanting-to-please look about him. The uniform listened very attentively to the attractive girl before him.

"And he's been watching out for me and my step-mom ever since my Dad died eight years ago."

The cuffs came off and apologies were made. The gun seemed the only issue holding up a happy resolution. Claryn had an answer for that as well since Mr. Fowler had often helped them out with the yard. To her the yard was as much his as it was theirs.

"Is there a law that you can't walk through your own yard with a gun?"

No, of course there wasn't. Claryn gave Officer Jones one of her best smiles as she walked him to the door. He gave her directions to be careful. "What with everything that's been going on, you can't be too careful." He also gave her his card penning his cell and home numbers on the back.

"You should feel free to call me if anything comes up, anything at all. You can call those numbers day or night."

Chess chuckled at how oblivious Claryn was.

"Thank you. I'm sure that won't be necessary, but thank you very much. Goodnight."

She came back up the stairs and gave Mr. Fowler a hug and thanked him as well.

"Does Sissy know you've got this man. . ." he said it like it was a pejorative ". . .here with you?"

Claryn was trying to move him toward the door, but he walked over to the sliding glass doors instead to inspect the lock.

"Sissy is the one who called him to come help, Mr. Fowler."

This received a harrumph. Mr. Fowler knew some of Sissy's track record with men as well.

"The lock's not broken. And you sure got in here awful fast, young man." To Claryn, "You've got to get a doweling rod to put there so that the door won't open even if the lock is busted."

Chess decided it was time to chime in. "Actually, I was going to suggest you take down the rod over the sink and use that right away. You can't be too careful." He was only slightly mimicking Officer Jones. "And it's good to know you've got neighbors watching out for you."

"That she does, and don't you forget it." Mr. Fowler's more than usually eventful night took its toll. He finally said a few words to Claryn and let himself out by the back patio door. Claryn took the curtain rod Chess handed her and put it in the door's track to keep it from sliding open again.

"Do you have him on speed dial? He's better than a guard dog."

"No point," she waved one last time and closed the vertical blinds. "He can't hear the phone ringing."

"Problematic." To Chess's eyes Claryn still looked tired and a tad down.

"But you've got JT's number and the shop's, right?"

"Justice doesn't even have his phone on him."

"True. Very true. Here. Let me give you my number."

She opened her phone to type the number in as he recited, having forgotten that it was listed as Justice's third number elsewhere in her directory.

"I'm first in the alphabet anyway. And I assure you I am faster as well." He was flexing for her.

"The only speed I'm interested in is how fast you can paint."

"And I would like nothing better than to amaze you with my considerable skills, but I think..." Her face really fell thinking he was going to leave her with the balance of the job. "But... I think you should trot right back to bed and get as much rest as you can."

Relieved, she still protested, "I can't leave you here all night doing this work for us while I sleep."

"Why not? I don't sleep at night anyway."

She hadn't considered that and her lips quivered into a small grin.

"And without the distraction of your lovely presence, I can finish the first coat, give it a full three hours to dry, and do the top coat."

She put her hands up in a gesture of submission. "I can't argue with that."

"I do, however, have another matter to check on tonight, and now my entry has been blocked."

She gave him the door key off her own set of keys. "I use the garage door opener anyway."

As she started wearily down the hall, Chess couldn't resist another bit of flirtation.

"You take my phone number and give me your key. In my experience, this means you are well on your way to throwing yourself in my arms."

Claryn didn't look back. "Goodnight, Chess."

Chapter 26

Kelley called Claryn at work the next day. As usual, Claryn was taking the dogs on walks. She rotated through them since there were too many to take each one every day.

She and Kelley talked for a bit about the missing women and poor Timmy Tony. At the mention of painting the front room, Claryn decided to omit Chess's help from her narrative, while Kelley went off on how they were decorating their apartment. They were allowed to paint and since Kelley had a light load this semester, she was very busily engaged in "nesting" as she called it.

"I wish you were here to shop with me. It's not like you've got classes to make or anything and Justice is out of town, right? Why don't you come up for a few days?"

"I've got work. And I think I should be really careful with my money situation. If the house does sell, I'll have to work on a nest of my own."

Kelley didn't think it was a nest if you were alone in it, but she wasn't about to say that to Claryn.

"Won't you get some money from the sale of the house?"

"It won't last forever. Remember how long my Dad's life insurance lasted?"

"Yeah, but that was Sissy's fault. Speaking of which, how are things going with those newlyweds?"

"Must be great. I don't hear much from her. She does these quick check-ins at odd hours. Mentions the school situation. Says how smart and responsible I am, and that's pretty much it."

"I'm glad we still talk. Do you need me to call more?"

Claryn was grateful her friend kept in touch, but "need" seemed a strong word. It was enough to know Kelley was her friend and always would be. Sissy was right. Claryn was pretty self-sufficient. Kelley called her the anti-people-seeker.

"I can always call you, you know."

Kelley said, "But you probably won't. So I'll take that as a 'no' but 'I miss you bunches.'"

"That's exactly how you ought to take it. No one else ever gets me like you do."

"I know." Kelley took compliments so well. "I am a very empathic-people-person. It's not just you I get. I've got lots of peeps."

"And I would not want to take too much of your time away from your peeps. You're practically a therapist. I still think that might be your calling."

"George and I have actually talked about that. I'm doing really well in my basic psych class."

School was another subject Kelley wanted to update Claryn on. So they talked for another half hour before Claryn needed to get off the phone for a visitor at the shelter.

Justice drove west till he hit the ocean and then walked out into the Pacific as if he could keep walking and never turn back. A pink sunset reflected on the waves making them look like vast stretches of silk undulating with dark serpents that crept onto shore in each dying breaker. In chest deep, he stopped and laid back, letting his heavy body sink to the bottom of his own gargantuan isolation tank.

He found he only needed to breathe about once an hour, a new discovery that he took full advantage of through the night as he let the currents jostle him and rock him deeper into the sand beneath great strips of seaweed making their way toward the shore.

He watched the sunrise through the water above him, and in a surreal haze of inward pain, wondered what would happen if he stayed there to rest during the day.

Like a pesky fly, one thought kept buzzing in the back of his mind, not even a thought, just a date on the calendar, the twenty-second. The twenty-second was looming; it was just around the corner. The twenty-second was coming; the twenty-second was close. What day was today?

It woke him up to an unnamed worry for Claryn, woke him up to a mission he wasn't sure was needed, woke him up to something more unbearable than the thought that he might hurt Claryn.

Someone else might come back and plunge her into a waking version of her seven years of nightmares. Someone else might hurt her while he was off wallowing in an ocean of self-pity and recrimination. He couldn't let that happen. He had vowed he would not allow it, and he had never broken a vow.

Chess was right. Justice was lying to himself if he thought he could drop everything and run away. Something else, he didn't need to be in Claryn's life to protect it. He would find a place to rest and go home. He rose from the water with his face to the sun.

It was time for a change. Chess had decided to sell his car, and though he and Justice hadn't talked about one of them taking the waiting '68 Pontiac Firebird Coupe, that didn't make a difference now. As Chess was listing the vehicle online, the phone rattled across the counter with its ring. He picked it up absently.

"You got me."

"Justice?" Claryn's voice was hushed and shaky. A cacophony of whining and barking dogs was drowning her out.

"It's Chess, Claryn. What's wrong? Where are you?"

"I can't hear you. But, I'm so scared. Someone's here." Her shallow breaths were against the phone, weaker and weaker. He was already in his car backing out of bay one. His hair stood on end as he shouted into the phone.

"Where are you?"

"The shelter, Smithson's. Please come. Someone's here."

"Hide, Claryn. I'm on my way. Hide!"

Claryn wished she'd let out Helene. The other dogs might be noisy and some kind of deterrent, but Helene was the only one with a vicious

176

enough streak to go after an intruder. Bull Mastiff's were very territorial and protective. Unfortunately, she was locked away.

When the headlights had flashed through the kennels and across the building windows, Claryn's heart had slowed alarmingly. Women were missing and she was alone.

No one should be here this time of night and if it were Mrs. Smithson coming home early, the dogs would not be in such a universal uproar. After a moment's indecision she called Chess. His words, "Hide, Claryn. I'm on my way. Hide!" only heightened her anxiety.

Claryn knew the approximate location of the visitor because the dogs, who could hear the movement outside the kennels, went from one gate to the next as each one was tested by the person intent on entering.

Claryn's body felt so heavy. She could hardly breathe, much less move. Her head seemed to roll heavily on her neck as she looked around the room for a place to hide. The supply closet was barely twelve feet away from her pallet on the floor.

"Felix?" The golden-lab left off his barking and responded immediately to her small voice. He came over and gave her several licks around her face. It was the encouragement she needed to drag her body off the pallet toward the closet.

The dogs moved in chorus, focusing on the door to the front room as Claryn dragged her heavy body across the floor inch by inch. Twice she lost her peripheral vision as darkness threatened to take her, and twice Felix came to lick her cheek as she sank to the cool concrete floor.

She got the closet door open and pulled the wheeled mop bucket out as she heard the glass in the front room entrance shatter. Whoever was coming, a locked door wasn't going to get in their way.

She pulled the closet door shut and felt her body give out against the supply shelf. Her head fell back against a row of bleach bottles and the smell of the chemicals brought tears. Her eyes swam and a light flashed across the crack of the door.

The barking was receding now, some of it off into the night as the front doors were left open. Claryn's limbs would not respond now as she tried to lift them to grasp a broom handle she thought she could use as a weapon.

The light flashed across a crack in the door again and rested there, getting brighter and bigger as it drew close.

Everything happened too quickly for Claryn.

The door opened and a dark silhouette shined the light up and down Claryn who could only squint her eyes and let her head roll off to one side. Helene growled fiercely.

The figure bent over her, put his arms under hers and dragged her limp body across the concrete back to the bed she'd made for herself on the floor.

Claryn tried to kick her feet but could not even feel them. They seemed so far away, like she didn't have legs.

"Who?" she asked feebly.

"Oh, little Claryn. You can't tell me you've forgotten our special time? It's just you and me now. And I've waited a long, long time to come back for you, Claryn. It won't do for you not to remember."

The voice was scratchy but familiar. The figure moved back across the room to retrieve the flashlight he'd left laying on the floor outside the closet.

Claryn tried to roll off the pallet. All she could move was her head, though, as the man came back and set the light so it shined in an arc across the top of her.

He was beyond the arc, taking off his ball-cap before leaning into the light. He pressed her arms into the covers with his large heavy hands.

His face came into the beam. He rasped, "I missed you, Claryn."

Claryn's eyes flew open wide and her mouth fell open for a silent scream that never came. She passed out as the handsome face of Richard Court stretched to laugh with pure pleasure at her terror.

Chapter 27

Justice pulled into the brightly lit shop, expecting to see Chess over on the couch even though his car was absent. Chess never left the lights on, never.

"Chess?"

He walked over to the couch and saw a blinking light on the phone. He picked it up and checked the message.

"Hello. Hi, this is Sissy calling for Justice. I don't know how this happened exactly but I got that call we were talking about and the parole went through, yesterday! Can you believe that? It was a day early and I'm just finding out. That's the system for you. Anyway, I thought I'd see if you could check on our girl. That would be great. Later."

Justice whirled on his heal dialing Chess immediately. He got an answer after three rings.

"Chess?"

"JT. Where are you?"

"I'm at the shop. Where are you?"

"I'm at the hospital with Claryn, bro. You better get down here."

Justice hovered outside the hospital room looking through the glass on the top half of the door. The curtain was pulled so he couldn't see Claryn or Chess and the nurse refused to tell him anything or let him enter without checking in with the family first.

The nurse came back out to say he could go in now, but only for ten minutes. Justice's feet felt leaden as he pushed the door open and walked around the edge of the curtain.

Claryn lay still, breathing easily, the sheets tucked around her making her look small. The hospital gown paled her skin. He couldn't discern anything amiss. Several wires were connected here and there and she had an IV, but Justice saw nothing else.

Chess sat in the only chair beside the bed holding her limp hand. He watched Justice's approach, unsure what state his brother was in or how he would handle seeing Claryn this way. JT came round to the other side of the bed, sat on the edge and took Claryn's other hand.

"I don't understand. Chess, what happened?"

Chess glanced back toward the door.

"First, if anyone asks or says anything, I'm Claryn's brother. It was the only way they'd let me have access."

Justice nodded.

"Claryn was at the shelter and called shortly after midnight, said someone was there and she was scared."

Chess looked at her instead of his brother as he continued rubbing her hand.

"I got there as fast as I could and there was this man. He'd broken out the front window and had Claryn laid out, and . . .I don't know. I don't think he actually got the chance to do anything to her. The doctors said there's no evidence of anything. She was out cold. So I carried her to my car and rushed her straight here."

"And the man?"

"I knocked him across the room as soon I saw him. When I left he was crumpled against the supply closet doors, but the police have been and gone and said they didn't find him."

"And Claryn?"

"I don't know. I told the doc about her condition and he said she's probably mentally protecting herself by shutting down. She'll wake up when she's ready. It's been about three hours, no change."

"Did you call Sissy?"

"I did. She flipped out so badly Brad refused to let her drive back here. Said he'd try to bring her himself. I told him there was nothing she could do so to keep Sissy with him till we have news."

Justice stood so he could look closely at Claryn's face. He pushed her hair back with one hand, then he caressed the side of her face for a moment.

"Claryn. It's me. It's Justice. Can you hear me?"

"I'll give you a minute." Chess went out with his hands in his pockets.

"Claryn. I'm so sorry. I should have been here for you. Please wake up. Please? Claryn. It's me, Justice. I'm so sorry."

He leaned down to kiss her forehead and caught it. That faint smell of the scumbag who put her here. His face went flat and his eyes turned white as he folded her hand over her stomach and walked to the door.

Chess met him there and seeing his face, pulled a pair of sunglasses out of his pocket and handed them to his brother.

"I'll be back. Don't leave her alone. Call me if there's any change."

Justice stood there straight and taut as he waited for his brother to return to Claryn's bedside. Once Chess was back at Claryn's side, Justice turned to the hunt. Three hours was a good head start, but not enough.

The police came back around early the next morning hoping to question Claryn, but she remained unconscious. After reviewing Chess's story, they left, leaving directions for the nurses to call them when the patient revived.

Around eight, Justice called to let Chess know the threat had been eliminated, so there was no need to request a guard for Claryn's room during the day. Chess told the nurses a story about having to get their mother and got home a few minutes before his rest time.

When Chess awoke, he used his key to Justice's room to check on his brother. The death taint from his early morning kill hung around him, a rank odor that would take several days to fade. Whoever the attacker was, he carried a lot of death in his veins.

181

Chess returned to the hospital hopeful but found no change. The new shift of nurses were very attentive to the attractive brother of the girl in two-thirteen, but he didn't notice.

Shortly before Chess expected Justice to arrive, Claryn's heart rate dropped and her breathing slowed. Chess hollered for the on-duty nurse, who in turn called in the doctor. Unwilling to disturb the patient by trying to wake her with medication before this time, the doctor changed his course.

A few minutes after the medication was in the IV, Claryn started to come round. Chess stood over her, relief playing across his features.

"Chess?"

"Yes, Claryn. It's me. You're safe at the hospital."

"Justice?"

"He's not here yet. Any minute now. How do you feel?"

"Heavy. Thirsty."

Chess held a plastic cup up and put the straw in her mouth not knowing what the nurse had poured in the cup before leaving them alone. Claryn sipped at it and nodded.

"The police will be coming back soon to talk to you. Do you think you'll feel up to it?"

"Do I have to?"

"I think so. I could try to put them off?"

"No."

Chess sat back down and Claryn raised her arm a little to reach for him. He took her hand in his and was sitting holding it when Justice returned.

"How is she?"

Claryn's eyes fluttered open.

"Justice?"

"Claryn."

He came to the bedside uncertain of how close he should get. He looked at her hand in Chess's and felt something inside crack. He started backing away.

"Justice?" A plaintive edge in her tone drew him back to her bedside.

"I'm sorry, Claryn. I should have been there for you. I'm so sorry. He'll never hurt you again. Do you understand?"

Claryn looked at him uncomprehendingly for a minute.

"It was Sissy's old boyfriend, Rick," said Claryn.

"I know. Richard Court. He's gone. He'll never hurt anyone again. Do you understand? You're safe."

Understanding dawned on Claryn's face as a mix of emotions played across her features. The relief he had hoped to see wasn't there. She shook her head back and forth.

"Oh, Justice."

The police came to the door and a nurse asked Justice and Chess to wait outside.

"She doesn't understand," Justice said.

"Nonsense. She just needs time to process."

"I should have been here. But no, I stopped over in Vegas, sold my car. Did a little hunting. I didn't get Sissy's message."

"Claryn's fine. Court is…" Chess looked around and whispered, "gone. Right now, she needs you."

"She doesn't need me. She has you. You can hold her hand," Justice's lip curled, "offer her some comfort. I can't do that. I've already done the only thing in my skill set."

"JT, that is . . ."

"Is what? This is your area. I'll leave you to it."

Chess wasn't sure what to say. He watched his brother's retreating figure and shook his head. JT was also good at being hard headed. That was something else in his skill set.

Chapter 28

"You can positively identify your attacker as Richard Court?"

"Yes."

"Can you tell us what he did?"

"Justice? Chess?"

Chess came back around the edge of the curtain.

"Justice had to leave. I'm here."

Claryn thought maybe it was better if Justice didn't hear everything.

"He broke into the shelter. I was hiding in the supply closet."

Claryn's heart began to slow and her breathing got shallow. She reached for Chess who took her hand.

"Then what happened, Miss Anderson?"

"He dragged me from the closet to the pallet. I didn't know then who it was, couldn't see in the dark."

"I think she's had enough," Chess said.

Her hand was falling loose in his and she blinked her eyes as if to clear the dizziness in her head.

"Nurse!" cried one of the uniforms asking if they could give Claryn something to keep her alert. The nurse complied, injecting more of the doctor ordered stimulant into her IV.

Chess began giving them all hard stares. Her heart rate recovered but it was artificial. If she couldn't talk about it without passing out, he thought, they shouldn't jack her up with medication to get her through it.

"Miss Anderson, you were saying you couldn't see your attacker? How do you know it was Richard Court?"

"He got the flashlight, shined it over me, leaned over into the light."

Now her eyes were filled with tears that came pouring out and down around her cheeks. She was holding Chess's hand firmly, though, and she looked at him as she sniffled and gave him her other hand as she tried to finish.

"He wanted me to remember, to know it was him. He said he was back for me." Her lips quivered and she began breathing short fast breaths.

"It's okay. Take your time. You said he came back. Had he attacked you before?"

Her shoulders caved in and she began to cry in earnest, gasping bites of air only to choke them out in long hacking sobs.

Chess moved to sit on the bed beside her and let her lean against him as great racking sobs shook through her.

"We can come back . . ."

"No!" she cried out, startling them all.

"I'm not . . . going…" she swallowed hard, "through this again." She pointed at the officer who'd been questioning her.

"You stay!"

She wiped her face on the arm of her nightgown and looked at Chess.

"Is Sissy here?"

"No. Brad wouldn't let her drive, said she was in an awful state. She doesn't know who attacked you."

Claryn nodded, reassured, and collected herself enough to speak again.

She rested her head back on her pillow and stared at the officer.

"I was asking if Richard Court had attacked you before and you appeared to nod yes?"

"Yes. He came after me before."

"And when was that?"

"He dated my stepmother." She took deliberate deep breaths. "He used to sneak into my room late at night." She cast a mournful glance at Chess before closing her eyes. "They dated for over two years."

"I'm sorry Miss Anderson. Can you tell me when that was exactly?"

"I don't know. One day Sissy told me she found out he was a bad man and he'd gone to jail on a misdemeanor, but it was his third strike so he got time. It must have been about four or five years ago."

"And when he said he'd come back for you, and you saw who it was, then what happened?"

"I passed out." New tears slipped down the sides of her face now. "I don't know what happened after that."

The officer nodded toward Chess and Claryn as he closed his notepad and clicked his pen.

"Okay. That's enough. I want you to know that we will find Court and bring him to justice, ma'am."

Bring him to justice. Claryn's mind turned the phrase over and over so much she lost track of what was being said. They were talking to Chess.

"We can go back over your statement if needed. Where can we reach you, Mr. Cain?"

Chess gave them his number and said he would be staying at the Anderson's home indefinitely. Then the officers left.

"Chess? What was your statement? Do you know what happened to me?"

Claryn's anguish was so plain that Chess had a hard time answering her.

"Please tell me."

"When I got there it looked like he was holding you down by the shoulders and I flew into him, knocked him across the room and carried you out of there."

"And my clothes?"

"They were on. Your top was torn a little just at the top."

Chess came very close to whisper.

"I couldn't smell him on you, Claryn. Not anywhere except your shoulders and across your top. They took your clothes for possible evidence but they won't find anything."

186

She continued to cry for a few minutes but she nodded and tried to smile too.

"Thank you, Chess."

"You're so welcome, Claryn. I'm sorry I didn't get there sooner."

"They said they were going to find him, bring him to justice, but justice already found him, didn't it?"

"It did."

She nodded and rolled over on her side, curling up and facing him as he moved back to the chair. She kept holding his hand between hers.

"Your skin is smooth, like Justice's. Is he coming back?"

"I don't know."

"I'm glad it's over. Really over."

She closed her eyes, tired and drained, the stimulant wearing off. Her eyes flew open.

"Will you call Sissy? Tell her I'm okay. I'll call her when I wake up next time, okay?"

"Okay."

"You'll be here, right?"

"As long as I can be."

"When is that?"

"Tomorrow morning, shortly before ten."

"All right. That'll work."

She closed her eyes and drifted off to sleep not long after. Chess slipped his hand from hers to step into the hall and talk to Sissy. Calls to Justice went unanswered.

Chapter 29

Chess stayed at Claryn's house only till the next weekend. By then Sissy and Kelley descended on the house and Chess knew it was time to get out of Dodge. The peaceful quiet days he and Claryn shared were a balm to her spirit and a revelation to his heart.

Chess longed for a coven family like the one he and Justice had with Sephauna, only better. Motivated by his own desires, without much concern for those of others, he formed one superficial relationship after another. His partners were too much like himself, seeking what they wanted, loving in their own way but with hearts set on their own pursuits. Staying young, living forever, or self-gratification. Passionate romances that burned hot and died quickly were the norm.

Answering Claryn's call and taking care of her was more about Justice and increasingly about Claryn as well. As his days became less about himself, Chess discovered a happiness he hadn't known since he fell in love with Sephauna, a joy he hadn't felt since he'd learned from her to always be fundamentally selfish as she had. Memories flooded back to him now as Claryn slept.

Chess had been sent from home at a very young age to apprentice with an artist of regional renown. Renaissance Italy was much different then. The Medici were the greatest patrons of the arts the world had ever known. Thousand-year-old traditions and norms were being cast aside daily. There were vast opportunities for anyone with any artistic talent at all. Even in such an environment, it was plain Francesco was something different. Francesco had a gift to be nurtured, his family said, Francesco was special and he knew it.

Sephauna was a sort of Italian courtesan of independent means and great reputation. She was courted, wooed, and entertained by a myriad of men from those who possessed wealth and power to those gifted with other types of prowess.

Francesco's master wooed Sephauna with daring and great admiration for her beauty. The master persuaded her to sit for him, and Francesco at the age of thirteen fell into a sort of love and obsession. Sephauna loved to be loved, and though she sometimes cajoled the young apprentice, she never allowed him too near her. She was as elusive as a wood nymph and as captivating as tongues of fire.

Later he understood that she'd held him at a distance because of the natural aversion bordering on revulsion that children rouse in their kind. Children all had a natural protection until they came to a physical point of maturity at which point their scent flowered into something else.

Sephauna compared it with the process of cooking. A great chef could take a repulsive main dish and treat it in such a way as to create a desirable delicacy. And Sephauna would know. The wealthy contended for invites to her sumptuous soirees as often as men tried to win her other attentions.

His master attended only one of Sephauna's parties. She remembered the youthful apprentice who so admired her, and sent Francesco a small parcel of the delicacies from her party. Determined to impress the object of his esteem, Francesco inspected each item carefully as he looked for aspects of its character he might then comment on to the Lady Sephauna.

Scents, tastes, textures. He prepared his accolades and questions. When at her next sitting he expressed his observations and praise and asked her to identify a very subtle aroma that eluded him, he won her attentions.

Within months she procured his apprenticeship, brought him into her household and began training him in her kitchen. In that kitchen, he first met Arvon, who appeared to all the world as just another of her admirers.

The most decisive gut instinct Francesco had ever followed was to pursue a relationship with Sephauna. From a thirteen year old boy procuring what she needed from the market or running secret messages through the streets for her to when he was a robust young man apprenticed to her in more intimate arts, he never lost his love for her.

When she at last revealed her true nature and asked him to join her, there was no question. What Sephauna wanted, Sephauna obtained.

She had an unpredictable temperament that would have seen her institutionalized as a woman at the turn of the last century. In her time, her unpredictability only added to her indefinable allure and the challenge of the pursuit.

Francesco learned over time that part of her mind was broken, though, and while the vampire venom transformed one's body and appeared to heal, it did nothing for the psyche. Conversely, her abilities as a vampire were corrupted. She herself was unable to change her young apprentice, though she never admitted it. When her attempt failed and Francesco's life hung in the balance, it was Arvon who'd saved him.

Chess and Justice saw firsthand the devastation wrought by the unnatural extension of the life with mental injuries. Justice experienced only the last seventy years of Sephauna's fall, but Chess witnessed a hundred and fifty year downward spiral. Even so, Chess had caught Sephauna's vision for their little family. He never lost that longing for a small coven bound by more than need and rules.

The mind and its recovery took center stage as Chess lived and interacted with Claryn those few days. Almost from the beginning Chess thought Claryn seemed pretty sweet, had taken the revelation well, and was someone Chess would have enjoyed hanging out with for a long time to come. Justice was pushing her away, perhaps for the wrong reasons, even though there might be even better reasons to cut her out of their lives.

Justice had patently not asked for Chess's assessment of Claryn's chances of making a successful transition. Beyond that, either the change itself was odious to Justice, who had never been given a choice as Chess had, or Justice knew her physiology was not the most looming question. Perhaps it was neither.

Chess wasn't much on giving up the things or people he wanted, while Justice seemed to easily put the needs of others before his own desires. Perhaps Justice had thought all along to give what he could, enjoy what there was, and let her go. The thirst that had almost seen Justice jeopardize her volition, and perhaps her life, was obviously the signal for the end to Justice. Chess found he couldn't put aside Justice's heart as effortlessly.

Fear cannot rule us, he thought.

Was Claryn's mind really broken as Sephauna's had been? He knew what her reactions to Justice were and also knew she was capable of physical warmth. The traumatic events of her young life shaped her, but did not hold sway. Chess suspected this was, in part, due to her focus on others.

Chess's feelings of comfort in her home were soothing. Given time off from the kennel, she worked on the house, creating a loose schedule for her days and adjusting her rhythms closer to his. She asked for what she needed, was easy to please, and enjoyed simple pleasures.

Though attractive, she didn't even rank on his list of beautiful women he'd known, at least not on the outside. Inside she was all heart, full of affection and friendliness, bolstered by unconscious ease. She was a comfort to be around, a low radiating heat that soaked into you and brought surcease to your striving.

Importantly, Claryn had a strength of character Sephauna had lacked.

One evening after he woke, they sat in the living room talking. She curled her legs under her leaning back on one arm on the back of the couch while he stretched out his long legs in front of the wicker rocker he was reclined in.

"I'm supposed to be here to take care of you and you turn it around," he said. "Why do you think you do that?"

Claryn seemed pleased by the statement. "I guess it's what my mother taught me. I remember her like a dream sometimes, where I'm not sure which parts are memories and which are fantasy. I remember her last day. She dropped me at kindergarten, and around lunch the principal came and took me in his own car to the hospital. He told me on the way that my mother was hurt and the doctors were trying to fix her.

"Dad was waiting there. I think Mom was in surgery because we had to wait and wait before we could see her. They did what they could, they said, even as they shook their heads back and forth. Dad sat in a chair with his head in his hands crying. I was small enough to drape myself over him like my blankie. I thought it would make him feel better.

"When we finally got to see her she was awake. She didn't let on if she was in any pain. Dad put me in the bed with her, I had to be very careful, and I curled up and fell asleep. I think she sent Dad out of the room to talk to me, because she shook me awake and said she had something very important to tell me.

"'Claryn, you and I are the same,' she said and she went on saying things like 'I have never had gangs of friends, but always, always there have been my best friends, like Daddy, who needed me, and that is where I was happy. You, Claryn. You will be happy where you are needed, where you can take care of your best friends even if it's just little things. I have to go now, and you need to take care of Daddy. He needs hugs, he needs laughs, he needs quiet. You watch. You and I are the same. You'll know what to do.'

"It was something like that, I didn't understand she was saying good-bye. Maybe I've added to it. I understood though those little things she'd done for us, I would do and do easily because I am like her. Dad said we could get through anything as long as we were together."

"How old were you when he died?"

"Ten. He used to sit there where you're sitting, different chair, same spot. I've never sat in it except in his lap."

"Should I not sit here?"

"No, it's good for you. It's good for me to see you there. It's just not a place for me."

192

Chapter 30

The Darkman hated giving up a doll, but after going missing for several days this gal now had some man staying in the house with her. Jealous rage whipped up bile in his stomach and he wanted to vomit.

Mine! Mine! Mine! He screamed in his mind. No one else touches my dolls.

Patience is a virtue, he heard answering back. Of course, he knew the stats. Ninety percent of people returned to their normal routines within a matter of days. He need only wait.

Dolls weren't allowed to make him wait. His eyes widened as he realized what needed to be done. His new doll would see; she'd see what making him wait caused.

He stopped in the hardware store the next morning and spent two hours choosing "punishing tools" according to the variety of marks they would leave on the doll. Pleased with his selections he spent the day putting them to good use. Later, he belatedly realized he'd have to replace this doll before taking his last if he was going to have any more quality threesome time.

Chess's last night at the house, a John Wayne festival ran on the classics channel. He racked his brain for a way to bring JT around. Stubborn people who know they're right are the worst, he thought. He set aside his pondering to enjoy a few of the old movies with Claryn.

And there it was in Technicolor. North to Alaska, the idea Chess needed. The Duke and his partner struck it rich, and the partner sent the Duke back to get supplies and also the partner's girl who, as it turned out, had already married someone else.

So the Duke brings back another dame for his partner who he knows will be heart-broken. The Duke falls for the gal without realizing it as she falls for him. She is meant for his partner, nothing is getting in the way of that.

The partner realizes the true direction of everyone's feelings and hatches a plan to make the Duke jealous so he'll realize it's the girl of his dreams he brought back. The plan works, and the last scene of the movie has all the friends arm-in-arm stretched up on the screen as they live their happy ending. That's it.

Claryn was surprised when Chess turned off the TV after the movie. It was still pretty early by his standards. She waited to see what was up without asking.

"I've made a decision. You are Michelle and JT is the Duke."

"The who?"

"John Wayne."

She nodded slowly, waiting for the punch line.

"It's you. You are the one for JT. He's just mixed up right now and can't see it. But we," he was gesturing back and forth, "can fix that. I'm the partner."

Claryn began to smile but it smacked of a silly-loveable-Chess look rather than the light-bulb-over-your-head-idea-that-would-work look.

"It's a movie, Chess, a comedy no less. They tie the ending up in a neat bow and hand it to you like a gift to make you smile."

"You're it, though, his only chance. And I'm not going to sit idly by and let him lose it."

Her expression sobered. "I don't believe in that either. The One, your True Love and there is no other."

"You don't?"

"No. My dad told me he found his greatest place standing next to his wife. And I, of course, asked him which wife and he said, 'Both.'"

Chess harrumphed, "That's your dad, but it sure ain't JT. Look how long it took him to find you! Besides, nothing ventured, nothing gained."

He moved over next to her on the couch, turning on the Chess charm. "And I will have you know that I am a great date, loads of fun. I can be a good listener, and I have a collection of the most titillating stories. I'm telling you, this is a package experience you don't want to miss."

Claryn thought she'd never met someone so full of themselves and yet still enjoyable to be around. Laughter bubbled out which only served to encourage him.

Chess got down on one knee. "Claryn Anderson, would you do me the honor of accompanying me to dinner this Saturday night?"

"Are we taking Kelley too?"

"Amendment--Sunday night? What's the worst that can happen?"

"One girl, two brothers, yeah, what's the worst that can happen?"

"Great, Sunday night it is then."

"Oh my," she responded, a faint flicker of nervousness in her stomach.

After a couple days out, Justice came back into town towing a new acquisition behind him that needed an incredible amount of work. And work was what would be best for him right now. He convinced himself it wasn't breaking things off with Claryn that was messing him up, but the death taint his body was working through.

The taint had effects he hadn't known. His control was slightly more tenuous and his thirst had a constant edge to it he'd only felt after injuries or in his first years as a Young One.

Normally, hunting trips were only necessary two or three times a year. It was the spread of Wild Ones into Justice and Chess's territories that demanded the hunts, not the brothers' needs. Yet another matter assuring him that walking away from Claryn now was for the best.

He half hoped that after living with her for a few days, Chess would come home ready to go north as well. No sooner had Chess walked in the door than Justice proposed the trip throwing out Vegas as their prime destination. Chess liked working the strip.

Chess inspected the car Justice brought and was slow to jump on the idea of a hunting trip.

"When were you thinking of leaving?"

"Sunday evening, bright and early."

"Tell you what, if you can hold off till midnight I'm on board."

Chess thought one more straight play was worth making. As they were going over the clunker, Chess asked him if he was going to call Claryn.

"No."

Not even 'I don't think so' but a quick unequivocal negative. Chess was unsure how to proceed. He took off his jacket and suited up to work side-by-side on the car, talking about what parts could be salvaged. After a while, Chess tried to bring up Claryn again, but Justice shut him down.

"Is she okay?"

"Yeah. She's doing well."

"Then, I don't want to talk about it. It's over. I should never have gone out with her in the first place. Lesson learned."

A few minutes later Chess tossed down a rag and unzipped. This isn't going to fix anything, he thought, and JT is a fool.

He whistled as he shook his head back and forth. He had this picture in his mind of the way Justice would torture himself, guarding the young woman he loved unbeknownst to her while she mourned him brokenheartedly. Chess decided not to do any more work on the car. Things were going to be ugly enough around here without him helping progress the work distraction Justice had chosen for himself.

Chess thought, my fool brother thinks he can simply walk away. Chess plopped down on the couch and wasted hours on Mission 2B Immortal increasing his frustration. Instead, he turned to one of his favorite games, World of Warcraft, to unwind.

When Claryn saw Kelley off on Sunday afternoon, she felt a guilty sense of relief that the weekend was over. It was hard to have so much kindly attention, especially since it included an element of constant vigilance about the state of Claryn's coping. Sissy gauged things quickly

196

and saw what she wanted to see, brave Claryn snapping back after another hardship.

Even though she was still unsure about the right and wrong of it, and she hated to think of Justice taking on such a burden for her, Claryn was increasingly grateful for what he had done, not only for her, but also for Sissy. Now it was really over.

Kelley was the one who read the footnote in the paper about Richard Court. He was found dead in a stolen vehicle on the outskirts of Phoenix. The intoxicated parolee had apparently taken a sharp turn too fast and landed at the bottom of a ravine. Dental records were used to confirm his identity after local wildlife had picked over the remains.

"Gruesome, but fitting," Sissy had said as she went to make a phone call. Justice didn't answer her call, so she left a message letting him know there was no need to worry and if he checked in the paper he'd see why.

No day in court for Richard Court. No day when Claryn would ever have to face him, or repeat what he'd done to her, or have Sissy find out. Since the case of her assault was closed, no one beyond those at the shelter and the hospital would find out where Court had been that evening before he died.

Mrs. Smithson called to check on Claryn and say Felix was missing her, but that she should take all the time she needed. Conferring with Sissy because it pleased her, Claryn let Mrs. Smithson know what day she would return to work that week.

She spent half of Sunday morning urging Sissy to return to Brad. The weather was beautiful, but storms were expected soon, and if she didn't get on the road that day she'd have a tough drive. Claryn had said she was fine many times and finally confessed that she had a date and wanted to meet him on her own.

"What about Justice?"

"I don't know. He kind of went off for a while and then seemed to feel bad that he wasn't here for me and I don't know what's going on there. But I'm not supposed to wait around on him, right?"

"Right. So I'll do your hair and then get out of it! Ha!"

It was twenty questions for a while with Sissy. Claryn liked to be private and Sissy knew that; it made the guessing game all the more fun. Was it one of the good-looking police officers she'd talked with? An old high school chum? Or, she gasped, a young doctor from the hospital? Claryn finally waved her out the door and was able to relax in the still house again.

Chapter 31

After carrying the light conversation through most of dinner Chess asked, "Why don't you have questions for me? Did you and JT have a talk about us? Our lifestyle?"

"No. We didn't have a chance."

"You seem woefully disinterested, and frankly, that's a little unflattering."

"I'm a private person usually. You've walked into the middle of my life, but I mean, there's lots I wouldn't really want to talk about so I tend to think other people won't either. I guess I'm afraid of being nosey."

"Well, there's nothing I don't like to talk about," he said expansively.

"Would Justice want you to talk about him that freely?"

"He made his coffin, let him lie in it."

Her fork stopped midair and she just waited.

"I'm just joking. When it comes time for repose, any surface away from sunlight will do, when not visiting the Andersons."

She was ruminating over what to ask. Chess was not very patient but propped his chin up on both fists waiting for her first question. She seemed to decide, yet still hesitated.

"I assure you," he said, "there are few subjects of conversation I enjoy more than talking about myself."

Her smile and headshake were exactly as hoped.

"Can you change the way you look at will?"

Claryn decided to keep her questions focused on Chess. Even though the same things might be true for Justice, she wasn't going to ask. That made it easier to say. It's just Chess, she thought.

"I can now. Self-control comes with age."

"How much older are you than Justice?"

Chess thought she'd ask how old he was, but this was different.

"Seventy plus."

"And your shop sign," she queried, "who is the Rook and who's the Bishop?"

"Depends on how you look at it. Do you play chess?"

"Not really. I know how the pieces move.

"All right then, think about the pieces and how they also carry connotative meaning. You tell me about the rook."

She thought about that.

"The rook. Moves straight forward and back, in the tracks, so to speak. Is a tower, also called castle. I guess I think of it as kind of straight and narrow, but it could maybe get up in your face."

"In your face, sounds like me."

She continued, "Further from center. The bishop sounds important, closer to the power. I guess on that one I think of it as stronger. It moves in straight lines but sideways, sneakier even. So both sort of seem more like you. Are there two of you on the sign?"

"Do they have to represent people?"

"Oh, yes. Especially if one is named 'Chess'"

"Then there are two of me…if only."

She smiled but again was quiet and expectant.

"I tried to put JT on the sign. Really I did. What piece is he do you think?"

"The knight?"

He reached over and touched her on the nose for correct as was done in charades. The touch was so light it tickled her.

"Also the knight comes laden with meaning, and while clear to you and to me, the connotations are objectionable to others. But enough about him! Let's talk about me."

She folded her napkin.

"Dessert?" he asked.

"I'm saving room for popcorn."

"Ah. I prefer it with garlic salt myself."

"Seriously?"

"Seriously not." He leaned in speaking softly. "Isn't there something else you'd like to ask about me?"

Her look was measured as she took in the nearness of the other patrons, their chatter, the music. Decision made, she said in a normal volume, "I was going to say 'No dessert for you?' but I didn't want you to think I was offering."

"Of course not," he said. His voice was reproachful but his look darkened and sparkled.

"You're incorrigible," she said.

"Prodigiously." His tone was lighter now. "And you are avoidant."

"Procrastinating."

He tossed his napkin down over his plate.

"Very well. Off to the cinema."

Justice might have driven a nice car, but Chess's flashy hot rod was obviously making a statement. He was reaching to open her door when she put a hand on his arm.

"Is it all right if we walk?"

"What?! And not arrive in the style to which I am accustomed?" His mock indignation was overdone and would have seemed out of place for anyone else.

"I'm sure you make an entrance however you arrive," she said.

He puffed out his chest with great pleasure as he tucked her hands in at his elbow saying, "We are getting along famously."

They started walking along closely like that. It was comfortable to Claryn, companionable. As if I'm walking along with Kelley, she thought. Boy, Chess would love to know that. She hadn't been sure how things would be after their initial contact at the hospital; that had all been so crazy.

The silence was not as easy as with Justice. Chess could only take so much of it.

Halfway to their destination, they went through an area that had no streetlights. A deserted warehouse was on one side and a scrub grass sandy field on the other. Not a single car passed them.

He sincerely inquired, "Does anyone know you're out with me?"

"No. I don't suppose so."

"It's not like when I was at your house and people knew I was there. And yet here you are." He stopped walking, standing close. "Do you feel safe even here with me?"

She looked around as if she hadn't noticed the surroundings and needed a moment to take in what he was inferring. She ended by nodding.

"I do. I don't see why here is really any different than my house."

"It feels decidedly different to me," he said.

They started walking again, but this time she stopped. She bent her head to one side and then the other as she scrutinized his face.

"Are you," she searched for the word, "hungry?"

"Thirsty. Somewhat. It's a feeling you learn to live with."

She bit her bottom lip.

"Just ask," he pushed.

"Would you . . . show me your scary face?"

He seemed squeamish. "Not a great idea."

"Why not?"

"It requires a certain concentration on things, a force of will." Gravely he added, "I let my mind go that way and, well, I'm not usually one inclined toward self-denial."

Chess knew she was unselfconscious. Unaware of her appeal, and oblivious to his growing appreciation of it.

She tilted her head closer and sternly directed, "You should practice then."

She straightened, gave a nod and stood waiting, all patience, as if she could stand and wait all night.

He focused squarely on her eyes, only her eyes, and transitioned more slowly than he ever had. Eyes increasingly reflecting the sparse light and losing all color. Teeth projecting. These were the externals, though. She couldn't see the change of attitude inside or know the cold heat that crept over him.

Rather than stepping back from his glare, she stepped nearer.

He pulled back with a furrowed brow, the discomfited one. Uncertain if curiosity drew her forward or if he unconsciously did it to her.

Her tone answered his unasked question.

"It is kind of scary," she said without a trace of fear.

He stepped within inches of her inscrutable face. "Then why is your heart beat the same as when you sat looking at your salad?"

His comment and nearness caused her pulse to change in an almost imperceptible way. He probably wouldn't have picked up on such a minute alteration were it not for his heightened attention to everything about her at this moment.

She raised her palms to the side of his face and the touch was, to him, lightly charged. Using her thumbs, she pushed his lip up to see his canines.

His vision, though crystal clear, was at the same time blurred on her face, making her a non-person in a way. His voice was almost husky and his eyes glowed white. "Why are you so certain I won't take what I want?"

The desire in his voice was new to her, but she simply stood erect. "Justice is your best friend."

Chess relaxed by degrees. "Yes. Yes he is."

He transitioned to his usual appearance promptly.

She patted his arm as she took it, starting forward again.

She said, "I think we'll be great friends. You've been a great friend to me."

"But I am scary, right?"

Her cheeks dimpled. "Yes, and strangely alluring."

Pleased as punch he laughed. "Fast friends already, working on bosom buddies." His innuendo was all play and Claryn laughed as well.

He bought the largest popcorn and soda package for her even though she protested. It was opening weekend for a new action comedy that was almost sold out. Running a few minutes, late they missed the previews all together.

Normally, Claryn hated coming in after the house lights were down. For her it would have taken a full minute for her eyes to adjust, and trying to find a seat in a packed house was misery. Chess didn't even hesitate as he easily spotted two seats against the wall near the back.

"Rear left on the wall. Follow me."

When he stopped at the row she asked for the wall seat, very conscious of the crowded room and close proximity of other moviegoers. Kelley always saved her a seat by the wall or next to one empty chair. She made her way easily to the seat now that a bright daylight scene was on the big screen.

The movie was a pretty fun romp. At some point in the dialogue, a joke was made about someone being long in the tooth, so Claryn playfully elbowed Chess. He leaned closer with a little light to his eyes and slightly protruding canines. Glancing over with popcorn already in hand, she pelted him in the face with it and directed her attention immediately back to the screen, which made him laugh at an inappropriate moment. For that they were shushed.

Because they ran late, Claryn hadn't made her usual pit stop before coming into the movie with a large soda. Almost on cue, about forty minutes into the movie, Claryn had to step out.

Once she was out of sight, Chess felt what he called his "spidey senses" tingling. It would never do to have something happen to her on his watch. So he made apologies as he headed out after her.

The theater they were in was fairly old and oddly designed. The restrooms at this end were added much later as well. He went straight to the ladies room, where he saw a greasy punk hanging out near the door.

Chess walked right past the guy and into the restroom. There was a narrow hall about as wide as a person that opened on the end right into the small stall and sink area.

Claryn, washing her hands, registered him in the mirror and spoke to his reflection.

"Wow, you really can't believe everything you read about vampires."

"Not by half."

As she dried her hands with paper towels Chess listened to the steady ba-thump, ba-thump of her heart.

"Is something wrong?" she asked.

"Not if there's nothing wrong in here."

She reached across him to drop the crumpled brown towel in the wastebasket.

"Only you," she said rather pointedly, jabbing her finger into his chest.

The young women they passed as they emerged from the ladies room together looked him up and down and eyed them both speculatively.

"Hanging out with you would ruin my reputation if I had one," Claryn said.

Dropping Claryn off later, Chess thought the next portion of his evening would be just as interesting, though probably not nearly as enjoyable. This would be an unprecedented experience for the Cain brothers. Chess had never offered to share, and he felt certain JT would not take kindly to doing so now. JT knew from his preparations that Chess went out on a date tonight.

He pulled into bay one with his car windows down and found his brother's legs sticking out from underneath their latest project. Chess was barely out of the car when the scent of who he had been in it reached his brother.

He was certain it was the only time he'd ever heard his brother hit his head on the under carriage of a car. Chess headed over to the couch, where he dropped his jacket over the arm closest to the bay. He decided sitting would be less confrontational.

"What have you done?"

Chess answered with the classic I-give-up gesture as if to say 'what's the big deal?'

"Nothing you wouldn't approve of, I assure you."

Disapproval, distaste, suspicion and more were written all over JT's face. He picked up the jacket and held it to his face breathing in the scent of her. Part of him wanted to go sit in the passenger side of the car, while the rest of him wanted to lay into Chess.

It felt like forever since he was even near her. He looked at the car and then back at his brother. Choosing the car, he walked to the open window, braced his hands on it and rested his forehead against the top of the door.

"How could you?"

This was unexpected. Chess really had prepared himself for the fact that he and his brother were going to rumble in epic fashion. According to his insight-jealousy plan, that's what was supposed to happen. At least that's how it happened in the movie.

The more time Chess spent with Claryn, the more his heart went out to his brother in a way it really hadn't before. He stood.

"Look, I thought since you're so bent up, and if this fight-flight thing is getting in the way, well, I thought I better look into the matter."

It had always been easy for Justice to let the feminine attention the brothers provoked rest on the more handsome and flirtatious Chess. It was almost an understood arrangement.

Justice found now he couldn't bear the thought that Claryn might find Chess more appealing. Justice knew he'd hurt her by pushing her away, but he hadn't considered toward whom he might have pushed her.

"I get it now," Chess said.

Justice wheeled toward his brother's subdued voice. For a split second he thought Chess was saying he felt the same for Claryn. Chess's

206

concern was fully focused on his brother, and the tightness in Justice's chest loosened. He walked over, still suspicious, and dropped down on the furthest corner of the couch.

"Get what?"

"Claryn is . . ."

Justice eyed Chess with veiled apprehension.

"She's perfect for you."

Maybe Chess really is trying to work out my problems, Justice thought.

"How perfect?" Justice said as he began to calm down inside.

"This life was never what you wanted, but you rolled with it. It wasn't some great gift to you but more like a turn of events that you took on the chin."

"What's your point?"

"You've never once supported my decision to bring someone else in, nor have you ever tried or even considered doing it yourself."

Justice was shaking his head back and forth to indicate he didn't like where this conversation was going. He stood as if to leave.

"I think now you've thought about and decided against it."

At least Chess knew him that well. Justice kept walking.

"She is perfect for you. And that's got to be unbearable."

Wordlessly, Justice went back to working on the black'67 Shelby Mustang.

The hunting trip didn't come up again till the sun was cresting in the sky. The brothers agreed it might be the best thing they could do. As far as Justice was concerned, Claryn was over and done for both of them now.

After a couple dry nights, the hunt on Thursday was unusually productive. For some reason Vegas was always ripe with some of the newest Wild Ones on the streets, but it was also fraught with risk. The North American Consortia sent regular teams to Vegas to keep the area under control. While the brothers were not unknown to the Consort, who considered themselves the only legal coven and rightful authority in the Americas, there was always a chance that a very old vamp might mistake youngsters like the Cains for Wild Ones and enter shoot-first-ask-questions-later mode.

Around two in the morning the brothers were walking past Circus-Circus when Chess adamantly indicated it was time to go home. In front of the giant jackpot wheel, Justice turned on him.

"What gives?"

"Nothing. I've got plans. I'm going out."

Justice shook his head in disbelief, inspecting his brother for duplicity. As far as Justice knew, Chess had spoken with no one else for days which could mean his plans were made Sunday night, but Chess had almost two hours of the day to talk to anyone he wanted while Justice rested.

Two hours for pure folly, he thought. "Who with?"

"That is a question you have never asked me before, JT."

Chess spoke this truth with both seriousness and mild amusement. He stood, waiting for JT to choose whether or not to pursue this line of questioning. Justice turned and strode toward the parking lot and Chess's car. Only the steady purr of the engine and the rubber on the road carried on a conversation during the four-hour drive.

Chapter 32

Kelley was back to checking in on Claryn with more regularity. In fact, Claryn suspected Kelley had an alarm set on her phone for when to call because of the repeated rings around four forty-five each afternoon.

"How are you?"

"Good. You?"

"Me? I'm fine and dandy. Is work treating you okay? No PSD flashbacks or anything?"

Claryn chuckled. "Nothing like that."

"And you still haven't heard from Justice?"

"No. I think he's written me off."

"His loss, my friend, his loss."

"Chess seems to be the only one holding out any hope."

"Yeah, or maybe Chess is smarter than JT."

"What's that supposed to mean?"

"I suspect the only way you'd go out with Chess is in this contrived manner, right?" She didn't wait for an answer. "And Chess came to your rescue, stayed with you. There is such a thing as Florence Nightingale Syndrome."

"It's not like that at all. Chess is like a big brother."

"Uh-huh, brotherly, I'm sure. Right up to the moment he kisses you."

"Kelley."

"Okay, maybe I'm wrong. He may be spending hours and hours getting closer to you so he can hook you back up with his brother. Sounds plausible? And if that's the case, and it all works out, what you need to be thinking about is how to get past your 'I wanna kiss you so much I'm gonna pass out' thing you've got going on. You don't have that problem with Chess?"

"Of course not."

"Hum . . .I've said it before and I'm saying it again, you would really benefit from some intense therapy. Hey, you still do yourself up for your non-date-dates. I mean, a date's a date."

"I do. Speaking of which, I need to wrap things up here at work."

"All right. Hearing about un-dates is not very exciting, but I'll probably call Monday anyway."

Claryn laughed at Kelley's sad tone.

"We all have to compromise sometimes. Till then."

"Till then. Ciao."

"Chow-chow."

Claryn had never eaten out so much in her life. On the menu tonight was the steakhouse she had thought Justice would take her to because he took her everywhere else her father had.

She was wearing the dress she bought for her nice dinner with Justice and starting to regret it. After talking with Kelley, Chess's admiration seemed to have grown by leaps and bounds.

The glances at her legs in the short skirt, the hand resting on her shoulder as it placed her sweater there. All of a sudden the impossible seemed possible. Claryn felt the need to revisit what they were doing.

They parked a few blocks from the steakhouse in order to enjoy the walk to and from dinner. Claryn realized this was their thing and wasn't sure they were supposed to have one of those. She felt more discomfit than at any time before. She realized it wasn't simply because of Chess, but also that prickly sensation as if someone were following them.

"You seem different tonight," Chess commented. "Is something the matter?"

"Do you ever get the feeling someone is following you?"

Chess laughed and gave her shoulders a companionable squeeze.

"I'm sorry, I should have mentioned it. There is someone following us. His name is Darryl, he lives on the streets, and he watches for my car so he can follow me to restaurants to get my full meal deal doggie bags. I didn't think to tell you."

That answers one question, Claryn thought.

"But you don't have to pretend to eat with me."

"Mercy, yes. Think of all the consequences if I didn't. The loss of tips for the waitress, the loss of income for the restaurant, and poor Darryl. You mustn't forget Darryl."

He held the door open for her as he went on.

"And remember, to you the ladies working here are staff, to me they hold the prospect of infinite other possibilities," he came close and winked, "especially the pretty ones."

Claryn felt better on all counts at that point, and gave Chess a smile so brilliant he forgot himself. He decided she might make his list of great beauties after all.

Chess got Claryn to talking about foods, eliciting her insights on what his meal tasted like, the various fragrances and such and found she didn't have a predilection for aromas like his or Justice's. It didn't help that she made all sorts of comparisons to items he'd never sampled as a human. Still, it was an enjoyable restaurant diversion.

Outside, Chess set his boxed meal on the ground out of sight behind a tree. Claryn presumed it was for Darryl and looked around for him, but didn't see anyone. Chess seemed unconcerned and moved on. They walked to Chess's car and then drove through Baskin-Robbins, where he insisted on getting Claryn a cup with three scoops of her choice. Then he cruised through town toward the secret destination he'd chosen for the duration of their date. He kept her talking ice cream right up to lookout point where he was hard pressed to find an open, secluded spot.

"Is this...? Are we where I think we are?"

"Yes we are."

"What is this about?"

"Is it that hard to guess?" He waggled his eyebrows as she continued to wait expectantly for her answer. He couldn't wait for her to comment.

211

"You never suspect me of my worst. I can't decide if that's a compliment or a comedown. Here's the beauty of this place."

He shined his headlights out into the sandy dirt in front of them.

Claryn cleaned another bite of ice cream off her spoon and played along. "Uh-huh."

"You don't see it. This place is a well-known hang out of repute that has very distinctive soil. It clings to your tires, gets into your grill, cakes in your tire wells even when it's dry."

"So Justice will know we came here."

"Yes." He was taking a bow as best he could inside the car behind the wheel. "And I think you'll be okay with the next part of plan execution."

Chess turned to rest his back against the driver's door, kicked off his shoes, and bent one leg up against the back of the long bench seat and held his arms out for her.

"Why?"

"Justice has a nose like a bloodhound, so this place only works for us if my clothes corroborate the story we're telling here. You can back up here and pretend I'm your pillow."

"Right."

Claryn gave him her hand and started to scoot over as he reached out with his other hand on her waist to drag her over. The sensation of strong hands pulling her body was too much.

Her heart and respiration seemed to stop all at once as she fell sideways completely limp against an incredibly alarmed Chess. Visions of her unconscious at the shelter, in the hospital, and finally in his arms at the shop as he tried to explain what happened to JT flashed across his mind before he realized she was trying to speak.

She's not unconscious, he realized much relieved.

"I'm sorry. I'm so sorry, Claryn. Tell me what to do."

He was holding her under the arms like a doll, trying to look into her face, which didn't help matters as Claryn struggled against her malaise.

212

All she could get out was a breathy, "Pillow," but he understood. He turned her around to lay back on him and took his hands away and stopped breathing. Her head wobbled from side to side as she tried to shake off the dizziness so it wasn't till she was still for several moments that she realized he'd stopped breathing.

"Breathe," she commanded and he did so.

"Talk."

He whispered behind her, "I'm so sorry, Claryn. I didn't think this happened with me."

"Not you. The pulling, the dragging."

"Ah, I'm an idiot."

"No. You're my friend." He didn't answer.

"Talk, please."

"About what?"

"People you've killed?"

Chess was totally thrown. "Seriously? That's your choice of calm down conversation?"

"Uh-huh."

Faces flashed across his mind like a high-speed slide show, but it seemed best to go with something more recent.

"Okay, so last week I was in Vegas and tracked down a Wild One. A Wild One is a vampire that has lost control, they get addicted to fresh blood, take too much and start killing people. That's not usually our MO, and we can't have 'em out there running amuck. So we take 'em out."

Claryn felt her strength returning a bit. Chess heard her pulse and breathing improving. Her voice was stronger as well.

"And people like me?"

"I don't think there's anyone quite like you."

She shook her head and waved a weak hand at him to go on.

"Humans."

"Humans you've killed?"

213

"Well, I guess everybody has an accident or two when they're young. The way it's supposed to work, or worked for us, is that you don't feed on humans without supervision. Heck, I don't think you should feed on humans for the first twenty years or more."

Claryn pushed away carefully, sitting up and looking at him confused.

"Shouldn't you eat more for control when you're that young?"

"If you have a coven you shouldn't have to hunt. We can feed off each other, drink water and go for months without anything else. Giving the blood from one vamp to another renews the lifeblood in some way, it's like it multiplies the fuel in the tank."

"Not indefinitely?" she asked.

"No. But you really only need one hunter. I don't know how many vampires a single hunter could sustain. A lot of factors going on there."

"But bou have killed people, humans, I mean."

"I have. Our sire, if you will, wasn't a hunter. She was more of a temptress."

"Justice said you were a player."

"Yeah. It takes a lot of self-control though, and you may find this hard to imagine, but I was kind of cocky as a young one, nothing like I am now. I had fed under supervision and thought I had this down. I didn't need Sephauna hanging around. How awkward is that? I underestimated the extent to which that accountability outside myself under-girded my ability to control my impulses."

Claryn saw his regret and understood that even the way he framed the event in sterile terms 'accountability' 'impulses' was a way of distancing himself from the events.

"You killed someone."

"Two. There were two of them with me at the same time."

"Why wouldn't they run? As least the second one?"

"It looks like necking and the bite itself produces a sort of mild euphoria that, when mixed with alcohol, is pretty debilitating to judgment."

"How many people have you killed?"

"Do vampires count?"

"You and Justice are definitely 'people' in my book, so yes, vampires count."

He was glad they counted; it was important to hear that from her.

"I don't know. It's not something I've kept count of. Not as many as most, I figure. My way of living might have been less honest, but it was also less deadly."

"Was?"

"Yeah. JT has talked me up on the wagon."

She spoke so softly then. "Justice has killed a lot of people, hasn't he?"

"You should probably talk to him about that."

Anger she didn't know she felt welled up in her throat and out of her mouth. "And when's that going to happen, Chess? Huh? What have I got to do, throw myself in front of a bus and land in the hospital?" Tears choked her as she went on. "So he'll come by and, and say a few words to me? When? Sure, he'll tell me he's gone out and killed for me, but he won't answer the phone when I call, will he?"

Chess handed her a handkerchief and the fact that he was carrying one made her laugh.

"You carry a hanky?"

"Yeah. Now you wipe all those tears on it, and blow your nose if you can. It'll drive him crazy."

She laughed low as she did it and sadly gave the soggy material back to him to put in his pocket.

"I don't want to drive him crazy. I'm only asking for another chance. Will he give us another chance?"

"He will."

"Why are you so sure?" She could see he was.

"I saw the most amazing thing happen one night." Chess began talking as if remembering an encounter from ages past.

"I saw this walk-alone man, who's traveled far and wide for two hundred years without so much as a flicker of interest in a mate, come home in a suit from a wedding one weekend and tell me he'd met the girl of his dreams. And if he was just a man with a simple life, we'd have a simple happy ending, but he's not.

"He's a monster. He's the only monster I know that could lay in poison, less than an hour from death's door, and say 'no' to a life-giving drink sitting in front of him because he didn't want to hurt you. I couldn't have done it, Claryn. You are the one, the only one for him. And we've got to make him see it."

Chapter 33

Justice worked while he waited for the probable confrontation with his brother, a cat already crouched to pounce. Well after Chess's departure for his evening out, Justice had called Claryn's house to see if she was home. He had called the shelter to see if she was working late. He had paced, he had fumed, he had plotted. He had sat down and collected his thoughts.

Chess needs boundaries, well-defined rules, that's all this situation calls for, he thought. Then he went to work on the car, hoping against hope Chess would come home and Justice would discover he was wrong. He had wasted a lot of time getting upset over something that hadn't happened...he hoped.

The Darkman was pleased his patience was paying off. He was equally pleased that the young man who had taken his doll out on a date was bringing her home and leaving without getting a kiss at the front door.

She still needs me, he thought. She's saving herself for me. He was certain now she would be his best doll ever. She needed something special.

He would get her a gift. He would find something she'd truly love and have it waiting for her when he brought her back to the house for their one night together here before they took their road trip.

He was elated as he went home for bath night with his latest doll, who seemed to be getting short shrift. That won't do. It's not your fault you weren't in the original plans. Fully clothed, he climbed into the claw-footed tub to hold her as he finished rinsing the shampoo out of her hair.

"I'll take a couple days off and devote them to you and you alone. How's that sound?"

Her head lolled forward as if in agreement and he hugged her to his chest tightly as her face rested on his shirt, half submerged in the bubbly water.

It wasn't yet midnight when Chess rolled into the last bay where Justice had parked his recently sold car. Justice was ready to talk reason, or so he thought, until he saw the distinctive dust and her scent filled his world. The urge to tear into his brother was almost overwhelming. He froze where he was standing in bay two as Chess got out of the car.

"You're still hard at work, I see," Chess quipped.

Chess walked up to Justice as nonchalant as he pleased on the outside but braced on the inside. His brother resembled a can of soda shaken and stretched to the limits within its aluminum binding.

Chess walked right up to him and took off his jacket. As he folded it over his arm the handkerchief fell out of the inside breast pock and slowly fluttered to the floor.

Losing control was not an option to Justice, it wasn't who he was. Her scents assaulted him like fumes surrounding a gas pump, they rolled off every inch of his brother, top to bottom. The images they conjured sucker punched his self-control, leaving it a shade flailing its arms as it began to fall away from Justice's body.

The moment he balled his fists, another mind-boggling odor distracted him completely, Claryn's salty tears caught on a handkerchief floating as it were on an invisible breeze.

Chess flinched as Justice sprang into motion.

Justice darted down, crouched on the floor and grasped the fabric he had saved from touching the grimy surface below. He stared at it as if Claryn's face were etched on the cloth like the holy relic, Veronica's Veil. What was she going through? Who was there for her but his brother? Whose fault were the tears?

Justice rose in one fluid motion, holding the hankie out to Chess.

"You dropped this."

"Thanks."

Chess warily took the hankie and put it in his back pocket, watching his brother return to his work on the car. He thought he had pushed the limits beyond the bounds.

Chess shook his head and walked down the stairs before returning with his art supplies. Back at his desk, he pulled an old crumbling drawing out of a folio and opened to a blank page in a new sketch book. He copied the familiar lines of Sephauna's face, transferring them from the past to the present in his art.

Justice worked nonstop till his phone rang the next morning. Seeing Sissy's ID he plucked it up.

"Sissy?"

"Yes, it's me. Is this JT?"

"It is."

"How are you?"

"Good. How are you?"

"Good, good. Did you get my message?"

"I did. Thanks for letting me know."

"It's nothing."

Sissy had something else to say but wasn't sure how to go about it.

"I know you're young, and young men tend to carry the weight of the world on their shoulders, but there are things beyond your control, things you can do nothing about. You can't beat yourself up for that stuff. Do you know what I mean?"

"I do, ma'am."

"Good. Okay, so I have a favor to ask."

"Shoot."

"Is your brother, Chester there? Can I speak with him?"

Justice smirked, thinking how his brother's new nickname lined up with the image Chess had of himself.

"Sure. No problem."

"Chester! Chester! There's someone on the phone for you."

Chess was already there scowling as he took the phone. Justice was singing the name over and over to some annoying tune as he went to his room.

"Sissy, how are you?"

"Oh, good. I felt so bad calling JT's number to reach you, but I didn't know what else to do."

"I'm dialing you from my cell right now so you can check your missed calls and save my number when we get off the phone."

"Oh, thank you. You're such a peach. Now tell me, how is Claryn?"

"She's doing really well, she's back at work without a hitch, and when we got together she was…she wasn't her old self, but she's sharing more and coping. I don't think we could hope for anything better." Chess knew Justice was listening in even as he worked.

Sissy sighed with relief. "Thank goodness. It's so hard to tell on the phone and she insists she's 'fine,' but she always does that. I'm so grateful to you, Chess, really I am. And you've been such a big help I hate to ask for anything else. I just don't want to put too much on Claryn's plate right now."

"You know I am happy to help in any way I can."

"I've decided to bite the bullet and go ahead with painting the rest of the house. The realtor thinks that will make the place pop and it's one of the least expensive renovations you can do. But I don't want strangers in there…and I could pay you out of the proceeds from the sale of the house."

"Don't be ridiculous. I enjoyed painting with Claryn. It gives me an excuse to hang around a bit and keep an eye on her. It's also such a good feeling of accomplishment to see it all looking like new."

Sissy thanked him over and over as she read off the color numbers and made arrangements. He noticed the time, which made him think JT probably heard part of his conversation before lying down.

The man didn't initially ask to see the dogs, nor did he ask any questions about adopting procedures. She tried to politely disregard the way his muscles twitched around his left eye when he spoke to her. He asked her about which dogs she liked. What breeds did she think served as the best guard dogs? When she told him, he didn't follow up by asking if they had any of those breeds.

Claryn's stomach did an odd turn when he walked around the edge of counter looking as if he were going into the kennel room. She was glad she'd already put Felix back in his kennel, but she couldn't say why.

Mrs. Smithson entered, having walked the couple hundred yards from her house to see if Claryn, who might be nervous in the shelter alone with a stranger, might like some assistance. The man looked at Mrs. Smithson strangely when she offered to show him the dogs that were available right now. She assumed the look related to the unavailability of some of the shelter dogs.

"Only a couple of the dogs are on hold due to their medical issues and treatment plans," she explained.

"I'll have to be going then. Good day," he said and then left.

Even Mrs. Smithson thought his exit odd.

"How bizarre. Did he even look at the dogs?"

"No."

"I guess he didn't want to take a chance on seeing a dog he might want, but couldn't have? Some people are like that."

Mrs. Smithson offered to finish things up so she could go home, and Claryn took her up on it. As she drove the winding road back to town, she had a vague apprehension that the strange man with the twitching eye might be waiting for her somewhere along the route.

"Chess?" Claryn's voice quavered.

"Hope it's okay. I still had a key and thought I'd get an early start. It's a bigger job this time."

"Wow."

Lights were on in every room of the house and furniture was gathered into the centers of the rooms. Plastic draped over and around every surface like the giant cobwebs in Mrs. Haversham's house in the old black and white movie of 'Great Expectations'. Dazed, Claryn pushed open her bedroom door, relieved to find it untouched.

"Sissy called you about all this, right?" A concerned Chess followed her to her room.

"Yes . . . and no. She left a cryptic message about you and a surprise tonight."

"Do you want me to stop?"

"No." Claryn stood unmoving thinking about how her life was changing. That was supposed to be the constant, change. So much of hers had stood still or run in circles and now she could picture the house complete, walls clean and bright.

It wasn't the future she was laying claim to when it might not be there, it was a different today that was already here. She looked at Chess and smiled.

"You're not breathing again."

"Didn't want to disturb." He returned to stirring the paint can in his hand.

"Are you going to tell me how things went with Justice when you got home?"

"I can tell you what happened, but I have no idea what it means."

"Is he jealous?"

"Yes. He exhibited barely contained rage one minute and then, I don't know. I honestly thought I was in for the beating of my life and then I dropped the hankie and he transformed into a different creature, one I don't recognize."

"I don't want to make you all fight," Claryn said, tugging at the hem of her shirt.

"A solid rumble amongst the boys is good every century or so."

"And if one of you got hurt?"

"We'd heal super fast."

Her brows furrowed and then her face lit with an idea.

"Let's call him."

"What for?"

"To see if he wants to help paint, of course."

"So we are continuing with the paint job?"

"Yes! You're the painter extraordinaire. This has to happen while I've got you in my clutches."

He eyed her with little hope Justice would respond, but her excitement was not to be squelched. He nodded his assent.

"You call and I'll get changed," she said. "We can do this together."

Justice hung up the phone uncertain what Chess was playing at. Come over and paint? Claryn didn't want the house painted; she wanted it left alone. He got online to order some car parts and try to get a line on some of the ones that were more difficult to find. The only sounds in the shop were electrical, making the place seem like a vacated ocean shell with nothing but hollow echoes of something that wasn't really as it seemed.

Were they really painting all night? Was Claryn asking for his help and waiting to see if he would deny her a simple request? Were they laughing and talking like old friends or something more?

Justice wasn't sure how he would take seeing her at this point, but there was only one way to find out. He decided to take his work overalls rather than change clothes and sat down to finish one last online part search.

Justice drove through town in the dead of night. Here too streets, parking lots, shops and restaurants stood empty.

In Claryn's neighborhood the atmosphere was serene, and Justice felt himself drawn along the walk to her front door as if guided by giant invisible hands he could not escape.

Chess opened the door to Justice's light tap.

"You came."

"I came."

Music was playing softly from a CD player in the kitchen where the first coat was drying. Justice listened a moment.

"Claryn?"

"Sleeping. I think painting wears her out. She went to bed a couple hours earlier than last time." When she thought you were a no show.

Justice didn't know there'd been a last time. "Where should I begin?"

"I'm almost done in the downstairs. Why don't you take one of the bedrooms to start? I've already got supplies set up in the master." Chess gave his brother an earnest expression, "I'm glad you came."

Justice nodded and they went their separate ways. Sure that Chess was somewhere below him, Justice stopped to look in on Claryn who was resting peacefully in the middle of the organized chaos she called her room.

It hurt to see her more than smelling the remnants of her scent had. He appreciated paint fumes for the first time as he closed her door and went to the next one down.

With his help they would easily finish in one night, but he could not, should not, would not be there when she came out of her room in the morning. Avoidance appeared to be the key to survival.

Chapter 34

The next night the Darkman came out to check on his potential target. Only time for one more and this one he would take with him on the road. He hated traveling alone. Besides, there was less concern and effort on the part of local law officials if only one body turned up even though two or three women went missing.

His last doll needed to be younger; up for the adventure he was about to take them on.

Edging around the corner of the darkened house, his eyes were on the other residences. No one on this street had an all-hour's kind of job, at least that he could tell. Every home was sleeping, its occupants tucked away and out of sight like the doll in the refrigerator. All resting peacefully after the day's activities. His dolls needed lots of rest.

Previously, the curtain at the kitchen window had been tacked back allowing a nice view into the house where other windows had blinds. Someone had graciously taken the curtain down providing a broader view.

Plastic, he thought excitedly. It was cool on the skin and convenient. The younger dolls sometimes wanted to get things started quickly. Insatiable youth. Plastic was a boon.

The walls in the front room were lighter now, reflecting more light. The blinds at the patio door were more thoroughly shut; further, a wooden brace had been placed in the sliding track to prevent entry.

Playing hard to get.

It mattered little. Tuesday night loomed large, and he had his ways.

Since Sissy scheduled all the house tours while Claryn was at work, Claryn lost count of how many appointments there'd been. One appointment was the day after the paint job, and then a call came saying there was a buyer who was only willing to meet Sissy's asking price if they could start moving in by the end of the week. Apparently the wife was close to her due date with their first child, so the young couple wanted to rent and settle in during the closing.

Claryn, who had so dreaded the moment, took it in stride. As she talked on her cell, she was walking a new Rottweiler who had a head so large it resembled a bear's.

"I can't believe you're taking this so well," said Kelley over the phone.

"It's time. I see that now."

"Uh-huh?"

"Really, I do. I just can't believe it might happen this fast. I'm ready, but I'm not ready. Know what I mean?"

"Yeah. I got ya. And you know if you got stuck between a rock and a hard place, it is a quick trip to open arms in Dallas."

"I know. You're the best. Enough with housing issues, I wanna hear about school and married life."

"All right. One thing first. Therapy for your issues, it might be your only hope for things with Justice."

"We're not even a thing now."

"Yeah, and you think Chess can do all the work by himself? Anyway, that's my last word on the subject."

Claryn could picture Kelley holding up one hand as if swearing to this complete falsehood. The thought broke out her dimples. She listened to descriptions of professors, classes, and library challenges that sounded wonderfully normal.

Up well before JT, Chess made a call to Claryn his first priority. Upon hearing of her impending homelessness, he declared it the perfect opportunity.

"Opportunity for what?"

"Let's take our game to the next level. Move in with me."

Claryn stopped in her tracks, confusing the wiry haired mutt who'd begun to pull her back to the kennel.

"I don't know what to say. I've got that personal space issue, you know."

"You certainly don't have a problem with being a little close to me as long as I'm not a dolt."

"That's different. You're just my friend, like Kelley. It's not like with you this is going someplace romantic or like you're really interested in me as a girlfriend. If you ever tried to make a serious pass at me I'd probably pass out cold."

Chess kept his expression neutral, thinking how different things might have been had he met Claryn first.

"And you think this is a reason not to move in?" he asked.

"I'm sure my issues are as bad as ever if I got close enough to Justice to find out. Living in the same space counts as too close."

"Then you have to move in."

"Why?"

"It will give you time to be in his space while you're not dating. Maybe you can work through some of this."

As crazy as the idea sounded, Claryn had been thinking that Kelley was right. If she could get past some of her issues, maybe it would be easier to work things out with Justice. Being forced into proximity would be like sink or swim therapy. What if she sank, though?

"I won't take 'no' for an answer. When do you have to vacate?"

"Thursday morning."

"Then come out to our place after nine. Justice will already be resting, and I'll have some time to settle you in before my own repose."

"I don't know."

"I'll be glad to move you into your new place as soon as you find it. I could even help you apartment shop when I get back up, so you'd be gone when JT wakes up."

Claryn wanted to take him up on his offer. *Maybe I'm grasping at straws. Maybe he doesn't even care about me as much as Chess thinks.*

What she knew was how much she cared about him. Even if it's a losing fight, she decided, I'll fight it till the end.

"Okay. Thursday at nine?"

"That's the spirit. I'll leave the door open in case you run late and I'm already…indisposed. Call me if you need anything between now and then."

Claryn surveyed her childhood home that night and saw a foreign place. The furniture was still under plastic and painting supplies were stacked neatly in the hall. The creamy white walls were fresh with possibilities that did not belong to her tomorrow.

In her own room she turned full circle and began filling a couple bags with things she wanted with her. One box, just an armload, now held her dearest photos, Dad's shirt, the baby blanket her mother made for her. Claryn pushed things to the middle of the room, covered the area with plastic and began her final work on her home to make it ready for someone else. She felt like she was white-washing the past and wished she could take paint to part of her memory. One layer tonight, another tomorrow, and she would move on into the unknown future.

Several hours later, she could barely lift her arms but felt a sense of peace. Setting up a fan, she lay down on a mattress in the master bedroom floor. She fell asleep with the feeling that the ghosts of her parents were hovering there with her closer than they'd ever felt before.

The Darkman had chosen two dogs, one for each of his dolls. It had been a long time since he'd played with neighborhood pets in southern Pennsylvania. It didn't have the same thrill it used to. He put one of the dogs in the fridge with doll two and closed the door rapidly.

"I really should do some research on making them last longer," he said to the empty room. The dogs! Of course, he'd start his experiments with small animals. He could do that back home. His wife might not like it, but taxidermy was a legitimate hobby.

The other dog he positioned on the end of the bed. He'll keep her feet warm. I'm sure she'll be pleased and he'll fit easily in the back of the car with her when we leave. He hummed 'Scotland the Brave' to himself as he plucked his keys from the dinette. The streets were fairly deserted this time of night. Still, he drove cautiously to the street four blocks over from his new doll's house. The driveways on this street were short, so there were lots of vehicles parked along the curb. It would probably take several weeks for anyone to report his abandoned vehicle. He reasoned with himself that dolls who traveled were more comfortable on the road in their own car. And he was always considerate of his dolls' comfort and needs.

Chapter 35

Chess turned off Mission 2B Immortal, determined never to be lured into playing the game again. If Arvon wanted information about the game he could darn well play it himself.

The only sounds in the shop were Justice's tinkering noises. Chess wondered what their place would sound like with Claryn there. Sighing at the thought of her human presence, he tuned into one of the classic rock stations out of Winslow.

A news update on a local woman who had gone missing reminded Chess of the predator they had in their territory. With all the happenings recently, Chess had almost forgotten that beast completely.

"I hope he hasn't taken another one."

"Excuse me?" JT's head popped up out of the hood.

"Another woman has gone missing."

"Another?" JT's expression was flat and hard.

Chess started talking about the details of the confirmed murdered woman and the still missing second woman and now this third. When Chess described his take on the crime scenes he had visited, the effect it had on Justice was electric. And it wasn't only about territory. Justice's reaction was an odd combination of wrath and out-right panic.

No, Chess hadn't been able to track the killer. This news infuriated JT. He fairly flew from the shop, tearing down the highway for town.

The Darkman left his car and started walking. It had been at least an hour since the last sounds of an automobile in the neighborhood had faded, and his goal was close at hand. He slipped around the side of the house to the back patio door.

The Darkman saw the wooden brace standing upright and laughingly thought about how hard it was for most people to change their habits and routines. He jimmied the lock and stepped into the dining room inhaling the scent of the fresh paint that still lingered. He crept into the living room and laid his supplies out on the plastic, so glad to find it still in place.

In Claryn's dream there was some kind of party going on at the steakhouse. Some tables had been removed to make room for the dance floor. She saw people she knew from high school and college dancing with random neighbors and townspeople.

The music changed to a slow dance and Claryn saw Julia Anthony dancing with Claryn's postman, Tom. Sissy claimed Chess as her partner, and Claryn searched the room for Justice.

She spotted him in a booth listening intently to what Claryn's dad was telling him. Her mom was at the table on her dad's arm. The three laughed at the punch line and Claryn wanted to run over and hug each of them in turn. Instead, she stood frozen unable to decide who to go to first.

A thick shadow was rising behind her in the corner like a dark ghostly presence. She kept her back to it as if ignoring it would make it go away, but it was bulging out into the room.

At first she thought it was Rick Court, but a glance off to her right told her she was wrong. The front end of his car poked out of the wall next to the drink station. People walked past his mangled body rotting on the hood as they refilled their sodas and ice tea.

Now Claryn stood frozen in fear as the oozing evil grew, filling the front entrance, the hostess area. It was nearer and nearer, getting larger as it went. None of the other partygoers noticed. She called out to her parents who continued talking and laughing.

When the presence touched her back, bile rose up in her throat, choking off all sound as she sank in slow motion first to her knees and then further. Her face came to rest against the cold rusty floor tiles and she was seeing the party sideways, out of focus. As the evil rolled over her inch by inch, she thought she saw a pair of glowing eyes in the haze of the party. She stretched out a weak arm toward the eyes and everything faded to black.

The Darkman held only the rag with the chloroform as he stood listening to the house. Whimpering came to his ear from down the hall.

Aw, he thought, someone's having a bad dream. Dreamless sleep was the best, and here he was ready to provide it. He smiled as he walked past the kitchen toward the sounds from down the hall.

His throat exploded in pain as he fell backward on the plastic, clutching at his Adam's apple. It was impossible that he'd run into something that hard in the dark.

Then a terrifying shape loomed over him with glowing white eyes and bared fangs. He tried to scream but his crushed voice box wasn't functioning. His brain couldn't register what he was seeing.

The shape stood to retrieve the Darkman's dropped rag as the bleeding man started backward crawling away on the plastic.

The shape was back on him in an instant. The fierce face with the glowing eyes terrified him senseless.

As the rag was placed over his mouth the Darkman gasped voicelessly, "Monster!"

The unmistakable odor of the dead animals and rotting corpse had assaulted Justice's senses the moment the patio door slid open. The murderer was carrying several items that might make noise if dropped. So Justice watched and waited. Fury broiled within him. Claryn's whimpers momentarily distracted Justice who thought, no one will ever hurt her again if I have anything to say about it.

Then he saw the broad smile that the sound of her pain brought to the killer's face and a deep rage burned in his chest. It had taken every ounce of his self-control not to hit that neck hard enough to leave the killer's head dangling over on his own backbone. Instead, Justice took the man down with precise speed and force.

Just after sunrise the next morning, Chess was astounded by the appearance of his very well fed brother and the heavy odor of the death taint that clung to him.

"You were able to track the killer back from the second victim's home?" Chess asked incredulously. Chess's tracking skills had always been the superior of the two and the trail was now much older.

"No. He came after Claryn."

That possibility had seemed so remote Chess hadn't even considered it. Now he shuddered.

"Porca madosca! I never thought . . ."

"You couldn't have known."

"What made you suspect?"

"I didn't. I just couldn't take the chance."

"I take it his death was not quick and painless."

His brother didn't answer, only turned to see that no judgment was on Chess's face. Chess understood and held his fist out to his brother.

"Justice," Chess said.

The brothers' fists met, knuckle to knuckle before JT headed off to clean up and rest.

"You can't do this again, bro," Chess called after him. "I know you can't smell it, but the bubble of death taint you're walking around in has got nothing on Pig-pen and who knows how many years you're taking off your life."

JT stopped short and turned a strange pained look on his face. "Have you ever thought maybe we live too long? Maybe only certain things make life worth living at all."

His brother was serious enough without getting all melancholy.

"I think that death taint has gone to your head," Chess said watching JT descend the stairs.

Good grief. At this rate he won't even make it to her thirtieth birthday.

233

The police report read that the body of an unknown man and woman were discovered in the wreckage of a rental house at the corner of 10th St. and Market after an explosive gas fire destroyed the structure.

Further investigation revealed the mutilated body of Julia Anthony, items belonging to Carolyn Johnson, and a dead dog, all stored in the home's refrigerator and thus partially protected from the blaze. The evidence indicated that the deceased man was in all probability a serial murderer and police were already tying him to other unsolved murders across the country. A raid of his house in Pennsylvania revealed mementos from at least a dozen murders.

In addition, Julia Anthony's car was recovered in the garage attached to the structure. The fact that the man was exsanguinated and dead before the explosion was covered up by the ferocity of the fire and his proximity to the point of origin.

Only a bare bones account of the fire and the subsequent discoveries made it into the local news outlets.

Chapter 36

Justice answered the shop phone Thursday morning.

"Chess and JT's Automotive."

"Justice?"

The sound of her voice cut him to the quick. This has to get better at some point, he thought.

"Oh, hey. Just a minute." He put the phone down on the desk and called out, "Chess, the phone's for you."

Chess watched him head down to his room. He'd figured Claryn was on the line. Just never pegged JT for a coward, but he'd hardly said two words to her.

"Good morning, my dear Claryn. How did the hand off go?"

"Pretty good, actually. I thought it would be harder to walk away from the house. I did say goodbye to it, out loud."

"That's good for closure, no pun intended." Chess was listening for the turn of the deadbolt on Justice's door.

"You know what else is good for closure? Walking around with their decorator. Did I tell you they're painting the bricks yellow?"

"The yellow brick house." After a moment he said, "The coast is clear. How far out are you?"

"I'm sitting maybe five minutes away."

"Then get your lovely derriere over here."

Claryn didn't know what a derriere was, but she put the car in gear and started moving it anyway.

"See you soon."

"See you."

Chess came out to meet the car, sheltering his eyes from the burning sun. Claryn rolled down the window.

"Where should I park?"

"In front of bay one is fine. We rarely pull anything in there."

Engine off, Claryn took a deep breath and got out of the car. She had several bags in the trunk but decided to leave them for later.

"Can I help you with your luggage?"

"Not right now. I'd like to look around first. I've never seen the bunker, you know." Noticing how he held his hand up she asked, "Does the sun hurt your eyes?"

"It causes some discomfort but not pain. It's one of the reasons there aren't very many of us living in more exotic locations. One can dream though."

The ringing of the customer bell seemed louder to Claryn knowing that Justice was asleep. She tried to be quiet as Chess led her down the stairs to the bunker. He seemed to take pleasure in speaking as loudly as possible without yelling.

"You don't have to tread lightly. You'd have a better chance of waking the dead than one of us resting."

The cinderblock hall was long and narrow with several doors all on the right side at regular intervals. The lights were bulbs with wire metal cages around them like what she'd seen in military movies.

Chess walked up to the first door and pounded on it with a flat hand. The noise was so loud in the confined space, Claryn put her hands over her ears.

"Justice's room." Claryn's mouth dropped open. "Promise you, he can't hear a thing."

He took out some keys and unlocked the next door down and held it open for her.

Expecting the same cold stonewalls as in the hall, Claryn was astonished to see that the walls and even the ceiling were covered with a beautiful mural of a garden in the moonlight.

"Chess. This is beautiful. Did you paint this?"

Without his customary grandiose acceptance of a compliment he responded. "I did. And I assure you that by the standards of my day it is sorely lacking. Although I think I have improved over time."

She put a hand out to touch the odd texture of the wall.

"It's . . ."

"Plaster. Frescos are painted into the plaster while it's still wet, so you have to work fast. But the effect is fantastic."

Claryn wanted to keep admiring the painting, but Chess pushed her along.

"The next two rooms are storage, but I could fix one up for you if you really want. However--" he walked over to the bed and sat down "--I was rather hoping you'd sleep here."

Claryn's response was mild alarm. She stammered, "Oh, no, I uh, that's ah. . ."

He kind of enjoyed teasing her, but for the first time something he'd said had set off her inverse fight/flight reaction. He realized how bad it made him feel to be the cause of her fear, even if teasing. He could only imagine how Justice handled it since it had apparently been a regular event.

"I wouldn't actually be here while you're sleeping, unless you take a lot of naps in the middle of the day."

"Oh, sure. Yeah. That's okay, though. I could just sleep on the couch upstairs."

"If it comes to that I'll move upstairs. It's safer down here. And there is a futon in the office."

Claryn wanted to ask safer from what. Then she realized that for all she knew they had regular vampire guests.

"I could sleep on the futon."

He got up shaking his head at her. "Not happening."

He led her back up the stairs.

"Water? Juice? Tea?"

"You've stocked up."

"Guilty as charged." He remembered the way Justice had watched him placing groceries in the break room.

"I'm fine right now."

"Then I'll get myself some water."

She followed him and saw that he served himself water out of the odd appliance she didn't recognize.

"What is that?"

"Reverse osmosis water filtration system. You get the purest water this way, free of chemicals and most other impurities."

"No wonder your water tastes so good." She claimed a glass and helped herself.

"Sometimes I call it The Still."

"Why?"

"If we drink too much of it too fast, it produces a state similar to light inebriation."

"That is wild."

He downed his glass and filled it back up. "There's something I wanted to talk to you about."

"Uh-oh."

He went back to the living room and sat on the couch. "It's nothing bad."

"Uh-huh?"

"I had this idea about your physical proximity problems, a sort of therapy, if you will."

"Kelley has been saying I needed therapy for years, but I'm not much on the idea." She sat down sideways facing him.

He laid his hand out on the couch, much as Justice had the night she'd confessed her dark secret. She eyed it a moment and hesitantly put her hand on top of his. He closed his fingers around hers, relishing the moment and noting that her heart's reaction was very minimal. They sat like that for several minutes. She grew uncomfortable but not increasingly fearful.

"This is silly. It's different with you."

"Because we're just friends."

"Yes. There's no real interest there."

"So I could do this."

He moved closer beside her and put his arm around her. She was still wearing her 'this is silly look' when he put his other hand on her leg. This produced a mild reaction as well and she engaged in a little self-talk.

"You'd never hurt me."

He took his hand back saying, "But Court did and that's where this all started."

Now her breathing got shallower. Talking about it made it worse. He felt a familiar protective urge. "Forget I said that. And let me get my idea out."

"Okay."

"What if the proximity was completely in your control? You could move as close as you wanted. Hold a hand, lean on a shoulder, whatever."

"I would know that the other person could move if they wanted."

"Not if they were resting, or as you would say, asleep."

She thought of Justice downstairs asleep.

"People can wake up if you move."

"Vampires can't." She was looking toward the stairs with wide eyes.

"I'm not suggesting we experiment on Justice without his permission. Besides, his door is locked. Look, I should go lay down soon. But I thought if you would like to come down and see how we rest, what it's like, you can. You could make a decision and then, whatever."

He stood up and put on his best flirty Chess face. "So what do you say, wanna come tuck me in?"

He walked over to the bay with the stairs and looked back at her. Then he turned and went down.

As Claryn stood up to follow him, a sense of déjà vu came over her. I'm Alice in Wonderland following the white rabbit down into another world. And follow him she did.

When she got to his door, he was standing just inside in sleep pants holding the door open.

"Oh, I'm sorry." She turned her back.

"It's just my pajamas. Come on in."

She backed into the small room noticing for the first time the small antique armoire on the wall beside the door. He closed the door and locked it handing her the key.

"I have another one in the desk."

She looked at the desk and the chair sitting next to it. She dragged the chair to the opposite corner of the room from the bed he was climbing into and sat down. The bed also looked antique and she knew it was an old style double, but it was barely wider than a twin. She wondered what Justice's room looked like on the other side of the wall. She was trying not to look at Chess.

He was laying with the dark burgundy sheets pulled up to his stomach and his elbows propping him up to talk to her. He blinked very slowly. It was harder to be in the room with him than she'd expected. A very attractive half naked male was laying a few feet away from where she sat. Now it hardly mattered that it was her friend Chess. She felt a wave of weakness.

He spoke very slowly.

"You are welcome to come over, hold my hand, curl up next to me, whatever. I trust you not to take advantage or stake me or anything." His eyes teased. "Just promise me one thing."

"What's that?"

"Don't draw on my face or chest. I've got a reputation to maintain, you know, and the ink doesn't always come off too easy."

His joking made it easier to be here.

"I promise."

As he laid back he said, "Thanks, love," and then was out like a light.

She couldn't believe how still he was. Now Chess was the statue.

"Chess? Chess?" No response.

She got up and walked over to him, shaking his upper arm, "Chess?"

She sat back down and looked around the room for a while taking in all the painting. The garden had trees off in the distance and a wall on one side with open archways going down the longest wall of the room. Vines grew up the columns and across latticework. It was almost like she was actually sitting in a little garden.

The sky had a few wisps of clouds across the three quarter full moon, and she could see stars off in the sky in the other direction. She thought one might be the morning star. It was magical.

The armoire's wall showed part of a house like an Italian villa off in the distance, and for the first time Claryn wondered if it was a real place. The door to the room blended into the wall, but she could see the dead bolt.

This door locked. Justice's door locked. She thought about the level of trust Chess displayed having her in here like this and was touched by it. If what he said was true, and she was sure it was, she could walk over and cut off his head without him raising a finger to stop her.

He was completely vulnerable. Him, not her. Excitement ran through her. She felt wildly elated. She was locked in a room with a large, strong, guy and he was completely vulnerable.

She had all the power here. She didn't know if this was a good or bad thing as far as her issues went, but it was completely unprecedented.

She dragged the chair back over near the bed and reached out to hold his hand. A hand that could not close to catch hers. A thrill ran through her. She sat beside him on the bed and took his arm and laid it across her lap. She spent a few minutes touching his face, then his hair. She played with his ears. For her it was an unparalleled experience. It was enough.

She stood, returning the chair to its spot by the desk. She twirled in a circle in the middle of the room and threw her head back and laughed.

Key in hand she walked back over to the bed and bent low over him to whisper in his ear, "Thank you, Chess. Thank you so much." Then she kissed him on the cheek as she had her father, turned off the light as she slipped out the door, and carefully locked it behind her.

241

Chapter 37

Chess woke to the very faint yet lingering scent of Claryn. She'd been gone most of the time, but hints of her were in the room. He knew she'd sat on the bed without lying down. He wished his own skin held scents as well as fabric. She was like a dayflower in his night garden, closed but present at the periphery of his perceptions.

His decisions to invite her to stay and to try his experimental therapy idea were both spur of the moment. He knew he was wrong not to consult JT about her stay.

Chess's impulses had not always served the brothers well. At least JT accepted most of them as par for the course. They had disagreements, dealt with consequences, and went on. Together through thick and thin.

Chess usually knew what to expect. The uncertainty about every decision regarding Claryn was difficult and the effects of Chess's impulses seemed to linger. JT was more distant than ever, while Chess was growing closer to Claryn than any woman since Sephauna.

To JT, Sephauna had been like a stepmother and younger sister rolled into one. She taught and guided him in his new life, and depended on his maturity and strength in every other area. For Chess, life with Sephauna had started out very differently.

His brother deserved a chance at this happiness, even if Chess had to make him miserable to try to give it to him. Chess had begun her therapy but he suspected it was JT who would have to complete it.

He got ready for his day and, finding Claryn absent, began reorganizing the storage rooms. He hoped that one of them would serve as a space for Claryn. His goal was to get as much done as possible before JT woke.

JT's body seemed to be trying to sleep off its recently acquired death taints. Disturbing as that was, it did give Chess greater opportunities to plot. He thought how much he would enjoy painting a room for Claryn and wondered what she would like on the walls.

Claryn turned her car radio on and scanned through the channels for something upbeat with which she could sing along. Mrs. Smithson had given her the day off, and she planned to make use of it. I should be apartment hunting, she thought. She felt a sense of freedom inspired by having no home to tend, no things to arrange or clean, and no plan to follow.

A Tom Petty song came on. Since she knew the words, she rolled down the windows singing at the top of her lungs as she drove through the desert cruising the county boundary.

She felt her phone vibrating and saw that it was Kelley. Suddenly she was bursting to tell her friend the news, but so much could not be said. She pulled over near the abandoned quarry to talk to her friend.

"Hello!"

"Hello yourself. Someone's awfully chipper today. What happened?"

"Well, I moved into the auto shop and began an experimental therapeutic approach that is already seeing results."

"I have to say, smashing! Therapy at last." Here Kelley took on a German accent, presumably to try and mimic Sigmund Freud. "And you moved in where?"

"It's just a temporary solution since I had to be out of the house so fast."

"I knew Sissy had a buyer on the line, but this is incredible, and you sound okay with it."

"I feel like the house and all that stuff was holding me back and now I can float above the cottonwood trees. Isn't that amazing?"

"I'm very very happy for you, but does your therapy happen to include drugs?"

"NO! You're hilarious. I have two duffels, a couple boxes in my car and could do anything, go anywhere."

Kelley started singing Free Bird, and Claryn, muting the radio, laughed and sang along.

"How on earth did Sissy get the house cleared out in time?"

"She paid a last minute mover to pack it all up and put it in storage. I'm sure that took a nice chunk of her unrealized house gains right there. And why go through today, what you can put off till next fall? It was a condition of the sale that they had to be in the house by today."

"And you moved in with Justice?"

"Not exactly."

"You moved in with Chess!"

"It was at his invitation, but no one's sharing private space really."

"What did Justice say?"

"I don't think Chess told him."

"Good golly, Miss Molly! Did you learn nothing from the summer of the Brent boys?"

"This isn't like that at all. Chess is only a friend."

"Oh, honey, you do know guys are always willing to play the friend card right up to the moment they can lure you into their bed? They all have one thing on half their minds all the time. I'm married now. I ought to know."

Kelley would be apoplectic if she knew Claryn had already been in Chess's bed.

"Keeping my own counsel here."

"If you're going down that road anyway, I think you may be shooting for the wrong Cain brother, if I do say so myself."

Claryn wanted to shift gears.

"I'm sure you didn't call me without news of your own."

"I do have news and I so wanted to tell you in person. Are you sure you can't use that new freedom to come here?"

"And wait to hear the news? Absolutely not. You will have to tell me right now."

"I'm pregnant."

"Kelley!"

"I know! I'm a wife for what, all of two months? And now I'm going to be a momma."

"Are you sure?"

"Pretty sure. I know you can get false positives early on. I don't think that's what it is."

"What did George say?"

"He froze with that deer in headlights look and then started jumping around as if I was giving him tickets to the Super Bowl."

"I'm so happy for you, Kelley."

"Thanks!"

"What are you going to do about school?"

"Keep trucking as long as I can and see what happens. Did I tell you George sold one of his characters?"

"What?"

"Yeah, he draws these cartoon character things that he puts on the web and he sold one of them for a nice junk of change. He's been drawing these things since he was in middle school as a hobby. Literally has a thousand of them lying around. I'm trying to figure out how I can become his agent and manage his talent. It could be a good sideline for us."

"I never heard of such a thing. I guess all those characters have to come from somewhere."

"I think he's feeling more like the manly provider, living the dream and all that jazz. It's a very attractive look for him."

"You don't think that could be the hormones talking?"

"Hah, either way, he is looking F-I-N-E, fine."

"There's my cue to go. I think I hear a rabbit calling my name."

"I love you, Claryn!" she half sang.

"Love you too, Kells."

Justice woke knowing he'd overslept again. It would be beneficial to know how much of his life expectancy each kill had cost him, but who was signing up for that experiment?

Anyway, their longevity was an unknown variable as well. He did feel the taint and was drinking as much water as he could in order to flush his system. That had side effects as well.

He walked into the hall and looked around for Claryn. Not possible. My system is so messed up. He went to the break room and downed a water before noticing there were already two dirty glasses.

He swung his head around and went back down the stairs to the hall following the no longer phantom scent to Chess's bedroom door.

He put his ear to the door, which is how Chess caught him. Relieved to see Chess down at the first storage room, Justice ambled down that way. The scent did not follow.

"What are you doing?" Justice asked.

"This may not be the best time for this."

Justice raised one eyebrow in response. There was seldom a best time for Chess's cockeyed schemes.

"Claryn got the boot from her house this morning and hasn't started her apartment hunting yet, so I offered to let her stay here." Chess was trying to put the damsel-in-distress card into play.

"Oh. Good. Good." Justice picked up a couple things to take to the other storage room.

"I thought you might not like the idea."

"When did you know?"

"Day before yesterday."

"I can see why you didn't tell me. The situation is partially my fault, though. When Sissy put the house up for sale, Claryn was upset. So I kept talking about how bad the market was, how long she probably had. Apartment hunting went to the bottom of her to-do list rapidly."

Together they cleared the space in minutes.

"Futon?" Justice suggested.

"Oh, yeah. That's a good idea."

Justice asked, "Where were you thinking she was going to sleep?" and then thought about where the scent ended.

"You offered her your room didn't you, dog?" This new Justice buddy persona did not sit well with Chess. He went after the futon with Justice on his heels laughing strangely.

"I know you think you've got Claryn figured out and you can ride in as the comforting friend and play your games, but she's a slow roaster," Justice said.

Chess was irritated by the game suggestion, even if that was his usual modus operandi. They already had the futon frame back down the hall. Now they got louder as Chess mumbled about how little JT understood women, Claryn in particular.

Justice grumbled, "The mighty Chess who understood Jenny, Polly, Ariana so well."

They got shorter with each other as they carried the awkward cushion that either of them could have carried alone, but instead were tugging and struggling with together.

"The only slow person around here is you, JT. When it comes to Claryn, you are about as thick as they come."

Justice was hot saying, "Oh, what? You trying to tell me after your previous forty or fifty relationships that you've finally found the one, your true love?"

"At least I'm willing to stick it out and take the risks. I never thought I'd see the day you turned tail and ran."

"That's not what I did and you know it." Justice had his hand pointed right in Chess's face.

Chess knocked it away.

After a moment's hesitation Justice laid into him with a punch to the nose.

They fought in the tight hallway, denting Justice's door, bending the hinges of the one on the cleared room, and busting the frame of the futon to smithereens. Chunks of masonry rained down.

They seemed to lose steam at about the same time and stopped with Justice straddling the larger Chess on the floor. His fists balled up in his brother's shirt.

"You just couldn't leave well enough alone." Justice gasped. "You had to come swaggering in, turning her head, holding her hands." Justice pushed off of him, staggering into the wall behind him.

"And what for?" he yelled.

Chess was resting on one elbow; one leg bent checking on his jaw movement.   "To make you jealous, of course."

Justice looked ready to go after him again. "That is the worst reason I have ever heard for playing around with a girl's heart."

Chess stood up and dusted himself off, shaking his head back and forth. He walked over, relaxed and cool as a cucumber as he got in Justice's face. His voice was low and calm. "The only heart I've been playing here was yours, JT." He picked at the torn shoulder of his shirt. "The other one wasn't available."

Their heads swiveled in unison toward the sound of the customer bell.

Chess pushed past Justice saying, "She's only here because of you." Chess went to greet Claryn and left his brother still trying to take in what Chess had said.

Chapter 38

"Hello?" Claryn called out into the shop.

"Right here." Chess jogged up the steps. "You ready for me to get those bags?"

Claryn had never seen Chess so bedraggled. He was covered in dust from top to bottom. His black cotton poplin shirt was torn in several places and the left sleeve was hanging by a thread at the shoulder. His dark jeans didn't look much better and his hair was sticking out all over the place. It would have been comical except that he seemed to have abrasions on every surface of his skin.

"Are you hurt? Did you get caught in a motor or something?" asked Claryn.

Justice listened from the hall, wincing at her concern.

She walked over and wiped away the scrapes of dust to see that the skin underneath was flawless as usual.

"What happened?"

"Brothers just have to work things out this way sometimes."

Claryn's heart fell. "Justice doesn't want me here," Claryn whispered.

From the hall Justice heard her disappointment, her pain. He was trying to make out how she felt about whom.

"No. He said that was good. He's glad you're here."

"Really?"

There it was. That twinge of hope.

"He said that?"

"He did."

"Then what?"

"I told him I went out with you to make him jealous."

"Oh. But you told him why, right?"

"It took awhile to get to that part."

"I'm sorry, Chess."

"It's not your fault. Some people are just more thick headed than others." Chess's voice was louder than necessary.

Justice knew this was being said for his benefit. Chess had been playing him. Claryn was here for Justice.

His heart rose as his stomach fell. He was back at square one with no good options. The woman he loved, under his own roof but still a thousand miles away. As quietly as he could, he went to get cleaned up.

"I'm a lot of trouble, aren't I?" she asked.

Chess walked over and rubbed her arms for a moment as if to reassure her. "And completely worth it."

"You're wiping your dusty hands on my shirt, aren't you?"

"What if I am?"

She laughed and gave him an ineffectual shove.

"Is Justice okay?"

Chess tilted one ear toward the stairs.

"He appears to have stopped listening in on our conversation and is getting cleaned up. I give almost as good as I take."

Claryn blanched and whispered, rather belatedly Chess thought, "He can hear us from downstairs?"

Chess waggled one ear back and forth with his finger, "Creature features. Come on. Let's get your stuff."

Outside Chess looked over her paltry luggage and the one bag of groceries sitting in the backseat of her car.

She interrupted his thoughts. "Can he hear us out here?

"This is going to be an issue isn't it? Probably not from downstairs and definitely not while he's in the shower. What happened today?" Chess noticed ker nervous excited look..

"Therapy!" She bordered on jubilant. "I can't explain it. You were all vulnerable, and I wasn't. I was…oh I don't know how to tell it. You had to be there. And awake."

He deeply wished he had been. Maybe my idea wasn't completely hare-brained, he thought.

"Anyway, I don't know what it changes. I feel different. Maybe hopeful? I wanted to thank you, while you're actually aware of it. I've been on cloud nine all day."

He took refuge in humor. "I tend to have that effect on women. I thought I had to be conscious to do it. Who knew? Same time tomorrow?"

She glanced at the shop. "Our secret?"

He winked.

"Now, what all's in the trunk?"

"Spare tire, jack, maybe a crow bar."

He took the duffels while she grabbed one box. "Traveling light, I see. You know, we'll be hurt if you don't stay for at least a few days."

"Uh-huh?" Her noncommittal tone made him suspicious.

"Did you go apartment hunting without me today? Cause I can lock you in that room if I have to." He thought about what was supposed to be her room door and the fact that it might not shut now, much less lock.

She wanted to tease as if she had found a place, but couldn't get her face to cooperate.

"No. I went cruising around the county, talked to Kelley out by the quarry, walked the dogs, and went to the grocery."

"What was Kelley doing out by the quarry?"

"Goofball."

They took everything inside and she unloaded her groceries of which organic canned soups and fresh fruit made up the majority.

"I thought you didn't have to work today?" Chess asked.

"I didn't, but the doggies miss me and get off their walk schedule if I cut out completely. You should come out one morning and help walk! They love morning walks, but I always have a lot of cleaning up to do."

"Dogs don't care for me much." He saw her immediate concern.

251

"No." She shook her head, eyes wide at this horror. "You personally or all of you?"

In the living room her bags disappeared down the stairs courtesy of Justice.

For a while they all acted as if everything was perfectly normal, so the evening turned out to be fun. Justice and Chess made up without ever saying a word. The three of them sat on the couch, Claryn in the middle, playing games. The brothers were especially amused by Claryn cleaning their clocks on Mission 2B Immortal. After watching her play a couple times, though, they got the sideways action of the game.

"Don't you all find this sort of ridiculous? Like you're going to play a game and become a vampire. Ooooo."

They weren't smiling.

She looked from Chess to Justice and back again, her eyes growing large. Then she tossed down the console like it was a hot potato making them laugh.

"It actually is being used as a. . ." Chess began and Justice finished.

". . .recruitment tool."

Claryn hadn't thought a lot about the others who were out there.

"Who are they?"

"A relatively young coven, getting stronger every day," Chess answered.

"And making their own rules," Justice added importantly.

Her stomach growled.

"Some hosts we are," Chess walked to the break room.

"There are rules? Doesn't that mean someone has to enforce the rules?"

Justice's face was all concern. "There's a lot you don't know about us. Didn't you ask Chess about us?"

"He thought you and I would talk." She tried to sound nonchalant, "That didn't happen."

They sat, the only sounds being the game menu screen and Chess's clattering around in the break room as if searching through the same three pans repeatedly for a missing one.

"I'm sorry, Claryn. After . . . that night, I thought it was for the best. The best thing for you."

"You were afraid of hurting me, right? But if I have something you need, Justice, it's yours, you're welcome to it."

"Don't say that, Claryn. You don't know what you're saying."

"No. Let me say exactly what I mean. I'm not laying my arms out for a snack--"

Justice tried to interrupt, but she put her hand on his arm to stop him. Her touch left him speechless as she consciously drew it back.

"What I am saying is that if you or Chess were hurt or really needed human blood then you can have it."

"Claryn, please don't." Justice had his head in his hands, knowing that she was sincere and wouldn't take it back.

I need to level with her, why is this so hard? Justice asked himself.

Chess had moved close behind them, though Claryn hadn't heard him.

"What JT is having a hard time telling you, Claryn, is that there are risks you can't understand without seeing them. And neither of us wants to see you in peril."

"What then? Just tell me. Are you so afraid you'll drain me dry?" She was defensive now. "There are worse things in life than death!"

Chess handed her the soup bowl and spoon. He sat down on the L across from Justice, whose look was clearly plaintive.

"Okay. There's too much to cover in one evening, so let's talk venom."

"Venom?"

"Yes. We carry venom in our bite. It has some healing qualities for human skin. So that movie thing where someone has bite marks, doesn't happen."

Claryn was eating her soup and being very attentive. She tried to gauge how Justice was fairing with her hearing this. Trying to spot which nameless fear was driving him away from her. "And how many bites does it take to, you know, three?"

Chess took a moment to search his memory for a fictional three bite reference. "Venom doesn't change people. Not like that."

Justice interrupted, "Moving on."

Chess continued, "Vampires like us can usually moderate how much we drink. The difficulty rises exponentially if we are in mortal peril. There are other risks to us--"

Justice broke in, "The risks to us can wait for another night."

"Agreed. Humans are not created equal, at least not when it comes to how their--your systems handle venom."

She could tell by Justice's countenance they were coming to it.

"Venom can cause a fever. Some people recover, others die. The percentages--"

"Don't matter, because we're not taking any chances," Justice butted in again.

Chess continued, "Another possible consequence is coma. Some people enter a coma from which they seldom recover."

"They die?" she asked concerned.

"They die or they remain in a coma indefinitely."

"Hundreds of years and counting," Justice threw in and went on. "Now what you should be thinking about asking is how many people have we murdered? How many people have we killed or doomed? And how do we live with it?"

Claryn's appetite was gone. It was a lot to take in and this was just the beginning. She was thinking about the drug commercials on TV that listed horrible side effects one after the other as they peddled something like a fancy antacid. The percentages did make a difference. Tonight she was too tired to argue, or ask, or think anymore about it.

She stood and announced, "I'm going to bed. I don't have to be at work till noon tomorrow, so I'll see you all in the morning."

They both stood as well. She supposed they'd lived through an age when gentlemen did that each time a lady rose.

She got partway down the steps and realized she didn't know where she was going. "Where am I sleeping?"

Justice stepped up to show her. "This way."

He led her down past their rooms to the one they were fixing up for her but had mostly destroyed. She ran her hands along the hall wall, touching the damaged masonry along the way. Justice was obviously embarrassed and that amused her now.

"I put your things in here, but it's not quite ready for you to sleep in."

"That's an interesting renovation." She pointed toward the splintered futon base. Then she dug through her green duffel for her yoga pants, big sleep tee, and toiletries.

"Yeah. I'm sorry about that. You get your pick of rooms, though, since neither of us sleep at night."

"Chess mentioned that."

"I bet he did," Justice said under his breath, heading back to their rooms. He unlocked Chess's and then his own pushing the doors open. She made herself poke her head in Chess's since it was the first she came to, but she really wanted to see Justice's room. She noted that the sheets had been changed.

She made no comment on the painting, only confirming what Justice suspected; she'd already been in that room. Then she went in his room and walked around.

He suddenly wished his room were different. It was so peculiar seeing her there.

Justice's room was basic and utilitarian. Blank walls, metal lockers, twin bed, and functional desk set a tone of a cold austerity, or it would have to most people.

To Claryn though, it was very much like Justice himself. Where Chess poured his passions out, Justice held them in as private treasures protected by personal strength. It was not a sad room to Claryn. It was one with possibilities.

Justice was about to suggest she stay in Chess's room when she said, "I can stay in here if I want?"

"Of course. It's all yours."

She nodded and smiled. "If you need anything, want something you could come back in. You guys can be silent if you want and I sleep like the dead anyway. . .no offense."

The silence between them was not companionable now as it had been on those first dates. Claryn missed it. She also couldn't joke like she did with Chess about getting tucked in.

Justice stepped out. "The lavatory is down there on the end."

Claryn looked back down toward the stairs seeing a small door that she had somehow missed previously.

"Are you going to be here tonight? Or going out for your day?"

"Chess will be here if you need anything, Claryn."

But you won't, she thought.

"Where are you going?"

"We have another property to check on. I'll head over there for a few days."

"I thought you were glad I'm here?" Confusion was plain on her face.

"I'm glad you came here. You need anything, we're here. One of us has to be elsewhere and seems better if it's me."

Claryn had thought the evening went well as if it meant something else, maybe picking up where they left off. At this point she wasn't sure who had the biggest issues.

She looked around. "Where's the key?"

Justice tried to think about that, what it meant that she was asking.

"Do you want to lock us out?" It was so convenient to say "us" instead of "me." It wasn't as painful to be around her as he thought it'd be. It simply felt hopeless; nothing good could come of it.

"No. I-I don't know why I asked. Goodnight."

"Goodnight."

He went back up the stairs listening. The sounds from the bunker were very faint, but he could hear them easier if he was working under his latest project. Getting some work done would feel good before leaving.

Chess turned off the TV and joined him for a while working beside him. They often used their bare hands for work that usually required tools. Soon no muffled sounds rose through the first bay.

"She was in your room this morning." A statement of fact, it required and received no answer.

"Did you lock the door?" Justice asked.

"I did. I gave her a key and told her to come and go as she pleased. We're not the only ones who find comfort in a dead bolt."

"It's weird seeing her down there. Was it funny seeing her in your room?"

"I thought it was nice," said Chess.

"Of course you did."

"She chose your room despite the fact it's boring, drab, uncomfortable."

"She did." He felt pleased despite himself.

"Bet you won't change the sheets tomorrow."

"I hadn't thought about it."

"Right." Chess stopped working. "I know you don't play games," he said. "I wondered, though, if I asked you to do something, would you consider doing it without asking a bunch of questions."

"Probably not. What is it?"

"You're no fun at all."

Justice said, "Arvon said we needed to maintain a presence at the homestead. Think I'll spend a few days there."

Chess was trying to think of the right response to this.

"Justice?"

They heard her at the same time and both jumped. Justice moved so fast it was as if he evaporated and appeared by Claryn's bed. He startled her.

"Are you okay?"

She was whisper-talking now. "Wow. You guys can hear everything."

"You're testing my hearing?"

"Shhh. I can't sleep. Would you talk to me for awhile?"

"Anything you want."

"Shhh. Close the door."

"Lights?"

"Definitely not. I plugged in my alarm clock. If I tap it the light comes on. That's enough."

He pulled the chair up beside the bed facing the headboard.

"I can't really see anything. You don't have a night light do you?"

"No." He chuckled.

"Can you see me?"

"Yes."

"How many fingers am I holding up?"

"Two on your left hand, one on your right and your right thumb."

She tittered, feeling like she was playing games at a slumber party.

"What will Chess think we're doing?"

"I don't care much about what Chess thinks we're doing."

"He's done a lot of maneuvering to get us here."

"Yeah, I can imagine."

She swatted at him but missed in the dark.

"You're too far away." He scooted the chair closer and leaned in.

She put out her hand to find him, felt his face and tucked her hand back under her pillow. The distance was acceptable.

"How many hours do you usually sleep each day?"

"Seven hours give or take. It's not really sleep. It's more like being unconscious."

"Chess showed me."

"Why?"

"Shh. He is more forthcoming than you are."

Justice growled, not liking the comparison.

"He also said now that I knew he'd probably have to kill me." She was smiling in the dark.

"Over my dead body," he said.

She tittered again. "Did you know girls get more giggly at night when they're tired?"

"No. Did you know you're very cute smothering your giggles with the sheet?"

"Yes. Actually I knew that." They both laughed. She yawned.

She was more relaxed in the dark, like she had been in the church. She was on the verge of falling asleep, but her thoughts alarmed her and her heart reacted.

"Whatever it is, let it go and go to sleep," he said.

"No," she swallowed. "Put your hand here."

He put it out on the bed next to her and she inched hers over till a few fingers overlapped. A feeling ran through him that rocked his heart.

She kept it that way for as long as she could, unable to fathom why such a simple thing should be so hard for her. There it was though.

"You should get some rest. Think you can sleep now?"

"Yeah. I don't want to though."

He almost asked why, but he knew the answer would probably lead to a discussion about his departure.

"It's for the best," Justice said.

Claryn closed her eyes, trying to ignore him. Otherwise she'd feel resentful. She relaxed, dozed after a few minutes, and then woke uncertain how long she'd been out. When she stretched out her hand to see if he was still there, he dodged silently back leaving her reaching.

Chapter 39

Chess planned to check on the homestead, abandoning the two lovebirds to their own devices. When Justice opted to leave immediately, it cramped his other plan as well.

He wanted to leave a note for Justice telling him to ask Claryn about her therapy. If Justice's door was the one Claryn had the key to, he thought, things would be better for all.

When they last checked there was still no sign of trespassers at the homestead, but Arvon thought the slayer was on the move. Arvon was rarely wrong about such things.

"You shouldn't rest there. Make your presence known and slip back here," said Chess.

"They got the slip on me once. What if they did it again? What if I led them back here?"

"You change out cars coming and going and drive like a fiend. Highly unlikely."

"Not worth the risk," said Justice.

"For someone you keep trying to write off, you worry a lot about her."

"There's not a predatory bone in her body. And I plan to keep it that way. She doesn't use people. That's not who she is."

"Funny how I've spent more time with her than you have, but you're the authority," said Chess.

Justice chose to ignore the comment even if it did get under his skin. What could he say, when by his choice he was leaving Claryn in his brother's arms…again.

"I've got a throw away cell near when I change cars."

"And will you actually call me away from here if there's trouble?"

Justice didn't answer as he picked up his bag from the sofa.

"I didn't think so." He threw one last taunt at his brother's back.

"If you keep throwing her in my lap, I might decide to hold onto her!" quipped Chess.

Now Arvon would have to be told about the Claryn situation. If Justice was unwilling to call for backup, Arvon had to know. Chess tried to do things his way.

I guess it's time I defer, thought Chess.

The homestead was an active ranch in that a local rented the land, worked it, and provided back a share of the profit in exchange for low lease rates. The clapboard house had seen better days, though, and the area around it and the barns was deserted. It would be an easy matter for someone to note the treads leading to the barn or any movement outside the house given how flat and deserted the land was.

They had spent time cleaning it out, trying to insure there was no lead back to Hallston. One issue with being there was that there was so little to do. Cars were Justice's past time, but someone could use that information to make a connection, so car tinkering was out. One option was to join the work outfit at the small turquoise mine. Maybe later he'd do that if they worked at night. For now reading fit the bill.

It was nigh on morning when he contemplated the security of the underground accommodations they'd built. Chess was right about the safety issue. A determined adversary with the right tools could get in easily. First they'd have to find it though. Justice smiled to himself as he went to rest.

Chess waited till business hours to call Arvon. He wondered again how ancient the old one really was, and how many hours he had to sleep. Arvon had an office and supposedly kept regular hours of operation on the premises. Arvon took the news of Justice's erratic behavior well. He cut to the chase.

"Humans are too fragile. What are her chances for making the change?"

Chess paused before answering, "My barometer says high. Justice is Mr. No-Risk when it comes to her and hasn't even asked."

"Justice isn't the only decision-maker. When was the last time you had a fresh drink?"

"Some time. I'm on the wagon and all."

"It's time to get off. If I make the call, you should be ready to do the deed."

Chess processed that. You would think I'd have known a fresh drink might be necessary, he thought. Chess always had theories about how things worked. Arvon's directive confirmed what he suspected. He remembered now reading that the mosquito needed fresh blood to reproduce. Looks like we do too.

Chess paused a beat too long.

"Problem?" asked Arvon.

"I have guard duty here, but usually date elsewhere. And, I want to remain a team, Justice and me. He tends to hold a grudge."

Arvon took this as extraneous commentary and moved on. The girl would either transition well, problem solved, or she would not. In which case, Arvon thought, there was no future anyway and the quicker Justice realized it the better.

"If it gets hairy down there, call my emergency line. No need to leave a message."

And you'll what? Chess thought. Send in the cavalry? Come down?

"In fact, give it to the girl as well," Arvon added.

"Seriously? Is open and honest the new operating procedure?"

"She doesn't need to know who the number reaches. Might even be good to have her around. She'll be alert when you're not. You've talked a lot about JT." Arvon avoided using his name. "Is she clamoring for the dream?"

"Don't think so."

"Asking a lot of questions?"

"Almost none. She's better at the 2B than either of us, though. How's that for irony."

"Has the temperament to survive, then."

Arvon got quiet. Chess heard an assistant come in with a verbal report and Arvon allowed Chess to hear. "The Mission 2B Immortal website had been hacked unbeknownst to its operators. Someone was collecting data on the rejects, not too hard to guess who. As if three of these slayers weren't bad enough."

Chess waited. Arvon was the one person Chess had patience with when it came to silence. Chess was shocked by the decision.

"Very useful asset. Bring her in on the current situation, at least some of the danger, the set up, the possible need for a daytime guard. Beyond that, tell her what you deem best with cooperation as the goal."

The word "cooperation" sounded ominous to Chess.

"If it ruffles JT's feathers, you're on orders. Get a taste of her blood if you can. It will improve your barometer. A sample sent my direction would be even better. We've seen some unexpected interactions between the populations recently."

Chess was too taken aback to wonder about the "unexpected interactions." Standard operating procedures were flying out the window, and he didn't care for the sudden change.

He regretted telling Arvon; suddenly he wished he had backed Justice's play to distance Claryn from them and their affairs. In this Chess and Sephauna were the same, Arvon's word was law. At least it always had been. "Arvon doesn't follow the rules," she'd told him. "He makes them."

Chess cocked his head toward the bunkers when Claryn started moving around. He started hot water for tea.

"I should get going," he told Arvon.

"Going, gone," Arvon said as he rang off. His way of saying to get a move on.

Claryn emerged with damp hair, and gratefully took the tea and exchanged greetings. Getting ready, Claryn had thought how comfortable she was. Here she was in the home of two monsters, almost contented. Then Sissy called.

"Hello?"

"Claryn! How did the hand-off go?"

"Not a hitch."

"Can you believe how lucky we got, and in this market too? I knew that realtor was working for the buyers, though. They totally paid almost the full asking price. Where are you?"

Claryn cringed. She hadn't told Sissy her plans.

"I'm out at Justice and Chess's place."

"It's a little early, are you…" Claryn heard Sissy take in a little breath before finishing her sentence, "are you staying there?"

"Chess said he would help me look for apartments this week. They have an extra room, said it was no biggie."

"Claryn, are you still dating one of them?"

She looked at Chess and headed out the shop door hoping he wouldn't hear her outside.

"Claryn?"

"No one's dating anyone right now."

"You sound sad about it. Look, I've got to go. I do not recommend staying with them as a semi-permanent solution even if you're not dating. But if you decide to move in there, however it's arranged, you can always tell me anything, you know?"

"I know."

"All right. I'll try to ring in next week."

"Goodbye."

"Bye."

She came back in and couldn't tell if he'd heard or not but decided against asking. She was disappointed by Justice's departure and didn't want to hurt Chess's feelings. She saw he didn't look sleepy for someone who had been up all night. It wasn't that long till rest time.

"Okay. So I'm behind on doggie walks and thought you could come out this evening and give it a go." She kept her eyes on her mug.

"Dogs tolerate us at best. They often flee or more often defend their master. Not a good idea." He thought this was not the direction his comments to her were supposed to go.

"Good idea or not, I think it's a matter of socialization and the character of the breed. I want to try. Will you come?"

He could see how important it was to her. "You want to ensure your dogs are properly socialized to vampires?"

Claryn crossed her arms and looked at him hard. "Is that a 'no'?"

Chess couldn't say no.

"Are your hours changing or is this later schedule for this week only?" he asked instead.

"I think Mrs. Smithson is seeing someone. She asked me about shifting my hours for a while and I agreed. It's hard to picture who she might be out with."

"I'm your gossip girlfriend now, aren't I?"

"No. Don't be silly. Isn't it almost your bedtime?"

"Ah, definitely not a girlfriend." His face clouded a moment, then perked back up as he stretched and yawned in grand style.

"Think I'll retire now." He gave her a key, waggled his eyebrows, and moseyed away.

Claryn came down so soon she thought she'd be right on his heels but he was ready for bed.

Considering his phone call with Arvon, he was thinking this would be one of their last sessions. He could have stood for this to go on for some time.

Necessity is the mother of invention, he thought. Chess was still Chess. "I had another idea," he said as she entered his room.

"Do tell." She stood leaning against the door, all attention. He stood as well.

"You said it wasn't the same because we're friends like Kelley or George."

"Yeah." Her brows were knit in confusion as he approached her but her heart rate was steady. He stopped in front of her and to the side so that the room was open to her.

"I thought for the purposes of real therapy, we should discuss a concept known as 'friends with benefits'."

She blinked at him as if he was joking, but he reached out and stroked her hair and searched her eyes. She barely reacted when he rubbed his knuckles across her cheek. Pulse slower but steady.

Then he put on his scary face and she knew he was joking around. He's not serious, she thought as he put his left hand behind her neck. She kept thinking that right up to the moment he leaned in too close to ignore.

"What are you doing?" Her fingers splayed on his chest pushing weakly.

He looked into her eyes and found he didn't have it in him.

"I don't know."

Claryn misunderstood his answer and her last thought was, "He's out of control." Her heart almost stopped, her legs gave way and she fell completely limp into his arms.

"Claryn." He hadn't meant to make her pass out. He lifted her up and carried her to the bed, laying her down. He looked around for something to serve as a fan. Her limp body and weak pulse scared him into an intense realization. He and Justice were more together than apart on all things Claryn.

With relief he heard her pulse strengthening. He was out of time.

"I'm sorry, Claryn." He kissed her on the forehead and laid down on the floor beside the bed, knowing orders or no orders, he would not violate her trust again.

267

Dizzy and disoriented, Claryn looked around confused. She couldn't think how she got here, and then she remembered. Chess had gotten close, too close, and she'd passed out. She felt at her neck, then realized it was a futile gesture since they didn't leave marks. Thinking on the conversation from the previous evening, she wasn't even sure that she didn't want him to have bit her. At least then they would know how the venom affected her.

"Chess?" She wondered if he was resting in the spare room. She lay still for a few minutes. His expression had been so intense, his eyes bright and then almost sad. Still she couldn't call up any real fear of Chess, despite his forwardness. He was such a flirt.

I should have expected this. Who knows, maybe it will help.

She sat up swinging her legs off the bed and spotted him laid out on the cold concrete without even a blanket.

He's so big. There's no way I'll get him up here. She took the pillow and placed it under his head. Then she took the sheet and covered him like she'd seen him do yesterday. His hands seemed larger, his arms stronger, his chest broader. He hasn't changed, it's how I'm looking at him.

She got down on the floor, sitting much as she had yesterday but on the opposite side. She took his hand and ran it through her hair as he had. Her heart reacted. She worked on being comfortable with that for a while.

Then she put his hand behind her neck. Nothing. She felt silly but still thought how wonderful it was to be trusted. To trust. What she needed to work on was something small. Something she could try with Justice. Holding hands. She closed her eyes, held his hand, and tried to imagine he was Justice.

The lookout Adams posted at the homestead house did his job and received his payment before returning to Santa Fe. It was an easy if boring task and the youth thought he would miss the easy money. The man making the payment was loaded for bear, a large caliber gun the likes of which the youth had only seen in movies or TV shows.

"You don't want to come back around here anytime soon. It'd be a shame if someone mistook you for a mountain lion," the gunman said.

It was all the warning the youth needed.

"You have my number if I can be of service."

"Best if you forget this place all together."

Definitely a threat. He hopped his ride and took the most direct route back to the city.

Mrs. Smithson rang in with a favor to ask Claryn. She wanted to know if Claryn would stay over and do a forty-eight hour shift sometime soon. Overtime would be in order, and she would make it up to her afterward with a couple paid days off. Claryn knew she'd still be able to get away from the kennel for several hours at a time when she needed to.. So even though she'd be on the clock there was no reason she could not get other things done as needed. Claryn happily agreed.

Chess's arrival at the shelter provoked barking and whining on a scale hitherto unknown. Dogs in their runs ran inside. Claryn was in the kennel area and thought some catastrophe must have befallen. It wasn't difficult to see that her extra dog walker would be no help at all.

Still she held out some hope. Felix tentatively wanted to go into the front room with her despite the presence of the vampire. If introductions were arranged properly, Felix might produce the courage necessary to make a new friend. This suddenly felt very important to Claryn.

Chess was anxious, and it sat very oddly on him.

"Claryn, about this morning."

"Did you?" She turned her bare neck toward him and gestured with fang fingers.

"No! No, I couldn't. I mean, I wouldn't."

Her clear disappointment confused him.

"Why are you….? Did you want me to?"

269

"No. I just thought if you were a little carried away, then, well, but here I am fit as a fiddle, so that means Justice couldn't, you know?"

"I see."

The raucous barking increased as he came over to the counter, which was closer to the kennel door.

"Told you," he said nodding towards the pandemonium at her rear.

"I'm not giving up that easily. What we need to do is make you as non-threatening as possible."

"I'm not going to sleep out here."

"You're on the right track, though. Do you mind?"

She wanted his button up shirt, which he was reluctant to give up, as it had no defense against the beasts in the next room. He would have rather given her his t-shirt but was glad he didn't. She had him lay down on his stomach with only his feet visible from the kennel door. His hands were down by his side. Then she went to talk with Felix.

Felix was so pleased to see her he jumped all around her. The canine must have thought his mistress's doom eminent. When he caught a whiff of the shirt she was wearing, he backed away and growled. She talked to him, sat down, and took the shirt off wadding it in her lap.

Felix wanted to come. He sidled up to her back and away again. She began talking to the shirt like it was a puppy, petting it, nuzzling it, so Felix couldn't stand it. She saw him from the corner of her eye cautiously. From the side he nosed her and then the shirt.

"See. That's not so bad. And you, what a brave good doggie. Good dog."

Now to try it with the real beast instead of his shirt, she thought. Felix was ready enough now to be coaxed into the front room. It didn't take too much. When the door to the kennel area closed behind him, he stopped near it, sniffed the air, and gave a little whine.

Claryn got down on the floor with the dog.

"Good dog. Who's that?"

She crawled over and put Chess's feet between herself and Felix. Felix didn't much like this. He went in a wide arch around to the front door and paced a bit, watching Claryn. She did the same act again, petting the back of Chess's calves, talking to them like they were wonderful cuddly creatures, and occasionally inviting Felix over.

Chess would have laughed but didn't want to sabotage Claryn. Felix did zigzags walking closer and closer till he sniffed a foot, poked it with his nose and backed off, though not as far. Claryn moved up to Chess's hands, stepping over to his far side while keeping her body down low.

Felix didn't much like not having her between him and the bad smell. He eyed her petting Chess's lower arms and finally came over to sniff them. She smothered him with praise and he relaxed a bit.

To Chess it seemed miraculous. He actually got to pet Felix with his hand down by his side. It was an unanticipated pleasure he could not remember ever having had.

"If you stick around here enough, he'll warm up to you." To the dog, "You just love your pats too much, lil' attention monger. You'd do better with Justice, wouldn't you?"

Chess moved his arms under his head, causing Felix to back off warily but only a few feet. What she said didn't make any sense.

"Why would he do better with Justice?"

She considered. "Well, you're bigger, more intimidating, physically, I mean."

"To a dog, right? Or have I unsettled things."

She didn't answer immediately, and he saw he had unsettled things between them. She wasn't as free and at ease with him.

"It's a good thing, though," she was saying. "It's more realistic for the therapy."

"I might be intimidating, even stronger. But Justice is more dangerous."

Claryn threw him an odd look. She wasn't baited into asking how.

"Are you stronger? Your fight seemed pretty even."

271

The reasons Chess was stronger were complicated and the reason he gave to her was the not the primary one.

"It's not size. It's age among other things. I wish he'd have let me go to the homestead instead of him."

An edge of worry crept into Chess's words.

"Why? What's going on at the homestead?"

He was relieved to have her ask. She asked far too few questions.

"There. Finally. You need to ask more questions, you know. The quick silver buck shots Justice had, he got them down there."

Claryn gasped. Her own discovery that night had eclipsed that part of the episode. Checking on the property at what sounded like a peaceful home-type place was not at all what Justice was doing. When she'd heard 'the homestead' she'd mentally pictured something as peaceful and safe like the house from "The Walton's". She realized this might not be the case at all.

"No." She stood, startling Felix, who took alarm and gave a bark at the unseen menace.

"You should go. He shouldn't be there alone, shouldn't be sleeping there." Her urgent tenor rose even as her heart slowed. "Why did he go there at all?"

"The man who led the first attack against Justice wants something. Wants it very badly. If he doesn't find it there, he'll look elsewhere and carry out his revenge as he goes. We need him to show himself and his intentions."

"Revenge?" Claryn didn't like to contemplate why the man would seek revenge against the brothers, especially since his reasons might be legitimate.

"It's not like that. He's set himself up as if he's a righteous ranger set on slaying our evil ilk. In truth, he is a Mission 2B Immortal reject who is angry enough to kill. At the same time he's trying to steal what he needs to become one of us."

"That's crazy. How could he steal--"

"The farther you go in the game, the more outlandish the scenarios become. There's a whole race of vampires who made themselves by taking blood from others of the kind. It doesn't help that when this guy actually took blood from . . ." he almost said her name, "a female. It probably altered his senses for a time. The blood will never do what he wants, though, without being given."

"How do you know all this?"

Her every question now produced a pleased expression on his part.

"We have a well-connected colleague of sorts to the north who keeps tabs on . . .well, I don't know everything he monitors or does. It's a lot."

"Should you be telling me all this?"

"He told me to tell you."

"You told him about me?"

Chess was apologetic. "Justice and I are at the center of this situation because we had connections to the female. Anything that affects our judgment . . ."

"...or disturbs Justice is problematic. I'm a dangerous distraction, aren't I?"

Chess nodded sadly.

Disheartened, her shoulders slumped.

"Or a valuable asset," he added after a moment helpfully.

"I should have stayed away. It's not like Justice would take the only thing I've got to give. The mercury, it can kill you, right?"

"It can. The priority is to get it out of our bodies before we rest. When we're down, our whole system goes down. The quicksilver would continue its work while we lay defenseless."

"You've lived for how many years? And then here I come, fouling things up. How would I live with myself if . . . and if it was my fault?"

"The situation is what it is, and you can still walk away. We're not the only ones at risk. Bullets are bullets no matter what they're made of." He half hoped she would walk away even if it meant she took their hearts with her and he'd have some explaining to do to Arvon.

273

"I don't have anything that madman wants. How can I be anything but a dangerous diversion?" she asked.

"There is an emergency number for Arvon, our northern neighbor that you could call if we were indisposed. Plus you are awake when we are not."

"But I'm here most days, not at the shop."

"It's unlikely any of this will come to Hallston. Adams knows about the homestead because the female had been there, likely followed her there. He would have to do some real digging to find anything connecting that place and this one. We're ready for him now. Justice will call me when Adams turns up and we'll. . .take care of it." He sat up causing Felix to engage in some round about maneuvering before he sidled up beside Claryn and kept her in the middle again.

Justice watched the hills knowing they had eyes right now. When would they make their move? Should he call Chess? His talk was big on going it alone, but two were stronger than one. A voice in the back of his mind spoke. A cord of three is not easily broken. Sometimes he felt like he had a cartoon character miniature sitting on his shoulder, feeding his mind perspectives that weren't entirely his own. Instead of a devil on one shoulder and an angel on the other, he had a tiny Chess and something like a perched owl claiming to be wisdom on the other.

There aren't three, there are two, and two have worked fine for a couple hundred years. No need to start mucking about.

And what if something did happen to him, alone in what was once a finely appointed home where they had tried to make a go of coven life with Jenny? Justice pictured Chess comforting Claryn. Claryn, who gave without thinking. How much would she give to be there for his brother? Too much.

He had been cautiously investigating the house for signs of entry during his rest. Certain the watchers remained at a distance, he prepared to rest again. Call for reinforcements, he thought, the voice on his

274

shoulder not making a suggestion, but giving a command. He decided to listen to the owl.

Rather than call Chess directly and leave a digital connection to their home, he called a line that Arvon had bounce around the continent before it connected to his location in Colorado. The woman on the other end took the note.

"For Mr. C. Cain from Mr. J. Cain. Come. They watch."

Justice knew Chess would work out his own relay area and Arvon would monitor the situation as well. He lay down thinking, at least if we go down together, Claryn can move on to a good normal life. Justice wasn't usually doom and gloom, but his recent experience with the quicksilver poisoning had shaken his confidence.

Adams wanted to find their new lair, knew if he found it he would have the leads and leverage he needed to get what he wanted.

He watched Fleets rubbing down the stock of his rifle with a soft yellow cotton cloth. It was reminiscent of watching a woman taking a shower as she caressed her body with the sudsy soap. Fleets would not miss, and this time they were ready for the chase. Adams had only to give the word. It was all so close and almost within his grasp.

Chapter 40

Claryn was locking up the last kennel when her cell phone lit up with Chess's number. She had asked him for a photo for the caller ID, but he'd said no. Photos weren't forbidden, just discouraged. She treasured the hard copy she had from Kelley's wedding reception of Justice with her, and had shown it to no one.

"Hello?"

"Hey, Claryn. I'm going to go join JT at the homestead. It's safer if there are two of us since we know there are a couple of them."

"Has something happened? Is he okay?"

"He's good. This is a precaution, that's all. Will you be okay at the shop on your own for a few days?"

"Sure. Do you want me to do anything at the shop like field phone calls or sort mail?"

"No. Best to leave that for us."

Claryn heard the engine of his car fire up.

"Do you have your key? I can bring one by."

"Not necessary, I've got it right here. When will I hear from you?"

"I don't know about that. If it's longer than a week, send up a flare to our friend in the north."

"Saying what?"

"That I told you to call if you didn't hear anything."

"Okay. You all take care of each other."

"Always. You take care of yourself."

"Will do. Be careful, Chess."

"Careful is my middle name," he sarcastasized.

"Uh-huh."

"Goodbye, Claryn."

Goodbye sounded ominous to her.

"See you soon," she said before ending the call.

Fleets, the sniper, radioed Adams when he saw the new arrival making an approach on the northern road. They hadn't been sure what Adams was waiting for, but Fleets could tell from the devilish, pleased tone of voice that this was it. He had to hand it to Adams, his gut instincts for these creatures were on the money. Fleets loosened up and stretched out, readying himself for the shots he'd need to take both the beasts down.

The prospect of a day off with both brothers away agitated Claryn as she puttered around the shop eating cereal for supper. The days went faster when she was working. She called Mrs. Smithson to ask if she could trade tomorrow's day off for a work day next week. Mrs. Smithson was happy to oblige.

Afterwards, Claryn played Mission 2B Immortal and found new resources on level two she hadn't collected before. At least that was something she could offer to show Chess when he returned.

Her thinking was that she would stay up in case they called. Knowing there was nothing at the shop she could do for them did not alleviate her sense that Chess would call, regardless of what he'd said. When she lay over on the sofa to watch television, though, she fell fast asleep.

Justice was up and the sun was down by a couple hours when Chess came rolling up in a well worn Pontiac Grand Am. Justice was laughing at Chess's choice of wheels when the first shot was fired. It passed over the hood of the car ripping into Chess's side. A second later Justice heard the rifle's report and pinned the origin to within a couple feet to the west.

Fleets would never have gotten a second shot were it not for the stupidity of his other target. That vamp moved so fast he appeared to teleport from the front porch down to the driveway where the first creature stood grasping his side.

277

Justice intentionally blocked Chess from the shooter's view and grabbed his brother by the arms. "Chess!"

Chess grimaced, "Let's get into--" Justice suddenly arched his back, eyes wide as two more rounds slammed into his body. He didn't let go of his brother as they walked over and into the car. Justice took a third and fourth body shot but successfully protected Chess from further injury.

Chess ducked into the car, pulling his now staggering brother in behind him and turning the engine over. He ignored the searing pain and drove straight to the east side of the house putting distance between himself and the shooter before cutting out by a track they once used to collect water from the distant wash in the springtime.

Justice was writhing on the back seat where he'd crawled to get away from Chess. The quicksilver wasn't just under the skin this time, it was lodged deep and caused him to spasm periodically from a fetal position out to a rigid plank, at least as much of one as he could make inside the car. Once he kicked the door so hard he thought it would come off its hinges and open the car up to the night. Chess slammed down on the gas pedal even harder.

The progress of the burning and poisoning of his internal systems began to shut down his senses. The jet engines landed in his ear canals again first, then the white iris of his eyes began overtaking his yellow pupils till he lost his sight. Finally, he could no longer feel the leather upholstery on which he lay. All he felt was a forest fire spreading slowly through his insides. He smelled his own flesh burning.

When Chess hit the paved road in a flurry of dust and squealing tires he looked back quickly and saw the headlights of a tail in the distance. Getting rid of it took some quick thinking. He intentionally slowed on a route notorious for its speed trap and fortunately the state troopers there were true to their routine. Chess's pursuer was into the trap, having to pull over as the cop gave chase with a flash of light. Chess then sped up in the higher speed zone beyond it and left the other car in the flashing lights of the trooper. It would buy them some time, hopefully enough.

The burn in his side was like nothing he'd ever experienced before. He'd gotten caught in the sun for a couple moments too long once when he was young and reckoned this was on par to that except there was no shade in sight.

By the time he made the trade out point for cars outside Albuquerque, JT was no longer responsive. Unseeing eyes stared wide and fear gripped Chess. Home was closer than Arvon, but he couldn't be sure of getting help at the shop.

He was heartened by the powerful fight JT put up against being taken into the other vehicle when they traded cars out. He knew where the right tools were at the shop and that made his decision.

Abandoning the Pontiac, he tore out through the night to the west as his ears heard a faint ringing in the distance like church bells.

Claryn woke with a start. Sleeping on the sofa without a pillow left a crick in her neck that she rubbed as she blinked at the shop. Lights were on all over and she knew she hadn't left them on.

Uncomprehendingly she saw the door going up on bay four, Justice's bay, as she thought of it. Her heart rose in her chest and she started to stand.

Chess jumped out of the car and practically tore the back door off in his haste as he threw it wide open. Claryn watched with mute horror as he carried a quivering balled up Justice over and laid him down on the couch Claryn had just been asleep on.

"Stay away from him!" he yelled at such a volume that Claryn put her hands over her ears and cowered. Chess ran through to the kitchen, back to the tool chests against the far wall. He yanked drawers out onto the floor and, finding what he sought, returned to the couch.

Chess held the silver-bladed knife that Claryn was intimately familiar with. Chess looked down at his dying brother and quickly lay open a two-inch section of his own wrist and tried to hold it to Justice's mouth.

279

Justice did not latch on and the small drops that made it into this mouth caused him to retch violently.

"I was afraid of that," Chess snarled.

Chess looked at Claryn's bloodless face, her hands over her ears and the way her eyes were locked on JT. He felt a rush of sympathy.

"I'm sorry I yelled. I can't hear so good right now," Chess explained.

Claryn seemed frozen, but her heart and breathing were steady.

"Claryn, this is going to be okay. We just have to get the quicksilver out, like you did before. Okay?"

"I can help?"

"Yes. You hand me what I ask for, okay?"

She nodded.

Chess took an oversized hunting knife from the coffee table and poised it over JT.

"The shots are deep this time. Don't freak out on me."

Claryn nodded again and watched him plunge the knife deep into JT's abdomen. It was only by looking at the holes in his clothes that Chess had any idea where the poison was lodged.

When he got deep enough he thought JT's body would expel the vile liquid. Some of it gurgled up very slowly but the cut began to heal around the knife, shutting the mercury inside again.

Chess told Claryn where in the shop to get metal tubing and how to cut it. He was impressed with how quickly and efficiently she worked under stress and she soon returned with the tubes. Chess took the cut pieces and stabbed them one at time into the bullet holes. His plan was to leave the tubing in place as a drainpipe for the mercury. He hoped it worked.

Claryn was asking him something, but Chess could barely hear her. He squinted his eyes as she repeated her question.

"Why didn't your blood help like last time?"

In answer Chess pulled up his jacket to show her the hole in his own shirt.

"My blood is poisoned too." He spoke loudly.

"I could--"

"No!" he cut her off. "That's not an option." I gave my word, he thought. He shook his head no and rolled JT over on his side hoping gravity would help the vile poison drain.

"I can get him blood, from someone I know the venom won't hurt." Chess said suddenly. "What time is it?"

"Six."

"It's early to call, but I think one or both of them will come to Hallston if I ask. Stay here and see if you can keep him turned. He's too weak now to be a threat to you."

Chess walked over to use the landline thinking the ID from the shop might get an answer faster than the Unknown ID from his cell phone. He glanced back at Claryn who was now cradling JT's head in her lap. Chess didn't want Claryn to hear his conversation with the good time girls, the facade he would put on for them. He stepped into the office and closed the door.

Claryn glanced up as the door shut and then let the tears she'd been holding back roll.

"Justice? Can you hear me?"

She was thinking about what the brothers had told her about the dangers of the venom, weighing that against Justice's condition.

Waiting.

She heard Chess cursing in the other room and knew one of his options wasn't one anymore.

Justice stopped quivering and got so still she thought he was dead.

"No, no, no, no!" Her eyes went wild looking around and fell on the knife. Justice's body rolled on its back as she leaned over to grab it up from the toolbox table.

She didn't hesitate at all. She cut her arm like she'd seen Chess do and hardly felt the incision at first because the blade was incredibly sharp.

281

She opened Justice's mouth and put her bleeding arm in it, afraid she was already too late.

He took a breath and with relief she watched his jaws flex wide before he bit down into the soft flesh of her arm.

The pain was like having something sharp pressed against her skin but not enough to break the surface, or at least it felt that way. In a couple moments her arm began to tingle and her whole body felt relaxed.

Justice's hands had come up from his sides to hold her arm on both sides of the bite as he drank. Claryn smiled and saw some of the mercury forcefully expelled out the drainage tube. She tried to roll Justice back on his side and realized he was no longer limp and compliant.

Familiar with the feeling of lowered blood pressure, she knew when enough was getting close to being too much.

"Justice?"

She tried to pull away, to push him off her lap, but she couldn't even budge his head.

"Chess!" She raised her voice as the office door opened.

"Chess! Help me!"

Chess leaped over the couch with white eyes and a roar.

He jerked both of JT's hands away from Claryn's and shoved her back from JT who snarled at him in protest.

Claryn fell away on the floor and sat holding her arm as the puncture wounds closed and healed over before her very eyes. The incision was long gone.

Chess easily wrestled his still weak brother off the couch and down the stairs into his room.

The quicksilver had forcefully erupted out of the tubes till nothing was left, but Justice's eyes were still opaque. He obviously wasn't registering what was happening. Claryn hoped it wouldn't be long till he was resting, with her new given lifeblood metabolizing in his system, he would wake better, she told herself.

Chess locked Justice in his room and came back up the stairs with a prayer on his lips for Claryn and her reaction to the venom.

"Chess?"

"I'm here. Are you okay?"

"Is Justice okay?"

"He's going to be fine, thanks to you. How are you?"

Claryn smiled tiredly, "I'm great."

Chess looked so worried as he patted her forehead, listened to her heart and looked back and forth in her eyes.

"What's the verdict, Doctor Chess?" she seemed tipsy.

He relaxed back across from her, leaning against the couch behind him.

"I think you're going to live."

"Yay!" She clapped her hands.

New pain seized him and he doubled over backing away from her.

"Now you," she pointed, concern coming over her face.

He held up a hand to ward her off and then took the knife and stabbed into his own side as Claryn crawled over with another tube. He sank it into his wound but it seemed he had waited too long. The burning inside was spreading and the pain brought clarity rather than thirst. He knew his poisoning wasn't as bad as JT's, that he had only the one spot getting broader.

Claryn picked up the knife again.

"What are you doing?"

She grinned, "Your turn."

"Stop. You don't need to do that."

She scooted over by him, "I'm not going to watch you die any more than I'd let Justice die. I love you too, you know."

He searched her face. "I'm okay. . . If I can get downstairs and rest, I'll be fine."

She squinted into his eyes, nodded and stood.

He stood too and they walked down the stairs together. When he was laid out on his bed she pulled up the chair beside him looking at the walls and ceiling again and then back at the tube.

"Nothing's coming out," she practically sang.

Chess thought how miserable it would be to be near her after a taste. How hard it would be to not want more. How likely it was that JT was going to want to kill him anyway for letting her feed herself to him when JT was in a poison induced mania.

"I'll be fine."

Claryn half sat on the bed and patted him on both cheeks like a small child.

"You are a rotten liar, Fran-ces-co Cain. A great painter, but a rotten liar. If you don't take what I'm giving now, I'll just wait till you're asleep and slit my wrist into your mouth. I'm betting you won't bite and without the venom I might just bleed out here at your bedside. What would your JT say about that?"

Chess looked pained but knew Claryn was feeling none. She was so matter-of-fact wagging her finger at him and talking about slitting her wrist. She was tapping the side of her head now.

"I remember what you told me. The only thing your body will do while you rest is metabolize blood. So you're getting it one way or the other."

She waved her arm around over toward his face, the opposite arm from the one she gave Justice.

He took it in his hands and frowned at her one more time as she turned to sit in the chair again with her arm draped over him.

"You won't hurt me." She sounded more sober. "I trust you."

Claryn had been playing up the euphoric effects of Justice's bite. It was easier to say what needed saying that way.

Chess closed his eyes and bit down much more gently than Justice had done. The pressure was soft and light and the prick of pain but a moment.

It seemed he drew a moment and pulled away quickly, as if testing himself to see if he could.

"I told you," she said.

He could feel his body pressing the burning back to a finite point. Still the quicksilver did not gurgle out. He closed his eyes and bit down again, long enough to make it the last. He pushed her arm away and turned his head to the wall watching the poison run out of the tube. After a few moments the mercury stopped pouring out onto the floor and Chess lost the inside burning feeling. He pulled the tube from his side and threw it down to the end of the bed.

"Chess? It's okay. It's mine to give, right? You're okay?"

He turned his head to face her, knowing he was moments from unconsciousness.

"Things won't be the same anymore, Claryn love. I'm sorry."

He closed his eyes and fell into repose.

She locked his door, leaving him a key, and took the one for Justice's room. In there she wrapped up in a blanket and sat in the chair with her head resting on one arm on the side of the bed and her other arm limp in her lap as she fell asleep.

Justice woke feeling a little strange, but grateful that Chess had gotten them home and was able to take care of the poisoning. He scanned his room, thinking a piece of Claryn's clothing must be nearby. The room was filled with her scent so strongly he would have salivated over it as a human.

He sniffed around and realized it was most pungent on his clothing. Alarmed he pulled the front of his shirt out and saw the blood, and without thought he held it up to his face and breathed deeply of it. He let his head rock back against the stonewall with force as he made fists and shook them.

"No!"

285

He thought he was paralyzed with fear for her, but when Chess, having heard his cry, opened the door, he vaulted from the bed and crashed them both out the door and into the hallway wall.

"Where is she?"

"JT--"

Justice could smell her on Chess as well and threw his brother like a heavy piece of luggage down the hall.

"She's fine!" Chess yelled. "She went to work! Everything is okay."

The fight went out of him as JT slid down the wall in relief and sat on the concrete floor with his elbows resting on his knees. He was shaking his head back and forth.

"How could you?"

"I wasn't even there, at first. I went to call one of the girls and the next thing I know she'd cut her wrist and, well, you know."

"She's okay?" Aside from being stubborn as a mule.

"Yes."

Chess sat across from his brother, watching him process it all. He was stretching his arms in front of him, making a fist and pressing it into his other palm.

"It feels so different," JT said.

"It does," Chess said it as if he was experiencing something new as well.

"What do you mean? It's not like this is the first time you've had human blood given to you."

"No, but what I've been 'given' was cart blanche, not someone knowingly giving their lifeblood for me. By the time Jenny knew what was what, she wasn't giving out of a care for me but because she wanted what she wanted for herself. This is different. Makes me realize how right you were about my way being dishonest. I avoided the death taint, but I've never received the life."

Justice heard what Chess did not say. There was no going back now to that dishonest way. Chess was on the wagon to stay. As glad as Justice

286

was that he could not remember what he'd done, he felt jealous that Chess could.

"I was first and then you—"

"I wasn't going to do it. Didn't think you'd like it much. Claryn threatened to slit her own wrist after I was resting and I'd already seen her do it with you…so"

"I didn't know she was so stubborn."

"She's a survivor. She'd do well—"

Justice turned a cold eye on Chess as they stood.

"We're not going there. You are not even to discuss it with her."

"You're not calling the shots anymore."

"What does that mean?" asked Justice.

"When you acted like you weren't going to call me in even if you needed me, I called Arvon. He knows about her."

"Chess!" JT was clearly hurt. "If he thinks it's in his best interest, he won't even give her a choice."

"Then I suggest you don't give him a reason to doubt your--"

"That's going to be hard line to walk, especially now. Leaving her alone and not leaving half my mind here whenever I go."

Chess hid his frustration. Claryn knew what they were, took the venom fine, had saved their lives, and JT's one-track mind focused on letting her go. There was nothing Chess could do. JT would have to figure out for himself how stubborn his Claryn was.

There was nothing else to be said. Chess hit the wall experimentally and his hand went through the cinderblocks to the earth beyond.

"This is freaky." The two exchanged glances, smiled, and jostled each other as they ran up the steps to find more things to test.

Adams reported the car of interest stolen and waited for the police to find it in the Albuquerque area. It didn't take long before the location went out on the police scanner and Adams went to search the Grand-Am before it could be impounded.

He hadn't expected to find a clue to the vampires' location in the car. What he did find was the previous owner of the vehicle, a small used car lot west of downtown Albuquerque.

Fortunately for Adams, the original salesman of the Pontiac was still around and remembered the late evening sale of the vehicle and the man who had made the purchase. Cash payment wasn't that unusual. What he remembered best though were the buyer's other set of wheels. A sweet Chevrolet Monte Carlo, custom rebuilt. Adams got a detailed description of the vehicle.

The salesman hadn't asked to that point why Adams was interested in the buyer, but the ready story of the missing woman in Santa Fe and the photo got the salesman to seriously rack his brain. He produced the smoking gun Adams needed, all but the last digit of the Arizona license plate.

Chapter 41

Claryn returned to the shop to find bay one a mess of torn metal. An engine block lay open and the guys were laughing over it.

Chess called over to her, "You have got to see this!"

Justice came to her, studied her face, and took in the way she was carrying herself. He was half in disbelief she looked so good and half concern over her welfare.

"You're tired. What did you eat today?" Justice asked her.

"I don't know. Fruit, some nuts, crackers."

Chess strode over. "I should have thought of that. I'll make a run. Be back in a jiffy."

Claryn's face showed confusion as Justice led her over to the sofa.

"The nuts were good, high in iron, but you need some red meat as well."

"That sounds really good."

Claryn winced as she sat on the black leather holding her right arm across her front as if ready to begin the pledge of allegiance.

"What's wrong with your arm?"

"Just a little twist. If I hold still like this it doesn't hurt too much."

"Show me."

Claryn shied away. not wanting him to see the pain. She only added to his concern and resolve.

"If it's that bad, I will take you to the emergency room right now."

"No." She was quick to answer and then very carefully took her jacket off her shoulder and gingerly down around her arm without moving the limb. At the elbow her arm was swollen and discolored with bruises that looked yellow and purple as if they'd been healing there for days.

"Oh, Claryn." He looked sick. "Did I do this to you?"

"No, not exactly." She could see he was already beating himself up over it. "You can't kick yourself every time I stub my toe."

"This is not a stubbed toe. How exactly did it happen?" He was trying to see it from every angle without her having to move.

"Exactly?"

"Yes. Exactly."

"Um, well, Chess grabbed my arm with one hand and—"

Justice glowered.

"And shoved you away with the other and I fell on the ground."

He knew it was his fault. He wanted to be angry with Chess, but his brother had done what was necessary. It had taken this kind of force to get him off her.

"We shouldn't have come back here at all," he said.

Claryn's throat closed with anxiety, her heart beat faster and her breaths came quick.

"Don't say that, please don't, don't say that."

He ignored her pleas, shook his head and stood.

"I'll take you to the hospital. Your arm might be broken and now partially healed wrong because of the venom."

She stood and turned on him, defensively.

"I am not going to the hospital. It's not broken. Look!"

She bit her lip, straightened her arm and broke out in a light sweat from the pain as she twisted her arm and folded it up.

"See? Not broken," she panted holding it out straight again in defiance.

Justice turned his head away eyeing her arm and frowning. She recognized the posture as what Chess had done the night before.

"Your eyes are turning white. Why?"

He tried to shake the thought he'd had and clear his vision.

"I'm a temptation now, aren't I?"

"You've always been a temptation."

"More so. You've never done that before around me. Or was it? What were you thinking. . .when it happened?"

She held her arm out again, walking toward him and seeing the effect she had on him. He backed away immediately with a look of panic in his eyes. It reminded her of something.

"Blood issues," she chuckled. "You have blood issues and not the kind that make you pass out. But you didn't do this at my house when I was dripping . . .What are you thinking?"

"I'm thinking you can be awfully stubborn and pushy."

Claryn grinned and responded, "I only get that way with people I care about. What were you thinking before that?"

He gave in with a sigh. "I was thinking if it's not broken, I could fix it."

"Oh," Claryn wasn't afraid. Her expression was all curiosity. "How?"

"Look, you don't simply tolerate the venom. It works on everyone's skin. But your bruises are healing, when you were anxious earlier your heart rate sped up instead of bottoming out. If you had more venom around the injured area your arm would probably heal quickly."

"Ah, you're already thinking up excuses to bite me again." Her eyes were teasing him.

"Claryn."

"What? I'm wrong? That's not what made your face go all--vampire on me?"

She said it so easily; she was too comfortable with it already.

"You're not wrong and you're not right. I don't have to drink to bite. I wasn't thinking of doing that."

"Oh." She expressed her disappointment.

"That's not the proper response."

"Proper response-schmonse." Her defiant stance spoke volumes.

"Why are you so willing to do this?"

She studied the floor before answering. "I don't make much of a girlfriend, do I? We've been out how many times and barely held hands, never kissed, and can hardly be close at all unless you're unconscious! I

291

thought this was something we'd have, for us, while I work on my other issues."

Exasperated and unwilling to continue the conversation at that point, Justice sat down and put one hand out for her arm. She sat down hesitantly and held it out to him.

He began in the bend of her arm, his canines making tiny gentle pinpricks as he went around her arm inch by inch. His mouth and other teeth were so light on her skin that it tickled and she tried not to twitch.

Watching his mouth on her skin, her pulse quickened with her breathing and she steadied herself for the familiar feelings of weakness that didn't come. The usual fear was there mixed with excitement, pleasure, and the heady elation the venom roused.

"Justice? I think. . ." She reached out for him as he watched the bruising disappear.

He dropped her arm and went to his feet scrutinizing her. She was certainly under the influence and needed a wake-up call.

"I think we should start apartment hunting for you your next day off. When will that be?"

"What?" She was blinking back tears as Chess came in.

"I know I was slow, but I forgot that Darryl would be waiting for my to-go box from the steak house, so I had to go back in and place the order again." Oblivious to the atmosphere in the room, Chess retrieved silverware from the kitchen and brought Claryn's dinner over to her.

"Thank you, Chess."

His head whipped up to her face in surprise at the sound of her voice. "Good grief, JT. You coulda at least waited till she ate something before you went at her again."

If Justice were a loony-tune cartoon character, smoke would have streamed out his ears. Without a word he stormed out the front door, letting it slam shut behind him.

"Huh. Have you noticed he's a tad sensitive when it comes to jokes about you?"

"He's kicking me out. Said it was time I looked for an apartment."
Claryn was hurt.

"Aw, Claryn. Look at it this way. How's he supposed to pick you up for dates if you're living in the same place?"

"I don't think that's the direction of his thinking."

"Yeah, well. Hey, why did he bite you again?"

"My arm was pretty messed up, twisted."

Chess inspected her arm seeing no remaining damage.

"I did that didn't I? I'm sorry. You didn't tell him how it got injured did you?"

"He was very demanding."

"Absolute honesty is not necessarily a good thing between a guy and a gal. Voice of experience here."

Chess moved down to the end of the sofa ostensibly to pick up a remote, but he didn't come sidling back the way he was prone.

Claryn chewed thoughtfully on her steak, though she'd never been one for much red meat, it sure tasted good tonight.

"You're avoiding me too, aren't you?"

Chess's face was apologetic. He tried to explain.

"Right now the smell of that steak, the taste of it, and even the texture are mixed together in your senses. Give it a day or two and those will sort themselves out."

I'm a steak. "Where do you think Justice went?"

"I don't know. He'll be back. You have an early day tomorrow right?"

She nodded.

"Don't wait up for him."

"I should find my own place soon, shouldn't I?"

"I think it's for the best. Now." He clapped his hands in readiness. "You are going to help me on my Mission 2B Immortal."

Outside Albuquerque, Justice paced around his Chevy in circles that delineated from an half mile out down to a few yards. He wouldn't have considered running this far before, but then again, he had never been this strong.

His heightened senses told him no humans had been near the car. At least it wouldn't be a lead for the slayer crew. He hopped behind the wheel and covered the distance back to Hallston in near record time.

"Sir, the person of interest we've been tracking is going west out of Albuquerque."

Arvon did not look up from what he was reading as he responded.

"Very well. Put Carson on standby with the Cessna. Report back if the target stops for longer than an hour anywhere within a fifty mile radius of ground zero."

"Yes, sir."

The vehicle registration took Adams to a small home off the grid between Winslow, Arizona and Flagstaff. The owner identified himself, admitted to owning the vehicle and stated he didn't know the current location of the car.

After going round a few times on questions, Adams happened to pull a large roll of bills out of his pocket as he was getting a business card out to leave with the man. The roll produced an instant light of interest and clarity in the man and a Ben Franklin with Adams' card jarred the man's memory. Turned out he was paid in cash to be the owner of the car which he had never set eyes on.

Adams peeled off another bill. "And from which direction on the highway does this regular cash payment come?"

"It usually comes from the postman who comes and goes that way. One time it came from a man who goes that way." The man indicated the west.

The forthcoming description of the man did not match either of his targets, but Adams was unconcerned. He thanked the owner of the Chevrolet Monte Carlo and went back to his car.

Pulling out from the driveway, he looked both directions and decided to backtrack to the east asking after the Arizona plated muscle car. The home outside Santa Fe was rural and he was betting their new place was fairly rural as well. There weren't very many communities to check to the east anyway and the fact that the one hand-delivered payment came from the west left Adams suspecting misdirection.

Observations at the old coven house had provided Adams with valuable information about the schedule of his target. Unlike those he watched in the city coven, the vampire slept fewer hours of the day. Adams had found it useful in his pursuits to do the footwork while his quarry was a ground and to find tactical positions for reconnaissance when targets were active. He did that as he went back through Winona and Gap Ranch, but no one was familiar with the cars he described.

Hallston was a tougher nut to crack. A recent killing spree on the part of an outsider involving young women in the area had people in the town wary and reticent. Bringing out the photo of the missing girl he was trying to find, reminded every person of the recent losses in their community. He was instantly suspect for stopping in their town and trying to talk with them.

Adams thought he might have better luck with the local service providers and wait staff who were hoping for tips. His waitress at the local steak house knew a bus boy who was saving for a nice ride and sent the kid over to talk. Adams was not disappointed.

There was a shop south of town that did great work but didn't sell local, the kid said, but he was hoping to make a deal and get a Dodge Charger at some point. He didn't know the names of the owners or anything about them except they were brothers.

The business was unlisted in the local phone book, making Adams all the more eager to check the place out. He left with a doggie bag and hoped he could find the shop during the day based on the directions the kid gave him.

He sat on a bench with a couple smokers and watched the light traffic on the dusty street. Occasionally he asked someone about the cars or the girl with no luck. It was a crazy long shot that one of the targets would drive by, wild to think the one with all the hits was still living, but patience and perseverance often paid great dividends. No one paid him much mind as he warmed the bench for the next two hours, no one he was paying attention to anyway.

He was ready to call it a night and had stood to walk back to his car when a man shambled out from behind a corner building to intercept him.

"Hey, mister. I see you've got some leftovers there, would you mind helping out a man down on his luck?"

Adams looked back into the alley and saw the makeshift shelter the homeless man had made for himself. He considered the man, who seemed ready to answer when he asked a question.

"What's your name?"

"Darryl."

"Darryl, I wonder if you might be able to help me."

"You want to know about somebody driving a car like Mr. Chess's."

"Mr. Chess?"

"I'm pretty down on my luck here and have to make a dime where I can, pick up meals here and there, you know?" Darryl eyed the bag and Adams passed it over and dug a few bills out of his pocket.

"Mr. Chess has a car like the one I'm looking for?" He held a bill out to Darryl.

"He does, but he wouldn't hurt a girl. The girls all like him."

Adams thought about this as he gave Darryl the bill.

"Mr. Chess is helpful. If he's the one who drives the car I'm looking for then he's also the one that loaned a car to the missing girl. He might have helped her in other ways too. He's not suspected of any wrong doing." Adams smiled at Darryl.

"Is Chess his first or last name?"

"First, but I don't know his last name." The bill was not forth coming for that.

"He lives out south of town though, I know that."

Adams gave him a bill, thinking this lined up with the auto shop the kid told him about. It was an odd question to ask if he was looking for the girl or wanting to speak with Mr. Chess, but Adams asked it anyway.

"Has Mr. Chess ever given you his doggie bag?"

"Oh, yes, they're the best."

"Why is that?"

"Almost the whole meal is in there every time." Darryl leaned in close enough for Adams to hold back a grimace as he smelled the man's body odor. "I don't think he likes steak very much."

"Suppose not." Pleased as he was with this news, Adams didn't give Darryl another bill to drink away. He went to his car whistling and decided it was time for a hotel rather than sleeping another night in his car. Tomorrow promised to be a very busy day.

Claryn worked late for no reason other than she didn't know how to face Justice knowing he didn't want her around. She knew he and Chess were concerned about the situation with the slayer and she was also. They didn't think there was anything to bring the man their way, but they had sent someone to watch the homestead. The watcher said there was no activity on the property other than the regular mining operation. They were unsure what their next step should be and Arvon, who had been digging up information on the slayer's past, was repeatedly unavailable.

Work finished, dogs in for the night, Claryn started to lock up the shelter when Justice and Chess pulled up out front throwing gravel as they skidded to a stop. Rushing out Claryn almost ran into Justice dashing in.

"What's wrong?"

"You're late and you didn't answer your phone."

Claryn pulled out her cell to see it had died, and she held it up for him to see as well. Claryn was confused by his worry. He obviously cared about her but kept pushing her away and she didn't know how to get through to him. She went back in for her jacket and locked up only to see him still waiting. It irritated her and she walked straight for her car without speaking to him again.

"Claryn. Claryn!"

"What!"

"We're going on a road trip to pick up Chess's car. We thought you should come with us."

"Do I have a choice?"

"Please come with us."

"Will you sit in the back with me?"

"If you like."

She turned on her heel and climbed in the back of the truck, sliding over and leaving the door open. Justice followed.

Chess adjusted his rearview mirror. "One of you let me know if any necking commences, I'll need to readjust my mirror for the best view." Chess winked at Claryn in the mirror and she let some of her irritation go.

Chess offered to stop in Hallston to pick up supper for her. Claryn found out their destination and said she'd rather get something from down that direction.

"Justice, why am I here?" She spoke softly

"We're concerned about your safety."

We not I. "You think the slayer might come here?"

"Maybe."

Justice was not cooperative.

298

"Who suggested I go with you?"

Justice kept his eyes forward. "I did."

Claryn watched the road in front of them for a while thinking about how he cared. He said she should find her own place on one hand, but came when she was late and wanted to make sure she was safe.

She understood now what Kelley had meant about having a status-of-the-relationship talk. She wanted to do that now, ask what they were to each other. She was afraid she wouldn't like the answer. While she had some daylight she unfolded the paper she had stuffed down in her purse.

Chess broke the silence. "How was your day, Claryn?"

"Pretty good. Felix stepped on something that had him limping on his front paw and then wouldn't let me look at it at first."

"I'm surprised you don't own a dog yourself."

"Dad said we weren't around enough to take care of one, and then Sissy was allergic."

Justice said, "And now?"

"Now I'm looking at apartments and most of them don't allow pets. Besides, my best friends don't get along real well with them."

"Hey now, Felix was really starting to warm up to me. Another couple visits and he and I will be pals. I'm certain."

Justice hadn't known Chess went to the shelter and watching Claryn and Chess exchange cheerful glances made him realize they were friends, whether he was in the picture or not.

It was reassuring to Claryn to know Chess would be coming around. Maybe I'm overreacting to being put out, she thought, giving Justice a tentative smile.

He returned the look before noticing she had circled a few listings.

"Can I see?"

"Sure."

He frowned over the circled ads. They were all for roommates, only one of whom was a female. He took her pen and put an "X" through that one.

"Not the best neighborhood," he handed it back.

"What are the options?" Chess asked.

"Well, there aren't a lot with roommates."

"You're looking for a roommate? I thought you liked being on your own."

"I did. Sissy thinks the new town homes are nice, where Julia Anthony lived. I guess with everything that's happened I got to thinking if I went missing on the last night of my work week it might be days before anyone knew to look. That could have been me."

Justice scowled, thinking how nearly it had been. Chess shot him a look and then coughed loudly. Claryn was looking out across the rolling land at the shadows reaching up from the crags.

Night is rising, she thought. She looked back at the paper she could barely read in the low light filtering in from the sunset at their backs.

"It's not my first choice, I guess having a guy for a roommate is better than having none."

Chess was surprised. "The ads are all guys?"

"There are only two."

Justice spoke up, "You should take out your own ad, put some notices around." Claryn turned to face him as he said, "There's no hurry."

She looked so grateful, Justice felt like a louse.

After taking another meal to Darryl and chatting him up for awhile, Adams sat on his bench again not far from the stoplight at 2nd and Wigwam Drive. He'd driven out to the automotive shop that day, watched it through binoculars because he didn't want to give away his presence.

In the afternoon he had called in his accomplices, who he now thought of as pawns. The sign on the door of the shop listed hours by appointment only. He also spent a portion of his day looking for staging areas for his eventual triumph.

Darryl, who was being paid to watch for the muscle cars, declined to sit on the bench preferring to stay near the top of his alley. So it surprised Adams when Darryl, squinting at the stoplight, came to sit by him.

"Did you get to talk with Mr. Chess yet?"

"I went by the shop but didn't catch him."

"There's his truck at the stoplight."

Adams whipped around to see several trucks waiting at the light.

"Which truck?" he asked edgily.

"White Ford extended cab. Doesn't drive it except with the trailer to pick up or drop off cars."

They watched the truck go past headed east. Adams was fairly sure the driver was the first target shot the other night. A glimpse of the man in the backseat was all he needed to feel the thrill of excitement.

They both survived. Amazing. He thought of the weak woman he had killed, how quickly and easily she had died. So much for immortality, he'd thought, but here is the power I've been looking for.

"Who's the woman?"

Darryl sighed. "I think it's Mr. Chess's girlfriend. They came to the Rancho here once not too long ago. She's the girl that works at the shelter."

This surprised Adams, "There's a homeless shelter here?"

"Only if you're a dog."

Adam's glance of the truck's occupants was so brief. "I hardly saw her, are you sure?"

Darryl walked around his corner and came back with a section of the paper. He turned to the back and held out a notice for pets needing homes. In a photo, the young woman from the truck was kneeling, petting the featured animal. Adams leered at the black and white scene.

"I see. Have you ever seen her in town during the day?"

"Oh yeah. She goes to the library, the grocery, and the outdoor market recently."

Adams pondered this information. Who was the girl if not part of the coven? Maybe she wanted to be part of it.

After a couple minutes he smiled, rolled off a hundred for Darryl and went to his car. Maybe she wasn't with the brothers. They were much stronger than any targets he'd approached before. If she wasn't one of them, and wasn't simply a meal ticket, then she was the weak link he'd been looking for.

Chapter 42

Chess found a radio station out of Los Lunas he liked and turned it up. Claryn moved to the middle of the wide seat, almost out of sight of the rearview mirror. Her heart sped up in her chest, a heady foreign reaction to her decision to take advantage of her captive audience. She didn't know if a chance like this would come her way again, and she was determined not to waste it.

Justice cocked his head to one side. "Are you all right?"

"Nervous." Pleased, she put her hand on her chest. "Can you hear that?"

"Clearly." He sounded uncomfortable.

"I've been on every medication there is for this; had the side effects of them all. Headaches, nausea, fatigue. The worst effects were nightmares, hallucinations, suicidal thoughts. Can you imagine prescribing a medicine knowing it gives your patients suicidal tendencies?"

Patently he could not.

"It's been one thing after another since I was fourteen, and now look at me."

She reached over and put her hand on his, her heart racing like a frightened rabbit's.

"Same fear, different response," Justice said not moving.

"I know, but it's more. I'm not going to pass out, I can still move, still do what I want without the threat of losing consciousness."

She lifted a hand to his face, feeling his jaw line and running her hand back through his hair. She leaned in, turning her face up to his, her hand behind his neck pulling him down to meet her. Her heart felt like it would burst through her chest but the smell of his breath was sweet and calming. Through heavy lids she watched as he closed the distance and gently kissed her.

He pulled away. "I'm sorry."

303

"No. Don't you see? You haven't taken anything from me. You've given me a gift. It's a gift, Justice."

He took the hand from around his neck, the one he had wanted to hold so badly a short time ago, holding it he heard her reaction but she was right, things were different. She could take it away from him at any moment, at least in the state he was in right now.

He turned her hand over to run his fingers over where he'd bitten her arm. He pictured how it must have been with him unable to stop drinking, holding her soft arm so hard it practically had to be broken to get it away from him. The pain of it etched his face.

"I could have killed you, Claryn," he whispered hoarsely.

"I did that. I picked up the knife and cut my own wrist from here to here." She drew a line with her finger.

He was intensely conscious of her closeness and the thought of her blood altered his features. Maybe she needs a good dose of reality, he faced her with his white eyes blazing.

She studied him, touched his face, ran her thumb along his lip to press it out of the way to see his teeth. She tested the point and accidentally stabbed herself, a puncture that closed as quickly as it had opened leaving a drop of blood on the surface of her skin.

In the front seat Chess leaned over to peek in the rearview mirror before returning his focus to the road in front of them. He was driving the speed limit for the first time in his life.

A dismayed Justice held her hand away as his nostrils flared. If anything Claryn's fear seemed to recede before his condition. She never responds appropriately, he thought.

Claryn tried to put her hand up to his mouth as he shook his head away.

"I don't want to hurt you. I'm dangerous! I could kill you."

She considered before saying, "Could you really suck enough blood out of my thumb to kill me?"

Chess choked trying to smother involuntary laughter.

304

Justice ignored his brother. "This is serious, Claryn, not some kind of joke."

"And you think what? If this weren't part of who you are you wouldn't hurt me? You think a regular guy is less dangerous or a different sort of relationship has fewer risks?"

"I do." Justice folded his arms across his chest and stared her down white eyed.

She crossed her arms and matched his gaze defiantly before taking a deep breath and folding her hands in her lap as she regarded her bloody thumb.

"Did I tell you how my mother died?"

"A car accident."

"Yes, an accident. Accidents happen. You think in an 'accident' no one's really to blame. Did I tell you who was driving?"

"No."

"My drunken, alcoholic father. A stubborn man who refused to give his keys to his wife, who refused to admit he had a problem till she lay dying in the hospital. He got help after that, became the man I remember. Life is risk, Justice. If you're not risking, you're not living."

She put her thumb in her own mouth, tasting the blood and wondering how it tasted to him. Then she took his hand and pressed it to her chest where her heart beat wild with sudden emotion.

"I'm awake to life right now instead of laid out cold because of you."

He laid an arm across the back of the seat to turn fully toward her with an expression of self-loathing.

"And what about tomorrow? Five years from now, or ten? Is this what you want to be? Do you want to kill to survive? Become a danger to others? What do you want, Claryn?"

"I want to be with you."

The tension stood out in the air as he searched her face looking for the proper doubt or concern and seeing only her honest desire. He seized the nape of her neck and kissed her hard.

Claryn tried to respond with passion but was overcome with sickening fear. Her flayed hands pressed him away and she cried out, still fighting the air after he'd let go of her. The car screeched to a stop.

Chess had a fistful of his brother's shirt as if to restrain him even though there was no need. They both watched Claryn on the opposite corner of the seat now cowering, alternating her hands between fists and spreading them wide as she tried to catch her breath in a throat too tight to swallow. She shut her eyes tight and heard Justice speaking.

"I'm no good for you, Claryn. I'm sorry."

He got out of the car. "Keys," he said to Chess who handed them over. They weren't that far now from where Chess had left the Pontiac. Justice headed down the road walking, then jogging, and finally running, full of anger at himself.

Chess climbed out of the front seat and opened the door to join Claryn in the back. He sat back against the opposite door, sympathetic and waiting. Claryn finally opened her eyes, her breathing close to normal.

"I messed it up again, Chess."

"No. You're doing great."

Silent tears traced down her face. Chess held his arms open and she backed up against him, picked up his arms, and laid them around her shoulders.

"JT is a hard case, darling. He's not used to floundering around in uncharted waters, and let's face it, he doesn't have much experience with the gentler sex."

"Unlike someone else we know."

"I resemble that." He said the joke with feigned resentment.

She altered her previous statement. "Someone else we know and love?"

"Much better."

"Shouldn't we go after him?"

306

"Nah, he'll have the car and be back this way shortly." He went on with what he was really thinking, "You know, things would be a lot easier if you had more of a hankering for the other Cain brother."

She scoffed. "Easy has never been the path marked out for me."

She turned around and eyed him, "Are you jealous, Francesco Cain?"

More than you'll ever know, he thought.

He kept a jovial face. "I simply want you to know that these lips and these arms and whatever else you might need to practice with, are at your disposal."

She clapped a hand on his arm, laughing in spite of herself and then stretched and yawned. "You are by far the more dangerous brother."

Chess puffed out his chest with pride, at the same time movement caught his eye out on the road.

Claryn couldn't yet see what had his attention and distracted him momentarily from it.

"Chess, would you change me if I asked you to?"

He did a double take. "Excuse me?"

Claryn was examining the floor bed thoroughly.

"I can't do that, darling. Justice puts up with a lot from me but I gave him my word. You might have noticed he's a shade volatile when it comes to you. I think he'd kill me before he realized what he'd done."

"I thought you were older and stronger?"

"Yeah, well, as mentioned previously, my skills lie elsewhere, and Justice? There's few to match him in a fight. Speak of the devil."

Justice reached them and spoke as he held the back door open for Chess to get out. "The car is gone, unless I've got your spot wrong. Where's that trail going to lead?"

Chess stepped onto the road and held out a hand for Claryn, who took it and slid into the middle of the front seat. Justice got behind the wheel and Chess whipped into the other side.

"To the cash lot I bought it from. Shouldn't be anything there."

"How close a look did the salesman get at your vehicle?" Justice asked.

Chess thought back to the way the man had walked around the Chevrolet, sizing it up before making an offer. He'd wanted some contact information that Chess was unwilling to provide.

"It's possible he noted the license plate," Chess admitted. "Let me call the cover."

A few minutes later they were speeding back to Hallston debating whether or not to call Arvon. Chess was for it, Justice against.

"I don't want him anywhere near Hallston."

"You don't want him anywhere near Claryn."

"And you do?"

Chess threw a concerned glance at her.

Claryn said, "I thought Arvon was some kind of uncle."

"He's some kind of something," Chess said.

"He doesn't play by the rules, Claryn, he writes the rules and then does as he pleases," Justice threw out.

"Let's not put the cart before the horse," Chess interjected. "There may be nothing to worry about."

"We have to find the slayer and take care of this situation regardless," Justice was focused now. Chess was glad to see it.

"Where should we take Claryn?"

"Not our place."

"Uh, I'm right here."

"Maybe we should put her up in Albuquerque, or stop in Gallup?" Chess suggested.

"I am right here," she waved her hand in front of Chess.

"We know that, love. Where would you like to go?"

"With you guys, but, I guess I'm a liability, aren't I? Somewhere close to where you are. Would you call me if you needed me?"

In unison they said, "No."

"Then wherever you leave me, I'll come looking for you."

308

Justice relented. "I'll call you and let you know we're okay."

She narrowed her eyes at him, "And I'll get to talk to you both, right?"

"Yes."

"Okay. Take me to the shelter."

"Are you sure?"

"Yeah. Besides, my car is still there, I've got a change of clothes and pretty much anything else I need. I think Mrs. Smithson is in town and I could go somewhere else from there if I felt like it. I could come to you if you needed me."

"Is her number on your phone?" Justice was asking Chess.

"No."

Claryn yawned again feeling spent.

Justice said, "You should get some rest if you can."

"Okay." She agreeably laid her head over against his shoulder and nestled in beside him.

Chess smirked thinking Justice was fighting a losing a battle.

Hank and Fleets arrived, the latter incredulous the second target still lived. Adams outlined a fictitious plan of attack that centered around taking the weaker female vampire first. Fleets was too trigger happy, so Adams decided to assign him a sniper position and take only Hank into the abandoned house he'd found.

It was early to bed and early to rise for him tonight. Tomorrow he hoped to say goodbye to both the sunrise and the sunset for what would be a very long time.

They were almost back in Hallston when Claryn started whimpering in her sleep. Without taking his hands off the wheel JT turned and blew lightly in her face till she relaxed again. Chess raised his eyebrows and Justice faced the road.

"I was thinking we should move on soon."

309

Chess wasn't surprised by JT's comment. "I figure we've got a good ten years left here."

"Not with the interactions we've had recently," Justice asserted.

"Maybe not." Chess rested his elbow next to the window. "We can wait a few years though and give her time to get ready."

JT scowled at his brother. "She's not going."

"As far as I'm concerned, she's family. She'll go if she wants. Either she's your girl and you want her with you or she's not your girl and you don't have a lot of say."

"You gave me your word."

"She doesn't have to be one of us to be family in my book, JT. Sephauna was my family for nine years before she changed me."

Chess watched JT struggling with this stance and decided to change the subject.

"Do you realize we both rested less yesterday? I was up fifteen minutes early and you weren't far behind me. It'll be interesting to see what happens today. That's what I call being juiced up."

Irritated, JT disturbed Claryn as he retorted, "She's not a juice bar." Then he breathed into her face again until she settled back.

"And what is she? To you, I mean, cause you certainly think you've got the say so," said Chess.

They pulled into the shelter leaving the motor running as JT nodded toward her purse. Chess got out her keys and headed to check out the kennel, but the noise of the agitated dogs woke her up.

"What time is it?" she asked.

"Hopefully early enough for you to go back to sleep," Justice answered.

She yawned broadly. "Probably."

"Why don't you stay here while we make your pallet for you."

"Okay." She shifted her head over to the back of the seat and kept her eyes closed.

When the brothers returned, Claryn was asleep again and Justice tried to blow in her face and pick her up to carry her inside. Chess held the front door and got back in the car.

Justice picked her up effortlessly to carry her inside. Resting against Justice, Claryn mumbled sleepily as she put one arm around his neck, "I'm awake, you know."

"I know." They had made up the pallet in the front room rather than agitate the dogs further. As he sat her down she blinked up at his pale face shining in the moonlight coming through the thin window.

He's beautiful.

"I love you, Justice." She closed her eyes and curled up with her pillow, neither waiting for nor expecting a response.

Justice crouched beside the pallet in stunned silence, unaware of the passage of time as her breathing evened out and dogs stilled.

Later in the predawn hour the sky lightened and he slipped out to the car where Chess sat staring off into the horizon. Neither said a word.

Chapter 43

Mrs. Smithson came by shortly after seven to check on Claryn because her car had been there since yesterday, but she hadn't been around last night. She was surprised to find Claryn had spent part of the night, but refrained from commenting. That girl's been through so much.

She invited Claryn up to the house for some breakfast and they talked shelter business. Mrs. Smithson was thinking about changing Claryn's hours and making a new hire because Mrs. Smithson didn't want to work assigned hours anymore. She also updated Claryn's contact information on an index card she kept near the phone.

"So you're apartment hunting?"

"Yes, roommate hunting is more like it. Seems only a couple guys have ads though."

"And that's what you're trying to get away from, right?"

Mrs. Smithson refilled the hot water for her tea looking at her carefully. She put the pot down and came around to sit next to Claryn on a padded bar stool near the island counter in her kitchen.

"You could live here if you wanted, Claryn. But, I assume you'd like to be closer to town and goings on."

"Thank you so much. You're right though."

"Well, think of places single women in your situation frequent and put a couple signs up there, the Laundromat, the grocery, the library. You'll get a better sort of response from those places than you'll get in the paper."

"Thanks, Mrs. Smithson."

"You're welcome, dear. Now I am off to the grocery. Do you need anything?"

"No, thank you."

Near the shop, Justice and Chess stopped a mile out and worked the perimeter searching for any possible evidence of the band of slayers. A few cars had passed on the road and one had parked on the shoulder of the road. Other than that, they saw nothing. This only served to put Justice more on edge. They secured all the doors and shut the bunker up tight to rest.

Adams surprised Fleets and Hank by springing for a big breakfast at the Hotcake House before taking them out to the site he'd chosen. Fleets tried one more time to convince Adams to take the operation to the auto shop they'd driven by. It couldn't be that hard to find where they rested and lop their heads off in their sleep.

In fact, Fleets wanted to stake them, see how they reacted, then behead them. The talk made Hank woozy, so he supported Adams more cautious approach of working toward more leads.

They had the modified ammunition they needed, the rifle, and two shot guns. Still they spent part of the morning in the local hardware store, the pawn shop, and the All-Mart.

By mid-day Adams was taking them to the Rancho Steakhouse where he bought an entire extra meal for a homeless man nearby. His mood was festive rather than apprehensive which confused both his companions. After talking to Darryl, Adams strapped on a large hunting knife at his waist.

Claryn saw that Mrs. Smithson was out as she walked a dog around a corner beyond the house. Then she spotted an unfamiliar car in front of the shelter.

Speaking to the large, flop eared Doberman she said, "I wish people would call ahead more often, Reggie. Course, the end of the day is the most popular time for drop-ins. Maybe you'll get lucky and have a new home soon."

She gave him a pat and went in the back door of the shelter to put him in his kennel before coming out to the front room. She spoke loudly as she stepped into the reception area closing the door behind her.

313

"Sorry, you caught me out walking one of the dogs. How can I help you today?" Claryn stood behind the counter with her hands pressed on the desk.

"She doesn't look much like a vampire, Jeff," said a doughy man with gray hair and a paunch.

Claryn's eyes flew wide and she started toward the door to the back room as the man named Jeff raised a shotgun from in front of the counter and leveled it at her. Her heart raced and for a moment she wished she could pass out and escape them.

"What do you want?"

"I want to have a pow-wow with you and with the friends you were hanging with last night. We're going to have a little talk and then you are going to call them and do exactly as I say so no one gets hurt."

"Jeff, I think we got the wrong girl."

"No, Hank, we have the right girl. She may not be what we thought, but she knows who to call, don't you?"

He had walked around the corner and was directing her out with the barrel of the gun. When she came around the counter she saw that the other man had a similar gun by his side.

"Please, there's been some kind of mistake." She tried to appeal to the man who was expecting her to be a vampire since the other man didn't seem to care.

"No mistake on our part," Jeff Adams said. "Where's your phone? Dial and read." He poked her in the stomach with the gun handing her a sheet of paper.

Chess cautiously emerged from the bunker area into the shop and scanned the distance through the small breaks in the blinds. He really wondered if they were wrong. The message light on the shop phone was blinking so he went to listen to it.

"This is Claryn. Mr. Adams wants to speak with you. Call my cell phone for directions when you get this message."

The sound of her voice made his own throat tight and his gut hard. He immediately called Arvon's emergency number and got a service. He left a message, slammed down the phone, and went to wait for JT to rouse.

Adams directed Claryn out of the shelter as she walked with her hands up and got in the passenger side door of the gray sedan they'd driven. Hank got behind the wheel and Jeff climbed in the back keeping the gun trained on Claryn.

"Where to, boss?"

"Let's just drive and talk, Hank, drive and talk."

Justice woke up to Chess's pinched features hovering over his bed. He swung around and stood up ready for anything, he thought.

"Are they here? Did you hear them?"

"They called."

"What?"

"They have Claryn."

Justice felt as if his insides were sucked down a sinkhole. He sat back down on the edge of the bed.

"How?"

"I don't know, but they had her leave a message and it's definitely the dogs at the shelter in the background."

"How long ago?"

"Two hours, give or take. I couldn't reach Arvon, had to leave a message. Come hear the message when you're ready."

Adams had a few questions to ask about the local coven, but wasn't pleased when Claryn resisted answering. He decided most of his questions could wait till they went to his staging area.

With no directions, Hank mainly drove in circles through the downtown area until he got tired of driving and asked if they could hit a drive thru and go back to the shelter.

Adams looked at Hank stone-faced. "Hit a drive thru? Think that's a good idea there Mr. Stephen Hawking? With a hostage in the front seat and me holding a shotgun in her back? See any issues with that professor?" Adams turned away in disgust and muttered under his breath, "Idiot!" He was silent for a moment thinking. "Let's go to the house. I think I'll get better answers at a place where I can exert pressure."

Claryn didn't want to think what that might mean, though the idea of torture leapt to her mind. Her anxiety rose to a new level and she could hear her heart pumping in her ears. She tried to be calm and collected while in actuality she nervously rung her hands and scanned for a way to call for help or escape without getting shot.

Chapter 44

Justice listened to the message three times, his face growing stonier each time. Claryn's fear was palpable on the line and she was obviously reading a message. Other than the dogs in the background, there was nothing else helpful on the message.

"You didn't call her cell?" asked Justice.

"I was waiting for you."

"I'm betting neither the sniper nor the driver who followed you from the homestead are Adams," mused Justice. "That means there's at least three. I don't know how many days they spent watching me at the homestead. They probably have a pretty good idea of when I get up. If so, we have some lead time before they start getting anxious."

"You want to try to track them from the shelter?"

"Yeah. Let's return their call from near there."

Adams gave Fleets a wave to indicate all was well as they drove down the dirt track to the abandoned adobe dwelling. At that cue, Fleets was to take his position in the hills.

Claryn didn't remember ever having been out this road before. In the car when she tried to talk about herself, Adams shut her down with a sharp blow to the head, much to his partner's consternation, who objected, "Easy there, boss."

"Shut up and drive, Hank," snarled Adams. "She's up to her pretty little white neck in this, aren't you, sweetheart?" He pulled back her hair searching that neck for bite marks. Seeing none, he turned back towards the front in disappointment.

The roof still covered one section of the house, an old adobe. Adams had put blankets across the windows on the front corner room. There, a battered, old wooden door with slivers of aqua paint still clinging to the inside hung at an angle. Claryn eyed the two office chairs that were sitting about twenty feet in front of the blanketed window.

Adams dragged Claryn out of the car and pushed her into the front room that had red-brown walls and a poured concrete floor. Dirt was everywhere blown into thick piles in the corners. The three chairs looked like recent additions and since there was nothing else in the room to suit, Adams had Hank handcuff Claryn to one of the chairs. There was also an old canvas camping cot folded in one corner, the sight of which made her heart race in panic.

"My name is Claryn Anderson. I've lived here in Hallston all my life. Please let me go."

When she tried to address Hank by name she got backhanded by Adams for her trouble. He hated the sound of her voice, hated the idea that she could easily have what he'd worked so hard for, hated that he couldn't find a mark on her neck.

Claryn was relieved to sit down, even handcuffed. Her knees had begun to shake and she was feeling weak.

"Why haven't they called back? And don't play innocent with me Saint Claryn or I'll make your head spin."

She cringed away from him and, seeing no reason not to answer, told him whatever popped into her head. She knew Justice and Chess were coming for her. She had to give the guys more time to prepare.

"They don't always rest the same amount of time each day," she explained.

"See, Hank, in it up to her neck."

Hank had his own question. "Why do you hang out with them?"

"I didn't know what they were at first. They were my friends."

Adam's voice was acid. "I'll bet they were. And how often do they feed on you?"

Claryn didn't think he'd believe the truth so she said, "Not often. They have others, other women."

Adams seemed pleased with this answer and was leering at her as the phone rang.

"Hello. Is this Chess or JT?"

"JT. Let me speak to Claryn."

"In good time. Is Chess there with you?"

"He is not."

"Too bad. Well, give him a call. You've got some time though since I have special plans for tonight. In the phone booth outside Basha's Grocery there are directions in the middle of the yellow pages. Both of you are to be at the top of the road leading onto the dirt track with the cattle driveway at midnight. My marksman will take out anyone crossing that point before time. Call me back then for further directions. No funny business or this meal ticket will be punched for the last time. Do you understand?"

"Perfectly," said Justice's cold voice.

Adams held the phone up for Claryn to speak and gave her a nod.

"Justice?"

"Claryn, I'm so sorry. Are you okay? Have they hurt you?"

"I'm okay."

"We'll be there soon. How many are there?"

Adams jerked the phone back, "The only one that matters is me. The top of the driveway midnight."

Chess and Justice didn't think they needed the directions from the phone booth and were already closer than Adams would have guessed.

Chess volunteered to do some reconnaissance while Justice doubled back to the Basha's. He wanted to make sure they were following the right directions and coming into the property the way they'd been told, but Justice held him off. Instead, they both retrieved the directions and were back at the gate waiting for their midnight directions.

"Hank, wait here," said Adams with uncharacteristic cheer. "Take a load off. I don't think anyone will be sneaking up on us tonight. You should take a nap if you can."

Adams had taken Claryn out to sit in the chairs out front with him as if they were an old couple sitting in their front yard enjoying the sunset. It might have been a nice scene except she was handcuffed and he was carrying a shotgun and a large knife.

"I think you matter more to JT than you think or than you let on. His voice was very strained on the phone. What do you say to that?"

"I would like to believe that."

He sneered, not liking this answer and went on with his own agenda.

"I brought you out here, Claryn, because I thought how nice it would be to enjoy this sunset with someone like myself. . .someone who wants to be more. And because I have some questions for you, that I would rather my associate did not hear."

Claryn looked at him askance remaining still.

"Tell me, is Chess or JT older?"

Not seeing any possible harm in answering, Claryn said, "Chess is older."

Adams was again pleased.

"Does it make him stronger?"

Claryn considered how best to answer.

"I think so. He sleeps less."

"Ah, very good to know. Did you know we shot them recently?"

He took Claryn's horrified expression to mean she did not.

"Yes. My sniper, who is out there now waiting for them to make a wrong move, shot them several times with mercury and they both survived. They are amazing. I've shot four vampires with mercury loaded shot, and they all died in less than two hours. That's how I knew they are the ones I want."

"Want for what?"

"To make me immortal, of course."

She frowned at him absorbing what he'd said. "You do know that doesn't work for everyone?"

"Yes, yes, but Hank and I have both passed enough levels of Mission 2B Immortal to know it will work for us. I beat the game and then was denied my prize." His voice was harsh and bitter. "So here we sit, having to play a game of another sort."

The sun dropped down behind the horizon and it seemed to Claryn he hadn't paid much attention to the growing shadows.

"Any idea how long it might be till I see another sunset?"

"No," she answered truthfully.

He came very close to her face to ask his next question. "And which vampire are you trying to get to change you?"

"Neither."

He slapped her again hard enough to rock her head backwards. His anger was disproportionate to her offense.

"I told you not to mess around with me! People who don't listen to me pay."

The brothers had been watching the low hills around them for signs of the sniper and seen nothing. An hour after sunset, an agitated Justice began pacing outside the car.

"We should do something," Chess said.

"You think his threats against Claryn are empty?"

"No. I think we can check out the area without anyone being the wiser."

Justice couldn't see taking the chance even though he was sure the sniper was an empty threat at this point. Even if he had a thermal or night device, their bodies barely gave off enough heat radiation to register on a scope. He gave Chess the okay to check things out and as Chess hopped a fence to begin looking around the property, Justice's phone rang. Chess loped back to hear the conversation.

"Hello."

"JT, you know what I don't like? I don't like when people don't listen to me."

Justice and Chess exchanged worried frowns and scanned the hills again for someone watching them.

"I'm listening to you," said Justice evenly.

"I know you are, but I need to set an example for other people so everyone understands what sort of man I am. You see, if I don't like what I see or hear outside my window, I might get to thinking Claryn here doesn't need all her fingers. Would you care very much if she lost a finger or two?"

"I would. I might find it very hard to cooperate or to see reason if she's hurt at all. Do you understand?"

"I do, and I'm so pleased we can talk like this. I want something from you, do you know what it is?"

"I think so."

"Good. And you want something from me. It's all quite simple. But I also need to know I can trust you to do as you're told. Are you both there now?"

That was a mistake, thought Justice. He wouldn't ask that question if he were watching us now. "We are."

"Hello, Chess."

"Hello, Adams."

"Ah, my reputation precedes me. That's very gratifying. All right, you all divide up your duties how you like, but one of you is to go on foot, find my sniper and take him out at midnight. He didn't listen and that's his punishment. Understand?"

"Yes. And the other?"

"The other can come to the house at midnight and sit in one of the chairs out front. Then we can have a nice chat. Got it? Good."

For once, Justice drove very slowly onto a property. When they caught the scent of where one of Adams' men had exited a vehicle earlier, Chess hopped out to follow the trail.

"Good luck."

"Justice." Chess struck his fist and darted off on the trail of the sniper. He disappeared into the dusty rose boulders littering the hills silhouetted in the wane moonlight.

Justice watched his brother run for a minute and then sat back to wait for the appointed time.

When he'd hung up the phone, Adams flattened the creases out of the front of the striped button-down he was wearing over kaki cargo pants. He walked over to a Coleman camp lantern hanging in the tree near the house to set it alight. The propane fueled lamp put out a surprisingly large circle of light that encompassed the chairs in front of the house.

"Which vampire would be the better sire, Chess or JT?"

Claryn was afraid of being hit again and chose one.

"Chess."

"Why?"

"He's older and stronger."

"That's what I thought." Adams grinned and lit another lamp on the side of the house hanging from a large nail.

"Let's turn these around to face our window, shall we?"

He stood her up, turned the chairs and pulled her along back into the house where Hank was engrossed in a pocket video game.

"I told you to get some rest. Your loss."

Having gotten up earlier than normal for an eventful day, Adams wanted to be well rested when his time came, so he'd intentionally built this interlude into his evening. It also pleased him to think of everyone waiting for his word on when to move and what to do.

Adams turned to Claryn and duct taped her mouth. "We don't want you to get to talking too much and distract your guard."

Then he opened out the cot and settled down for a nap. He wondered what his sleep would be like the next day. Of what would a new vampire dream?

"Hank, wake me up at a quarter till and be ready just in case."

"A quarter till what?"

"Midnight, you twit," Adams put his back to the wall and closed his eyes. He fell asleep listening to the peaceful lull of air moving lightly through the valley.

Justice wished he'd asked to speak to Claryn again, if only to hear how she sounded. The amount of tension in her voice might have been an indicator of how easily she thought he and Chess could handle the situation. Of course, she knew very little of how they operated together.

She had been with these men for hours now. Justice stared off in the direction he imagined the house was. She's in no immediate danger, he reassured himself, she's their only leverage.

He thought a lot about Claryn and how she'd come to be where she was right now. He wasn't berating himself for a change, he was focused more on who she was to him. Chess said she was family, always welcome.

Justice remembered his family like a vague dream. He remembered losing them one by one and being left with a sense of injustice and the consuming passion to make it right. He'd used his training and weapons in what seemed an extension of a soldier's career. He had always thought justice was served, believed it still, but it hadn't changed the loss he felt. Gone was gone.

When Sephauna changed him he just became what he already knew he was, a monster. He still had a continuing mission, an ongoing purpose, a never-ending walking death.

Claryn seemed to hold out life, protecting it with goodness and courage, nurturing the grieving stepmother, giving whatever was at her disposal. Justice saw in Claryn the greatest contrast to himself; she walked into the room giving, caring, and pouring herself out for others. When she saw others were in need, she walked without fear.

In a moment of inspiration, Justice realized that when her fear was greatest it was tied either to a violation or to her own needs, to what she wanted for herself. He tried to dismiss the notion as empty arrogance that she might need him, his companionship, his love.

There were so many things he was willing to die for, but it wasn't the same as having something, someone to live for. Focused on the path in the darkening night, he thought what Adams really held hostage at the end of that lane was priceless. For Justice, it was life itself.

Chapter 45

As the wind picked up, Chess wove his way back through the rocks to the car. The sniper wasn't much of a sentinel, sitting as he was playing a game on his phone and glancing up at the house periodically. It would be so easy to dispatch the man sitting with what was no doubt the same rifle he'd taken down JT and Ches a few days ago. JT was calling the shots, though, and the hard part was waiting.

From the next rise over behind the sniper, Chess could make out the old abandoned house nestled in a bit of valley with a couple of straggly trees around. It was such a small affair, two rooms with the square footage of maybe two bays of their shop. He barely made out the tracks where the men had taken Claryn into the weather stripped front door. Tracks leading off in other directions were now being filled with heavy dust as the wind picked up.

The windows were partially boarded and a lamp like those outside the building was hanging inside. The diffuse illumination indicated the indoor lamp was turned down low. He could tell a blanket was tacked across the boarding on the main window by the way the light rippled when the wind blew the fabric aside.

Chess couldn't get close enough to hear anything without risking the sniper spotting him. He stayed long enough to ascertain that there was only the one lookout and that he wasn't going to get to see anyone in the house. Then he slipped back over the hill in a wide arch and returned to the car.

The dust moved across the road like sheer curtains obscuring even Justice's view of the hills outlining the horizon around them. Chess approached from the rear in a deliberate effort to sneak up on his brother who simply waved him in.

"How's it look?"

"Hard to tell. Only the one lookout and he's not much of that, our sniper from the other night. One of those tiny boarded up adobe places. Camp lamps set about, although we could probably come at the place from behind, take care of this whole mess in the next twenty minutes."

Justice shook his head.

Chess nodded and sighed. "Other than that, not much to tell. Did you try Arvon again?"

"No luck."

Being an optimist, Chess felt the stress differently than his brother. JT usually spent time mapping out worse case scenarios in order to prepare. Chess took in the stiff posture and taut features so far beyond the norm.

"How are you?" Chess asked.

"How is she?" JT countered.

"It's like that, huh?"

"It's like that."

Claryn jerked her head up with sudden anxiety, realizing she'd dozed off. The steady moaning of the wind and the low light lent a foggy dreamlike quality to the scene around her.

Hank dozed in his chair and Adams snored under a throw blanket. Dust moved through the air in constant swirls and pricked her dry throat as she breathed it in through her nose. She ached to wipe the powdery dust from her face and eyes but had to settle for sliding her face against her shoulder.

She wished she could signal for help somehow. She tried to shift her chair toward the window. This immediately caused a loud rousing squeak that brought Hank's head up swiveling along with the shotgun he'd had draped over his knees in her direction. The blanket stirred as well and she coughed through her nose to cover up her movement.

Adams sat up stretching and yawning as if he'd had the best sleep of his life. His entire demeanor said life was good. With a confused look at his pal, Hank stood up and peeked out through the blanketed board to the front where the wildly swinging camp lanterns threw circles of light around. Hank experienced the visual sense of being on the carnival rides that had always made him sick. Sandy dirt blew in sheets across the area reducing visibility so much that Hank couldn't see the branches of the tree furthest from the house.

Adams clapped his hands, rubbed them together and laughed at how he'd made Hank jump. Claryn leaned uselessly away as he came over to her and ripped the tape from her mouth. She felt a sudden searing pain like she'd gotten her lips and the whole lower part of her face waxed. She gasped in pain, sucked in dust and coughed in earnest.

Her captor sneered and pounded her on the back.

"It's time to get this show on the road, and you have a starring role, young lady."

Hank watched as Adams made the call and stepped out into the night. Sometimes the boss didn't make much sense at all.

Chapter 46

The phone rang in the silence and Justice stared at it as if it was a bomb. Chess took it from his hand and answered, his furrowed brows the only indication something was amiss.

"Hello."

"Chess?" Claryn's worry filled her voice, and for a moment both brothers hoped she had escaped.

"Claryn!"

Adam's smug tone oozed over the line. "Now that we have that out of the way, it's time to begin."

Arvon's service reached him with the message after a forced landing due to weather on a remote airstrip.

"Really could use that car now." He growled to Carson, his private pilot who had retired from the Air Force last year. Having to set down so far from his destination irritated Arvon.

"It should be here anytime now. Shall I go with you, sir?"

"No. I'll drop you in town in the courtesy car so you can get some rest. If I'm not back by sunset tomorrow, take the plane back home."

"Yes, sir."

Justice drove at a snail's pace on the approach to the house with his headlights on high as directed. Had Chess not described the way the drive hugged the bottom of the hills, he might not have been able to drive at all in the dust storm. He smelled dampness in the air and knew the rain would soon pound the blowing earth back down where it belonged.

When he came around a bend and saw the small structure with the cottonwood trees out front, he killed the engine to walk the last hundred feet with the headlights beaming behind him. Although certain the humans could not yet see him, he held his hands up straight over his head as ordered.

Fleets didn't care what Adam's orders had been, it was foolishness to sit out on a rock waiting when he could no longer see anything but the light of the lantern in the distance. He wrapped his weapon to protect it from the dust and began slowly picking his way back down the hill.

Halfway down he saw the two glowing headlights and paused in the shadow of a rock to make sure the vampires did as they were told. On the side closest to him, Fleets saw one emerge and move slowly forward. He strained to see if the other was on the far side.

He couldn't be sure but decided he better get in closer to cover what approaches he could just in case. He also thought it would be nice to be closer to their car, whose second set of keys jingled in his pocket, if the whole deal went south.

Hank spotted the headlights in the distance although the grit blowing around reduced them to two fireflies flashing through the darkness.

"They're here," he said with nervous excitement.

Adams took his cue and pulled Claryn up out of the chair. He backed them both into the corner where his shotgun was propped up. He ordered Hank to cover the door with the other shotgun and wait. Then Adams pulled out a large Bowie knife and held it in front of Claryn's face.

"You will be still, and quiet, and cooperative, or you will bleed. Do you understand?"

Claryn nodded her head 'yes' as much as she dared feeling the edge of the blade at her throat as she did so. Her heart was now pounding in her ears again. Her stomach and throat were tight with apprehension.

"Hello?" Justice's voice brought tears to Claryn's eyes. Her heart raced a mile a minute out of fear for him.

Adams barked, "We're in here. Come on in real slow-like with your hands on your head."

Chess was a few feet behind the sniper moving like a mountain lion across the rocks and relying on the wind for cover. When he was almost on top of the man, Chess's cell phone rang and the man turned with the big gun in hand shooting off a wild shot before the barrel swung all the way around.

Chess grabbed the automatic rifle at both ends as he jumped on top of the sniper and pressed the gun back into the man's throat. The man fired off two more rounds uselessly as his own weapon crushed his windpipe, and Chess's phone continued to ring.

Arvon listened as the cell phone went to voice mail and dialed another number. Apparently both his boys were otherwise engaged. Catching their trail on a night like this presented interesting challenges he thought he'd rather not tackle when a quicksilver slayer was on the loose.

Everyone froze in the little shack as the distant sound of the sniper's rifle was carried to them on the wind. Hank looked with wide eyes at Adams who was grinning toward the blanketed window with satisfaction.

"He was a liability." Adams explained. "The kind that doesn't take orders. Understand?"

Hank nodded as it dawned on him that the man he'd been following might actually be crazy, not for believing in vampires, but just plain crazy. Hank swallowed hard and faced the door again.

Adams smiled and waved the knife in front of Claryn. "Come on in, Mr. JT, nice and slow."

Chess tried to signal to JT from the hill to wait, but JT was already opening the door, placing his hands back on his head and elbowing through the opening. As ordered, Chess fired off the last two shots as well as the five shots from the spare clip before heading down the hill at a jog.

Holding the rifle in one hand and his cell in the other, he checked to see who his missed call was from. Moving through the rocks like a slalom

331

racer he tried to return the call only to find he no longer had adequate reception.

Justice pushed the door open slowly, peering around the corner of the wall. He saw Adams holding the large knife close to Claryn's throat. His lackey was clearly agitated by the demise of their partner, but Adams looked pleased as punch with the progression of the evening.

Justice let his anger sweep over his face and stepped into the adobe covered cinderblock room slowly, his fingers interlaced and resting on the top of his head.

Adams smiled at him. "Take a seat, JT," he nodded toward a chair on the far side of the room, "or should I call you Justice?"

The flat answer caused Adam's genial expression to falter. "You should definitely call me Justice."

Claryn looked pale and weak, her face was bruised, but she wasn't bleeding. Justice took these things in without moving his white eyes off Adams, who he judged to be the greatest danger. The other man held a shotgun, but had backed away automatically on seeing Justice's expression.

"And Chess is up on the hill, I assume."

"No. He should be outside the door about now."

"He's very fast isn't he?"

"He is."

Justice kept moving across the indicated end of the room to distance himself from the door where Chess would enter. If there was the least chance of taking advantage of a distraction it would only work if he and his brother weren't both being covered by the one shotgun.

Adams noted the movement. "You can stop right there unless you want to see this pretty young lady here bleed."

Justice froze in his tracks so completely every human eye was drawn to his still form like tourists at Buckingham Palace watching for the Queen's guard to blink, flinch, or breathe.

At that moment, Chess's entrance was spectacular.

A large branch crashed through the boarded window, Chess threw back the door so hard it almost flew off. As he'd planned, it was a distraction extraordinaire.

Unfortunately, it backfired completely.

Hank stepped back between Justice and Adams pulling the trigger of the shotgun. The shot went wild and spread into the blocks beside the door. The buckshot also caught Chess's right arm and stitched a bloody crescent on the side of his body as he attempted to cross the threshold. Chess fell back against the wall.

At the same time, tense and excited, Adams with his arm around Claryn's shoulders jerked her back so she lost her footing. As she fell, his blade slipped into Claryn's jaw line making a matchbook length cut under her chin and eliciting her involuntary cry.

Justice responded immediately as both he and his injured brother registered the scent of her fresh blood.

Uncertain of the extent of her injury, or Chess's ability to control his urges under the circumstances, Justice jumped forward into a crouch halfway between Chess and Hank to both protect and better see Claryn. Adams wrapped his knife hand around Claryn's waist yanking her upwards again on her feet. She was breathing in a way reminiscent of Lamaze.

The fierce beast-like expressions on the vampires' faces caused Hank to trip backwards over the chair, seeking desperately to get to the far side of the room with Adams and away from the two nightmare creatures.

Adam's voice bellowed over them, "Stop right there! Nobody move!"

Half sitting on the floor where he'd fallen, Chess put a hand on Justice's arm and gave it a controlled squeeze as his right arm dangled uselessly beside him.

They both judged Claryn's injury as comparatively minor, though it bled in a distractingly profuse manner. Adams failed to notice this at all till his knife hand felt slick with the red flow.

Blinking and following the direction of the vampires' focus, Hank turned and almost dropped the shotgun as he reached toward Adams and Claryn.

"She's bleeding something awful, Boss."

"Hank, move back to your position, now."

"But—"

"Now!" he bellowed at Hank without taking his eyes off Justice and Chess.

"Alright, blood-suckers, how bad is it?"

"Needs to be staunched, but it's not fatal," Justice spoke concisely, his fury barely in check. He reached into his pocket for a handkerchief and held it out to Hank.

"Pass this to your boss."

Uncertain, Hank looked to Adams.

"Yeah, give it to me."

Claryn's breathing was fast and shallow, but she tried to give the guys a reassuring look.

Hank gave Adams the hanky while he kept his finger on the trigger of his shotgun.

Justice and Chess both winced with Claryn as Adams reached around holding the blade lower on her throat and placed the fabric against the slashed skin.

After all his preparation, Adams thought he had come within an inch of seeing it fall apart. It was time to take back the reins.

"None of you want to see more of that, or do you?" he suggested maliciously. "So this is how this is gonna work."

His eyes took on the light of a voyeur as he surprised them all with the next part of the plan.

"You," he jutted his chin toward Justice, "are gonna change Hank here into a vampire so I can see how it's properly done."

Hank blanched. "What? What are you talking about?"

334

Justice stood, opening his hands wide like a supplicant and tried to reason with Adams.

"If I do what you want, she'll be dead in minutes because your buddy here won't be able to resist. I need some assurance that it won't go down that way."

"You get nothing!" Adams spat. "Maybe you get your blood bag back alive and maybe you don't. I'm in charge here and this isn't a negotiation! Do it!"

Confused and half panicked, Hank was still holding the shotgun leveled toward the general vicinity of both Justice and Chess. Justice took a step toward Hank, who saw the door moving. In panic, he pulled the trigger.

Outside the wind had died making the noise of the shotgun blast reverberate off the stone in the room all the more as a dark figure stepped inside. The shot caught him squarely midsection, but he stood un-phased.

Adams put his back into the corner using Claryn as a shield. The shotgun behind him pressed reassuringly into his leg.

Hank wildly swung the shotgun to and fro over the room.

Having caught a few wide pellets again, Chess groaned and crawled further from the doorway to the wall opposite Adams.

The new player let the door slam and cleared his throat. He spoke with an odd-clipped accent. "Uh-hum. Greetings, Mr. Adams, Mr. Jeff Adams I assume. I am here to work out a resolution of the situation in which we currently find ourselves."

"Who are you?"

"I am, Arvon, the acting authority for the Council of Elders, and as such I am here to offer you a place with our kind."

Adams warily watched Arvon. Hank kept shaking his head back and forth murmuring to himself.

"You're here to change me?"

"To change you, and to insure that no more of our kind suffer. We have been watching your steadfast pursuit of your goals with interest.

Your adaptation of weaponry is impressive. Your hunting prowess noted. We have come to the conclusion that it is time for us to step in and grant you a place with us."

"I want to see it done, see how it works. These guys aren't much on cooperation."

"My young associates will cooperate fully, now, let me assure you."

"Really? Who says?"

"They, like others of our kind, answer to an authority. I am that authority."

"Prove it. Change him."

Hank wasn't about to stand there and take it. He raised the shotgun up and emptied his last three rounds into Arvon.

Unmoved, Arvon said, "Justice, Francesco, change him."

Claryn shut her eyes turning away as Justice helped Chess to his feet, and they closed in on the whimpering man. Adams stood riveted, eyes wide like a child standing in front of the tree on Christmas morning.

Covering her ears to Hank's screams, Claryn saw Arvon frown at the front of his shot riddled clothing. Ignoring the others, the elder raised his cupped hand out beside him, furrowed his brow with concentration, and focused on his hand.

Claryn couldn't fathom what he was doing until she saw his hand fill up with the mercury from his body. Finished, he poured the liquid metal out of his hand into a depression that edged the room's floor. Hank lay inert on the floor, and Arvon tossed Justice a silver knife. With lightening speed, Justice released every shot of mercury form his brother.

The motionless Hank groaned, shook his head, and then snapped back to life. His nose led his focus to Claryn, and with feral eyes and bared fangs he lunged for her. Arvon's arm shot out and catapulted the young vampire against the far side of the wall below the window.

"Restrain him," Arvon ordered before turning his attention back to the wanna-be.

"As you can see for yourself, all that you desire is within your grasp, Mr. Adams. Are you prepared?"

Adam's expression was wonder, hope, and suspicion.

Arvon continued, "I'm sure you are aware that the girl is a special pet belonging to my young associates. So you will have to release her."

Adams was torn. The girl was his safety net. Yet, he desperately wanted to be immortal.

"I have your word that you're going to change me."

"Yes. Justice will change you."

"I want Chess to do it."

"Unfortunately his system is still processing mercury poisoning, and, as I think you are aware, quicksilvered blood will not produce the desired result."

"Then I want you to do it!"

Arvon spoke as an firm parent with a demanding child. "You have much to learn. In order to successfully change someone we must have metabolized fresh blood recently." He turned to Justice asking, "When was your last meal?"

"Day before yesterday."

Adams threw in, "Liar! You just fed on Hank."

Arvon turned silvery eyes on him. "He fed that meal back to your associate rather than into his own system processes. Alas," Arvon nodded with one hand on his chest, "mine was a couple weeks ago. Trust me, Mr. Adams, this is a matter about which I know a great deal."

Adams considered a moment longer and then released Claryn with a push toward the door. Weak in the knees, she almost fell. Arvon steadied her with one arm and set her against the doorframe while Chess continued to restrain the wild Hank. Justice was at her side, holding her and stroking her hair. She blinked at the expression in his fierce countenance and found hope.

"Handcuffs?" Arvon held a hand out to Adams who handed over the key that the elder passed to Justice.

Claryn knew Justice would attack Adams now that he no longer held her captive, but he did not. She realized that, no matter what had transpired before, Justice followed his elder's orders. It was a revelation.

The handcuffs dropped from her chaffed wrists, and she opened the door and stumbled outside. Justice eased her back down the wall outside the doorframe as she sat with her head turned away.

She heard enough there.

Soon Adams was triumphantly celebrating. She couldn't see him lick the knife he'd held on her throat. Didn't see him ecstatically sucking her blood from his own arm and shirtsleeve as if it was pure heaven.

"She smells so good. How can you just stand there?" He turned on Justice, "Let go of me!"

"There is," Arvon hardened, "the matter of the rules."

"Rules!"

"Rules. There are only three. You must submit to your elders. You may not reproduce without permission. And, imminently important at this juncture, you must not take lifeblood unless it is given. Do you understand?"

"I happen to know that not everyone lives by your little rules."

"That is true. Sometimes the Council is slow to punish for these offenses. Not today. Both of you will stop struggling to get to that girl right now, or you will suffer the consequences."

Adams growled but was able to restrain himself. Hank was wild with his thirst and struggled all the more.

"You wanted to see one of our kind perish today, were you not, Mr. Adams?"

"Yes!"

"The consequences may include death by exsanguination," Arvon nodded to Chess and Justice who quickly drained Hank down to a shivering heap. "Death by poisoning," Arvon kicked Hank into the mercury pooled at the wall where the liquid burned into his skin. "Or by combustion, among other options." Hank's unseeing eyes hazed over.

338

Arvon growled out his next words. "Unfortunately, you have already taken lifeblood, stolen it from your own kind. Therefore, the judgment of this Elder upon you, Mr. Adams, is conflagration. You did want to see one of us burn today, didn't you?"

"What?"

Arvon stepped toward the door and turned to Chess. "Handcuff him in his vehicle."

Adams slipped his hand behind the chair to the shotgun. He grabbed it up and shot round after round into the three vampire shouting, "To hell with all of you and your rules!"

Chess and Justice fell back as quicksilver ripped through their clothing and skin.

Claryn looked back through the door and saw Chess and Justice fall to the ground. ""NO!"

Arvon, unused to disobedience, took a moment to glare at Adams before he stepped up, gripped the barrel of the shotgun with both hands and batted Adams against the wall.

Claryn crawled weakly toward the brothers, who both scooted away from her. "Stop! Stay away." She paused, remembering Justice's hands holding her wrist captive.

An odd gurgling sound drew her attention to the other side of the room. With one hand, Arvon held Adam's suspended in the air by his neck.

"Cuffs," said Arvon.

Neither Chess nor Justice moved, and Claryn realized the ancient vampire spoke to her. She retrieved the cuffs and tossed them over.

Justice shakily got out the blade he used on Chess's wounds and tried to pass it off to his brother.

"No. You first. You're in worse shape than I am, bro."

Justice shook his head back and forth against the wall.

"Why? Why is Justice in worse shape, Chess?" asked Claryn.

Arvon cuffed Adams, stuffed part of his shirt in his mouth, and draggede the struggling young one out to the grey sedan.

"Justice made two of them." It obviously hurt Chess to speak. "Used a lot. . . of his own blood to do it. I couldn't help because of the poison." His own hands shook almost as violently as Justice's. He tossed the blade to her. "Help him, Claryn."

Claryn took the blade, but Justice pushed her hands away. Haltingly he said, "Chess, first." Justice wheezed, "Might need him."

Chess tore open his shirt. Across his broad chest and abdomen spots of bulging embers blackened his skin. Claryn felt slow and clumsy, but when she cut, the pellets popped out one by one through the lacerated skin.

Meanwhile Arvon laid Hank's remains on the hood of Adam's sedan for disposal and returned.

Claryn pleaded, "Mr. Arvon, can you help, please?"

Arvon observed the trio for a moment with creased brows. Then he took the knife from Claryn. Arvon turned and cut one of Justice's protrusions. Instead of popping out, the mercury oozed so slowly the skin began healing back over part of it.

"Justice needs blood and ours is useless till this poison is flushed." Arvon eyed the young woman. "Can you take care of that while I take care of this?" He motioned toward Chess.

Claryn nodded dumbly and watched Arvon carry Chess out the door..

Justice tried to move away from the scent of her blood, so fresh on her skin. "No, it shouldn't be like this. Please go, Claryn. Go and have a life."

Salty tears welled up, and Claryn grabbed both sides of his face to make him look at her. "My life is right here. And what it should be is this." She kissed his lips firmly, heart racing, holding his face, until he gave in to her demand and kissed her back hungrily.

Claryn pulled back certain now he wanted her as much as she did him. It wasn't just her blood. He had the strength to take that now, but he didn't.

"There's what should be, and there's what is." She moved her hair back from her neck. "And what must be."

Justice's was unable to move his white eyes away from her throat as it drew closer.

Claryn deliberately jerked the handkerchief from under her jaw setting the blood to flowing down her neck again. She placed her arms around Justice's shoulders to give him her lifeblood in a manner he hadn't the power to refuse.

His mouth was firm and warm against her neck, the prick of his teeth quick. Claryn sighed and leaned into him. In a moment, he withdrew and searched her face.

"Are you okay?"

She blinked happily. "I will be when we get that poison out of you."

Arvon had returned though neither of them knew when. He took the knife to Justice's wounds and barely incised the skin before it forcefully ejected the liquid metal balls.

Justice stared at Claryn as his eyes returned to crystal blue. When he stood and offered her a hand, she wobbled to her feet. Justice swept her in his arms out the door.

Arvon surveyed the dim shelter, the set for so grisly an ending to this portion of the tale. Clearly, the Mission2B Immortal Coven demanded attention. He tucked his knife into the holder on his belt and walked out the door into a desert pink sunrise.

When he approached the car, Arvon noticed Justice and Chess place themselves between himself and the girl, Claryn. The protective instincts of the brothers Cain border on the ridiculous, Arvon thought.

"May I?" Arvon indicated the wound on Claryn's chin. Sitting in the open back door of the car, Claryn glanced to and from each of the brothers and back to Arvon. She nodded tentatively.

With all his fingers extended, Arvon put his thumb in his mouth, cut it open with his teeth, and pulled it back out bloody. Then he rubbed his thumb lightly across her chin.

The wound tingled and itched, within seconds it closed and healed over. Neither Justice nor Chess had seen this done before, and both wondered if they could have done it themselves.

To their consternation, Arvon sampled Claryn's blood by cleaning his thumb in his mouth. Then he dismissed them all with a distracted wave of his hand. "I'll see you back at your shop."

As Chess started the car, they were silent each keeping their own counsel as to what they thought of the events of the night and Arvon's role in them. Justice sat in the rear, and both brothers turned their attention to Claryn.

"Are you all right?" asked Chess.

"Are you hurting anywhere else?" Justice still had his arm around Claryn who felt vibrant, as if her body hummed to the tune of her venomed blood or to being alive after such a night.

"I'm fine. I'm better than fine."

Justice kept one arm around her and loosely held her hand. Although her heart rate was slightly elevated, she reveled in his nearness, half afraid if it ended he would begin distancing himself from her again.

"Looks like we're having company whether we want it or not," said Chess. He resented Arvon's highhanded ways. Justice, on the other hand, related to Arvon as someone who did what was necessary, when it was necessary, whether it was a pleasant task or not.

"Do we have time to check on the dogs?" asked Claryn. "They might need water, and I know they could use a walk about. I'm not sure if anyone is around to check on them this morning."

342

Leave it to Claryn to think of all God's creatures at a time like this, and to put them ahead of other beasts, Chess thought. The brothers shared a moment and then laughed.

"Yes," said Chess.

"By all means," Justice responded.

"Let's go check on the dogs." Chess was pleased to have a reason to make Arvon wait.

Only Arvon watched as the sun rose high enough over the hills for sunshine to creep toward the dirty sedan. It reached the papery remains on the hood first. They shone bright with fire before vanishing into a fine dust. The destruction of the quicksilver slayer, handcuffed to the wheel and snarling, took longer but was just as complete.

Chapter 47

At the garage, Arvon made himself at home which meant engaging in a routine security check and looking into the provisions. He saw that the brothers had not made much progress on the M2BI game. He poured some water, inspected the automobiles, and waited patiently on the sofa enjoying the change of scenery.

The trio arrived as the hour for Justice's rest drew quite close. Arvon stood as they entered.

"Justice, would you do me the honor of introducing your lovely friend?" he asked pleasantly.

"Claryn, this is Arvon, our elder from the north. Arvon, this is Claryn Anderson, my hero."

Claryn wanted him to say "my girlfriend" or something to indicate where they stood with each other at this moment. It was not to be. She offered her hand to Arvon, who bowed low to kiss it, turned it over and smelled at the air around her.

"Enchanting. It is so nice to meet you, Claryn. If you don't mind me saying, you have a very unusual bouquet about you. It is such a pleasure."

She would have found his sincerity disturbing had not Justice and Chess distracted her. The former was pleased, the latter glared. These weren't the reactions she expected.

"It's nice to meet you. Thank you for coming today for us."

"Justice needs to rest soon." Arvon said. "Perhaps the two of you would like to excuse yourselves and have some privacy?"

Justice walked over to Arvon as if to shake hands but instead stood as if he was a soldier at attention.

"Will you be staying on?" Justice inquired.

"No. Sadly I must return to the city to attend to other matters."

"We'll see you when we see you then."

"Till then."

"Till then."

Claryn was thrilled as Justice stepped back over to her, gently took her by the hand and led her down the stairs of the bay. Her heart pounded in her chest. They didn't speak till they were behind the locked door of his room.

"Are you afraid?" He listened to her heart.

"Should I be frightened of him?"

"Arvon? No. He won't hurt you or do anything to even upset you, I imagine."

"No?"

"No. He values his relationship with us too much."

Still her pulse throbbed.

"What are you afraid of?" he swung his legs up on the bed sitting against the wall, knowing they had scant time.

Claryn resolutely sat down next to him, her face a mixture of emotions.

"I'm afraid you'll send me away or go yourself as soon as you wake up. Please, Justice--"

"Oh, Claryn." He held out his arms as an invitation.

She fell into them not caring how her pulse raced, how she could scarcely catch her breath.

"I'm not going to leave you again," he said. "It seems I can hardly live without you." He let go of her as he laid back to rest.

She clung to him. "Promise?"

"Promise," he said as unconsciousness overtook him. She stayed there for a while, running her hands through his hair, holding his hand, touching his face, and, finally, kissing his cheek. Her heart throbbed and her stomach fluttered, but she stubbornly held on.

There was a part of Chess that had always resented Arvon's role in Sephauna's suicide, her assisted suicide. She asked for Chess's help first. He flatly refused.

Arvon showed up one night not long after, and by midmorning the next day she was gone. Chess respected Arvon, had at one time revered him, but he did not trust him to serve any but his own purposes.

Aware of Chess's feelings, Arvon watched his young friend pace the floor. Justice showed not a care that shortly Arvon would be alone with Claryn. Chess could hardly stand it.

"You're killing Justice piece by piece out there today. Those were the 3rd and 4th pieces of riff raff he's dealt with in about as many weeks. Do you have any idea how much of his life expectancy he lost out there today?"

"The death taint of so few is negligible compared with the life gift of the one. I assure you, Justice has not lost one day."

Chess paused his pacing. "The blood that's given, it gives more life than the death taint takes?"

"In the proper circumstances, yes."

"What do you mean?"

"Seduction and games may fabricate a giving response, but in such a case the blood does not carry the life force as it does when given out of sincere concern and love. We can give to each other and refresh the life by the act of giving. Exponential multiplication of the life is derived from human compassion, though." He sipped his water. "It really is quite remarkable."

Arvon commented to the room knowing and not caring about the agitation he produced. "She really is quite remarkable, as well." Arvon went on. "And she is absolutely devoted to Justice. Would do anything for him, I suspect."

Chess stopped his pacing to come sit across from Arvon with narrowed suspicious eyes.

"Tell me, Chess, how deeply devoted to her are you?"

Chess was taken aback. He had tried not to think about or analyze his own feelings too much. Claryn belonged with Justice. He knew it the same way he'd known as an adolescent boy that he belonged with Sephauna.

He glanced toward the stairs. Much less agitated now, he answered firmly. "She's family."

Arvon knew what that meant to Sephauna, and, thus, what it meant to Chess. Whatever mild concern Arvon had had about a lover's triangle dissipated. The Cain brothers remained united, strengthened even.

By the time Claryn came back up, it was almost time for Chess to rest. Chess didn't veil his amusement that whatever position Arvon held over them, it did not bear on Claryn. Her priorities were her own, and Arvon's guest appearance ranked somewhere below the needs of the dogs. She sank down on the couch near Chess.

"Chess, you are not being a very attentive host," Arvon said.

A rueful Chess didn't want to be attentive to the elder whose water glass was half full anyway.

"Claryn's blood sugar is quite low." Arvon commented. "It's a good thing you're not prone to blood sugar sensitivity, my dear. Perhaps some juice? Or apple sauce?"

Claryn hadn't realized how weak with hunger she was.

Contrite, Chess put a hand on her shoulder. "Let me get something for you. What would you like?"

"Honestly, everything sounds good right now. Thanks, Chess." She pressed his hand with her own, and the elder watched.

Arvon was content to sit, drink his water, and observe the girl as she ate. She seemed rather unaware of the effect she had on Chess.

"We are now in your debt for, what? Twice you've saved the lives of my young friends," said Arvon.

"They're my friends too."

"Of course. And you are privy to a reality that perhaps you were not prepared for but which you have grasped with alacrity and moved into with audacity. I find I am your great admirer, as are others."

Chess grew quite still, not showing his discontent.

Arvon continued, "I am at your disposal. Perhaps you have some questions?"

Claryn's expression was thoughtful. This was certainly not an opportunity to let pass. "I've heard there are rules for you all. Are you the one who enforces those rules?"

"I hadn't really thought of my personal place in that light. I guess I am one of the enforcers, though, as are Chess and Justice on certain matters. There are others, however, who take that job much to heart."

"I saw what you did with the mercury when you were shot," she said.

Chess was scrambling to recall what Arvon did after being shot. He remembered hearing the gun fire while he and Justice were disposing of the Wild One. Other than a glance to see Claryn was safe, he hadn't given it a moment's consideration.

Arvon held up one finger to postpone. "Chess, would you mind retiring early and giving Claryn and me additional time alone?"

Chess very much minded but didn't see the point of objecting. He was minutes away from forced retirement as it was. He got up to take his leave and reconsidered. If Arvon was of a mind to answer questions, perhaps he would pose one. "Arvon. Did you come down here to protect your assets?"

"Ah, Chess," Arvon acknowledged the young one. "I am sorry I have not made more of an effort on your part. I did not come down here to protect assets. I came down here to protect the sons of Sephauna."

Chess thought about his own lack of knowledge about the relationship between Sephauna and Arvon. Had Arvon sired Sephauna? Cared for her? Chess considered the idea that he might have misjudged their elder on some points. Chess gave a curt nod and turned away. As he exited the room, he heard Claryn saying.

"I'm not the kind of person who's likely to keep secrets from my closest friends."

"And I will certainly not ask you to do so. They did not see me handle the quicksilver, and I simply did not want to discuss it at the moment. Beyond that, all I will say is I haven't the deadly allergy to the substance that others have."

Below them Chess closed and locked his door. Arvon was certainly old. Would they outgrow their weaknesses, become like him, or was Arvon all together different? It was the last question of the day for his conscious mind.

"Did you love Sephauna?" asked Claryn.

Arvon took a moment and spoke with slow introspection as if self-analysis was a difficult labor of the mind. "That is a very good question. I cared for Sephauna a great deal. She was special to me in a way that only a handful of others have been. Among those, I have driven away, abandoned, or killed more than I care to remember. It is little wonder Chess distrusts me so." Arvon gave her a sad smile. "In my experience, the type of love to which you refer is not readily cultivated among our kind. And it is a very rare bridge between you and us that is both fascinating and powerful. So. . .no. I myself have never loved nor been loved in that way."

"Do you hope to be?"

"At one time I did. I wanted it badly. And I suppose Sephauna embodied the last of that hope. Yet here I am." Arvon tilted his head admiring Claryn. "Am I, the mighty elder, now somewhat pitiable in your human eyes?"

"Yes. I think so."

"You really are a singular creature." His earnestness caused Claryn to blush. "Tell me, Claryn. What is it that you want? What do you most desire?"

"I want to be with Justice."

"Yes. And do you want to join our ranks?"

"Are you offering?" she asked without hesitation.

349

"What if I am?"

She sat still, her eyes seeming to study the air in front of her, perhaps seeing optional futures. "That's not where I am right now. I want to be with Justice. Of that I'm certain. That's where I am right now."

"Living fully in the present." He put his water glass down. "It is commendable. If, however, the time comes and you decide to change your possibilities, I would like to suggest that you call me rather than asking one of your young friends for assistance."

"Why?"

"Why? Yes, why indeed." He contemplated. "You can only receive of your sire that which they have to give. The possibility of healing blood, for example." He nodded at her chin. "If the time comes, speak to your friends, tell them of my offer. They will appreciate the beneficial nature of it and best advise you. And now, I see that you are ready for repose as well." He stood, and she did likewise.

"I am honored to have had this time with you, Claryn Anderson. I do not often have the leisure to visit like this with and appreciate your kind." His hands were folded in front of him, and he bowed forward expressing his honor like an ancient Japanese samurai in a movie. Claryn thought the gesture peculiarly suited him.

On the way to her futon, Claryn paused outside Justice's room. As much as she longed to lay down beside him, her heart sped up at the thought. Not a reaction very conducive to sleep, she thought. Under a blanket, only one room between them, Claryn closed her eyes thinking of endless dates with Justice. She daydreamed as she dozed off that she was opening the door of her new apartment to Justice as he picked her up to go out.

Let it be, she prayed.

Epilogue

The Desert View Cemetery was perched on a small knoll looking out over dust-swept hills, rocky vistas and crumbling crags where the night was now rising. It was a beautiful place Justice had never visited before.

He studied the flat headstone of Thomas and Cheryl Anderson doing a little quick math. From the ribbon carved above their names with their engraved wedding date to Mrs. Anderson's death, the couple shared eight short years together.

Yet look at what they did.

Claryn knelt in front of the stone, carving out a hole in the dry soil for the bottom of the potted cactus she brought to leave as a token of her love for the forever young couple. The small barrel cactus bloomed pink on top with tiny bright blossoms. The pebble covered hard baked earth wasn't yielding, and Claryn accidentally stabbed her hand with a few needles.

"Ouch."

"Let me see," said Justice holding his hand out.

Justice crouched and took her hand in his listening to the slight change in her heart rate as he plucked the needles out with quick care. A couple drops of blood sat on the edge of her palm, and she watched for his reaction.

"Better?" he asked.

She extended her hand to him. He responded with a frown. She shrugged sticking the tiny wound in her own mouth to clean it off. That caused him to scowl as well, but the risk of infection was minimal.

As she stood, Justice reached down tracing the etched bas-relief of flowers between the names.

"Looks like the violas Kelley had on her wedding cake," he said.

Claryn's cheeks dimpled. "Almost. These are Johnny Jump Ups. They're only about this big." She spread her fingers to show him. "Dad said Mom planted them around our house, and I used to bring fistfuls to

351

her as soon as they came up in the spring. Absolutely refused to leave them alone. Poor little guys hardly had a chance."

Justice dusted off his hands and stood smirking.

"What?"

"I guess when you dig in your heels, big or little makes no difference. Guys really don't have a chance."

Poking at his chest, she said, "That's right. And I hope you've learned your lesson." Her words teased but her eyes worried.

He reigned in the urge to take her in his arms and offered her his hand instead. Whatever time we have, he thought, I'll take that worry out of her eyes, one day at time.

In companionable silence, they walked back to the car hand-in-hand, both conscious of the effect this had on her. It was getting better little by little, day by day. Hadn't he told Kelley he was patient, had all the time in the world. But now the time seemed to slip by too quickly. Claryn told him she'd rejected Arvon's offer. How much time will we have like this?

He studied her profile as she stopped beside the car to gaze at the colors painted across the big sky. Content to live in the present, Claryn continued her course of not asking what he considered the most important questions.

Topic Avoidant, Chess called her. She wasn't the only one. Chess joked a lot about crucial issues. Justice could see what his brother never joked about though. Happy as he was for Justice, Chess wasn't the type to be alone. Justice, who had always been fine on his own, suddenly found the thought of a future without Claryn unbearable.

Her pulse increased as she stepped in closer beside him tentatively placing her arm around his waist. He let his arm rest on the car behind him, but this didn't suit her. She took his hand trying to find where she was most comfortable with it. After trying the shoulder and bicep, she tucked it beneath her arm and pressed her arm down on top of his. Then she slipped her other arm back around his waist, trying to wait out the anxiety the contact brought.

Lingering in the soft breeze with Claryn tucked beside him, Justice found new sympathy for his brother. Chess had always known what he needed and had been searching diligently for over a hundred years. Justice found it without hunting at all, and sincerely hoped his brother would too.

Death Taint

Begotten Bloods Two

Prologue

Chess Cain had never been so grateful he knew how to knit. The long bamboo needles made rhythmic sounds as he worked yarn between them, knit two, pearl two, knit two, pearl two. He held the work in front of him like a shield and kept his eyes focused on the abomination less than ten feet away.

Its gray skin stretched back over pointed chin and cheekbones that were so sharp from lack of flesh they threatened to tear through their mottled covering. The mouth hung open, every tooth a fang, and acrid air scraped in and out its maw like gaseous waste. Eyes filled with blood from one lashless gray lid to the other followed the movement of the needles without blinking, mesmerized as Chess inched his body between the creature and the prize it had come to take.

The woman bleeding on the floor was unconscious and not badly injured. Chess' own acute senses told him her small wounds were clotting over while her respiration and heart beat were strong. He knew the moment his body cut off the creature's peripheral view of its victim because its eyes jerked to his and a long guttural protest screamed up its throat. Less than a day old, the abomination was stronger and quicker than his 300 years, and no matter what he felt for the woman the creature had been, he could not afford to pause.

Chess rocketed toward his adversary hollering at the beast, hoping to secure her attention. She could tear him limb from limb but if she darted past him to those behind there wasn't a thing he could do to stop her.

The abomination threw back its arms, rippled with muscles thin and hard as bone, clawed hands with fingers whose length was doubled by their talons spreading to rake Chess' flesh from his body. Within arms reach Chess smiled sadly. The creature's nails stabbed into his sides as his weight slammed into its chest and its fangs descended ready to rip the side of his neck from his spine.

His agonized scream rent the air, but his right hand drove the wooden knitting needles home and through the creature's heart. Entangled, their bodies dropped as stones to the marble floor. The one immobilized, the other wrenching the ten unnatural daggers from his sides.

Chess began to scramble away, and the creature coughed out a mist of browned blood. Its limbs and head convulsed and fell useless to the floor, however its jaw hinged back and forth like a puppet's moving to formless words. Unsure Chess glanced about for another likely weapon.

"Chesssssss..." it wheezed at him. Its lids fluttered open reveling human eyes, not whitewashed like his own, but alert and rich with color. "Can't. Move."

He slipped arms around her and pulled the slack gray body onto his lap. "Ah, God forgive me. I didn't know anything else to do. Please, forgive me."

She shushed him. "You," her body bucked as if hit by a charge from cardiac paddles. "Good man. You are."

He shook his head vehemently.

Great bloody tears, dark with death taint ran down her hollowed cheeks. "I killed those men," she wheezed, "I was going to kill her."

Chess wished he could cry too. "That wasn't you." He knew what it was to fight the bloodlust but not as the kind of creature she had become.

She closed her eyes. Her arms twitched. One hand landed near the bamboo needles. "Don't. Don't let me--"

"I won't."

Their eyes met and her lipless mouth tried to smile. "You'll take care of me now." Her hand flapped over on the wooden protuberances and he pressed his own over hers frowning. "Now, Chess," her voice was stronger, "You have to do it now." Blood crept from the corners of her

355

eyes through the labyrinth of vessels to her pupils pooling there and spreading back out.

Impossible. No creature was that strong, he thought. She convulsed in his arms. The hand under his closed in a fist grasping the wood in her chest. Chess braced her body, binding and lifting as he raced out the apartment door to the stairwell praying the sun would take her before she took him.

About the Author

Kristin King first saw a vampire in a coffee table book of Hollywood monsters and has been hooked on paranormal creatures ever since. Inspired by her husband, adored by her golden lab, embraced by Jesus, and well-grounded by her four sons, Kristin can be found on Facebook (KristinKingAuthor), Twitter, and Pinterest where she enjoys hearing from readers.

14672967R10209

Made in the USA
Charleston, SC
24 September 2012